"Nelle McFat

mystery, and p

—Romantic Times

TEARS OF FIRE

"I didn't run away that night for the reasons you think. I promised you I'd pay you back, and I will."

Andre looked around the room—at the cozy fire, at the champagne, at Deirdre's expensive lounging ensemble—and raised his eyebrows. "I suppose this is better than working as a valet. Do you really think your father would approve of what you're doing now?"

Deirdre lifted her chin. She had no idea of how entrancing she appeared in the firelight, with her elfin curls catching the gleam and her rich blue eyes reflecting the ambivalent emotions of meeting Andre Devereux under these intimate circumstances. "My father no longer has the right to approve or disapprove of anything I do. Nor do you."

Andre reached out and caught her hands, pulling her toward him so that her face was a breath away from his. "I don't disapprove at all," he said softly, though there was something about his eyes that was not at all soft. "I paid very dearly for you tonight, my dear...Deirdre. Enough for you to clear your debt with me totally. But I warn you—I expect to get my money's worth."

Other Books By Nelle McFather:

LOVESPELL

ECSTASY'S CAPTIVE

WOMAN ALIVE

TEARS OF FIRE

NELLE MCFATHER

LOVE SPELL NEW YORK CITY

LOVE SPELL®

February 1994

Published by

Dorchester Publishing Co., Inc.
276 Fifth Avenue
New York, NY 10001

Printed in the United States of America.

For the legendary Minnie Pearl [a.k.a. Sarah Ophelia Colley Cannon] and all the Grand Ole Opry greats and for all the Sons of the Confederacy, including my brother Buzz [Ret. USAF Major]. The South shall rise again!

ACKNOWLEDGMENTS

I wish to thank my readers, Aleece Jacques and Marlene Bush, for their usual patience; my agent, Meg Ruley, for her never-ending belief in me; and my editor Alicia Condon, who appreciates my sometimes off-the-wall adventures. Add to that kudos to *Atlanta Constitution/Journal* columnist Celestine Sibley, who has been a writer friend and supporter for going on twenty years! Thanks, you people.

"Oft o'er my brain does that strange fancy roll
Which makes the present (while the flesh does last)
Seem a mere semblance of some unknown past."

—from Samuel T. Coleridge's "Sonnet"

TEARS OF FIRE

Prologue

Summer 1988

My name is Fable.

I have always lived at Moncoeur. When our family's famous stable of Tennessee Walking Horses was to be featured in the *Nashville Banner* Sunday lifestyle section, I was interviewed by the lady writing the article. She asked me how long I had lived on "the old plantation" located between Nashville and Franklin, Tennessee.

I told her "all my life," though I could have added, "and beyond." But the journalist lady would not have understood my feelings about having been a part of Moncoeur for more than my lifetime. She might have tried to link me to Shirley MacLaine or some "new age" theory in the article, which would not have set well with my father. Daddy was thinking seriously at the time about running on the upcoming conservative ticket for Congress.

"How does it feel," she asked, "to be the great-great-great granddaughter of Deirdre O'Shea McAfee Devereux, the famous lady moonshiner of the Civil War?"

Usually, I call non-Southerners down on applying that misnomer to what was actually the War Between the States, but this time I didn't bother. I was currying my favorite horse, Gambler, when she asked this. Gambler, by the way, is not a Tennessee Walking horse. I do not share my family's passion for forcing prancing gaits on beautiful animals. My father and I, however, have made a pact that if I do not speak out in public on this matter, he will not pester me to attend and ride in the shows.

I curried Gambler a few more slow strokes before answering, giving myself time to deal with the emotion that always wells up from my deepest insides at the mention of my long-gone great-great grandmother Deirdre. At least the subject of my sister Celeste had not been dredged up. I was dreading that one even more. About my ancestor, Deirdre, I said simply, "She was a great Southern lady." I kept on at my task, currying Gambler's mane to a sable gleam. "She saved Moncoeur and all the people in it. I thought you were going to write about our horses and the Shelbyville Celebration."

"Well, a little background never hurts with these things. Old money, old houses, old legends—your family has it all." She looked down at her notes and I braced myself for the question I knew would come next.

She fooled me. Celeste's name still was not brought up. This lady was apparently hung up on Deirdre. "Is it true your ancestor started out as a penniless Irish refugee who turned to prostitution before she wound up in the Devereux family?"

I was only twenty-two at the time, but I'd been to enough uppity muckety-muck Belle Meade social functions to know how to bring an unwanted encounter to an end. "My daddy said that if I kept you out here in these ole smelly stables too long, he was going to put us both to work shoveling out the manure. He and Mama are on the veranda by now, I'm sure, waiting for us to come join them for something cool and refreshing." I threw the curry comb aside and, after patting my horse's sleek backside, strode toward the stable door.

Ms. Journalist stepped carefully around one of Gambler's larger horse chips, having no choice but to follow me up to the big house. I looked longingly up toward Deirdre's Mountain, where my great-great-great grandmother's still had toiled and bubbled during troubled times, brewing up her famous "Whiskey Mountain" corn liquor. The big white oak under whose spreading arms I had spent many a dreaming moment was banked by threatening dark clouds. Maybe it had looked like that when Deirdre had stood up there, weeping as she watched the red glow of the Battle of Nashville.

"We're in for some weather," I said, feeling the puckery little ripple of goosebumps that always comes with thinking about Deirdre. It's like there's a veil fluttering between me and something that I know has always been there and is getting closer all the time.

Ms. Journalist sped up her pace at the first spatter of raindrops, and I very soon delivered her to my parents and a tray of mint juleps in silver cups under the covered veranda. It was not long before I was able to excuse myself and retreat to my favorite place atop Whiskey Mountain. My father loves a new audience who hasn't heard any of his stories, and he didn't try to stop me as I slipped away from the little gathering.

I have always loved a good storm. It excites me, seeing the sky perform its dramatic Götterdämmerung, cleansing itself and our part of the planet. What was it Coleridge said in his famous ode? "And may this storm be but a mountain-birth" . . .

The lights of Nashville were obscured by the jagged sword of lightning that ripped the sky. I found myself counting "one . . . two . . . three" between the brilliant flashes and the inevitable roll of thunder following. My tree—Deirdre's tree—seemed to tremble with each onslaught.

A leaf drifted down onto my hair, and I pulled it from my long, tangled locks.

I'd had my long blond hair permed over a year ago, but I have never changed its color. The lock blowing across my mouth was bright red. Excitement grew deep inside me, like the feeling one has at the airport, waiting for one's plane to take off. A crash of thunder racked the tree, and I found myself adrift between thoughts that seemed at the same time foreign and familiar. Cards? I play bridge and that silly game of hearts, but not poker. Yet I began seeing a five-card hand that . . .

The lightning lit up my mountain. The white oak leaves shivered and shuddered, and every time the lightning flashed, I saw new, old shapes outlined like photo-flash negatives.

A very loud crash, then a limb was breaking away from my old oak tree. There was another brief flash, then cursing somewhere around me in the room that had gone dark. Room? Was I in a room? Deirdre? Papa!

Why was I dressed like this?

"Papa!"

I had pulled down onto my back, and I pulled it into my long tangled locks.

I'd had my long blond hair permed over a year ago, but I have never changed its color. [illegible] across my mouth [illegible] red. [illegible] deep shade [illegible] like the [illegible] at the [illegible]. Waiting for [illegible] to take off. A crush of [illegible] packed the [illegible] and [illegible] of [illegible] which [illegible] the [illegible] and [illegible]. [illegible] Yet I [illegible] that.

The [illegible] up my [illegible]. The [illegible] and [illegible] and even [illegible] the [illegible] light to [illegible].

A [illegible] then a [illegible] was [illegible] from [illegible] tree. There was [illegible] the [illegible] in the [illegible] I [illegible] a [illegible] face. [illegible] regular.

Chapter One

Spring 1859

The two fugitives went unnoticed in the flurry of last-minute boarding of passengers and cargo onto the *General Robertson*. Even if the constable on dock duty hadn't been busy watching the precarious hefting of an ornate harpsichord destined for a fancy brothel in Nashville, he wouldn't have noticed a shabby pair like the O'Sheas.

For one thing, Deirdre O'Shea was dressed like a boy, her flaming hair stuffed under an oversized cap. For another, Riley O'Shea had shaved off his flamboyant whiskers just that morning. Too, even though it had been seven years since the terrible potato famine had prompted mass migration to America, New

Orleans was still teeming with Irish immigrants. The two O'Sheas didn't stand out in the crowd.

The fugitive pair sighed in relief when they were finally safe on board the steamboat. They found a stretch of railing to themselves, and Riley braced himself for the tirade that he knew was coming from his daughter.

Deirdre didn't disappoint him. Her dark-blue eyes flashing fire, she vented her frustration on her father.

"Didn't I tell you it was stupid, getting into that game with those men last night? Didn't I tell you, after just one look, that they were slick and too smart for your shenanigans? But, no, you wouldn't listen, you with your slippery fingers and padded bankroll!" Deirdre paused for breath, angry not only about their close call with the law, but disappointed. She'd liked New Orleans, which was as far from the dreary farm in Ireland and its grief and problems as any place could be. It had seemed that Riley O'Shea had settled down at last to being a sensible father, making a good home for his remaining dependent and himself with his job at the wharf.

But then he'd had to get back into the cards, had to put himself on the dark side of some powerfully mean men, as well as the law! Deirdre glared at the man beside her, words failing her.

"Now, now, darling," Riley soothed, patting his daughter as he looked around for some distraction to take his mind off Deirdre's unhappiness with him. He found just the thing. There was a barrel of Monongahela whiskey being off-loaded. The Irishman licked his lips. "A crying shame," he muttered, hoping there were still other barrels left in the steamboat's saloon. He could use a bit of up-lift right now, with all the business of the ill-fated game last night. And Deirdre's scolding made him thirsty. "A crying shame," he said again, with real sorrow as the whiskey was rolled out of sight.

"Forget about that barrel of whiskey, Papa. What do you have to say about nearly getting us thrown in jail? The next time you get into a flim-flam like last night, I'll thank you to leave me out of it!"

"Now, now, darling, don't be marring that sweet face with your spite." Riley patted his daughter's stiff shoulder again, noticing that the loose cotton shirt and baggy pants effectively concealed Deirdre's womanly figure. A good thing, too. Every man on hand last night would be able to describe his daughter to a constable. She wasn't a girl to go unnoticed by men, his Deirdre. Only eighteen, she was, and she already had the fine form and thoroughbred beauty of her late mother. "Ah, girl, I needed the distraction of your pretty face to keep those fellows from watching the cards too close. They were a slippery crowd, and I needed the advantage."

"Well, a lot of good my pretty face did when

you were found cheating. It's lucky we were to escape with our lives."

Riley O'Shea stifled a grin at the memory. He found shuffling cards much more exciting than wharf work, and certainly more satisfying than nursing potatoes. This was a fine country, full of opportunity. Now that Deirdre was up in age, he'd start seeking those opportunities a bit more selfishly. "Ah, but that was a smart thing you did, girl, knocking over the lamp and spying the back door just in time." He could see a twitch at the corner of his daughter's full mouth and knew she'd soon be laughing with him over their escapade. He winked and whispered, "Lucky I am to have such a smart daughter. Lucky, too, I can see in the dark like the old cat I am. I escaped with most of the pot!"

"Oh, Papa!" Deirdre sighed deeply. "Someday, you'll be getting us into trouble that I can't get us out of." She stopped suddenly as a fashionably dressed girl, followed by a huge black woman loaded down with parcels, boarded the steamboat. "Oh," she breathed, drinking in the exquisite details of the girl's costume. She wondered how it would feel to be wearing green velvet with black piping and soft ruffles. She tried to imagine the feel of the bone-handled parasol and the tickle of feathers from the charming hat. "Look at that, Papa. She must be a plantation owner's daughter."

Riley O'Shea looked at the lovely young passenger, to whom every man on board was paying homage with bows and smiles. He got a lump in his throat at the thought that his own daughter was dressed like a ragamuffin, and a boy at that. By damn, he'd find a game on this boat and win enough to set his Deirdre up in fine style! "One day I'll see to it you wear clothes like that, Deedee, my darling."

Deirdre scoffed at that secretly. Her father couldn't hold on to enough money to buy her an outfit like that if he had molasses stuck to both hands! She watched the young woman everyone was admiring sweep past, her skirts held daintily safe from the rough deck.

"Good afternoon, Miss Devereux." The young mate approaching blushed and stammered as the object of his admiration fluttered dark lashes and smiled at him. "It's always a pleasure to have you traveling with us. You've been shopping in New Orleans, have you?"

Gabrielle Devereux gave a throaty laugh as she rolled her eyes prettily at the mound of packages her overburdened servant was balancing. "Obviously! Perhaps you could give Prudy a hand getting these to my cabin?"

The young mate stepped forward to assist but was stopped by a gruff command from the bridge. "Oh, I'm sorry, ma'am, but I'll have to attend to my duties." He scurried off, leaving the spoiled young woman looked miffed.

Gabrielle looked around, the annoyance on her pretty face plain. Her gaze fell upon Deirdre, who was lounging against the railing, watching the little tableau with interest. "You, there. Boy."

Deirdre realized after looking around that the arrogant miss was talking to *her*. "Huh? Me?"

"Yes, you," Gabrielle said with exasperation. "There's a coin or two in it for you if you'll give my maid a hand with the parcels. It seems there's no one else around at the moment to help." Her dark eyes moved rather disdainfully over Deirdre. "You don't appear to have many muscles, but I suppose you'll do."

Deirdre made no move to take the coins Gabrielle held out to her. Her eyes met the other girl's levelly. "What's wrong with *your* muscles?"

Gabrielle's mouth opened and then shut abruptly. "Well, I *never!*," she finally sputtered.

"Never what? Carried your own packages instead of making that poor lady behind you act like a packhorse? You're young and strong; carry your own stuff," Deirdre said, shrugging as she turned her back on the plantation heiress.

Riley O'Shea stepped forward smoothly from his daughter's side and bowed to Gabrielle Devereux. "It's my pleasure, miss, to assist you with those packages. And keep your coins to yourself; no Irishman would take payment for performing a task that's altogether an honor."

Gabrielle sniffed, but led the way forward to her cabin. Deirdre couldn't miss overhearing her parting shot, which, after all, was filled with irony:

"You, sir, are a gentleman, as apparently your son is not!"

Deirdre had to chuckle quietly at that. *How right you are about that, Miss High and Mighty!*

It wasn't easy sleeping on the hard planks of the main deck. Not only were the O'Sheas hard put to stay warm, the constant noise and confusion of the steamboat's frequent stops kept them awake. At almost every muddy little country landing, the *Robertson* stopped. Then there were the trampling feet of freight hustlers and roustabouts, all vying with one another for the scant profits to be made back in Nashville. But finally all was relatively quiet, except for the ship's boilers groaning in agony and the squeak of the paddle wheels.

Deirdre finally slept, exhausted from the chase out of New Orleans. It was hard work keeping her father out of trouble and herself with him.

She woke after a couple of hours of deep slumber, for a moment forgetting where she was. But the chilling spray of lather from the paddle wheels and the rhythmic motion of the ship reminded her.

She reached over to touch the dark lump next to her. "Papa. Papa, are you awake?"

The soft bag stuffed under the blanket didn't budge, and Deirdre sat up, fully awake now and aware that her father wasn't safely asleep next to her as she'd assumed. She cursed softly and angrily, "Damn you, Papa! I can't turn my back on you for a minute."

The sound of music and laughter from the saloon reached her ears then, and she rose resolutely to her feet. Pulling her cap down over escaping wisps of hair, she hitched up her breeches and, lips grim, went in search of Riley O'Shea.

She had no doubt that she would find him in the saloon, already deep into a card game that undoubtedly would be out of his league. Well, dammit, half that money was rightfully hers, and she wasn't going to stand by while he lost it to some smooth, ruffled-front gambler! Enough was enough.

"Now, boy, this ain't a place for the likes of you." The burly man at the entrance to the ornate, gingerbread saloon was indulgent but firm as he blocked Deirdre's entrance.

Deirdre ducked her head, not wanting the bouncer to see the trouble brewing in her eyes. "I've just come to see if I might scrounge a bit of fresh water, and maybe a bite, in return for a touch of work at your tables," she muttered.

The man laughed and patted the slender shoulders. "For sure, you could use a little more meat on those bones, lad. And our barkeep's a kindhearted man. No doubt he'll let you fill some glasses in return for a bit of food." He lowered his voice to confidential tones. "There's a hard-drinking game in progress right now. Though, between you and me, it's a sucker's game, since Devereux is on one of his streaks."

"Devereux?" Deirdre forgot to keep her voice muffled, letting the question come out in a high squeak.

"Andre Devereux." The burly man just grinned at the high-pitched sound of puberty. He had a boy this one's age and felt a kind of tenderness for the undersized youth with the squeak of adolescence in his voice. "The best riverboat gambler afloat the Cumberland, as anybody can tell you. Honest, too, which makes 'im more welcome than most of the weasels what comes on board to gain their fortunes through cheating ways."

Such as Riley O'Shea, Deirdre said to herself with filial disdain. She peered around at the big table in the center of the saloon. She couldn't see her father's face, since he was sitting with his back to her, but one look at the man opposite Riley was enough to tell her what the situation was. Her heart sank. "That's Andre Devereux, the tall man in the dark coat?" He was a man most would call handsome, and he seemed quiet and pleasant enough from what she could see. But she knew instinctively that he was a professional who wouldn't put up with a Riley O'Shea's shenanigans any longer than it took to pull out that silver-handled derringer and shoot him between the eyes. "The one who's dealing the cards?"

"That's him, all right. You've heard of Devereux, lad?" This with surprise, since this scruffy boy, even with his fine features and appealing ways, didn't look like someone who'd travel in upperclass gambling circles.

"I've heard the name." Deirdre's throat felt dry and scratchy from the tension of the past few hours. And from the looks of things, more trouble was ahead. She could see the dark stains around the throat of her father's best shirt. Riley O'Shea sweated profusely when he was losing at cards. And when he was losing at cards, he started cheating. "I guess he's related to that young woman I saw come on board with about half the store-bought goods in New Orleans." She was just making conversation until she could figure out what to do.

Her companion was effusive on the subject of Miss Gabrielle Devereux. He chuckled. "Ah, so you've taken notice of our prettiest passenger! Well, no surprise, that, since there ain't many young men aboard what don't have a dream or two concerning Miss Devereux. But don't get your hopes up, lad. The young lady's Mr. Devereux's brother's ward, under protection of all that family money. They say Mr. Andre and his brother have some bad feelings for each other, but both of 'em is fierce when it comes to looking after kin."

"I'm not one bit interested in Miss Devereux," Deirdre protested warmly. "As a matter of fact, from what I've seen of her, she's a spoiled, conceited brat who wouldn't lift her finger to hit a lick at a snake." It was time for action; Deirdre couldn't afford to stand around discussing the Devereuxs all night. "It's lucky some folks are, without even knowing it—unlike some of us that have to grub for a living."

That brought a sympathetic look and the offer Deirdre needed. "Right you are, lad. Now if you'll be off to fetch that round of whiskey for the men at their cards, there'll be a bowl of stew and mug of milk waiting for you behind the counter afterwards. I'll see to it myself. Now mind you don't spill nothing! Ain't nothing worse than dampening a table where the cards is working."

Deirdre took great satisfaction in the look on her father's face when she appeared at the table with a tray of drinks. It was all Riley could do to hold onto his equilibrium when he spied his daughter standing behind the dealer's shoulder.

"Great Dublin Demons!" he muttered.

Andre Devereux raised a dark eyebrow. "I'm sorry, Mr. O'Shea. Did I understand you to say you'll take two cards?" His well-manicured hand hovered over the deck.

Deirdre looked down at the three queens in Andre's hand and inwardly groaned. She hurried around to stand behind Riley, her heart sinking when she saw the two pairs he was holding. She almost groaned aloud when her father said smugly, "I'll stand. And I'll raise you fifty."

Deirdre knew it was now or never. She set down the mug of beer just at the moment that Riley O'Shea reached out to sweeten the pot. Beer went everywhere—onto the ante, onto the cards, onto the players' laps. The man next to

Riley jumped up, cursing, his cards scattering helter-skelter as a torrent of beer landed in his lap.

In the scramble, only one man did not jump up or curse the Irishman or lose his cards.

Andre Devereux looked first at Riley O'Shea and then at Deirdre. He waved aside the bartender, who came up with obvious intentions of bodily removing the culprit from the scene of disaster. "Never mind that, my friend. Just get another table prepared. And bring fresh cards, since these are ruined." Dark gray eyes with specks of black met Deirdre's with a combination of menace and amusement that the girl found most unnerving. She was in deep trouble this time, she knew. "Tell me, young fellow," Andre asked softly, "Have you been waiting tables long?"

A flurry of snickers went around the table, breaking the tense silence that had followed the accident. Deirdre's chin lifted. She hated being laughed at more than anything in the world. "No, sir. Tonight's the first time."

Andre looked down at the undisturbed, winning hand he was still holding as if nothing had happened. "It wouldn't be possible, would it, that what just happened was deliberate—would it?"

Riley O'Shea half-rose, blustering, "I'll thank you not to make such insinuations, Devereux!"

"Insinuations?" Andre Devereux dropped his cards in the basket the bartender had brought for the ruined deck. He looked from Riley to

Deirdre, his eyes the cold grey of a cannon Deirdre had seen in a park. "I ask the rest of you gentlemen—doesn't it seem a little odd that Mr. O'Shea has been losing steadily all evening, and on the hand that would've wiped him out completely, along comes his little companion with his convenient awkwardness?"

At the murmurs around the table and the devastated expression on her father's face, Deirdre decided she had no choice but to confess. "All right, Mr. Devereux; I'll admit it. That was no accident. And it wasn't my father's idea." Deirdre's gaze locked courageously with that of the gambler. "I saw that Papa was losing, and I just couldn't stand it. That's all. I'm sorry." Deirdre's eyes swept over the other men at the table. "I'll say that to all of you. I'm sorry." Her eyes stopped at Riley's flushed face. "Except to you, Papa. I won't tell *you* I'm sorry!"

" 'Papa'," Andre echoed softly, looking from the offspring to the parent. "Ah, so we have here the classic situation of the pure son trying to save his father from the evils of gambling."

Riley O'Shea glared at Deirdre. "Pure, my Aunt Fanny! It's a thrashing he needs, but I'll not delay the game no more on his account."

"I'm not sure you should continue playing with us, Mr. O'Shea," Andre Devereux said coldly.

The wave of good-natured protests around the table overruled him. "Oh, come on, Devereux; give the Irishman a chance to get some back." "All right, Devereux, admit it: you're going soft on us, letting a young pipsqueak break up a good game."

"Very well," Andre said reluctantly. "Mr. O'Shea can continue playing, but on one condition." A smile tugged at the gambler's lips as he looked at Deirdre. "Our young—er, waiter will be off to his bed and leave the whiskey-serving to someone a bit more—ah, graceful."

Deirdre blushed at the ripple of laughter that went around the table. She looked at her father, her eyes smoldering. "All right, Papa, he gave you your chance to get out while the getting's good. Since you don't have the good sense to take it, I'll tell you this—when you leave here tonight with empty pockets, don't come whining to me in the morning." She meant it, too. Deirdre O'Shea was sick to death of her father's irresponsible shenanigans. She spun on her heels and walked ramrod-straight to the door.

Andre Devereux watched the proud figure leave the salon before saying to Riley O'Shea. "A spunky lad you've got there, O'Shea. Are you sure you haven't had all the cards you need for the night?"

The Irishman mustered up the confident charm that Deirdre's little scene had momentarily shaken. "Now, Devereux, you know a man can't let a stripling dictate his pleasures." He rolled his eyes and rubbed his hands together. "Oh, to have back the hand I had! I can tell you, gentlemen, that pot there has to find its way to my pockets on this game—else there's no justice in this world or the next!"

Andre smiled, knowing that his hand from the previous game would have taken the pot. But he liked Riley O'Shea, and there was something about that boy of his that was almost disturbingly appealing. . . .

"Shall we move to our new table, then, gentlemen?" When they'd done so and the cards were being dealt, Andre said casually, "You will save a bit back for that boy of yours, won't you, O'Shea?" At the Irishman's defensive expression, the gambler added mildly, "I don't intend that to sound critical of your ability to provide. But I note that your son, while a notably handsome boy, doesn't seem to have inherited his father's robustness of frame."

"Well," the Irishman stammered, "He—uh, takes after his mother, God rest her soul." He thought about how angry his daughter was with him and was momentarily contrite. Then he remembered the pretty clothes she wanted, and here he was on his way to having a full house, if the next two cards would only fall right. . . .

He'd have the money for them both to live like real folks when they got to Nashville. And his Deedee would have all the dresses she wanted, as well as one of those fancy parasols. . . .

Deirdre was too angry to go back to her comfortless bed. She walked up and down the deck, careful not to step on an occasional sleeping form, and wondered about the legality of disowning one's father.

"Oh. I didn't know anyone was awake this early."

Deirdre had stopped at the back railing to watch the spray from the paddle wheels catch the light when Gabrielle Devereux spoke.

The Irish girl laughed. "I don't know how early it is. For some, it's 'this late'!"

"If you're talking about those men hanging about in the saloon, like my cousin Andre, then don't expect to see them in bed at all. You men are all the same. All you think about is drinking and playing cards." Gabrielle pouted prettily and fluttered her fantastic lashes.

Deirdre stared at her with astonishment as the realization dawned on her, *Dear heaven, she's flirting with me!* "You're wrong about them. I mean us. I mean, not all of us drink and gamble."

It was the wrong thing thing to say. Gabrielle's dimples appeared. "I could tell you were different from the first time we met, even though you were so horribly rude."

Deirdre moved quickly away from the softness that was pressing closer to her at the railing. "Uh, I guess I ought to tell you right out. I don't have much time for girls and stuff like that. Tell the truth, I don't even *like*'em."

Another mistake. She'd just offered a challenge that a Southern belle couldn't possibly ignore. "Even me? You mean you don't like me even a teensie, weensie bit?"

Oh, lord. Deidre groaned inwardly. "I . . . uh . . . well, your clothes are pretty."

Gabrielle wasn't about to let someone of the opposite sex get away with that. "What about me? Don't you think I'm pretty, too?"

Deirdre looked up at the stars and closed her eyes, for the second time that night seriously contemplating patricide. It was all Riley O'Shea's fault. He and his damned foolhardiness had gotten her into this mess! "I—er, haven't really thought about it." Since her father wasn't here for her to kill, maybe she could just bolt. But Gabrielle was blocking the aisle with all her damned layers of petticoats. "Like I told you, I don't think much about girls."

"Have you ever kissed one?"

Deirdre's hand jerked away from the railing as though a snake had just covered it rather than Gabrielle's soft hand. "Good God, no!" she burst out with sincere horror.

"Well, would you like to?" Gabrielle held her face alluringly close to Deirdre's and closed her heavily lashed eyes. Deirdre stared at the pursed, pink mouth in utter repulsion.

"I'd rather be shot!" she exploded.

Gabrielle's eyes flew open and filled with anger. "Well, I never!" She stamped her feet. "You're the rudest, the most insufferable, the most vulgar . . . *ragamuffin* I've ever met. I've *never* met a boy like you before!"

The girl flung herself off in the direction of her cabin. A moment after the whirling petticoats had rounded the corner of the deck, Deirdre was surprised to hear a soft chuckle from the shadows of the deck near her. She turned to see Andre Devereux, the ruffled front of his shirt catching the irridescent moonlight.

"She's right. You're not an ordinary boy." Andre held out a covered dish that had a wonderful, savory smell. "Here. I won't say that your performance tonight could be classified as help, but I understand you were promised something to eat in return for helping at the table."

Deirdre looked down at the bowl, mentally salivating at the thought of the rich, thick stew. But pride overcame the temptation of her appetite. "Thank you. But I'm . . . I'm not hungry. Is that why you came out here, to bring this out to me?" The game must be over, she thought with relief. Where was Riley?

"Partly. But mainly I came to wait for your father to return with the money he owes me. He promised to meet me here after he'd gotten his stash out of the Captain's safekeeping."

Deirdre stared at him, then burst into laughter. "And you fell for that? Mister, the only 'stash' Papa had was what he had in his pockets in that saloon!" She shook her head sadly. "And I was telling myself earlier how you were too smart to be taken in by one of my father's shams."

Andre's eyes narrowed. "There's no place your father can hide from me on this ship. And he knows that if he lied about the money, I'll take it out of his hide when I find him." A frown appeared on the broad forehead. "Oh, my God—I just remembered. We'd pulled up to the Donelson dock that last hand before O'Shea left to fetch his cash. You don't suppose . . ." Andre's face cleared then when the boy didn't react. "No, he wouldn't jump ship with you still here. He's a fool about the cards, but he's not the kind of man to abandon his boy."

He might be if his only choice was that or facing Andre Devereux over a bad debt, Deirdre thought. Besides, he couldn't face his daughter after tonight.

"You're the O'Shea boy?" The first mate was standing there holding out a letter. "Your father gave me this for you." Deirdre and Andre's glances locked. "And this for you, sir." The gambler took the envelope and opened it.

"His I.O.U.," he told Deirdre, a grim smile on his mouth. "And a note telling me he'll send the money and come for you just as soon as he can find work. What does yours say?"

Deirdre's throat caught on the "DeeDee darling." But of course she couldn't share that part. "Just that he's sorry, that he had no other choice, and that since you seemed to feel sorry for me, maybe you could look after me until we got to Nashville." She swallowed hard, looking at Andre, her eyes huge and hurt. "I guess I was too hard on him in there tonight. My father . . . my father has never welshed on a gambling marker in his life, Mr. Devereux. And getting off the boat, leaving me . . . That just shows how desperate he was. I promise you, he'll make it good someday. And you don't have to worry about me; I won't trouble you." Deirdre started off, but Andre caught her by the arm.

She looked down at the strong, brown hand circling her forearm and wondered why it was causing such crazy sensations in her. Andre looked down at his hand, too, and dropped it from the boy's arm as though he'd been burned. "Just where do you think you're going?"

"Why, back to bed," she told him with a weary smile.

"And then what?"

Deirdre shrugged. "I'll find work in Nashville."

Andre looked the slender body up and down. "Doing what? Waiting tables?" He ignored Deirdre's bristling at the sarcasm in that. "I have a better idea. You can work for me. I can assure you, a frail lad like yourself has never had a better offer! You can be my valet temporarily until I get you to Moncoeur and figure out something appropriate for you to earn your keep. You'll be a hell of a lot better off there than in a strange town."

"I . . . I can't," Deirdre whispered. She wondered if she should break down and tell him everything—about New Orleans, about her father's terrible weakness, about her ridiculous disguise. But something stopped her—perhaps the strange way he'd made her feel when he'd held her arm.

"Can't? Or . . ."

The young mate came up then, his face full of embarrassment. "Mr. O'Shea, I'm sorry to be the one to tell you, but the Captain said . . ."

He coughed and let it out rapidly. "I'm afraid your father left without taking care of his fare or yours. We're not quite sure how—well, I'm afraid you'll have to talk to the captain about what's to be done!"

Deirdre closed her eyes and counted to ten. She wondered how many other people on the *Robertson* her father owed. "I . . . I don't have any money."

"But I do," Andre Devereux said easily. He smiled at the mate as he pulled out his wallet. "There, that should take care of both O'Sheas," he said after counting out the money. "And there's an extra bit for not saying anything about Mr. O'Shea skipping out. There are a couple of other—er, interested gentlemen on board."

Deirdre clenched her fists. *Damn Papa's eyes!* If he didn't have the courage to stay and face his creditors, at least he could've taken her with him. Now here she was under obligation to Andre Devereux. God knew how long it would take her to pay him back.

"I suppose I should thank you," Deirdre said after the sailor had left.

"Never mind the pretty words," Andre told her. "Just go see if they've brought the tub I ordered to my room and lay out fresh clothes for me. I could use a bit of freshening up after all that liquor you spilled on me." He looked at Deirdre's rumpled, grubby appearance with some amusement. "You could do with a bath yourself, my young friend."

Deirdre backed away from him in horror. "Oh, no. No, not me."

Andre smiled. "Oh, so you're a modest lad along with all your other eccentricities. Well, I'll leave the tub for you after I'm done and stroll the deck till you're finished. The thing is, I expect anyone working for me to stay neat and clean. And my relatives at Moncoeur are downright fastidious." He looked at the misshapen hat atop Deirdre's curls. "Tell me, do you always wear that peculiar hat? I haven't seen you without it."

Deirdre said quickly, "I catch cold easily." Anxious to divert the subject from her appearance, she repeated the exotic name Andre had used. "Moncoeur?" She loved the sound of it and said the name again, letting the word ripple over her tongue deliciously. "Moncoeur. Is that the name of your plantation?"

"It is. Moncoeur—my heart. It's my anchor. When I'm not on the River, I go home to Moncoeur." His face clouded; Deirdre suspected he was thinking about the rift with his brother. "Even though I'm not always afforded the prodigal son's welcome I'd like."

Deirdre suddenly had a terrifying thought. Gabrielle! If Deirdre had to spend all her time dodging the spoiled girl's advances, she was in serious trouble! "Does your—uh, cousin stay there, too?"

"Gabrielle's in school in Nashville, though, of course, she comes home for holidays and summers. She's not much use around the house.

Says the slaves should take care of all that." Andre laughed. "My brother's ward is a bit pampered, I'm afraid!"

Deirdre didn't have to be told about that. "Are there many slaves at Moncoeur?"

Andre's face grew shadowed. "Not now that we're concentrating on horse-breeding instead of crops. Jean-Paul and I haven't always agreed on the morality of owning another person body and soul."

Deirdre suspected this was a touchy subject. "Yet that's kind of how it is with you and me right now," she said.

"Good God, you make me sound like some kind of monster! Look, my lad, I'm keeping you around not so much for the money but because I feel sorry for you." Andre ignored Deirdre's indignant protest. "And because I think you're a spunky boy who's gotten a bad shake from his father. I just don't like the idea of turning you loose on the streets when we reach Nashville. There are some pretty sordid elements there, my young friend. Now, speaking of sordid—would you mind awfully getting along with that tub business? We'll be docking in a couple of hours, and I'd still like to get an hour's sleep after my bath."

Deirdre followed Andre's tall form to the corner cabin, which was his. She stepped wide around him and into the room, expecting him to come inside, too. But he said lightly, "I have some business to finish up on deck. I'll be back for my bath shortly. In the meantime . . ." Andre grinned and bowed. "Make yourself at home, my young friend."

Deirdre was incredulous at hearing the key being turned in the lock on the outside. Andre was making her his prisoner!

"That's so you won't jump ship like Papa," she said grimly to herself. "Another O'Shea owing him money." She frowned, catching sight of herself in the oval mirror over a washbowl. Again she considered just blurting out the whole truth when Andre returned. But, no; he'd take that for an open invitation to seduction, since she was all alone and at his mercy. "Well, you can't go to bed in your cap, my girl. So what do you do now?"

As if in answer, her eyes were drawn to a pair of shears lying on the dresser next to Andre's silver-handled brush. Deirdre took off her cap and sighed as she viewed the cascade of flaming hair that tumbled to her shoulders. Then she took a deep breath and started snipping away. . . .

Chapter Two

Andre Devereux's "business" on deck was sorting out some very confused feelings. He leaned on the railing and smoked a thin cigar as he tried to figure out why, for the first time in his thoroughly masculine life, he was attracted—in a way he didn't care to elaborate on, even to himself—to a member of his own sex.

He muttered to himself, "I would've shot anybody on the spot who even hinted something like this could happen to me." The boy was appealing and certainly on the effeminate side, but that didn't explain the magnetism Andre had felt between them when they'd touched.

Thoroughly disgusted at himself for even acknowledging such repellent reactions, Andre flung his cigar into the churning wake of the ship and, cursing softly, started back to his cabin.

At the same time that the gambler was agitating over his troubled thoughts about her, Deirdre O'Shea was looking for a place to hide her shorn locks. The porthole was sealed, so that was out. She briefly considered the chamber pot behind the tiny curtained alcove, but discarded that idea with blushing images of how that hiding place might be discovered.

He was coming back. She could hear him stopping outside the door to unlock it. Desperately, Deirdre stuffed the gleaming red mass under the mattress of the bunk. She'd get rid of it later, when she could sneak out to the railing.

Andre laughed when he entered and saw his "valet" without his cap. "God, no wonder you keep your head covered all the time! Either your father cuts your hair with a bowl and a meat cleaver or some Indians left you for scalped." The unattractively short hair restored his male confidence. What in God's name had gotten into him, thinking he might be undergoing some terrible personal revolution? "What's your name, anyway?"

"Deir—Dearborn. Dearborn O'Shea." Deirdre averted her eyes from Andre, who was yawning and unbuttoning his frilled shirt. She turned her head when he got down to snowy underwear and only looked again when there were just muscled bare shoulders showing over the rim of the tub. "It's—uh, an old Irish name. My great-great grandfather's, to be exact."

Andre wasn't interested in her family tree. He yawned again and pointed to a brush on the side of the wash basin. "Scrub my back, will you? I'm too tired to reach it, and my shoulders ache like the devil after sitting at the cards so long."

Deirdre swallowed hard and started doing as she was told. "Harder," Andre mumbled, relaxed in the warm water to the point of not caring if his back were being scrubbed by a boy or a chimpanzee. "Ummm. Last time I had my back scrubbed, it was a beautiful woman doing it." He was enjoying the memory too much to notice how Deirdre's hand shook on the brush. "At Madame Julia's. Ah, now there's a brothel madam who knows what her customers like." His eyes opened and he grinned up at Deirdre. "Maybe I'll take you with me sometime. The girls would have a fit over such a pretty fellow, and so young, too. You ever, uh . . . ?"

Deirdre shook her head vigorously, noticing that in her consternation over the direction of the conversation, she'd scrubbed part of the broad back almost raw.

"Hey, ouch!" Andre took the brush from her and waved her off. "It's just the dirt, not my skin I want taken off!" He looked at Deirdre, who was standing at the porthole, her back to him. "Sorry; I didn't mean to bark at you. You're still thinking about your father, aren't you?"

No, I'm thinking that I can't possibly stay here with you or go to Moncoeur no matter how wonderful it might be. The uncomfortable sensations he'd been causing in her ever since this ridiculous masquerade had gotten out of hand were troubling her. She had to get away. Somehow she'd get money and repay him for the steamboat fare, but not by working for Andre Devereux or his kin. "I was just thinking how much I'd like to take a turn around deck while you're dressing." She had heard the gangplank scraping against a dock. This could be her chance.

He saw right through it. "Not a chance," Andre said pleasantly, the strong lips parting in a smile that revealed even, white teeth. Deirdre wondered if he cleaned them with a cloth and gritty soda the way she'd done since she was small. "The Captain tells me we're taking a load on here at Gallatin. You could get lost in the shuffle with all that burley tobacco and pickled pork they're bringing on board." Dark brows quirked humorously. "And I'm beginning to like you, Dearborn." Damn it, why did he feel so protective about the boy? There was more to it than feeling responsible because he'd let the older O'Shea stay in a losing game. He couldn't stand the thought of Dearborn roaming around a rowdy town, seventeen thousand strong, with no one to look after him.

Deirdre fought back the tears of frustration. "Mr. Devereux, I'll just say it straight out. I don't feel right working for you like this. It's . . . it's like charity, and my family's always taught me, even when times were the hardest, that it's best to stand on your own two feet."

Andre shook his head slowly. "You're a proud little fellow, Dearborn. I admire that. But why is it I have the feeling that the moment you got away from me, you'd be over your head in trouble again? Tell you what—you give me your word as a man that you won't strike out on your own when we get to Nashville, until I've figured out what's best for you, and we'll talk about this again very soon."

Deirdre turned back to the porthole so Andre wouldn't see her smile. She could make the requested promise "as a man" and break it with a clean conscience at the first opportunity. "You've got my word as a man, sir."

"Very well. I'm holding you to it." Andre stood up and wrapped himself in the big towel Deirdre held out to him with carefully averted eyes. "Reach in my trousers over there, the ones I was wearing. Just to show you that I trust you, I'll let you be guardian of the cabin keys!"

Deirdre hesitated only a moment, until the guilt feelings subsided. Then she extracted the keys, reminding herself of the way the promise had been worded. She wasn't morally bound to keep it. "I thank you, Mr. Devereux. I'll put 'em right up here on the dresser so we can find 'em in the morning."

Andre, clad in the fresh underwear Deirdre had laid out for him, stretched mightily, then tossed a blanket and pillow over to the girl. "Here. I'd let you have the bed, but you're more used to making do with hard sleeping places than I am."

"This will do just fine," Deirdre said cheerfully. From the corner where she quickly curled up, she had a perfect view of Andre's head on the bunk. As soon as she saw that he was sleeping soundly, she would quietly make her way to the deck, to be the first one off the steamboat as soon as it docked in Nashville.

It wasn't long before she could tell from the gambler's even breathing that he was dead to the world. Deirdre eased across the room, taking care not to bump into the tub—he'd forgotten about insisting she bathe, she thought, grinning. Taking the keys, she gently unlocked the cabin door, looking back after the door cracked open to be sure Andre still slept.

For a moment, she hesitated, feeling a pang at the unexpected, almost boyish vulnerability of the handsome face. "Don't worry, Andre Devereux; you'll get your money," she whispered. "And that's a promise I make as Deirdre O'Shea—*not* as a man!"

Moments later, after the *Robertson* pulled into the dock near Fort Negley, she was free. No one even noticed the slender boy who leapt nimbly over a sack of shelled corn to disappear into the grey dawn surrounding Nashville.

Deirdre stopped briefly to admire the handsome St. Cloud's Hotel. Then she set off at a brisk pace down deserted Second Avenue.

"Ho, what have we here?" Deirdre awoke with a jerk at the sound of the hearty voice. She hadn't intended to fall asleep. She'd just stopped to rest for a moment on a secluded bench in a cosy little garden. The last thing she remembered was thinking how pretty the roses were with the early dew sparkling like diamonds. "You're a bit young, lad, for being a tramp. No doubt you're lurking out here hoping for a free glimpse at one of my girls?"

Deirdre rubbed her eyes and looked at the woman standing on the porch, her hands on broad hips, dark pompadour gleaming in the morning sun. Nearly black eyes in a rice-white face held more good nature than irritation. No linsey-woolsey dress for this ample figure; the silk and lace costume marked Madame Julia Poston as what she proclaimed to be in spite of her profession—a well-to-do lady. "No, ma'am." She sat up straighter, alarmed at the significance of that "my girls." Obviously, she'd chosen the porch of a brothel for her stolen nap. "No, ma'am!" she said with strenuous conviction. "I'm not that kind of boy."

Madame Julia's keen eyes rested on the opening of Deirdre's loose shirt. A swell of creamy bosom exposed by buttons that had come undone during the night betrayed Deirdre completely. Madame Julia knew human flesh very well. This was no young man! "No, I can see that you're not," she said softly. "As a matter of fact, I can see that you're not a boy at all." The dark eyes moved expertly over Deidre's slender figure and came to rest on the spikey red curls. "My, my, you are a sight to behold! That's an . . . er, interesting hairstyle you've got there. And I don't think you'd see that outfit pictured in Godey's."

Deirdre grinned. She liked Madame Julia at once and felt no menace from the woman at all. And it was a relief to be lightened of her burdensome masquerade. "I guess I am a pretty sight, all right. Would you kindly be telling me how I can find the Nashville Female Seminary? I heard in New Orleans that they're partial to Irish help in their kitchens."

Madame Julia smiled. "You wouldn't stand the chance of goatscheese in hell getting in even the back door, dressed like that." She said more gently, "Run away from your family, have you, my dear? It's no way to start life in a place like this, you know."

"I've got no family to run away from," Deirdre said. Well, hadn't she decided to disown her father? So she was being truthful. "And I really would like to try for a job at the college, if you'll just please tell me which way and how far."

Madame Julia looked at the girl standing straight and proud before her. Then she reached a decision, partly out of charity, partly out of the same instinctive protectiveness that Andre Devereux had felt. "It's not likely they'll have anything, what with all the folks pouring in here, looking for jobs. To tell the truth, you'll get your food and a mean bed and nothing else for back-breaking work at almost every place in this city. The Irish come here to escape their heartbreaking famine back home and every bastard in town has taken advantage ever since. Come inside. I'll feed you and get you some clothes and then we'll talk." The friendly smile reappeared as the woman held out her well-kept hand to Deirdre. "Oh, by the by, I'm Madame Julia. Or, to some few respectable folks who have no earthly idea what I do for a living, Mrs. Poston."

Deirdre's face showed surprise. "Oh, you're the lady . . ." she stopped just before disclosing Andre Devereux's name. "The lady that someone on the steamboat said has the biggest heart in Tennessee." She gave a polite little curtsy. "I can attest to that already, ma'am."

Madame Julia beamed so broadly that Deirdre didn't repent her little exaggeration at all. "Oh, my dear, you *are* a little charmer!" She winked. "I'll bet you made an absolutely *delicious* young man who drove all the girls wild on that boat."

Only one, Deirdre said to herself, beginning now to see some humor in her experience with Gabrielle Devereux. She grinned, knowing Madame Julia would appreciate the funny side of it, too. "Well, I did cause a couple of hearts to flutter," she admitted with an exaggerated swagger that made the older woman giggle.

There was no sign of the "girls," Deirdre was relieved to see. She followed Madame Julia through the cosy parlor, whose tapestried furnishings and painted, fringed lamps might have been found in a straight-laced parsonage. The kitchen was warm and welcoming; Deirdre came close to fainting when Madame lifted a lid and the delicious odor of ham drifted her way.

After three slices of the savory Tennessee meat, two helpings of potatoes, and four thick, doughy biscuits with honey, Deirdre sighed and polished off a second glass of fresh milk. "I'm eternally grateful to you, ma'am. And I apologize for eating like a farm-hand."

Madame lit a thin black cigar, an event which simultaneously fascinated and shocked her guest. "*Au contraire, chérie,* you managed to look dainty and polite the whole time you were devouring enough breakfast for at least four people. You know, there's that about you—Deirdre, you said?—which intrigues me. You look like a ragamuffin, a scalped one at that; yet you have the air and manners of someone with good breeding."

Deirdre said with sad pride, "My mother was such, though her life was hard. She ran away from a noble family, just to marry my father, and never let us forget what she once was." Deirdre sighed, thinking of the charming Riley and how he had been a thorn in her mother's side while she lived, just as he was to his daughter now.

For Deirdre, it had been a strange childhood—working in the fields till dark and learning "how ladies conduct themselves" at night. Her mother had been relentless, perhaps because of her bitterness at how her own life had turned out.

"Then you see what it can mean to run away," Madame Julia said. She leaned across the table so that her huge bosom came dangerously close to her mug of hot tea. "Tell me what's happened to you, girl. I've been dying of curiosity from the moment I found you curled up in my garden. I see a story in your face, that chopped-off hair. Was it some man caused you to get so desperate?" *Men!* Julia thought. She loved 'em dearly on the whole, but they were at the root of every woman's troubles.

"Yes," Deirdre said, with no intention of telling Madame everything. "It was a man—a horrible man." She put her hands over her face and mumbled, "I . . . I don't want to talk about it." She peered through her fingers, seeing that her hostess was all sympathy. Deirdre thought sheepishly that she was getting to be worse than her father about using drama to advantage.

Madame Julia was not one to probe an aching tooth. "Then let's talk about what to do with you. Would you like to stay here? You say you're good in the kitchen. I've had a time getting help since all these abolitionists started making trouble for us. I'll offer board and a better salary than you'd make any place else in Nashville."

Deirdre's elation faded when Madame Julia named a figure. She knew it was fair, but it wouldn't come close to being enough to pay Andre back as she was determined to do, just as soon as she could. The knowledge that she was as bad as her father, running away from her debt, still rankled. She was anxious to clear the decks with the gambler. "I guess . . . I guess that would be fine, at least till I figure out what else I can do. And I thank you, Madame Julia, for being so kind to me." In a burst of gratitude, Deirdre elaborated on the second-hand praise she'd "heard" about Madame Julia. "I even heard it said when I was in New Orleans, from some of the girls in Storyville, that yours was the finest brothel in the South, run by the best madam in the business!"

Madame Julia's black eyes gleamed like the jet beads around her neck. "They even know about Madame Julia all the way down there! My, my—oh my. That does make a body feel good! And I *do* try my best to run a nice, genteel place!"

Deirdre decided that maybe she did have a bit of Riley O'Shea's blarney in her after all. But what was the harm in it when it brought a sparkle to the eyes of this very goodhearted woman?

Deirdre liked most of the girls at Madame Julia's. Except for Lilianne, whose almond-shaped eyes often viewed the younger girl as though she were an unknown quantity which might turn into competition, they treated Deirdre like a puppyish little sister. She wasn't that much younger than most of them, but the girlish cotton dresses she wore and the infamous haircut contrasted sharply with their studiedly alluring attire and fancy coiffures, setting her completely apart.

She didn't mind her chores—shopping daily for food, keeping fresh flowers in the parlor and bedrooms, mixing special pomades and salves for the girls from the herb garden that was Madame's pride and joy—next to her roses. In contrast to the glamorous residents of the house, Deirdre felt childlike and unexciting, although she kept those thoughts to herself. Though she secretly wished Madame Julia would stop overprotecting her, she didn't want to hurt the older woman's feelings by telling her that.

Madame Julia was strict about keeping the girl "backstairs" when evening came and customers starting sauntering in through the stained-glass door of the house on Second Avenue. Once, just as she was disappearing down the hall right on schedule, Deirdre thought she heard Andre Devereux's baritone voice as the front door opened.

But though she was curious, she didn't stop to look. What would he say to her, or she to him, if they ran into each other in a place like Madame Julia's?

As the weeks passed, Deirdre found herself growing restless. As fond as she was of Madame Julia, her over-protectiveness bordered on smothering.

Pegean, another Irish girl, was the first one to give Deirdre the idea. They were upstairs, Deirdre using the irons to curl the other's straight hair, which reached halfway down her back. The girl was looking not at her hair, over which Deirdre was painfully toiling, but at the reflection of the other girl in the mirror.

She said suddenly, "You know, Deedee, you're prettier than the rest of us put together—except maybe for Lilianne. And she's so stuck on herself, she doesn't count."

Deirdre was honestly shocked by the unexpected compliment. She'd gotten so used to feeling plain around the others in their fancy clothes and dressed, flowing hair, that she really thought Pegean was making fun of her. She screwed up her nose and crossed her eyes comically. "Do you want me to go fetch Madame's eyeglasses for you?"

Pegean laughed. Everyone—except Lilianne, who never laughed at anything—thought Deirdre was a stitch. "Well, your hair is still pretty awful, but aside from that . . ." Pegean looked at Deirdre, her eyes lighting up. "Hey—is Madame in her room?"

"No, she's off at that tea we've all been teasing her about." Deirdre held up an imaginary teacup and crooked her little finger exaggeratedly. With her eyes squinched and her full mouth pursed like a catfish going for the bait, she looked uncannily like the Reverend Bobo's wife, who passed their house each day with her nose stuck in the air. "You know—the one that Mrs. Reverend is going to without knowing who she'll be standing next to in the receiving line."

Pegean giggled. "Oh, you. Forget Mrs. Reverend. I want to see how you'd look in something not so prissy—and with real hair."

Deirdre said solemnly, "We could try sprinkling my head with some of that cow manure Madame got for her rose plants and maybe it'll grow faster."

"I have something a little more immediate in mind. Come on!" Pegean dragged the other girl, both of them still laughing, down the hall to Madame Julia's room.

Madame Julia, her eyes sparkling, marched into the kitchen, pulling her gloves off and unpinning her very proper hat as she went. "Stop stuffing yourself between meals, dear; you'll get fat and then where will you be in this business?" The automatic rebuke was directed toward Pegean, who was having a slab of ham and a thick biscuit at the kitchen table. "Where's Deedee? I want her to hear what a lark it was, seeing some of those biddies' faces when they realized who I was."

"She's upstairs," Pegean mumbled, her mouth full and her eyes dancing at the thought of the surprise in store for Madame when Deirdre came down. "No, I'll go get her. You just stay right there."

Madame lit the fire under the teakettle and stood at the stove humming happily. She had so enjoyed popping that Mrs. Bobo's eyes out—her with her constant nagging at the Reverend to use his pulpit to help run Madame Julia out of town.

"Well, what do you think of her? Isn't she just *beautiful?*"

At Pegean's question, Madame Julia turned and nearly scalded herself with the teakettle she was holding.

There stood Deirdre, resplendent in a low-cut silk dress whose midnight-blue sheen matched her sparkling eyes. Pegean had applied makeup delicately, adding only a touch of color to eyelids, cheeks, and mouth. Madame's newest and most expensive wig from Paris, a cascade of glossy raven curls, topped the vision.

Deirdre's happy smile faded when she saw the look on Madame Julia's face. "Don't . . . don't you like it?" she asked uncertainly.

Julia glared at Pegean. "This is your doing. Go, leave us. And you're excused from the evening meal."

Deirdre was crushed by the older woman's reaction. Did she look so awful? In the mirror in Madame's bedroom, she'd looked like the other girls. (Much prettier, Pegean had insisted at the end of the transformation.) "Madame, please don't blame Pegean. It wasn't her—"

"Shh." Madame waited until she'd heard an upstairs bedroom door close, signaling that Pegean had indeed gone to her room. "That girl! I'm fonder of her than all the rest—except for you—but she'll be the death of me yet! Now, what's all this, Deedee?" She shook her head slowly, her eyes sad as she looked at the younger woman. "What on earth do you think you're doing, getting yourself up like that? My darling, you can't be like Lilianne or Pegean or the others. You don't *want* to be like them, or like I was when I was their age. My precious, it's a life of heartbreak, and old age comes ten times earlier."

Deirdre was sorry that Madame Julia was so upset, but she couldn't help that. The moment she'd felt the silk on her skin, had seen the haughty beauty staring back at her from the mirror, she'd realized that she was hungry for things that she could never have if she spent her life tending herb gardens and the like. "But what good is life if you spend it poor and doing dull things day in and day out?"

Madame Julia looked hurt. "Darling, I thought you liked your life here."

"I do, Madame Julia; I do. You've been so wonderful to me—and all the girls have. But I don't want to be a maid in a brothel for the rest of my life." Deirdre stretched her arms dramatically. "If I'm going to be working in a brothel, I want to be a star! And make lots of money," she added hastily.

Madame Julia hid a smile at that, some of her distress dissipating. The child in Deedee was showing herself again, in spite of the alluring womanliness of her new appearance. A plan was already forming in the madam's head, now that she realized the course her protege was set upon. "Tell me," she asked; "if I put my foot down and said no, absolutely not, you can't be one of my girls—what would you do?"

"I'd go to Madame Justine down the street," Deirdre said promptly. "Pegean says she's *desperate* for new blood in her place."

Madame Julia made a mental note to put the kitchen off-limits to Pegean for the next month as punishment. "Wearing my wig and that dress, which I just had delivered for a pretty penny or two?"

Deirdre's face fell. "Oh, Madame Julia, I *do* sound so horribly ungrateful. I want to work for *you!* Please give me the chance. Please trust me to know what I'm doing." She had already figured out from what Pegean had confided that she could make enough money in one week to pay Andre Devereux back for her and Riley's passage on the *Robertson.*

Madame Julia put her hands on her young friend's shoulders and looked deeply into the rich blue eyes. "My dear, I trust you completely, but I can see you don't know one whit about what you're getting yourself into. However, since you seem determined, I'm certainly not going to give Justine LeFarr the satisfaction of luring you away from me. At least if you stay with me, I'll be able to look out for you in what can be a heart-breaking business. Now, let's have that spot of tea and plot our strategy for launching you properly."

Madame Julia had already planned her strategy—one that would protect the girl whom she'd begun to love like the daughter she'd always wanted but never had. She looked at

Deirdre and said crisply, "By the by, since you're determined to go into this profession, I'll tell you right at the start—I'm the boss. And I'll be the one to negotiate your services your first night. Understood?"

Deirdre, a little put off by Julia's sudden transformation into all-business, nodded, her eyes big at the realization that Madame was talking about selling her virginity. "Yes, ma'am," she said meekly. "I understand."

Chapter Three

"They're all staring at me," Deirdre hissed from their velvet-lined box high up in the Music Hall. "I think it's the wig. I declare, I don't feel right as a brunette. Everybody's laughing at me."

Madame Julia, resplendent in black velvet and pearls, chuckled behind her fan. "I assure you they're not laughing. Every man I know who's seen you here tonight will be over to see me to find out who you are. We'll drive a fine bargain tonight for your precious 'first time out', my love."

Deirdre cast a nervous look at her companion, not sure she liked Madame's total, cheerful capitulation to Deirdre's career decision. "Uh, maybe we should wait a few days, Madame Julia. I mean, after all, I'm very new at this and . . ."

"Definitely not, my dear. There's no time like the present, as they say. Strike while the iron is hot and all that, you know." Madame Julia's fan hid her secret, smug smile. "And you, darling Deedee, are causing quite a heat wave down there amongst my gentlemen customers. Why, did you see how everyone stared at you when we entered our box?"

"I . . . I guess I did," Deirdre said uncomfortably, adjusting the lace at her neckline to give her more decorous coverage. Dear God, how had she gotten herself into this? And Madame Julia seemed determined not to let her out of it. Maybe, as Pegean had said in a miff after she'd been cut off from in-between snacks in the kitchen, their mistress *did* have a sharp eye for the dollar.

"Dear heart, would you stop twitching?" Madame Julia whispered. "The performance is about to begin."

"My dress is too low," the girl whispered, averting her eyes from the nearsighted stares of a stocky, bewhiskered man in the next box. The powdered wig he was wearing probably hid a shiny head as bald as a baby's bottom. Dear lord, what if he were the one to ask for her tonight? She could swear she'd seen Madame Julia exchanging significant nods with him over Deirdre earlier. "And I can hardly breathe, my waist is so tight."

Madame looked at the creamy swell of breasts above the fine silk burgundy gown. "No man wants to pay top dollar for a pig in a poke, my dear," she said unsympathetically. "Now, remember what I've told you. No conversation with anyone, here or after the concert. I've posted my man at the door to prevent anyone coming in our box, and we'll be hustled out the back door immediately after the diva's last song. Oh, I *do* wish you'd been with me a few years ago when Miss Jenny Lind performed here. The *Gazette* called her high-pitched and over-rated, but she was just like a nightingale! Now just smile mysteriously at no one in particular and keep on looking divine."

Deirdre did just that so successfully that Madame Julia posted her considerable bulk at the door during intermission. At least two of the girl's admirers did their best to meet the mysterious Irish beauty on the pretext of bringing refreshment to the stall.

But Madame Julia was firm and had them barred without mercy. Her plans did not brook unscheduled encounters.

One of the reasons for the consistent success of Madame Julia's establishment on Second Avenue was her tasteful arrangement for "selection." Unlike the rowdier houses in the city, there was no jumble of men and women in the waiting room, sizing each other up over beer and laughter. Sleaziness was not part of Madame's mode of operation.

In her infinite canniness about men, Madame Julia had learned that they adored efficiency, even in their pursuit of pleasure. Consequently, everything was run very smoothly and in organized fashion.

The downstairs parlor was a "receiving room," where gentlemen were served glasses of sherry by a selected hostess, whose only duties of the evening would be making the clientele welcome and comfortable. Then, as each man subtly made his desires for entertainment known to the hostess, he would be sent upstairs to a "viewing room." Here the upstairs hostess would take over, subtly determining the client's selection and handling the transaction, unless it were a special situation that Madame Julia wished to handle personally. Then she would assign the room, sending the selected girl ahead to await her gentleman caller. Beyond the bedroom door, organization was left entirely to the client and his partner.

The viewing room was quite cozy and private. From a mirrored window overlooking a comfortable salon where Madame's girls awaited their evening call, its occupant could leisurely select the lady of his fancy. Then the deal would be struck with the hostess and the chosen partner would melt away to the room assigned her for the evening.

It was in the lounging salon that Deirdre sat, nervously awaiting the call meaning an end to both her virginity and—hopefully—her financial obligations, for Madame Julia had hinted that a 'first-timer' often brought a high price. She kept her eyes modestly averted from the smoky mirror that she'd learned was the viewing window, saying ambivalent prayers. *Dear God, maybe no one will want me and I won't have to go through with this after all.* That was followed by *Oh, please let whoever selects me be kind and not fat or bad-smelling.*

Behind the mirror, Madame Julia was completing the negotiation for the evening's most popular choice amongst the gentlemen. She had already turned down three requests for Deirdre and was chiding Dr. Geoffrey Markette for being late getting to the house from the evening's concert.

"Now, Geoffrey, if you weren't my dearest and most loyal client, I would not have waited another moment for you to get here. Have you any idea how much in demand our darling Deedee is after being on show tonight?"

The stocky, grey-whiskered man's eyes glistened with forgotten yearnings as he nodded wistfully. "I could hardly keep my eyes off her at the concert." Julia hid a smile at that; the poor fellow could hardly see beyond his nose! "But it's a steep price you're asking, Julia." He tried to look stern, which made the madam's smile even broader. He was a lamb trying to look like a lion.

Julia leaned over and whispered something in his ear.

Geoffrey Markette's face brightened. "On the other hand," he said hoarsely, "I've finished paying for the dispensary and Mrs. Markette is visiting her sister in Gallatin tonight. . . ."

Unbeknownst to Madame Julia, Andre Devereux had come upstairs before he was called and was letting the hostess in on his frustration.

"Dammit, Pegean, Julia and I are old friends, and I'm sure she would be mad as the devil if she knew I was downstairs cooling my heels when I already know who I want."

"Now don't you go getting your dander up, Mr. Devereux. Lilianne is probably still available." Pegean added cattily, "You're the only one who ever asks for her regularly, anyway."

"I didn't come here tonight for Lilianne," Andre said coldly. "Not that it's any business of yours, but there was a girl in Julia's box this evening . . ."

"Oh, ho," Pegean said, her dimples showing. "So our Deedee caught your eye, just as she did every other man's here."

Andre muttered. "I thought it was more damn crowded tonight than usual. Why have I never seen this—Deedee before?"

"Maybe because Madame Julia keeps her under special wraps for very special customers," Pegean said, her Irish devilment rising. "Madame Julia ain't one to have favorites, but I'll tell you this much—she's got it soft for *that* one. Has ever since Miss Deedee showed up here last month."

Andre's face was thoughtful. He hadn't been able to keep his eyes off the girl sitting with Julia at the concert. Aside from a troubling sense of familiarity, there'd been an enchanting innocence about her. Even with the flamboyant gown and raven hairstyle. Andre had half hoped he wouldn't find her in residence at Madame Julia's, half hoped she wasn't what she appeared to be. The other half of him longed to meet her, to find out who and what she was and why he was so attracted to her. And to make love to her, whatever the price.

So she'd been here for weeks. That was a grim testimony to the mockery of her "innocence." "Pegean, I want to see Julia. Right now."

"Sorry, me darling. She's not to be disturbed." Pegean winked and whispered, "She's settling with Dr. Markette—and I'll bet at a pretty penny, too!—for his evening with our Deedee."

Andre groaned, "Not that old fossil!" Not Geoffrey Markette, with the powdered wig and whiskers and old man's gait—and half-blind to boot! *Wig!* Andre's eyes looked beyond the hostess at an image of glossy masses of fire-red curls, pressed beneath his mattress. He relived the excitement of realizing that "Dearborn" had really been a girl—and the relief that revelation had brought. His attraction *hadn't* been unnatural; it had been instinctive and true to his masculinity.

He was suddenly sure that "Dearborn" and this "Deedee" were one and the same. She was wearing a hairpiece over the mangled, flaming hair. Anger mingled with excitement. His mind whirling at the prospect of seeing the Irish girl again without the pretense between them, Andre concentrated on what the hostess was saying.

"Now don't you be talking about one of our sweetest customers," Pegean chided. "And, speaking of talking, I can't stand around jawing with you all night—unless you came here for business," she added with a wink.

Andre put his hand on Pegean's arm when she would have walked away. "I have, indeed. I don't need a viewing room." He certainly didn't want to run into Julia now, not with his current, rapid plotting to thwart her plans for the girl. "I'll take Lilianne."

"But you said you didn't . . ." The Irish girl's good-natured face was perplexed.

"Pegean, you've always seemed like a girl with a good sense of fun. How would you feel about helping me play a little joke on Lilianne?"

Pegean's eyes sparkled with impishness. "Oo, I'll have myself in hot water again, I can just tell. I'm already on Madame's bad side, Mr. Devereux, so how could I—"

"There's a box of cane sugar candy and a ham, sliced and cured, in it for you. And I'll have 'em sneaked in so Julia won't know a thing," Andre told her.

He couldn't have come up with a more effective bribe. The enforced "diet" Pegean was on was driving her crazy. She'd even been caught snitching raw herbs from Julia's garden. "On the other hand, this place *could* use a bit more fun," Pegean said promptly. "Now just what sort of joke did you have in mind?"

"Well, you're the upstairs hostess tonight and in charge of assigning the rooms—right?"

Pegean nodded, her eyes narrowing. "Oh, ho. I get it. A bit of the switcheroo game—that's what you have in mind, eh?" The impish eyes gathered mischief and her voice lowered to a conspiratorial whisper. "There's a fine powdered wig we used in the New Year's farce last year—it's in the chest in the hall two doors down from the rose room."

Her emphasis on *rose room* and accompanying wink told Andre what he needed to know. He grinned and kissed the girl on the cheek. "Ah, Pegean, you're a lass after me own heart. May the saints in heaven be good to you for being such a fine sport."

"I'll probably be seeing them personally when Madame hears about this," Pegean said. But secretly she exulted that it would be handsome Andre Devereux introducing her little friend to the mysteries of love instead of poor old Geoffrey. What on earth had gotten into Madame, anyway, matching those two up on the most important night in Deirdre's life?

"Leave Julia to me. And for God's sake, keep her out of this until it's a *fait accompli!*"

Pegean took the money Andre handed her, eyes widening when she counted it. The handsome gambler really had his heart set on Deirdre! "Save the fancy phrases for my funeral when Madame Julia finds out who hoodwinked one of her oldest customers," Pegean muttered darkly. But she scurried off to tell Lilianne that her gentleman would be calling on her in the tapestry room, being very vague when Lilianne asked his name.

Now if she could just manage to avoid bumping into Madame Julia before she got Lilianne and Deirdre settled, she might live to see morning—and breakfast was the only normal meal she was allowed to take.

The thought of food prompted a happy image of the goodies Andre owed her. Pegean went about her assignment with a blissful, faraway look on her pert face. After all, she *was* doing her little friend a big favor, as well as having a laugh on Lilianne.

As for Madame Julia, Pegean wasn't all that worried. Five minutes of scolding and then she'd be shaking her head over Pegean's scattered brain. She'd soon be giving that robust laugh of hers over the joke on Lilianne. . . .

Deirdre's heart stampeded into her throat when she heard the soft tap at the door. "Come . . . come in," she whispered.

Though the man outside could not have heard the invitation, the door opened and Deirdre could see the silhouette of the man who would be spending the evening with her. In the semi-darkness of the candle-lit room, she saw the powdered white of a thick wig, and her heart sank.

Oh, God—it had to be the man who'd stared at her from the next box at the concert. He hadn't seemed so tall, and she could have sworn he was stout, but the hairpiece was unforgettable. Deirdre braced herself and made her mouth shape a welcoming smile. She backed over to the loveseat in front of the fire and sat down, nearly knocking over the ice bucket containing French champagne that Madame had provided for her special guest.

"Will . . . will you have a glass of champagne?" Deirdre's hands shook as she poured some of the sparkling liquid into one of Julia's finest stem glasses. "The fire's very nice. Perhaps you'd like to warm yourself." She blushed, wondering if that was quite the thing to say.

"I'd like that very much." The familiar baritone voice made her come close to dropping both champagne bottle and glass.

Andre Devereux!

Deirdre was paralyzed with shock. Had he recognized her, too? She shrank back into the shadows of the high-backed sofa, wondering if he'd come to snatch her up again for running out on him.

"That champagne—you offered me a glass, remember?"

Deirdre held out a glass, her face turned away as he came closer to her to take it. Andre's hand closed around hers, making their flesh burn together. He slowly brought the glass, still holding her hand captive in his, to his mouth, looking at her intently all the while.

"Turn your face to me, Deirdre," he said softly.

"How did you know my name?" she whispered, not meeting his eyes, knowing the worst.

Andre reached out and, before Deirdre could protest, pulled off the cascading wig. "Ah," he said, staring at the soft, short curls of flaming red thus revealed. "It's my little friend Dearborn. We do meet in the strangest ways." He reached into his pocket and brought out a small snuff box from which he extracted a glossy red curl of hair. "I do believe you left something in my cabin," he said, holding the sheared tress up to Deirdre's ear. "See? A perfect match. God's name—do you know what a fool you made of me?"

"I . . . I'm sorry. Things just . . . well, got out of hand. And I didn't run away that night for the reasons you think. I promised you I'd pay you back, and I will."

Andre looked around the room—at the cozy fire, at the champagne, at Deirdre's expensive lounging ensemble—and raised his eyebrows. "I suppose this is better than working as a valet. Do you really think your father would approve of what you're doing now?"

Deirdre lifted her chin. She had no idea of how entrancing she appeared in the firelight, with her elfin curls catching the gleam and her rich blue eyes reflecting the ambivalent emotions of meeting Andre Devereux again under these intimate circumstances. "My father no longer has the right to approve or disapprove of anything I do. Nor do you."

Andre reached out and caught her hands, pulling her toward him so that her face was a breath away from his. "I don't disapprove at all," he said softly, though there was something about his eyes that was not at all soft. "I paid very dearly for you tonight, my dear . . . Deirdre. Enough for you to clear your debt with me totally. But I warn you—I expect to get my money's worth." His face lowered even more. "After all," he murmured. "You've been working for Julia long enough to know how to give a man his . . . money's . . . worth. . . ." His mouth was touching lightly around her cheekbones, her chin, her lips.

In the turmoil of emotion, Deirdre tried to hang on to what was wrong with what he'd just said, but it was hard to concentrate. "Mr. Devereux," she whispered. "The champagne. It's . . . it's very expensive."

"So are you," he whispered back, his mouth finding the tip of a delicious earlobe. Without moving his lips from the burning trail they were tracing down to her mouth, he pulled off the powdered wig he was wearing and flung it atop the dark tumble of curls that Deirdre had been wearing. "So here we are—just you and me," he murmured against the hollow of her throat. "Without fake hair, without aliases and, very soon, without everything. And I warn you that I expect sweet payment for the anguish you caused me when I thought I was feeling lust for a damned stripling boy. Sweet . . . sweet . . .

payment, my darling Dearborn," he murmured as his mouth crushed hers.

Deirdre, breathless from the bruising kiss whose intimate demands shocked her, protested when Andre's lips moved abruptly to the swell of her breasts. "I . . . you go too fast. The champagne," she said desperately. "It's being spoiled by the flames."

"So am I," Andre said, sighing as Deirdre managed to wriggle away to play hostess. He ignored the glass she held out with a shaking hand, instead placing his lips on the deep dimple in her left shoulder. "Fill *this* with your champagne and I'll gladly finish off the whole bottle, one sip at a time," he whispered, his tongue growing playful and causing strange sensations in Deirdre.

Deirdre closed her eyes, took a deep breath, and downed the abandoned glass of champagne in one swallow. It was her first encounter with strong spirits—one she would not soon forget. "I feel a little dizzy," she whispered, wondering if all those little bubbles were responsible for making her float to the ceiling.

"Wonderful," Andre whispered back. "That gives me the excuse to help you into that rather magnificent bed." He scooped her up in his arms and carried her to the high, canopied four-poster, gently lowering her onto the satin covers.

Deirdre squeezed her eyes shut and waited for the inevitable.

It didn't happen. After a long time, she opened her eyes. Andre was lying next to her, his chin propped on his hands, watching her with amusement. "What's the matter?" she asked faintly. "Is something wrong with me?"

Andre's eyes danced with excitement. God, she was an artistic tease! Already a month into this business and she still managed to maintain the naive innocence of inexperienced virginity. He ignored the persistent instinct for protectiveness, reminding himself that Julia, generous though she was, had no proclivity toward charity. The girls who lived with her earned their keep. "That remains to be seen, since you're still fully dressed. Maybe if you'd take off your clothes . . ."

Deirdre blushed. "I—uh, thought the man always liked to do that," she said faintly.

Something flickered in Andre's eyes before he said, a little harshly, "Some men, perhaps. But this is you and me—remember? And I'm paying for the pleasure of what I want. I'd like for *you* to take your clothes off." He smiled slightly. "I took mine off for you once, if you'll remember, so turnabout is fair play."

Deirdre turned red, remembering. "Yes, but that wasn't the same thing at all."

"It certainly wasn't," Andre said in a low voice, his eyes holding hers. "If I'd known then what I know now, I would've insisted on that bath for you, too." He waited as Deirdre stood there nervously fingering the tiny buttons at her bodice. "Well?" He felt his impatience threatening to halt the slow, sensual game he was enjoying so thoroughly. The girl had mastered the pretence of innocence to a fine art. His desire was climbing uncontrollably.

Deirdre finished with the buttons, then with a shy look toward the bed, let her gown slip into a shimmering puddle around her feet. As Andre watched, his dark eyes growing darker, a petticoat followed the dress. And then another. Deirdre closed her eyes when she was down to only her chemise. *I can't do it,* she said to herself.

But before she could say the words aloud, there were strong arms around her and Andre's lips were pressed against her bare shoulder. Deirdre felt the cascade of the remaining barrier of cloth slip down her body as Andre finished undressing her.

"I couldn't wait any longer," he whispered, his body warm and hard against her shivering one. He was naked, too, now. Deirdre felt the hair on his strong chest against her breasts with a shock of unexpected sensuality. Then they were on the bed together with Andre's urgent need for her guiding Deirdre along the path of passion which, like the champagne, she'd never experienced till now. "Oh, Deirdre. Sweet, sweet, tantalizing, devious Deirdre . . ."

He made lingering love with his eyes, with his mouth, with his hands, till Deirdre's whole body was aflame, her senses clogged with confused sensations, her brain reeling from the newness of what was happening to her. He would allow no modesty. When Deirdre pushed his face away from one nectar-tipped breast, he found the other and demanded its sweetness as unrelentingly.

"Do you have no shame at all?" Deirdre asked in a choked whisper when she could finally speak. Never had she dreamed that this was what lovemaking was about. She'd naively assumed that the man took the woman, there was a bit of discomfort on her part, a kiss or two, and then it was over. Her body was learning otherwise, under Andre's tutelage, and it both shamed and excited her.

"None where this is concerned," Andre whispered. What kind of lovers had she been exposed to? he wondered angrily. The jump on, jump off, "thank you, ma'am" variety? Deirdre was exquisite; he could not imagine any man not tuning that voluptuous body to its finest note of ecstasy. "Passion is the only honest emotion, darling Deirdre. Enjoy it; revel in it; be a part of it."

I think I already am, Deirdre thought wildly as Andre's lips charted an intimate, burning trail back to her mouth. She was aware of his male yearning hot against her thighs and wondered if it meant she was a real trollop to feel excitement at the image of it filling her body. . . .

Andre lifted his mouth from hers, passion making his words come out hoarse and ragged. "God, you are a lovely thing, Deirdre. You taste and smell like a ripe peach. You have the body of a French courtesan and the face of a Raphael angel! I just wish I were . . ." It had been on the tip of his tongue to say *I just wish I were the first man in your life.* But he changed it to "I just wish I were as young as the mythical Dearborn and as fresh and wholesome."

Deirdre shyly wondered if it would be bold of her to ask him to kiss her again. As though he'd read her thoughts, Andre murmured an endearment and rolled over, placing his head close to hers on the pillow.

He turned her face gently so that their eyes met, barely an inch apart. His were the color of dark, warm smoke as he murmured, "I can sense the fires inside you, Deirdre. You're a passionate woman." His mouth came closer to hers. He said huskily, "Kiss me while I caress you, my sweet Deirdre."

Deirdre pressed her mouth against his and sensed Andre's pleased surprise at her initiative. "That's right, darling Deirdre," he whispered. "Open yourself up to me . . . ah, yes . . . like that. Yes!"

His hand, which had been gently, insistently stroking the throbbing peaks of her breasts, moved slowly down her belly to the curly thatch between slender thighs. Deirdre's breath caught in her throat when Andre's manipulations brought hitherto unknown sensations to the depths of her being. She moaned feebly when her legs were carefully parted, but had no desire to betray her own honest needs.

Then Andre was there, his strong body pressing her down, down, down into a velvet abyss. One tearing jolt of pain, softened by feminine curiosity, and she was part of him, he of her. Deirdre felt the thrusting, building passion of Andre inside her with a sense of unreality. She felt his hands slide beneath her to cup her buttocks, holding her tight against the final, strong thrust. Then she lay quiet and trembling as he lay heavily against her.

Finally: "My God, I didn't know. Deirdre, I didn't know! I swear I thought you were . . . oh, lord, girl. Why didn't you tell me you hadn't known a man before? Damn that Pegean to hell and back. She's the one, telling me you'd been here for a month. Naturally I just assumed . . . And Julia! She was parading you at the concert like a choice piece of stock!" Andre hugged Deirdre to him, his heart still pounding from the ecstasy of male triumph. Yet, he didn't understand. How could Deirdre still be a virgin after working for Julia over a month?

Deirdre gave him the answer. "Tonight was my first night. I've been working as a domestic for Madame Julia up until now." She felt very strange, as though she were someone else, not Deirdre O'Shea at all. Did all women feel that way after their first time? she wondered.

Andre groaned inwardly. He felt like a bastard. Yet if it hadn't been him tonight, it would have been that dolt, Markette! "Why, Deirdre, why? Why would a girl like you voluntarily enter such a business? God knows you're beautiful enough, but think about five years down the road! It's a dead end, girl!"

"You're a gambler," Deirdre said. "That's a dead end too. Why don't you stay at home and work on the plantation with your brother?"

Andre smiled grimly. "*Touché*. I gamble on the riverboats because it's risky, exciting, and I can make money at it."

Deirdre said, "Well, I've decided on this profession for precisely the same reasons." She hated his patronizing air toward her. What right did Andre Devereux have to look down his nose at her for choosing to be part of a profession that he himself supported? She said airily, "Actually, I may decide to become a madam, like Julia, at an early age. Or I may find some rich, attractive gentleman who wants to marry me. . . ." She hadn't thought about either prospect. She just wanted Andre Devereux to know he wasn't in charge of her life.

"In a brothel?" Andre laughed harshly. "Not likely. Deirdre, are you sure this is what you want?"

"Yes," Deirdre lied, thinking of Dr. Geoffrey Markette and how she'd felt when she thought he was coming to her bedroom. She wasn't sure at all, but Andre Devereux didn't need to know that. "It's better than working as a housemaid or in the fields for the rest of my life."

"Then, if you're absolutely sure, I'd like to make love to you again." At Deirdre's reflex, he asked, "Did I hurt you that much?"

She said reluctantly, "It . . . it wasn't *awful.*"

Andre chuckled and kissed the tip of her nose. "Not really awful, she says! I guess you know I can't leave things like that, just as a matter of pride." His hands played with the curls over her ear as he looked deeply into her eyes. "Actually, it's not my pride at all. I just want you again like the very devil." He whispered, "But I won't take you again unless you want it, too."

By the end of the next half hour, Deirdre had discovered that her body was full of treachery. Andre took full advantage of that treachery, never letting up until Deirdre whispered in his ear that she wanted him as much as he did her.

At her moment of excrutiating intensity, she cried out a vulgar Irish curse that embarrassed Deirdre and delighted her lover. . . .

Andre smiled at the sleeping girl in the bed he was easing out of. She looked enchanting, with the gamine wisps of hair lighting up the pillow and her hands tucked under one soft cheek like a child. She was all woman, though, he thought with a resurgence of the emotion she'd caused in him.

He dressed without waking her, then tiptoed over to kiss her lightly.

Andre stood for a long moment before knocking on Julia's door. He dreaded telling her the trick he'd played, but had decided he had to talk to her about Deirdre.

Julia was a good woman. Surely she would see that Deirdre O'Shea wasn't suited for working in a "house."

"Well, who in the world . . ." Julia stood there in a voluminous flannel gown, her face greasy with cream, her hair up on multicolored rags. She tried to shut the door again, but Andre laughed and slipped inside her bedroom.

"Julia, you look absolutely adorable." Andre dodged the pillow she threw at him. "Look, I really have to talk to you. It's about Deirdre O'Shea."

The look of annoyance on Julia's face at having a man catch her *en déshabillé* changed to complacency. "Ah, my sweet Deedee. You and every man here tonight wants to talk about the darling. Well, I think after tonight I'll be able to talk some sense into her; she was already on the verge of backing out. After a night with that sweet old fool, Geoffrey, she'll have had enough! And since he's been impotent for so long that he doesn't even take his pants off when he's with one of my girls, it isn't too late for Deedee to change her mind!"

Andre stared at her. "Oh, God!" *Impotent!* "Then why, I ask you, does the man come to a place like this?"

"Not for the reason you might think. Geoffrey is sweet and half dotty, but he would never try any of that stuff that I've heard goes on down at Justine's. No, he just likes to cuddle and kiss and rock a girl like she's his little dead daughter come back to life."

"Oh, God!" Andre said again, sitting down and burying his face in his hands.

Madame Julia, mistaking Andre's reaction, said, "I suppose it sounds bizarre to you, but actually, it's all very touching. The girl who used to take care of our Geoffrey left last week, so when I told him that Deirdre had just lost her father and needed comforting from someone like him . . ." Julia finally noticed that Andre was not apparently enjoying her story about Dr. Markette. "Andre, for heaven's sake, what's the matter? You look like someone just shot your favorite horse."

Andre looked up at her, his handsome face solemn. "Julia, I have something to tell you that's going to make you mad as hell. But first you have to give me your solemn word that you won't take it out on Pegean."

Julia sat down very slowly, her eyes on Andre's face. "I'll decide that after I find out what she's done."

Andre sighed heavily. "She's not the culprit, believe me. I am."

"Then I'll take it out on you. Now, tell me what it is you have to tell me. Is it about Deirdre O'Shea? I didn't know you knew her."

"It is, and I did know her. Well, not *her,* but—oh, hell, just let me get on with it."

Madame Julia took it pretty well, Andre thought when he was finished. Or at least he *thought* she did.

That was before she calmly took a pearl-handled derringer out of her desk drawer, pointed it steadily at Andre's head, and said with fire in her black eyes, "You get out of here and never set foot in my house again, or so help me, I'll blow your brains out!" She marched back to the desk and took out a wad of bills and stuffed them in Andre's pocket. "There's the money she owed you. I'd say you've been paid in full, buster!"

When he'd gone, Madame Julia put the derringer down and sat down and cried, not for Deirdre's lost innocence but because this was such a rotten business. And now that sweet, vibrant girl was a part of it.

In the middle of her tears, she glanced up and caught sight of herself in the mirror. In spite of herself, she started laughing. What a comical sight she must've been to Andre Devereux, looking like a greasy, fat scarecrow waving a fancy pistol under his nose.

The fact that the derringer wasn't loaded made her laugh all the harder. And by the time her mind rolled around to imagining the look on Lilianne's face when she discovered that doddering old Geoffrey in her bed instead of Andre . . . !

Julia laughed until her sides hurt. Dammit, life could be a bowl of peach pits, but laughing at it once in a while made it a lot easier to swallow!

Chapter Four

Madame Julia did something unprecedented the next morning. She took a breakfast tray up to the girl in the rose room. Tiptoeing in, she expected to find Deirdre still asleep.

Instead, she found her in her robe at the window, laughing at Julia's cat, who was being chased by a noisy blue jay. She turned as the older woman entered. "Oh, do come look, Madame Julia! Chauncy has apparently been after that poor bird's babies again. He's getting murdered."

Julia set the tray down and came over to look. "Serves him right, the fat old rascal. I feed him a gracious plenty without him going out robbing nests." She looked searchingly at the girl beside her. "I expected you to sleep late this morning."

Deirdre laughed, for no good reason at all, and stretched out her arms as if to embrace the morning. She cradled the mug of tea Julia handed her and took deep breaths from the fragrant steam. "Umm. How lovely! Thank you." She went over to sniff the fresh rose on the breakfast tray. "Oh, what a beautiful rose! Madame Julia, you are so *good* to me!"

Madame Julia sighed. Things were certainly not turning out the way she'd planned. By rights, Deirdre O'Shea would by now be meekly agreeing with Julia that life in a brothel was not for her, that she would turn her thoughts to other, happier ways of earning her living. Damn Andre Devereux for interfering!

"Deirdre, I saw Andre last night," she said. "I paid him the money you owed him out of what was coming to you. And I told him his business was no longer welcome in my house." Julia left out the part about waving the derringer around. In the cold grey of dawn, she'd regretted her foolish histrionics. After all, Andre Devereux had always been a gentleman on his infrequent visits to see Lilianne. Besides, he was influential up and down the river, often sending clients Julia's way.

"Oh." Deirdre slowly put the rose back on the tray, not quite meeting Julia's eyes when she asked, "Then . . . then I won't be seeing him again?" She blushed, realizing how unprofessional this must sound to Madame Julia. "I mean, I hope he didn't—well, *complain* about me to you."

"No, he didn't complain about you," Madame Julia said quietly. "Deirdre, last night was a terrible mistake! You see, I never intended for Andre Devereux to visit you. . . ."

Deirdre listened without saying a word while Madame Julia told her the whole story. When Julia was through, she said softly, "I see. So he thought I had been working for you like Lilianne and the others all this time since I left the ship." So that was why Andre had talked to her and treated her like a woman who no longer had her innocence.

Well, she would have to get used to men treating her that way from now on, wouldn't she? Deirdre swallowed hard when she thought of the nights to come when the Geoffrey Markettes instead of the Andre Devereuxs would be coming through that bedroom door! And then she thought about how hard Madame Julia had tried to protect her, and she felt like bursting into tears. "Madame Julia, you really don't want me to work for you like this, do you?" she asked softly.

Julia's black eyes glistened as she shook her head. "Oh, my dear, if you only knew how wrong the life is for you. You've a heart that's as tender as a ripe peach, ready to fall for a man like Andre Devereux—and be burst in the falling! It hurts me to think of the pain ahead of you in the years to come."

Deirdre already had a foretaste of that pain. To think of not seeing Andre Devereux again, to think of the silly things she'd said about staying in the brothel—it hurt terribly. "Madame Julia, you were right about me all along. I . . . I realized it last night when I thought it was Dr. Markette coming into my bedroom. I can't do it. I can't be a Lilianne or a Pegean, no matter how hard I try."

Madame Julia's smile was a joy to see. She held out her arms. "Oh, my precious Deedee! You just don't know how happy that makes me!"

After they'd hugged and kissed each other, Madame Julia said practically, "Now, we can't have you working in my kitchen and garden for the rest of your life. But until the right man happens along, you can stay here and help me just like you've been doing."

She started giggling a few minutes later as they were finishing the pot of tea and plate of muffins. "Oh, my dear, I just happened to think about it—how on earth am I going to explain the sudden disappearance of my raven-haired beauty from my salon?" But Madame Julia was not long in recognizing the potential of having a "mystery woman" legend make the rounds amongst her Second Avenue clientele.

In the weeks that passed, Deirdre enthusiastically earned her keep. She kept the bed linens fresh in all the receiving rooms, saw to the changing of flowers in the parlor, took care of the marketing, helped the girls with their nightly wardrobing, and was even more indispensable than ever.

The day after she worked till dark planting the new spring garden, she couldn't get out of bed. Madame Julia anxiously nursed her with bowls of steaming chicken soup. "I hope it's not the croup, love. Have a spoonful of this, Julia's own brew. You've been overworking yourself, and that's the truth." The truth was that Madame Julia had been eyeing her charge worriedly for the past two weeks. The dark shadows under the lovely eyes concerned her, as did some other changes in the girl.

Madame Julia prayed that Deirdre's malady wasn't what the older woman suspected it was. She sat by the girl's bed, trying to decide if it were time to ask some significant questions.

The wave of nausea she felt at the bowl Julia was holding out to her made Deirdre see dark spots. "I . . . I don't think I can eat anything, thank you." She barely made it to the curtained alcove holding a dainty, flowered chamber pot. Reappearing, her face pale and wan from the retching, she smiled weakly. "I just hope you don't catch it—whatever I've got, I mean."

"I don't think I will," Madame Julia said solemnly, putting the bowl aside. She had not missed her charge's occasional bouts with dizziness in the past few days, nor another disturbing fact. "I haven't noticed you hanging out the monthly cloths, Deirdre."

Deirdre put her arm over her eyes. The light hurt. "I'm a bit late; that's all. Good gracious, with all that's happened to me, to be just a few days beyond the time I should be . . ." She sat up suddenly, her eyes wide and scared. "Oh, my God! Julia, you don't think . . . ! I'm not! I couldn't be!"

Madame Julia nodded slowly and sadly. "Pregnant. Oh, my dear, I'm afraid so. But we'll wait a few days before we get all addled about it. After all, it's not that long. And as you say, there's been so much going on with you that . . . that . . ." Her words trailed off as the two women stared at each other, both knowing that Madame's words were only wishful thinking.

Deirdre flung herself face-down in the bed clothing. "Oh, God," she said, her voice muffled and miserable. "Oh, dear God, what do I do now?"

"I think," Madame Julia said firmly, "that it's time we found you a nice, Irish husband." Mentally, she started ticking off the eligible, hardworking young men she knew. Not one who came to mind was suitable or worthy of Deidre O'Shea.

Still, Nashville was a strict town for people who were observed to be stepping outside certain moral boundaries. Julia had lived with snubs and snobs since she was Deirdre's age. She certainly didn't want that for this tender, beautiful girl.

Deidre raised a tear-streaked face. Her frightened eyes tore at Madame Julia's heart. "You mean, fool some man into marrying me?

Why, Julia, even if I knew someone to marry, I couldn't fool him about the baby. I just couldn't."

They looked at each other, both thinking the same thing at the same time. It was Andre's Devereux's child, if indeed Deirdre were pregnant.

Deirdre shook her head slowly, reading Madame Julia's face accurately. "No," she said quietly. "I can't, Madame Julia. I can't go to Andre Devereux. I just can't!"

Well, I can, Madame Julia said to herself, her lips set in grim determination. It fell to her to at least let the man know about the situation.

She waited another week, at the end of which there was little doubt that Deirdre was, indeed, expecting. Then she sat down, pen in hand, to write to Andre Devereux.

Two weeks later, Madame Julia realized that time was running out. There'd been no response from Andre Devereux—not that she had really expected to hear from the man, but she'd held onto hope. There'd been something in Andre's voice when he'd come to her about Deirdre, something that had made her think he really cared about what happened to the girl.

"Well, that's that. We'll just have to do something else," she muttered to herself as she went in search of the Irish girl. Men! You could put all their honorableness where women were concerned in an acorn shell!

She didn't tell her charge about the letter she'd sent to Andre. "My dear, it's time we started thinking practically. You need a husband, and that's that. Don't call it deception; call it surviving a world in which we're at the mercy of men. God knows, the men in this world practice enough deception on us women to make a little secret like yours seem like nothing."

"I guess you're right," Deirdre said after a long time. "After all, if I do find a husband, there's no way he would know it's not his child, is there?"

"Not unless you tell him," Julia said, pleased that the girl was beginning to listen to good common sense. "But here we are talking like we've got you a husband, and we haven't even laid eyes on the right one yet!" Madame Julia chuckled. "Guess I'll get busy shaking the bushes in this old town!"

But as it happened, it wasn't Julia who found a candidate for Deirdre's hand. It was Sean McAfee who found Deirdre O'Shea. And from the moment the young Irish horse trainer set eyes on Deirdre, he knew there'd never be another girl in the world for him. Cropped hair and all, Deirdre was the most beautiful girl he'd ever seen in his life.

Deirdre, for her part, had noticed the tall, blond fellow staring at her as she passed on her way to Morton's General Store. He was going into the shipping office next to the pier and stopped, open-mouthed, to stare at the girl whose short, glossy curls seemed to have captured the sun.

He was coming out when she passed the office again on her way back—a happy coincidence that Sean McAfee was ready to take advantage of.

"Miss! Excuse my forwardness for asking, but I'm new in town and the streets being so confusing and all, even after Dublin. . . ."

Deirdre smiled, liking the keen blue of Sean's eyes and the neat beard. "Dublin? You come from Dublin?" Her own village had been only twenty miles out from there, she told him. Her smile dazzled poor Sean to the point that he forgot what he was going to ask her. "Isn't it wonderful here? And the potatoes . . ." She patted her bag. "Imagine—you can just buy them out of a barrel at the store." Deirdre made a charming face. "I don't know about you, but if I never have to dig another potato, I'll die happy."

The sack Deirdre was carrying had by now somehow made its way into Sean's strong arms, and the two were chattering like old friends as they walked down Second Avenue. Then they were in front of Madame Julia's. Sean held onto the bag tightly, as though by giving it up, he might be giving up ever seeing this wonderful girl again. "You . . . you live here? It's such a pretty house."

Deirdre prayed that one of Julia's girls wouldn't choose that moment to lean out an upstairs window for a look at the morning.

"It's not mine. I live with a . . . an old friend, Mrs. Julia Poston."

"Maybe I could meet her sometime," Sean said eagerly. "I don't know anybody here. I mean, except you."

Madame Julia rose at the end of the porch, where she'd been snipping roses and shamelessly eavesdropping. Deirdre hadn't even known she was there. "Don't be rude to one of your fellow countrymen, Deirdre darling. Ask him in for a cup of tea." She came over to meet the young Irishman, her dark eyes assessing him with satisfaction and then going back to signal Deirdre her approval. "And perhaps Mr. McAfee can take supper with us tonight, him being on his own in a strange place and all."

Deirdre said, alarmed, "Julia, what about the—uh, company you're expecting tonight?"

Madame Julia's dimples appeared, knowing exactly to what kind of company Deirdre was referring. "Oh, land, I forgot to tell you this morning when you went off shopping. That company was canceled. Matter of fact, I'm having no visitors for the next two weeks while I do my annual redecorating in the parlor."

Deirdre relaxed. She'd heard the girls talking about their annual vacation on Madame Julia's farm; she just hadn't realized they were leaving this morning. No wonder she hadn't seen anyone at the window!

It was too fateful to ignore, the coincidence of the house being empty with her meeting

Sean McAfee. Deirdre looked sideways at the young man, who was listening politely to Madame Julia. He was nice-looking and apparently had good breeding, from his manners. Young, maybe twenty-four, she calculated, which was just right. There was a strength to his jaw that she liked, too.

The blue eyes turned to hers unexpectedly, and Deirdre blushed, glad Sean couldn't know what she was thinking. "What do you think about it, Miss O'Shea?"

Deirdre struggled to reconstruct the snatches of conversation she'd overheard. "About the uh—new drapery material or the rug Julia's talking about buying?"

Sean laughed along with Madame Julia. "Your friend, here, has been offering me some fascinating advice for the last ten minutes. She says I'll do a lot better finding myself a good job with somebody's horses if I have a wife. People out in the country like a settled man, not some jumping jack that's likely to go running off just when he's needed."

Madame Julia, looking smug as the old calico cat on the porch railing, didn't quite meet Deirdre's eyes. "I was just pointing out to Mr. McAfee that he'd best stay in Nashville for a while longer before he goes job looking. We have the prettiest girls in Tennessee."

Sean gave Deirdre a lingering, admiring look, his blue eyes warm and no longer shy. "I'll go along with that, ma'am, from what I've already seen."

"Well, you young people probably have a lot to talk about. Tell you what—instead of that tea I offered you, why don't you take Sean to that new sweet shop on the river, Deirdre? Here . . ." she took some coins out of her pocket and held them out to the girl. "Buy him one of those new chocolate sodas somebody was telling me about the other day. And you have one, too, darling."

Sean's jaw set hard, and he said quietly but firmly to Madame Julia, "I'll buy the treats, ma'am. You put your money back where it came from, thank you all the same."

Madame Julia all but purred. "Well, now, it's a proud young man you are, Mr. McAfee, and it's a pleasure to have you visiting us. Where *are* you staying, by the way?"

"Well, I don't have myself a place just yet, but the shipping office was telling me about some rooms that—"

"Just so happens I have a room to spare for the next few days. Oh, not for free," Madame Julia added hastily, remembering Sean's pride just in time. "But you can be sure it'll be just as cheap and a lot cleaner than any public boarding rooms."

Sean's eyes came back to Deirdre's face and stayed there, filled with yearning. She had pity on him and smiled, nodding her approval. "It's lucky you are, Mr. McAfee, to have this lady liking you at first sight. Madame Julia doesn't make that kind of offer to many people." Deirdre thought humorously, *Not unless they're paying dearly for one of her girls!*

"Then I'd like to take that room, Mrs. Poston, and thank you from the bottom of my heart for being so kind to offer it." Happiness spread over the young man's face as he realized that he was going to be living in the same house with the girl of his dreams. "And now Deirdre and I will be off for that—chocolate soda, you said?—to celebrate."

No more "Miss O'Shea" or Irishman-right-off-the-boat diffidence now. Sean McAfee had already decided that when he left Nashville, Deirdre O'Shea would be at his side—as his bride!

Madame Julia waved the newlyweds off in the buckboard she'd lent them. "It's kind of a wedding present," she'd insisted, when Sean protested. "And Billy Akin at the Holly Gap Inn where you'll be spending the night says he'll bring it back to me when you young folks get settled somewhere."

She saw Deirdre turn and wave back to her and call, "I'll write you, Julia, just as soon as Sean finds work! And I'll come back to see you—I promise!"

Julia wiped away a tear, knowing that she would miss Deirdre O'Shea as much as the real daughter she'd never had. She knew, too, that she might never see the girl again, which filled her heart with indescribable sadness. "God bless you, child," she whispered as the wagon turned a corner and was out of sight.

"God bless you and that child you're carrying. And I pray that young husband never learns the truth. It would only hurt you both." She was an astute woman when it came to knowing men. And, in addition to recognizing his good points in the past few days, Madame Julia had seen a side to Sean McAfee that was stern and unyielding.

He was not a man who would take deception lightly. Madame Julia said another little prayer and went back into the house. The girls would be back the next morning and it would be business as usual.

Only, with Deidre and her vibrant spirit gone, the little house on Second Avenue would never be the same.

It was her wedding night. Sean would be coming up any moment now with the mugs of ale he'd buoyantly suggested they drink to toast their marriage. Deirdre stood at the window of their bedroom in the Holly Gap Inn and looked out at the mountains. Beautiful, they were, these Tennessee hills that ringed the valley, creating a sense of safety and peace that Deirdre had never felt anywhere else.

Though she had no intention of confessing her secret, Deirdre knew Sean would be hurt and angry when he discovered that his bride was not virginal. She should have told him before they married, but she had succeeded in convincing herself that the right moment would present itself.

Well, this was that moment if she were going to tell him rather than let him find out for himself. Deirdre braced herself as the door opened and Sean, his face beaming with happiness and excitement, entered.

"Well, it's not champagne, darling, but since we're saving my money for the place we want to buy someday . . ."

"The ale's just fine," Deirdre said, moving to take the mug he was handing her and holding up her face for a kiss. "Sean, you're so good to me. I feel it's you who does all the giving, and me the taking."

Sean grinned wickedly. "Before this night is over, we'll have changed that around some, my love." His hand caressed the soft silk of her robe. Julia had presented Deirdre with the exquisite peignoir and matching gown with their hand-embroidered, tiny rosebuds, making the girl burst into tears for the third time in as many days. "You are so beautiful, Deirdre. Did you see that Billy Akin's eyes pop when I walked in with you? Every man who sees you wonders how I got so lucky."

"So lucky," Deirdre murmured with guilty cynicism. She put her head on his shoulder. They were sitting on a loveseat by the fire and Sean's arm was strong and comforting around her shoulders. "Sean, there's something I have to tell you. I should've told you before now, but . . ."

His lips were at her jawline, nibbling gently toward her mouth. "Umm. You taste just as pretty as you look. What should you have told me before now?"

Deirdre closed her eyes as Sean's lips found the little pulse in her throat, making her remember Andre, who'd touched the tip of his tongue to the hollow there, making her shiver. "Sean," she whispered; "I . . . I was with another man once." She felt Sean grow very still. The mouth stopped its demanding journey.

"Once? Only once?"

She opened her eyes. His were regarding her thoughtfully, but without the shock she'd expected. "Yes. I could never explain it to you; all I can say is that I . . ."

Sean put his finger over her lips. "Shh. That was before you met me—right?" He smiled at her. "There was a girl in Ireland that had me jumping over hedges, but that was before I found you. So why don't we call it even and start from right now?"

She laughed and threw her arms around him. "Sean, you're incredible! Now I know why I let you talk me into getting married so fast."

Sean hugged her fiercely. "I couldn't believe it when you actually said yes. But I didn't want to give you a chance to reconsider or for some other man to come along and snatch you out from under my nose."

"Sean," Deirdre whispered, her finger going to touch his mouth, lightly outlining it and making a little path in the crisp beard. "You talk too much. Sean's mouth trembled under her fingers, then he quickly moved his lips to capture her fingers, one at a time. Deirdre felt the moistness of his tongue with a shock of sensual feeling, mixed with guilt.

"You taste so sweet, every part of you," her bridegroom whispered. "I want this night to be as special for you as it is for me. Please want me, Deirdre my love. Please tell me that you want me."

She swallowed hard, thoughts of her night with Andre intruding on what she was feeling with Sean. But those intrusions she denied, reminding herself that this was the start of her new life with a man who dearly loved her. Her husband was strong and masculine and certainly not unattractive; it was easier than she thought to let his desire stir her own natural passions. He was her husband, after all, and Andre was far away, not only unavailable but illegal as far as a newly married woman was concerned.

"I want you, Sean," she whispered, slowly removing her wet fingers after a brush of his open lips and putting them to the task of unfastening the tiny buttons at the neck of her gown. "You are the most wonderful husband, and I'm your wife. I want to be good for you, the way you've been good for me."

He looked at the rosy perfection of her flesh emerging from the unfastened gown and closed his eyes. "Good for me?" he groaned, his passion overwhelming him so that it was almost all he could do to release his pants and shirt without stumbling. He'd never been with a girl like Deirdre. The hot, hurried fumblings in the fields with bold daughters of the potato field workers had been furtive and unsatisfying. Sean thought he might die in the moment of ecstasy with this beautiful young woman whom he desired so much that he was trembling all over.

Then they were in the rope-slung bed, their bodies rolling together in the dipped center, and Sean's male passion was timidly asserting itself against Deirdre's tender female shyness.

That didn't last beyond the first contact Sean had with sweet breasts that he found responsive to his fervent assault, nor the first parting of soft thighs that could not be closed again until Sean had felt the last tide burst from within. . . .

Deirdre lay awake long after Sean slept, his flushed face warm upon her bosom, his breath light and untroubled, unlike her own thoughts.

She had tried, she really had, to match his passion, to give of herself as he had, but it had been no use.

"Are you happy?" he had asked her, his hands stroking the parts of her that ached from lovemaking that had left her yearning and unsatisfied. "Is there anything I can do to make you happier? God, Deirdre, I want you to be as happy as I am."

She had stroked back and whispered the half-lies that she knew she must. Sean did not deserve to have his manhood struck down in the triumph of his wedding night, not at the hands of his bride or the ghost of Andre Devereux whom Deirdre could not forget—not on this night or any other.

"You've made me happy, darling," she'd told him. "Now go to sleep. It will be a long, long day tomorrow."

When Sean had rolled over, content, Deirdre added silently, *And a long, long night for me.*

But, miraculously, she slept. Her wedding night was over and with it vanished a few old, girlish dreams that had no place in her new life as a married woman.

Deirdre had just finished her breakfast of beaten biscuits, eggs and jam when her husband burst into the Inn's dining room. He'd reluctantly left his bride in the company of Tansie Akin, the innkeeper's wife, while he looked at a horse that someone had brought into the stable with a lame foot.

"Deirdre, my sweet bride!" He picked her up and swung her around exuberantly, setting her down only after a resounding kiss. "You'll never guess what wonderful luck! It always pays to do a good deed. The traveling bellman whose horse I just helped shoe is on his way back from his rounds of the plantations hereabouts. And guess what? He says they're looking for a man to train their fine horses at one of the prettiest plantations in these parts. Not only that—the mistress is in need of a woman to take over the household, her being ill . . ."

Deirdre caught her breath after her husband had come close to squeezing it out of her. "Now, slow down, Sean. For goodness sakes, one thing at a time!" She saw Billy Akin and his wife exchanging smiling glances and smiled herself, thinking how charming Sean could be when he was excited. "All of this sounds very interesting, but after our talk last night, I thought you'd decided to start your own blacksmith shop, perhaps in Murfreesboro."

"That's for *someday,* love. At any rate, get yourself all pretty and I'll help you with the packing and we'll go take a look. Billy says they have a nice little cottage on the place for the horse trainer and his missus; it's just made to order for us, darling!"

Billy winked at Deirdre. "The man's addled all right, or he could look at you and see you're already pretty enough to make the womenfolk at Moncoeur look to their men."

Deirdre felt a cold shock go through her. "Moncoeur!" She turned to Sean, who was gulping down a steaming cup of coffee and finishing off the rest of his wife's biscuits. "Sean, not . . . not Moncoeur?"

He was still too excited to notice the strangeness in her voice. "That's what they call the place. Miz Devereux had her husband Jean-Paul remodel the old place to look just like her home down on some sugar plantation near New Orleans."

Tansie Akin nodded. "Saint Bernard Parish, that's where she's from. Aurelia Gerard Devereux was a famous Creole beauty back when she was young. It's a crying shame that she—" At the stern look from her husband, she didn't finish the sentence, much to Deirdre's disappointment. Deirdre was sure she'd been about to say something about Aurelia Devereux. "Well, I'll just take these dishes back and then help you pack, Mrs. McAfee."

Deirdre looked at Sean, her heart beating fast at the idea of going to Moncoeur, of seeing Andre Devereux again. She could imagine the contempt in his eyes. After all, when he left her he thought she was continuing her profession in Nashville! And what would he say to Sean, who knew nothing of the real situation at Madame Julia's? "Sean, don't you think it would seem, well, *arrogant* to show up there with a wife and your things all loaded on the wagon? As though you were taking it for granted that they'd hire you?"

Sean looked thoughtful. Then he kissed his wife on the cheek. "Now, that's good thinking, honey. Tell you what. You stay here with the Akins—you folks mind looking after my wife?" At the couple's joint acquiescence, Sean said cheerfully, "That means I can take a horse instead of the buckboard and be back here by nightfall." His eyes kindled as they sought Deirdre's. She knew he was thinking about their lovemaking the night before. "I won't be too late, honey. You wait up for me now," he said in a low voice meant for her alone.

"I'll be on pins and needles the whole time," Deirdre said truthfully.

"Just keep your fingers crossed," Sean said as he kissed her.

"Oh, I will," Deirdre assured him. *But not for what you think,* she told herself. Dear God, let the Devereuxs have already hired somebody else!

"Well, honey, this is it! The place where we'll be staying until we have our own big old plantation." Sean drew the buckboard up at the turn-off to Moncoeur. "You ever see anything so pretty? And just wait till you see the inside! Miz Devereux had the bookcases sent all the way over from France, some of the fellows on the place were telling me. And some fancy cabinet maker from New Orleans special-made her bedroom suite—all mahogany, they tell me."

Deirdre hardly heard her husband's excited chatter. She was looking at the gracious, white oak-lined driveway leading up the big house and wondering if the sudden calm feeling she had came from knowing that she'd always been fated to come to Moncoeur.

As they neared the house, even Sean got quiet. It was so beautiful, so serene, this gracious Greek Revival manor with its Doric columns, dormer windows, and open-air galleries, that both the McAfees were filled with admiring awe. Sean whispered, "Our place is separate from the main house. They call it the *garçonnière* and it's part of the kitchen house. You'll love it, honey."

Deirdre's hand squeezed her husband's arm. "Sean, that mountain behind the house! Oh, just look how the sun's coming up through that big oak tree and the whole mountain looks like it's on fire!" She could almost forget her anxiety about Andre and what he would say when he saw her. All she could think about was getting up one morning before anyone else was awake and climbing that mountain and owning the whole world. . . .

"Oh, by the way, I forgot to tell you that Mr. Jean-Paul Devereux's brother won't be here to meet you. He left to meet a man about some kind of deal on the steamboat out of Nashville."

So Andre was gone! Deirdre breathed a silent prayer of thanks. "Then I guess it'll be up to the other brother as to whether I'll do for taking care of things at the house."

"Oh, that won't be a worry," Sean said confidently, pulling the buckboard up in front of the three-story brick kitchen house. "I already told 'em all about you, about how smart you are and hardworking." Sean grinned at her as he jumped down and held out his arms to her. "Didn't tell 'em, though, how pretty you are or about that crazy red hair and the temper that goes with it."

"Thank goodness for that," Deirdre said with relief. Andre would probably have recognized her from the description. She let Sean's arms stay warmly encircling her for a moment after she descended from the buckboard. Maybe everything would work out for the best, after all. If she proved herself indispensable to Aurelia Devereux and the household, and was obviously expecting a child by the time Andre returned, maybe he would stay quiet about what he knew about her.

She took a deep breath of the crisp mountain air. Somewhere, from one of the slave cabins nearby, someone was singing with dulcimer plaintiveness, "Me and my boy and a bob-tailed dog went across the river on a rotten log . . ."

Deirdre, smiling, strained to hear the rest of the song. She loved music. But the song faded out, and Sean was tugging on her arm to let her know she'd best start minding her p's and q's with what was happening in the more important part of the plantation. "Welcome, Miz McAfee. Welcome to Moncoeur. You done come at the right time. Miz Aurelia, she so gloomy when Mister Andre and Miss Gabrielle goes off. That bright, pretty face and sunshiney smile of yourn, that's just what Miz Aurelia needs."

Deirdre grinned back and took off her dark bonnet, which was covered with dust from the ride from the inn. She shook out her red curls and looked back at her mountain. In her mind, it was already *her* mountain! It seemed to give her power and confidence, just looking at its protective serenity.

Then she kissed Sean lightly, picked up her skirts daintily, and followed Prudy, entering

Moncoeur for the first time. Never, from the first moment inside its cool elegance, did she feel like a servant or even a stranger.

From the first moment she saw Moncoeur, and the mountain shadowing it, Deirdre O'Shea felt she was home.

Chapter Five

Summer 1988

"Fable, what on earth . . . ? You're drenched. Where in the world were you? We looked everywhere. That awful woman wanted a picture of all three of us. Your father finally got rid of her, but not before telling her every scandal in the family history he could think of. I declare, if you aren't a mess . . . even your hair's all full of oak leaves. . . ."

My mother's "hissy fits" are interminable but harmless. I was just glad that she was talking too much and was too agitated over my bedraggled entrance into the front hall of Moncoeur to notice how shaken I was by my experience atop Deirdre's Mountain. "I'll go clean up before dinner." I looked around the spacious entry hall, seeing it as though for the first time, through another's eyes. Had Deirdre felt intimidated by the fine old staircase, imported from Louisiana? Had she stared at the thousand-light chandelier that hung above the foyer? I closed my eyes, imagining how it must have felt to enter Moncoeur for the very first time.

I had come home.

"What? Fable, how many times have I asked you to please not go around murmuring to yourself as though the rest of us aren't around to talk to. You've been acting so strange this whole year, as though you were the only one who had the grief to deal with." Mother's pale, blue-veined hand fluttered like a white spider, finally coming up with a snowy handkerchief which she touched delicately to both eyes. "You've been like this ever since . . . ever since . . ."

"Mother, go ahead and say it out loud. Dr. Velkoff said in my last session that all of us have got to come to terms with the fact that she's dead. Celeste is dead, and, no, I haven't been the same ever since. Neither have you; neither has Daddy. But at least I know there's something wrong with the way I feel about my sister being gone while you and Daddy . . ."

The dreaded, deep voice of my father made my mother stop sniffling and me stop mid-sentence. "Go on, Fable. 'You and Daddy' what?" My father can be a scary man when he is not around people he's trying to either charm or impress into doing something he wants them to do. "Have you decided to begin the practice of psychiatry without benefit of license or qualifications?"

I felt the sting of tears that I have fought back in the presence of Hadley Morton Devereux ever since I first discovered that he liked having the power to make people cry. My father and I are old enemies, having long battled each other for the soul of my mother. "I was just trying to tell Mother that Dr. Velkoff thinks we all denied ourselves a sufficient period of mourning after Celeste was killed." I looked at him defiantly, my greenish-hazel eyes locked with his. Except for my hair color, my greenish eyes are the only other resemblance I bear to Daddy. It may be unfair of me, but I have never been attracted to fair-haired men, perhaps because my father's blond handsomeness has always slightly repelled me. Underneath the soft-spoken Southern gentleman exterior, I have always felt, lies a menacing layer of very dangerous ice.

Celeste and I had individually reached that layer and learned of this man's ability to cut off internal feelings forever. Daddy's idea of the function of children is that they are born to bring glory to their parents. My sister and I, ultimately, failed to do this—to his notion, at least—and Daddy cut us out of his heart like so much excess flab.

It was too late to retreat from the skirmish my father had me trapped in, so I just threw myself into the ring with him. "You flung yourself immediately into politics, and poor mother had to keep up with all the social responsibilities." I shot my arm out toward my mother, who flinched as though she thought I was trying to strike her. I wanted to cry but instead said vehemently, "Look at her! She's lost almost thirty pounds and lives on Valium and vodka. For God's sake, Daddy, you're killing her!" *Like you'd do to me if I didn't have your kind of strength.*

It was as if he heard my unspoken accusation. His full lips curled with contempt. "Your mother is a strong woman from good coal-mining stock. Half her family died violently before she was half-grown. She doesn't come from people who mope around whining. Nor do I, or you. Now, if you think you can make yourself presentable in half an hour, I'll invite you to join us for cocktails. Judge Parrish is coming by, with that up-and-coming young lawyer son of his. I'm sure LaMont is a cut above those trashy country-music people you seem to favor over our kind."

Our kind. My nails bit into my palms. My parents would never accept what I was or love me in spite of it. I couldn't leave home yet because I was sure it would mean the slow death of my mother who, in spite of her inability to stand up for herself, was almost pitifully grateful to have someone besides my father in the house. "LaMont? A 'cut above', my Aunt Fanny! LaMont's father paid someone to tutor him for six weeks straight before he took the bar—and then he almost didn't make it."

My father's eyes narrowed dangerously. He takes perverse pleasure in our little confrontations but despises my habit of poking large leaky holes in his shield of snobbishness.

Maybe that's why I became a country singer, to thumb my nose at Daddy's attitudes about everything, including music. But, no, I didn't fall in love with my chosen field of music just to annoy my father. I have to be honest about that. I truly care about the simple honesty of country music. The simplicity suits my soul, and the rhythm suits my voice which, I'm told, is both plaintive and carrying.

Daddy decided to let my crack about poor LaMont wilt in the air between us. "I'm sure you want to freshen up before dinner, in any event," he said in cold dismissal.

I had no argument with that. I needed a long, hot shower about the same way Mother probably needed her Valium.

After my bath, I stood on the balcony of my upstairs bedroom, looking out on the rain-cleansed sweep of grounds surrounding the house. As always, my eyes sought out the dark shape of Deirdre's Mountain, where I always seemed to feel these strange links to another life. Then I closed my eyes, recreating in my mind the vivid journey through Deirdre's past. It had been so real! But how had I lived through such a long period of Deirdre's life when in fact only a short time had elapsed? More importantly, *why* was I being drawn back into the past?

When I opened my eyes, I almost expected to see a shadowy figure, long skirts blowing in the wind and tangled red hair catching the gleams of the late sun. But this time there was nothing to see except the wind rustling the huge oak that held so many secrets to the past.

The woman on the mountain with long flowing hair—I first saw that spectral vision a month after Celeste's death. Another person saw her before that, but I'll get to that later. That's when I started seeing Dr. Velkoff, an eminent Nashville psychiatrist, because I thought I was going crazy.

He convinced me otherwise. "Emotional trauma does strange things to all of us, Fable. You lost your sister in a terrible accident at a time when you two weren't speaking to each other. Naturally, you feel guilt over that. At the same time, you still have your resentment over what she did to you. Death doesn't necessarily erase our feelings about someone. Add to the hard feelings between you and Celeste the strain between you and your father and the pure and simple fact of grief. Whether you loved your sister or hated her, you still have to deal with the fact that she's gone."

"But why am I hallucinating? I look at that mountain, and I feel myself slipping into another world. And why would I see *her*—my long-gone grandmother?"

Dr. Velkoff polished his funny little round glasses. I often accuse him of impersonating

Freud, even to the pointy grey beard, but he ignores that along with my "Vell, Dr. Velkoff?"

"Because, as you told me at the start, your sister is said to be the spitting image of your late, late grandmother, and you are choosing a gentler way to explore your feelings for Celeste by going back in time."

"Going back in time?" I laughed. "Hey, I never thought I'd hear you admit to the possibility of that."

"Going back in mind only, of course," Dr. Velkoff harrumphed. But I knew that he was fascinated by my accounts of the dreams I'd had since my sister's death. The dreams, which I recorded in the first two minutes of awakening, as the psychiatrist had instructed me, had been about a peculiar incident in a country which we later pinpointed as Ireland during the potato famine. They had progressed to images of a voyage to America. My seasickness aboard the refugee-packed ship had carried into my awakened state. I was sick for a week.

And now I had gone back—actually gone back to live as Deirdre when she first came to Moncoeur, pregnant and newly wed and clearly anxious about what would happen when she saw Andre Devereux again.

I smiled as I fastened on earrings and dabbed perfume behind my ears in preparation for going downstairs to meet LaMont Parrish, his father, and my family for drinks before dinner. In a way, I felt caught up in an old-world soap opera. What would Deirdre do when she saw Andre again? What would he think, seeing her entrenched in his plantation home, married to another man? How would it all turn out? How did Andre really feel about Aurelia, who obviously had stronger feelings about him than she should? What did Deirdre, so fond of Aurelia, think about this? Did she wonder about it as she went about her daily routine of caring for the mistress of Moncoeur?

"Tune in to last century, same place, a different station." Dr. Velkoff would say I was kidding too hard about things that really mattered to me. Maybe so.

In the meantime, I donned summer-pale hose and shifted from the past to the present. LaMont cornered me as soon as I entered the living room and made that shift very real with his talk about his new BMW, his condo near Brentwood Country Club, and the most recent antics of his eastern-transplant law partner.

I listened to all of this blather with the patience of an angel, with sweet smiles from time to time in the direction of my father, then LaMont. I wondered how Deirdre would deal with a diabetic conversation like this one. I was dozing off, looking straight into LaMont's tinted contacts. Not until he ventured a slight sneer about my singing did I come to life. But I caught Daddy's stern gaze on me and bit my tongue. This was not the night to go into a defense of country music, nor did I really care what LaMont Parrish thought about the genre.

I contented myself with staring in fascination at the strings of spinach struck to LaMont's big white teeth. "Isn't Azalea's spinach-caviar dish simply divine?" I asked sweetly and was rewarded by another green grin.

About the time in the evening when, in the old days, Celeste would have been summoned into the cavernous living room to play her harp while looking like a descended angel, I excused myself politely.

"Aren't you going to have your daughter play and sing for us, Hadley? My wife said 'Lonesome You' was on the Billboard charts last week."

My father looked at me with sheer hatred, and I knew he was thinking of Celeste and her harp and Mozart-drenched evenings with a beautiful daughter who stayed at his side and said "Daddy Dear" till I wanted to throw up.

"Thanks, Judge Parrish, but I have a taping early in the morning, and I don't want to strain my vocal cords." I gave the old fart a kiss just for asking. Maybe LaMont wasn't really his son, I hoped. I gave LaMont a peck, too. It didn't hurt to have a cheap lawyer around these days. I might need one when I got around to filing for divorce from my father.

Growing up in a wealthy old Southern family setting has its moments, not all bad but not all good. The Devereux name comes with papers, but there are a few varicose veins in the old blue-blooded background. My father has spent a great deal of his life trying to make people forget that our fortune is based on bootlegging whiskey during the Civil War. I personally have always been proud of that particular part of our history. Imagine how much courage it took for my ancestor, grandmother Deirdre, to go out peddling her corn liquor in an area torn apart by war! Add to that the fact that she was a woman in an era of feminine gentility, and you come up with a pretty good picture of how remarkable this lady was.

Though we live between Nashville and Franklin, Tennessee, way out in the country, we are included in Belle Meade "society." The money from our famous whiskey is seldom sneered at even by the hoity-toity. Besides, having a long line of fine horse stables which consistently bring in trophies at Shelbyville's famous annual Celebration provides an automatic "in" with the ton of Nashville. As I've mentioned earlier, I dislike the whole idea of the Tennessee Walking Horse tradition. It has never pleased me to think of a beautiful animal being trained to perform simply to satisfy some human vanity. Naturally, my father takes great joy in this particular hobby of controlling horses.

This is another burr between my father and me. He even broke his promise after Celeste died and tried to make me ride in the Celebration, but I refused. "You know how I feel about walking horses, Daddy. You and I have an agreement on this subject, remember. I'll ride Gambler at home, and that's it. Besides,

I'm not the show-off that Celeste was."

My sister was born to be shown off. Celeste was gorgeous, talented, popular, and the apple of her parents' eyes, especially her father's. A natural ham, she soon became an entrant in every pageant there ever was. Most of them she won. Daddy groomed her for "the big one" from the time she was eight years old. How many times did I hear the same prophecy—"When you're ready, honey, you'll be Miss America. You're the prettiest girl in the whole U.S.A. and one day you'll be wearing that crown."

My father is an intelligent man. Except for his having an inordinate need to have glory attached to the Devereux name, I don't know why he had this compelling need to turn my sister into a public Barbie Doll with no purpose in life but looking beautiful and winning pageants. I do know that my mother went along with it as she always went along with anything her adored husband wanted. I, on the other hand, stayed silently behind, alone and perplexed, as I watched the three of them trundle off to some pageant or other, the specially built trailer that held Celeste's harp trailing behind the limousine like an ill-shaped coffin on wheels.

It was a sight to behold, I can tell you that. Right about then I started writing country songs about the depths of despair. My old worn-out Gibson got a workout on those weekends and every other one that excluded me from the interests of my very strange family. Being mournful helps you sing better country, so I guess everything turned out for the best.

I suppose I should point out about now that growing up in Celeste's shade stunted me in confidence and in every other way but the physical sense. Food became my closest ally in a world that steadily perplexed me. By the time my sister was molding herself into a size six, seven-hundred-dollar swimsuit by a California designer for the big, grown-up beauty contest, I was squeezing into a size 14 polyester pantsuit. My hair was blond and straight and lackluster; I had no idea whatsoever about makeup after eighteen years of being the "other Devereux girl" and had no interest in learning.

That's when the big change occurred in my life. Up till then, the only boys I'd ever had anything to do with were the classmates who copied my homework and dutifully tried to get inside my bra and pants at high school proms.

That was before I met Royce McColl, who had leased Barksdale Farms next to our place.

Looking back, I've tried to be honest with myself about that first meeting in view of what happened later. Granted, I was overweight, hoydenish, unfinished and not the most appealing young woman in the world, but I could swear that the magic was there for Royce McColl as well as for me. It would not be until much later that I learned how well this man could project whatever impression served him best. Maybe I was no beauty queen, but my jeans and old shirt suited my riding style.

Not only that, I'm damned good on horseback. Gambler and I melt into one when we ride, and I think probably that Royce's first glimpse of me galloping past, my hair flying, was not an unpleasant one.

Anyway, that's how he made me feel when he caught up to me at a pretty little stream on our land, just next to the property he was leasing.

"It's not often you see a woman ride full-out like that. I'd begun to think there weren't any horsewomen around. All I've seen are prissy little things in smart derbies and jodphurs mincing around with their noses stuck in the air."

I was startled to hear from this virtual stranger what I'd often thought with private derision. I would hear that sharp edge in Royce's comments many, many times more, but right then, all I could think about was that at last I had met a man I was really attracted to. To be honest, I didn't think about anything except the sensation of being in close proximity to one of the best-looking men I had ever laid eyes on. Royce McColl was born to sit a horse like the magnificent Arabian he was astride when I first saw him. His leonine head full of flaming red hair that was made fierier by the contrasting iron-grey beard was the initial eye-catcher. Then one's attention was drawn quickly to the rest of him—to lively green eyes, broad shoulders, and long, lanky limbs that were made for faded chambray and denim. Everything about his looks suited me, including his "good ole boy" attire. I liked him from the tip of his scruffy cowboy hat to the well-worn roach-kickers that might have belonged to a rodeo rider. It never occurred to me that this image was deliberate, designed to impress me from the start. Why should it have? I was a young woman who had never set foot out of Tennessee, much less had any real experience with men.

He grinned at me, and I grinned back, glad that I was on my horse so that he couldn't see how pudgy I was underneath the loose shirt.

"You must be one of the Devereux girls." Why should I suspect at that point that I was not the Devereux girl that Royce McColl was after? In a way I'm glad I had that time of an innocent girl's joy at being sought after by a handsome man. And joy it was when Royce put his horse into a slow gait that matched Gambler's ambling stride. "I've been hearing about how pretty they are, but I just hadn't got an invitation to come find out for myself. Hear your dad doesn't care much for outsiders."

I looked at him, startled. The easy drawl, the calm air of not being in a hurry about anything certainly didn't fit into any Yankee profile I was familiar with. "You're from the East?"

"New York, if that's what you call East. I call it a sewer. Couldn't get out of there fast enough after I closed up my business there. Wound up there a while back plumb by accident, and I'm proud to be gone."

"You had a business in New York?" I was still trying to put together the puzzling picture. Royce was a mystery from the start to me, and I guess that's one of the reasons I fell so hard. All the boys I knew had their pedigrees embossed on their Rockports. Well, except for my Music Row buddies. "What in the world are you doing down here?"

"Looking for some land to invest in. Trying to get myself back to some basics I seem to've lost track of in the fast lane." He looked around the sweep of grounds we were coming to as Gambler got wind of home stable and turned us in on Moncoeur property. "This is really nice. Must be a good feeling to grow up where you've got real roots." He shielded his eyes against the sun and pointed at Deirdre's Mountain. "I saw you up there one night, late, when I was out riding after dark. You were wearing an old-fashioned kind of nightgown, like, that was streaming around you, and your hair was all wild and blowing . . ."

The chill that went down my spine was not caused by the sudden ducking of the sun behind my grandmother Deirdre's mountain.

It was caused by the mention of the nightgown, by the description of the woman on the mountain, and also by the fact that I do not possess a nightgown (I sleep in the nude) and have never gone up on the mountain after dark.

Our black cook, who is very superstitious, says that when Deirdre's ghost is seen on the mountain, there is trouble ahead for Moncoeur.

"Hey. Hey, you okay?"

I managed a smile, although my mind was whirling with the off-hand remark Royce had made about seeing a woman on the mountain. Maybe it had been Celeste on a late-night stroll. But I knew better. My sister was not one for strolls of any kind except those made down a runway. Besides, she had said more than once that that old mountain was spooky.

"I . . . I'm just a little hot from the ride. Azalea will be looking for me and worrying." I saw the little smile at the way I pronounced our cook's name and thought hopelessly, *I'm a goner.* That smile did me in. I smiled back, explaining, "Yes, it's pronounced 'Az-uh-lee-uh,' not like the flower. Don't ask me why. That's just the way Azalea wants it. She's an original, all right. Hey, I'd better get on back to the house." I didn't want to leave him, but the green eyes were scrutinizing me with a curiosity that I didn't want to turn into critical appraisal of my less than perfect figure.

"Well, whatever happened to that famous Southern hospitality I've always heard about? Can't I escort you back to the stable, help you unsaddle?"

"No, really." I flung my hair off my face where the early evening breeze had fanned it. "My father doesn't like me to entertain guests when he and my mother are gone. He's a little old-fashioned about things like that."

Royce put his hand on my bridle when I would have flicked Gambler into motion. "Nothing wrong with that, but you look like a grown-up young lady to me. Can we have a ride together tomorrow morning? I'd like to have a guided tour of some of these back roads. And I am your neighbor after all."

I let that smile melt my innards down into my boots, and for the life of me I couldn't do anything but nod.

"You an early riser? Say seven-thirty, before the heat comes up?"

I nodded. My family wouldn't be coming back for two more days. Daddy had no way of finding out that I'd broken one of his rules about seeing a man while my parents weren't around to chaperone. Besides, how could it hurt to go riding with a man who obviously was just lonely and feeling neglected by his closest neighbors?

I could feel him watching me as I rode on to the stables, and just before I entered them I turned to wave to him. Thad Wilkins, our trainer for the walking horses, was cooling down Celeste's horse, Blue Boy, after a workout, and I let him help me unsaddle Gambler, something I don't usually do.

"You comin' down with something, Fable?" he asked, eyeing my flushed cheeks and taking over the rubbing down of my mount.

I shook my head, but I knew better. I was coming down with something all right, but it wasn't anything that one of Azalea's home remedies would fix.

I was on the way to having a bad case of "love-at-first-sightis."

Anyone who has grown up in the South will be quick to tell you that the heart of any house is the kitchen. I cannot remember when ours was not the center of delicious activity involving canning, pickling, or baking of whatever happened to be coming in that season.

This particular night the kitchen was cold, and there was not one sign of the "good groceries" Azalea was famous for. I found a warm pot of coffee on the stove and that was all. When I poured myself a cup and messed it up with sugar and cream, I jumped halfway out of my skin to hear Azalea speak from right behind me. "That's right. Load up on that sweet stuff and then finish it up with the rest of the cake you been stuffin' yourself on ever since your mama and daddy left."

I came close to choking. After I'd gotten over my paroxysm, I glared at the black woman who had had a large role in raising me from skinny, unheralded infancy. "Azalea, you scared me just about half to death. What are you doing hiding out in the dark like this? And where's supper? I'm starving, and I don't see one blessed thing being fixed for my supper."

Azalea took my coffee mug and emptied it, then replenished it with unadorned black Luzianne from the stove. She might have been comical with her pink hairnet tightened over close-cut grey frizzled hair, but I wasn't laughing. Azalea's face was set in the same stern lines that had accompanied many a lecture during my lifetime, and I knew I was in for it. "And there won't be, 'cept a bowl of thin soup." Azalea got herself a mug of coffee and sat down across from me at the butcher block table. "Look at you. Just look at you. Everytime they go off, you start in moonin' around, eatin' everything in sight, feelin' sorry for yourself, actin' moody and not doin' nothin' with your face, your hair, your clothes—just look at them clothes you're wearin'! Look like you're dressed for a cock fight. Shoot, girl, I didn't help bring you into this world to see you go to hell in the devil's handbasket."

"Azalea, are you mad at me about something?" I was shocked, no two ways about it. Hurt, too. Azalea had always made me feel that anything I did in the world short of killing somebody was all right. Even Celeste had always been jealous of the way Azalea petted me from the time I was born. "I didn't mean to stay out this late, but I got to riding and—"

"I ain't mad at you about ridin' that horse of yours, and I ain't mad at you about stayin' out too late. I'm mad about a lot of things, but not at you." Azalea poured me and her another cup of coffee and took out her rumpled pack of cigarettes, which meant she was really getting down to business. Lighting a bent-up Lucky, she asked me, "Did I see you messin' around with the fellow moved next door?"

Messin' around? "I was just being neighborly, Azalea. You gonna let me have one of those?" I took the cigarette she'd lit for herself and waited till she lit another before asking, "You know anything about that guy?" If anybody did, she would, I knew.

"I know there's something funny about him." Azalea puffed on her Lucky and squinted around the smoke. Daddy would not have approved of the scene in the kitchen, I thought with some satisfaction. "He don't have no family, for one thing. That woman cleans for 'im told me there wasn't nobody but him. He don't have his own stuff. Place is just like it was when he moved in, no photo albums, no personal junk, no nothing. She said he even went down to Brentwood Pharmacy and bought all new shaving stuff, things like that."

I thought about the nice smell of Royce McColl. He'd bought some new scent, too, apparently. "Well, that's not exactly a crime, is it? Maybe he'll boost the economy around here." I reached for the cookie jar in the middle of the table, but Azalea deftly rescued it from my reach.

"That's another thing." I wasn't sure what the first was, but I was pretty sure what Azalea was getting ready to light into. "We gone have to do something about you. I been thinkin' about it and it's time."

"Time for what?" As if I didn't know.

"To git you lookin' better'n your sister ever thought about lookin'. I been thinkin' about it. It's part my fault, bakin' all them cakes you like 'cause nobody . . ." She stopped, but I knew she would have said what I already knew, that nobody cared about me. "And I been bad about lettin' you eat all weekend when they're off som'ers. But that's come to a halt, right now.

We gone go on a diet, startin' right now. Don't you even look at those cookies."

Everybody could use a friend like Azalea. That night in the kitchen, she started melting me down, and my life took on a whole new tilt.

Chapter Six

I had been secretly meeting Royce McColl for several months before anyone in my family noticed the changes in me. Celeste was riding high on her win in the Miss Tennessee pageant and several accompanying honors at the university she attended in Knoxville. She flitted in for only occasional weekends.

On one of these occasions, she shocked me by asking me to go out with her and some of her friends. I was a sophomore at Belmont College by that time and trying hard to keep my place on the Dean's List. That left me time for very little social life except that which Royce and I maintained secretly.

"Come on, Sis. We'll even go to some of those crummy little places where they sing that country stuff you like so much."

One of her friends commented to me as we entered the cobwebby side door to "Dusty Roads," a Nashville institution for more years than I can count, "Hey, Fable, you've lost bunches of weight. You look great."

My sister had never said a word about my new slimmer figure. Looking back now with more charity than I felt then, I honestly think she hadn't noticed. Celeste's self-centered focus was not her fault; she had simply been programmed from birth to think about no one but herself.

Still, I remember that night with a little bit of tenderness. For one thing, it was the first time I'd ever performed in front of my sister, and I can still remember the look on her face when I took my place on that silly little stage and sang one of my songs. She was shocked, I think, to find out that I wasn't some no-talent twanger.

Dusty Roads is a funny little dive in a sort of bad area of downtown Nashville where numerous big-time country singers have been discovered. The deal is that if you want to perform, all you have to do is get up there and do it. Most performers are amateurs with more talent for drinking beer than for singing. Sometimes, however, currently well-known singers show up there. So do agents. That particular night, a representative of one of the better known recording studios on Music Row happened to be present. I didn't know that at the time, of course, when I got on the little stage and clowned around with "Lucky Me, Lonesome You," a song I'd written on a blues-clouded night. I wasn't trying to impress anybody except my sister and her buddies. I did notice the same guy watching me afterwards as I danced with anybody who asked me, including one jerk who was too drunk to keep his hands where they belonged.

I had drunk a little too much beer, but I wasn't too drunk to be embarrassed when I realized that the man who'd been watching me all night was witnessing the scene. I pushed my partner away from me and went to the ladies' room. When I came out the door, my all-night observer was leaning there against the wall, waiting for me.

Royce McColl was, at the time, the only man in my life, but that didn't mean I was blind or dead. The stranger looking straight into my eyes had something about him that sent a chill to my marrow. It was as if he knew that sometime, somewhere down the line we were going to be important to each other. Deep down I knew it, too.

Maybe that's why I acted silly and flippant, to head off any exchange of sexual signals. This was no ordinary pick-up attempt, and we both knew it. "You know, the girls at my table have already picked you out as the best-looking guy in the place. They think your pony-tail and dark scowl make you look like Steven Seagal."

He quirked one eyebrow and looked even more like the movie star. But then he smiled at me, and the resemblance ended. That smile started melting away the insulation around my heart; I just didn't realize it until later. Much later. Too much later.

"I grew my hair out long before he did. I'd ask you to dance, but I'd rather hear you sing again. After seeing you out there on the floor, maybe I ought to warn you about slow-dancing with strangers."

My blush was swift and pure. Suddenly, I knew that this was a man that I wanted to respect me as more than a pub-crawling air-head. "Thanks—not for the advice but for a great idea for a new song. Give me five minutes, and I'll give you a song you'll leave here humming."

I meant it as a joke, maybe a little showing off in the company of an attractive man, but by the time I'd scrawled the lyrics and melody that were crowding into my head faster than I could write them down, things had changed.

People in the club realized it, too. When I started up on the little stage, some gin-soaked Opry aspirant handed me his guitar. The proprieter, who'd heard Hank Williams and Chet Atkins singing from where I now stood, folded his elbows and shushed some of his customers to listen. As I got into "Never Slow-Dance with Strangers," I looked right into the eyes of the man who'd inspired the song and sang straight to him. Dusty Roads had turned into my Casablanca, with a suddenly quiet room listening intently to history being made.

It didn't stay quiet and magical. When I finished to enthusiastic applause and hooting, I tried to make my way to the man in the back of the room, but people kept grabbing me, and I was herded back to my table by Celeste's friends. When I looked next, the man was gone. He had, though, left his card with a simple "Call me" scribbled across the address of a major recording studio on Music Row. At least now I knew his name and that he was interested in my singing. Harrison Judd was studio manager for one of the top producers of country music records in Nashville.

What I didn't know was if he was as interested in me as in my talent. This wasn't a time to dwell on that, however, since my table was treating me like a newly discovered star and I wasn't just my sister's little kid sis anymore.

I listened to Celeste leading the others in a whining version of "Stand By Your Man" in an attempt to recapture her place as center of attention, but I wasn't bothered at all. I even joined in with a few doo-wahs as I thought about how tonight might have changed my life.

I also thought about Harrison Judd—and not just about what his Music Row connections might mean for a hitherto undiscovered country singer.

Royce had not been unobservant about my new dedication to face and figure. We met as we had been doing for weeks at a quiet little creek on the back of Devereux property. As Gambler and Hurricane grazed together over spring dandelions, Royce stroked my hair—which I was letting grow out and had recently permed into rather becoming cascades of corkscrew curls. "There's something different about you, all right. You going famous on me after that fellow telling you he liked your song?"

"No," I told him, laughing. "Harrison Judd is the man I called about my song, but I don't see myself going famous or anything close to it. Celeste is the one who's set on being famous." I rolled over on the grassy bank to catch a tiny butterfly on my finger. "She's on her way to Atlantic City next week, by the way. Daddy had the harp all spit-polished, and I can't tell you how many hours Mama's spent getting all the clothes up." I could, but I wouldn't. I didn't want Royce McColl knowing how ridiculous my family was about this final leg in my sister's lifelong career in pageantry.

Royce chewed on a dandelion stem, then stuck it behind my ear. When he pulled me over to him, I felt something deep inside me turn to pure, quivering jelly. "You know what I think?" he whispered, making the jelly turn warm and even more quivery. "I think you're the major talent in that family and I think your talent lies in more than just singing."

He kissed me in a way that made it hard to remember that I wasn't supposed to be out here or seeing a man that my parents didn't know or approve of. When his hands dug into my hair and pulled my mouth open to his, I felt like fainting with all the warm gushes of feeling that were coming from everywhere. I couldn't even speak after he'd left my mouth to go to new spots of feeling. I heard him murmur something against my breasts after he'd freed them from my shirt and was having his way with them.

"You are so very beautiful," he whispered.

"You almost make me believe that," I whispered back.

He rolled over on his back and brought me down onto his chest. I felt my nipples graze his chest and shivered in the April sun. "You should believe more good things about yourself, Fable Devereux. Why do I get the feeling that nobody in your family gives you credit for anything?"

I kissed the tip of his nose and trailed my finger down the crisp outline of his beard. Royce was in his thirties, I'd learned by now, and had been married before. Two more strikes against him as a suitor for me, if my father found out. "Because Celeste was the fairy princess in our family. Daddy just always thought she was perfect and wonderful. He didn't want another child. He never kept that a secret, even from my mother when she was carrying me. I was an accident, a disappointment to him from the time I was born. It was mutual, too. Daddy and I have never been able to stand each other."

Royce played with a dripping curl and used it as a rope to pull my mouth down to his. "Your sister can't be more gorgeous than you." I still think about how easily that man could lie and I wonder at my naivete.

I raised myself off his chest. "That's right! You've never even met Celeste. Oh, I'll tell you what. When you do meet her, you'll see why nobody ever pays any attention to me when my sister's around. She's drop-dead beautiful." I ruffled his hair. "Her hair's about the color of yours and reaches nearly to her waist. She's got my great-great-great grandmother Deirdre's hair. Sometime when my parents aren't around, I'll let you come in and see the portrait of Deirdre. She was an incredible woman, let me tell you."

"And your sister's like her?"

I had to stop and think about that. The legends about Deirdre abound in our family, and not one I'd heard made her sound much like my frivolous sister Celeste. "I don't really think so. Hey, what are you doing?"

"Trying very hard to find the zipper to these jeans of yours."

"No, Royce." I was battling my own feelings more than him. "If Daddy caught us down here like this, I'd be run off the place. As a matter of fact, I got really scared the other night at dinner. He asked me if I'd met you, been over to your place."

Royce's hands froze at my waist. "What did you tell him?"

"I said yes, I'd met you—casually, like neighbors—but that no, I hadn't been over to your place."

"Was that the end of it?" I could feel his tenseness and I wondered about that. I should have wondered about a lot of other things, but I was young and insecure.

"Well, no." I hoped what I was about to tell him didn't make him mad. "My father tried to talk to me about you and didn't have much luck. Then he got mad and said he'd had a few inquiries put out on his own about our 'mysterious neighbor.' "

Royce was as still as deep water. Then, "And what did he get back on these inquiries?"

"He said there was something funny about not being able to trace a man who obviously had the money to move into our neighborhood. He said he's heard there are people trying to bring the horse-racing rackets into Tennessee, and maybe that's what you were down here for."

The tension left him and Royce laughed vigorously. "Well, that's a relief—that he thinks I'm part of a big-time criminal element and not just a small crook trying to weasel myself into your social circle."

I couldn't help asking the question that had been plaguing me since I'd first met Royce. "Well, just what *are* you doing down here, Royce?"

He hesitated just the briefest time before drawing me into his arms and kissing me soundly. "Right now, I'm trying to make time with a certain young woman who's bound for the big time in country music if what I hear is true. Hasn't 'Lonesome You' gone into a crossover hit?"

"Not a big one, just enough that Harrison says my next song may get me a place on the Saturday night Opry."

"And I can say I knew you when. But right now, I want to know you in some other ways than your singing."

I couldn't stop him from doing what I wanted as much as he did. He had brought protection, and I just couldn't think of a good reason to say no to the idea of losing my virginity with a man as attractive and compelling as Royce McColl.

Besides, I was in love.

That night on the creek bank, I said good-bye to girlhood forever. Royce was a lover who left no part of my body untouched by his passion. When he made every fiber of me want more of him with each caress, each kiss, I just gave in. It had to happen someday, and why not with someone like Royce?

"Don't move," he whispered hoarsely when we were at the moment before physical union. "I'll try not to hurt you, but I can't wait any longer."

He was a big man. His entry did hurt, but I was caught up so much in the passionate moment of having a man I cared about reach a part of me that had never been touched that I soon forgot the pain.

He was very gentle and tender afterwards and dried the tears that I didn't even realize were on my cheeks. "I'm sorry, honey. I wouldn't hurt you for anything." He kissed me over and over again and whispered the sweet things that every woman wants to hear at such a time. And then he made love to me again with a kinder passion that soothed the rawness of losing my innocence. I held him close and shut my eyes against the sun that was setting behind Deirdre's Mountain.

"I cannot believe that you are telling me this, Fable. You are not going with us to Atlantic City, not going to be with the family on the most important night of your sister's life?"

The eggs and bacon that Azalea had put in the silver warmers on the buffet in the huge dining room were sticking in my throat as my father scolded me. He was in riding clothes, having been out for an early morning run with his favorite horse Triplet and the Irish setters. Celeste had accompanied him and was upstairs packing, he told me when I stumbled in for coffee.

"I just told you, Daddy. When I got in last night . . ."

"Where were you, anyway? Your mother said you wouldn't be in for supper, but I didn't hear you come in last night."

"Out. I was out. I am grown up, for God's sake."

"Don't curse, Fable. Now tell me why you think you can't join the family in this trip that may be most important event of your sister's life."

I flung my napkin down in frustration. "I'm trying to tell you, damn it! I have a life, too, in case none of you has noticed! I have a taping set up at ten o'clock tomorrow morning. That's what the call was about. Harrison wants to get it finished in time to release before the fan fair this June. He thinks one of my new songs has a real chance at the big time and he—"

"Harrison?"

"Harrison Judd. And, no, you don't know him, just like you don't know any of the people on Music Row, because they don't belong to your stupid clubs or have tickets to the Symphony or—" I got up and poured another cup of coffee, sloshing some of it on the linen tablecloth when I sat back down. My eyes were red from lying sleepless, I knew, and the call from Harrison Judd at eight o'clock had interrupted what little sleep I had gotten after leaving Royce. My father was looking at me with one of his narrowed-eyes stares. I wondered what he would say if I blurted out that about twelve hours earlier, his younger daughter had lost her virginity. "Never mind. I just can't go, that's all. Celeste doesn't care; Mother doesn't either. They've never wanted me along. Neither have you."

"So you think your little country music career is more important that your sister's chance at the biggest title in America."

I looked my father dead in the eye and said with the slowest, coldest, most venomous tone I could muster, "To me it is. As a matter of fact, I wouldn't give you two pieces of horse turd for that title that you and Celeste think is so all-fired important."

My father did something unprecedented. He got up from his place, put his napkin down very carefully, and walked around the table to where I was sitting. The slap he gave me reverberated in the huge room. I don't know where the shocked gasp came from—my father, me or Azalea, who was entering just then with a fresh basket of toast.

I do know that when I slowly rose from my seat, my eyes never leaving those of my father, I had a compulsion to pause under the portrait of my ancestor, Deirdre Devereux. The painting, by one of the traveling "house painters," had always seemed to me to be more alive than anything else in the formal, cold dining room. "Did you see that?" I whispered to the woman looking down at us from her eternal, serene stance. "Your father was a gambling Irishman, but I'll bet he never struck you or treated you like dirt. . . ."

My words trailed off when I saw the apparition in the door.

"How do you like it?" Celeste said, pirouetting gracefully as she modeled a gown that was the exact replica of the one in the portrait. "I'm doing a little skit for my part in the talent division. The Southern woman behind the war scenes." My sister kissed our father and patted me on the cheek on her way to the buffet. "Good morning again, Daddy dear. Fable, you look a little flushed. I'm really sorry you won't be going along with us. Are these eggs fresh, Azalea?"

"What about your harp?"

"What about it?" Celeste nibbled daintily at a piece of toast.

"Aren't you going to play your harp in the competition?" I wanted to scream the question, but it came out very calmly.

"Oh, yes." She crunched a morsel of bacon, quite loudly it seemed to me. "That will be part of the skit—our ancestor playing to soothe the ladies back home. I thought I might use the 'Brandy-oh' song she sang back then. That is, if you'll teach it to me this morning after breakfast, Fable."

They stared at me, waiting for me to answer—Daddy with that curling smile, Celeste with a bit of toast on her beautiful mouth that still munched bacon noisily, and I with the bright pink imprint of my father's blow to my cheek.

I looked up at Deirdre and laughed. "Do you mind sharing your old song? I mean, it's not exactly what it was meant for, but if it's okay with you . . ."

Celeste giggled. "Fable, I declare if you aren't the craziest thing, talking to that portrait. Daddy, did you ever see the like?"

My father didn't smile. "Your sister has been doing a lot of . . . unusual things lately." He gave my sister a little peck on the cheek. "Practice your song, Pumpkin, and finish your packing. I'll see you later."

He didn't look at me or utter one word to me, which suited me just fine.

If Celeste and I could have been sisters in the best sense of the word, how much we could have shared! I thought about what had happened between Royce and me and how much I would have loved to talk with someone close about all the feelings that accompanied my first foray into the adult sexual world.

But Celeste was too full of her own feelings to think about mine, even if I had been able to share them. We worked on the song that she wanted to use in her skit. "What in the blue-eyed world is a white oak stump, anyway?" she asked impatiently after I'd gone through the little song with her.

"It doesn't matter," I told her and then I played it through again, very slowly.

"Coffee grows on the white oak stump.
The river flows with brandy-oh . . .
Go choose you one
That'll stand by you,
As sweet as sugar candy-oh."

She found the strings on her harp to play the melody and worked on the lyrics with her sweet, high, slightly off-key soprano voice. "I guess that's it. Ole Deirdre is probably plugging up her ears to hear me singing her favorite lullaby." Celeste picked up my guitar, plunked a few strings, and asked casually, "How did you learn that song, anyway?"

I looked at her in surprise, not because of the question but because there was no answer. I suddenly realized that I had no idea where those lyrics had come from. Celeste was giving me one of Daddy's "well she really has lost it now" looks, so I made up a rational response. "I guess from Azalea. You know how she's always humming the things her folks passed down to her. She comes from the old blood on this plantation, too, you know."

Celeste strummed a little more. I realized that she was trying to pick up the tune of the song I'd sung that night at Dusty Roads. "So, you're doing some taping down at a studio, and that's why you aren't going with us to the pageant." She was still idly picking at the guitar, but I knew she was interested in my response. I realized from what she said that she'd overheard most if not all of the confrontation at breakfast. I felt a little guilty about making that awful crack about her lifelong ambition to be Miss America.

"I'm sorry I won't be there." But I really wasn't and neither was she and we both knew this. My sister had never given a flip whether I was along on what I had long ago named her "S&M" trips—self and myself. "As for my taping gig, it's no big deal. Harrison thinks I may get a shot at an Opry appearance if this new song goes over with the d.j.'s like he thinks it might."

"Opry!" Celeste's snort of derision told me what she thought of my career ambitions. "Are you singing that song you wrote that night at that dreadful place, the one you just thought up on the spot?"

I laughed. "I was drunk as a skunk. I guess maybe I ought to always do my songwriting after a few beers."

"I thought it was pretty good."

We were getting to the end of the long, slow curve, I could tell. "Thank you. And, no, that's not the song we're taping tomorrow. Harrison has something else he thinks is perfect for me." When I had called him a week after he'd given me his card, he'd had me come in to do a demo. After that, things started happening fast. Harrison said the studio biggies were real excited about me and wanted to get me on the air pronto.

Celeste hit me with the short, fast pitch. "Then, do you think there's a chance I could use your song as the modern part of my skit? I was thinking, it's going to be a little old-fashioned the way it is now. Besides, I've noticed that the contestants who usually win the talent division are those who actually come up with something they created. . . ."

I just stared at her. "Are you saying that you want to sing my song and pass it off as one you wrote yourself?"

"Come on, sis. Don't make it sound like big-time criminal stuff. You can dash off another one without even half-trying."

My sister was as close as she ever got to begging. I actually felt sorry for her. Here she was at the threshold of the Big One, the event that she had been preparing and hyped for all her life, and she was scared to death of not winning.

What the hell. It was just a dumb song that I'd written to impress her friends and Harrison Judd. "You'll need the guitar. The harp would look and sound ridiculous with a country song."

Celeste squealed and came over to hug me. "That's the whole idea. Here I am in the first part of my skit, Southern lady to the hilt, dressed up like my grandmother and singing corny lullabies. Then, *shazam!* I shed the old-fashioned clothes and do the torchy bit with your song."

I had to admit her idea was good. And Celeste was damn good at these things. Lord knew she'd had enough practice.

I sat down with her and taught her "Never Slow-dance With Strangers," even showing her a neat little run on the guitar that she could put in for show.

If Celeste didn't win the crown, it wouldn't be because she had a mean-spirited sister. I have always been proud of that fact.

Chapter Seven

What happened in our family after Celeste came home, untriumphant—she had not placed even in the top ten finalists—defies even my understanding. And I grew up with these people!

Azalea and I had watched the pageant finale on television, so we figured we were in for heavy-duty sulking on my sister's part and some tight-lipped cursing about stupid judges and the like from my father. But we did not expect the complete change that occurred at Moncoeur when it turned out that Celeste was not, after all, destined to become the crowned fairy princess of America.

My mother retreated into her world of diet pills and bridge parties, my father turned his attention to his walking horses, and Celeste turned on me.

It didn't help that I was getting to be something of a celebrity in those days. "She's a Quiche Girl in a Barbecue Town," the song that Harrison had gotten from a writer friend, Clyde Edgerton, for me to record, was on the radio every time you turned it on. Celeste sneered about it, saying I'd be wearing a stupid hat with a stupid price tag like that corny Minnie Pearl before long.

That really burned me up. Sarah Cannon, a.k.a. Minnie Pearl, is one of the finest, most cultured ladies in Nashville and everybody who knows her absolutely adores her. I told my sister that in no uncertain terms, adding, "Why don't you get a life? I'm sick and tired of seeing you mope around making everybody miserable." I didn't point out that anybody dumb enough to major in beauty pageants and fail the final didn't have any business pointing a finger at someone succeeding in the country music business.

"And I'm sick and tired of you acting like Miss Goody Two-Shoes when I know for a fact that you sneak off everytime you think Daddy's not looking and . . ."

She finished that sentence with some blue language that I'm not interested in repeating. "Just shut up, Celeste. Shut up."

"Why should I? Because you say so?" She got right in my face, then, and told me low and mean, "Just because you've dropped a few pounds of that baby fat and started slathering on all that Maybelline doesn't mean you've turned into the beauty of this family. And if I wanted to, I could call a few guys and have every song you've ever thought about singing black-balled." Those green eyes got even meaner. "As for this man you're screwing, I could take him away from you like that!" She snapped her long, red-tipped fingers under my nose.

"If you can, he's not worth having." I didn't really mean that. Royce McColl was the only thing worth having in my life right then, and I knew I would curl up and die if I lost him.

"We'll see, won't we, little sister?" Celeste's lips curled in my father's contemptuous smile, and I shuddered.

I think that was the moment that Celeste decided what she would do to amuse herself that summer, now that she was washed up in the world of beauty contests.

If I am beginning to sound like Little Orphan Annie, let me hasten to correct that image. We Southerners thrive on drama. Blood matters. No matter how much we might despise somebody close kin to us, we'll stick to that person through thick and thin. We may fuss and feud within the family, but let some outsider come in and do the same thing, and the family rises up and sticks together. Somebody asked me once why Southerners are like that, and I had to think about it pretty hard. I have several theories. One is that it's the heat and the humidity that makes us cranky sometimes but always stick together. Another is that we've been made fun of by other regions for so long for the way we talk and our slow-moving ways that we circle up our wagons when outsiders try to get at us. Faulkner wrote about the the moral decay beneath Southern aristocracy, but I think he's off-base about that. I think the South is still in a healing process and the family acts as the bandage protecting the old wounds.

At any rate, Celeste and I started hating each other big time that summer. She had a streak of mean in her a yard wide anyway, and I had a big mess of old resentments. Think about it: she was an also-ran and I was a just-coming-out-of-the-gate participant. My sister really could not bear my getting all the attention now. She had never given me any particular notice before; now she did. Everything I wore or said or did brought sarcastic comments until I thought I'd go crazy.

What I had dreaded all summer finally happened.

Royce McColl and my sister Celeste officially met. I know now that Royce had waited for this meeting for a long time, but Celeste had never laid eyes on him before. I think the term for what happened when she saw him for the first time and he saw her close up instead of from a distance is spontaneous combustion.

Looking back, I realize that Royce was probably secretly laughing at me when I bitched about Celeste and what a shrew she'd become. How perversely exciting it must have been for him to have me in his arms and Celeste on his mind the whole time. His lovemaking, as I look back on it, was more ferocious after we'd been discussing my sister.

It all broke loose at the little poolside party my father was giving for my mother's birthday. Royce saw Celeste across the patio and left my side without a word of apology.

I saw those two blazing red heads together over the champagne fountain, and my heart sank. They looked like a Viking god and goddess about to burst into flames and leave the rest of us mortals gasping off-stage.

Celeste was breathtakingly gorgeous in a skimpy cobalt-blue dress that was tattooed to her breasts and fanny. She'd worked on her tan all summer, finally getting past the redhead-skin blister-and-peel stage, and was a glowy-golden color that set off her brilliant eyes and hair like crazy.

Royce McColl was no slouch, either, when it came to looks. He was no sun worshipper, but his working-man's tan was better than my sister's. Gone were the faded jeans and plain chambray cowboy shirt. That night, his bulky handsomeness was encased in a casual suit that had "designer" written all over it. Gone, too, were the scruffy boots; a handsome pair of Guccis showed spit-polish. I wanted to throttle all the men who kept coming up to ask me to dance; every time I looked over my partner's shoulder, I saw those two glowing heads of red hair together, and every time I felt my heart go a little bit more numb.

Daddy came up to me after Mother's cake had been brought out and guests were fanning out after we'd sung "Happy Birthday." "I don't know what's happened to your sister. People keep asking me if she's going to sing for us, and I don't know what to tell them."

"She's showing one of our neighbors the stables," I said. I had seen Celeste leading Royce off into the night, and I had a pretty good idea of what she was showing him by now. "Why don't you let me be the one to sing?"

My father gave me a grudging look of admiration. I had a feeling that he was aware of what was going on. "You mean you would actually break down and sing for your poor old daddy and mother? That would be a first." My father, after both his daughters had "let him down" according to his lights, was heavy into his martyred King Lear role these days. Celeste and I were Regan and Goneril, with no Cordelia in sight.

"It's my mother's birthday," I said quietly, "and it's not much of a birthday present, but I'd be honored to sing for her."

So I sang to my mother while the man I loved was doing lord knows what with my sister down in the stables. I sang and I sang and cried deep down all the while, and before it was over I knew why people say that country music is the keening wail of the wounded heart.

They got married a month later in Las Vegas, sending us a wire from San Francisco, where they spent their honeymoon. Azalea reported that Royce had bought off his lease on the house next door. His cleaning lady told her that her boss was buying a big house on Hendersonville Lake, right next to the one owned by Johnny and June Cash.

At least that was clear across town. I picked up the shattered pieces of my heart and wrote a new song that Harrison told me was the best thing I'd ever done. "Hand-me-down Love" went to the top of the charts in two weeks, and I was in demand all over the place. Azalea told me I was getting too skinny, and I came home every night and filled up on cold fried chicken and heated-up Luzianne, then went to my room to rest up for the next day.

Azalea caught me one night and turned me every which way but loose. "What in the world do you think you're doin', girl? You cain't go on actin' like nothing in the wide world's happened here. Yore mama, she's goin' crazy, yore daddy he's been there and back, and now you goin' the same place, sure as shootin' and takin' me with you. When you gone talk to that sister of your'n, git things straightened out betwixt you? It just don't do to have too many suns go down on bein' mad with yore kin folk."

"Azalea, I'm not mad. Hell, Celeste probably did me a favor, getting that two-timing turkey out of my life. Now I can get on with my career, make something out of my life. It's getting clear to me that no man helps a woman do that." Well, maybe Harrison was an exception, I thought.

She set me straight on that. "Don't you be makin' statements 'bout men like that," she told me sternly. "They ain't much good, but we need 'em, and they need us, and that's what keep this ol' world goin' round. That man your sister's married to, I've allus had my doubts about him, but one thing I ain't got no doubt about. You got to get things squared up with Celeste and you got to do it purty soon. I smell a hurricane brewing up, and I been seeing little grey fogs at night." Azalea swears that she has the power of prophecy, that a little mist floats toward her when something bad is about to happen.

I rolled my eyes and reached for one of her Luckies. She grabbed them out of my way. "You're a singer, and them things ain't good for your throat. You promise me, now. You make it up with your sister. Your daddy tells me those friends of yours out there, Donna and Austin, that airline fellow, are havin' a party, some kind of pig roast. Your sister's invited and so are you. Now don't you be sayin' no to that"

"She went after a man I loved, Azalea," I said.

"So that's the end of the world? Ain't no man worth fallin' out with your sister over. They got something we don't, but that's all any man's got and that don't last. Blood do. Your sister, she's got your blood."

"Sometimes I wonder about that," I said darkly. "Are you sure I wasn't adopted?"

* * *

I went to Donna and Austin's pig roast. If indeed the newlyweds did attend, it would be the first time I'd laid eyes on my sister and her husband in the six months since they had eloped.

Donna, bless her, prepared me for my first sight of Celeste. "Fable, I don't know what's the matter, but there's definitely something wrong with your sister. We're all worried to death about her."

I sipped my mimosa and looked out at the wild geese that come back to the lake each spring. Austin once turned over his very expensive boat to one of the nesting females to have her babies in. "She won't have anything to do with any of us, so I wouldn't know." I shrugged. "Maybe she's pregnant."

Donna shook her head. "No, it's something else. I think there's something wrong in that marriage. How well did you actually know Royce anyway?"

I laughed without a smidgeon of humor. "Not nearly as well as I thought! Daddy still thinks he's some kind of secret agent or something. What does Austin think? You guys have been living next door to each other all these months."

"Royce keeps us at arm's length, like he does everybody else. This is the first time he and Celeste have accepted an invitation that I know of. They've bought that huge, gorgeous boat and spend all their time going up and down the lake . . . hey, I think I see the Wanderer right now." Donna shielded her eyes against the brilliant sundown rays.

I braced myself for my first sight of Celeste since she'd become Mrs. Royce McColl.

The shock of seeing her as she came up the path from the dock to where I stood watching from the upper deck brought an audible gasp from me. "Donna! She's emaciated!"

"I told you," Donna whispered back. Then she waved and called out gaily to Celeste and other newcomers. "Hey, you people! Austin has mimosas waiting by the pool. We'll meet you down there."

Celeste turned her face up to where I stood next to Donna. She was pale and hollow-eyed and no longer glowy from last summer's tan. At sight of me, her haunted countenance registered shock—and something else. Shame? I cannot put a label to what I saw on my sister's face. But if there had been stairs down from the deck, I would have been careening down them to greet my sister, no matter what had gone between us before. As I said before, we're *blood.*

Royce was still at the dock, so I didn't have eye contact with him. By the time I made it downstairs, Celeste was gone, making some hurried excuse to Austin, I heard later, and the Wanderer was half a mile down the lake.

"Why would she run from me?" I asked Donna, who has known me and my sister all our lives.

One of the pilots who'd been down at the dock came up to us. "That your sister? Wow, what'd we do to run her off like that? Hey, I know that guy from somewhere. Lessee . . ."

"Greg, you know everybody." Donna knew I was still smarting from Celeste's pointed avoidance of me and tried to take my mind off it. "Greg has shared a New York apartment with three gorgeous stews for years and he tries to pretend it isn't platonic, but we all know better."

"You throw a wrench into all my new relationships," Greg told her, holding his hand out to meet me.

"Where do you think you've seen my sister's husband before?" I asked after we'd minced carefully through the who-are-you and what-do-you-do part of the conversation.

"Dunno. Could be *The New York Times.* I subscribe and read it religiously."

"You were down there just now." I waited until Donna was turned away talking to someone else before asking this. "You've never met my sister before, so you don't know about the tremendous change in her. Just seeing her for the first time, what do you think?"

The pilot's sunny smile disappeared behind a cloud. "Lady, I hate to be the one to say this, but I think your sister is in real trouble."

"Cocaine?" I whispered.

His nod wasn't necessary. I'd been around enough of that stuff on Music Row to be able to recognize an addict when I saw one.

But why? My sister's only addiction in life had been to winning beauty contests.

Royce McColl had to be the key. It was time to find out about the man who had not only driven a wedge between my sister and me, but who was also apparently involved in mysterious activities that were now driving Celeste to self-destruction.

My sister's haunted look permeated my dreams. I started trying to reach her by phone, but her answering machine always gave me the same message: she was out and would return calls when she was available.

She never did.

I even drove out there and tried to get someone to answer the door at the huge rock-and-cedar house, but to no avail. After that, Donna offered to ride me over to the house by boat. We couldn't get past the tightly locked gate in the security fence that guarded the grounds against unwanted visitors.

Apparently, I fit into that category. I was pretty sure, even though the house was shuttered and deserted looking, that my sister was inside, suffering whatever hell she was going through, and that she knew of my attempts to make contact.

Daddy was incredibly callous about the situation when I tried to bring it to his attention. He had never forgiven her for "letting him down," and he could not stand Royce or the idea that Celeste had married him against Daddy's wishes. "She made her bed. Let her lie it. She hasn't even called us, not since she made her jackass decision to marry somebody nobody in town knows anything about. Obviously, this Royce fellow is after her money. Well, he'll find out pretty soon that the Devereux fortune isn't up for grabs by carpetbagging fourflushers." My father is good at shifting loyalties. Once he decided Celeste wasn't going to bring fame and luster to our family, that was it.

My mother was no good at all. She just burst into tears every time I brought up Celeste's name.

In desperation, I went to Harrison Judd, who I knew had some contacts with the Williamson County Sheriff's Department. "It's driving me crazy, Harrison. I think my sister is in deep trouble, deeper than I ever thought. Can you have this guy checked out, maybe find out if he's into the drug or money-laundering business?" I remembered what Austin's friend Greg had said about seeing Royce's picture somewhere. I told Harrison about that.

Let me talk about Harrison Judd and me and the way things were between us during the time of my early success. If Royce had not been still in my life, Harrison and I would have taken off like a rocket together. But he was careful not to tread on the boundaries between a business and a personal liaison, and I was grateful. I don't have the emotional stamina to be a two-man woman, and Royce was very much in command of my time and energy. Harrison Judd knew this, though he wasn't being altogether unselfish in honoring the embargo.

He wanted me all to himself, free and clear, he told me later, with no hangovers.

Those crazy electric vibes still flickered every time we were around each other, but we both put in our own power-surge controls. Other women didn't. I saw every green young girl singer who came to the studio go crazy over Harrison. He was kind to them and kept them at bay somehow. Sometimes I watched him when he didn't know I was watching and marveled at the way he kept those big-eyed girls adoring but distant.

Maybe, I decided, it was that college professor air he had to him—the distracted gestures, disheveled clothes, tousled dark hair that sometimes crept out of its ponytail.

What always struck me as sexiest about him, though, was his walk. He had a hunched-up power to his shoulders and hips, though he was bony as hell. I always likened him to a big lean, powerful cat when he strode across the studio floor.

Maybe, though, the reason he always kept the starry-eyed ingenues from getting hurt when he didn't respond to their kittenish advances was his wonderful talent for not taking himself seriously. Harrison is a master at putting things in perspective, keeping everything in balance.

Harrison has a unique talent, too, that breaks us all up at the studio. If someone gets on an ego trip or starts showing out around Harrison, he looks at the person with this deadpan expression and *wiggles his ears.*

It is very hard to stay mad or serious when Harrison does this.

He never gains weight, though he has terrible eating habits. I've seen him go through an entire box of Goo-Goo clusters at one recording session. For the benefit of those uninitiated into the country music cult, these sinfully rich peanut, caramel and chocolate patties have been part of the advertising base of Grand Ole Opry since long before the show moved from historic Ryman Auditorium in downtown Nashville. They are even older than Tootsie and her Orchid Lounge—no longer extant, either of them—where the big stars would quaff beer up till two minutes before their on-stage call at the Ryman.

Harrison Judd has an in with everybody who is anybody in the country music business, which is probably why my career took off so quickly. He was married at one time, he tells me, and "got that out of his system once and for all."

Country music is a huggy/kissy kind of business, but it was a very long time before Harrison kissed me. He told me after our relationship changed that it was very hard to keep his side of our association platonic, since he felt electricity around me from the start. He had learned to be a patient man, he tells me now, and he knew if he gave me enough space and time I would come to my senses and realize he was the man for me.

After my experience with Royce McColl, I appreciated that patience.

But back to the mystery of my sister. Harrison's friend in the Williamson County Sheriff's department called two days after I'd seen Celeste. "Miss Devereux? Deputy Sheriff Laney Ford here out at Franklin. Any chance you could come over here and take a look at what I got on this McColl fellow?"

It took me about fifteen minutes to drive the 18 miles from our house to the little town of Franklin. I had a cold feeling in the pit of my stomach even before I saw what Laney Ford had to show me.

The faxed copy of a *New York Times* tear sheet was poor quality, and the man in the picture was without a beard, but I recognized Royce McColl—or whoever he was—right away. I didn't recognize the pretty dark-haired lady in the photo who was identified as his wife. "That's him!" I fell into quiet puzzlement as I read the eight-year-old article, then shook my head. "I don't understand. Does this mean Royce McColl was part of the mob or something?"

"Bryson Daves is his real name. I found one of his old saddles out at that place he rented next to you and ran the fingerprints through. He's from Louisiana, did his Service bit, then wound up in New York." Ford pointed to the picture. "He'd been up there around five years when this happened."

I stared at the picture and the glaring headline: "BRIDEGROOM VANISHES ON HONEYMOON!" I read the startling story again, trying to make myself believe what I was reading.

Laney Ford lit up a cigarette and belatedly offered me one. Too numb to remember I wasn't smoking these days, I accepted. "Crazy, ain't it? Like something outta one of them teevee cops-and-robbers things. Man gets married, takes his bride to one of them fancy Eyetalian restaurants, then flat disappears."

"She says here that two men walked into Luigi's looking like they were trying to find somebody. Before they spotted her husband, he saw them and turned white as a sheet. Then he gave her a wad of bills, told her to get the next plane to her family's home out in Kansas, and he'd get there as soon as he could." The deputy added his own epilogue. "He never made it to Kansas."

I shook my head, still not believing it all. "That was the last time she saw him. He went out the back way, and the two men followed. She went back to Wichita. Did you follow up on the woman?"

"She's married to somebody she met after the seven years went by, freeing her up. Got a kid. She said to keep her posted if anything came up on the guy, but I had the feeling she hoped we wouldn't find anything. The woman went to hell and back, and I'm pretty sure she's not anxious to have an old husband come in and mess up her nice new life."

"I can imagine. What about the New York police? Did they have anything on Roy—Bryson?"

"That they did. Just get ready for this. Turns out Daves was doing undercover work for the L.B.I.—that's the Louisiana Bureau of Investigation. Had been the whole time he was in New York. Some of the big-time crooks down in Baton Rouge were getting political payoffs from New York, and the D. A. down there was about to crack the whole business wide open. That's when their key witness—your sister's new husband—disappeared. After a few months of trying to find the guy, they wrote Daves off as fishfood and closed the case."

"What do we do now?"

Laney Ford shrugged. "Do? You got a complaint against the guy?"

I gave a grim little laugh. "Nothing that would hold up in court. I don't give a damn about Royce. I just want to help my sister."

Laney Ford pondered, and I could tell he was debating about whether to tell me something else. "There is something about her I guess I ought to tell you." I was getting used to the knot of cold dread in my stomach. "Me and the folks over at the Hendersonville P. D. are pretty tight. They say she's on the hard stuff big time. Hasn't been caught buying just yet, but she's come close. I'd say that sister of yours is walking on the edge."

"I know," I whispered. "What can I do?"

"At least get the word to her that she could be in a peck of danger." Laney Ford leaned forward so his words wouldn't carry through the noisy office. "*We* found him, didn't we? What makes you think that pack of birddogs from bayou country can't do the same thing? Or that other crowd from New York?"

I shuddered. "That's why she won't come to the door or answer the phone. That's why she's taking that damn dope—because she's scared out of her mind!" I felt more helpless than I'd ever felt in my life. And then a horrible thought crossed my mind. "This little investigation you've made. Will it stir those people up again?" If anything happened to Celeste, it could be my doing!

Laney's eyes were sympathetic, recognizing the guilt I was undergoing. "Girl, I hate to tell you this, but that bunch is already on to where your sister's husband can be found. What I didn't tell you yet is that the Hendersonville Sheriff investigated a mysterious explosion at the McColls' house last week. It seems like somebody rigged Mr. McColl's Lincoln to blow up the moment he turned the key in the ignition. Fortunately, the man's cagey. He has one of them gadgets that unlocks the car door, then turns on the lights and ignition from several yards away."

My gasp made everybody in the office turn and stare. "So they've already found him! My sister is in terrible danger! Isn't there something you can do?"

The deputy shook his head. "Hendersonville tried to get your brother-in-law to bring charges when the car blew up. He refused, saying the Lincoln had a gas leak and it was an accident."

I left the office in a daze, not even remembering whether I'd thanked Officer Ford for all his help. All I could think about was what I could do to save my sister's life.

I couldn't make up my mind about whether to tell my parents about all this. Knowing my father, I was pretty sure he would do something that would endanger Celeste even more. Plus, once he found out she was on dope, that would be it as far as he was concerned. My father has no patience with anything outside the realm of proper W.A.S.P. behavior. Celeste knew this as well as I did. I'm sure that's why she had cut herself off from her family as soon as her life started going sour.

My inability to come up with some kind of action kept me awake more nights than I can count. When I did sleep, I dreamed about Deirdre, only she was Celeste and somehow me at the same time. After one of those tormented nights, I got up at dawn and saddled Gambler and rode up on Deirdre's mountain to watch the sun come up.

When I got back to the house, Azalea was waiting in the kitchen with a big pot of fresh coffee. After she'd poured me a cup, she said glumly, "I saw the grey mist last night. It was over my head this time."

Once she had seen her grey mist at knee level. The next week, our beloved cocker spaniel died of a heart attack.

Celeste is half a head taller than Azalea.

"Azalea, I don't know what we can do. I've called her, I've sent her letters, I've gone out there. She just won't see me." My coffee went down like grit in my dry throat. I lit up one of Azalea's Luckies. Azalea didn't say a thing, which showed how worried she was about seeing her grey mist the night before.

"One thing you got to do is start thinking about your own self for a while." Azalea looked at me critically. "If you ain't a mess, I never seen one. That hair needs trimmin' and permin', and yore eyes look like two holes burned in a blanket."

I blew a smoke ring at her. "Well, thanks a whole bunch! You don't look all that glamorous yourself this morning." I felt a wave of tender love for the black woman sitting across from me. She was the only person in the whole world who'd ever given me complete, unqualified love. And she was getting old and dried-up to the point that I really worried about her. Daddy had scoffed when I'd pointed out that Azalea didn't need to be doing so much of the work around the house, but had grudgingly agreed to hire a new servant when I'd insisted.

"I'm ser'ous. And you need to be gettin' you a boyfriend that takes you out jukin' once in a while stid of workin' and stayin' by yourself all the time."

"The right man will come along one of these days," I told her.

But she was right about me not looking after myself. I had to stop worrying about a situation that I apparently had no control over and take charge of my own life.

I spent the afternoon in the Brentwood Fair Lady salon, and I must say it did wonders for my looks if not for my spirits.

Harrison really liked my hairdo and spruced-up appearance when I met him for breakfast the next morning at the Loveless Cafe. Telling him the crazy story Laney Ford had divulged about Royce made me feel a less little alone in an increasingly troublesome situation. So did the breakfast, which has no equal in Tennessee and maybe in the whole world.

The biscuits and ham with redeye gravy at the Loveless are another Nashville country music institution, along with the waitresses who serve them. The wonderful 60's beehives and I ain't-takin'-no-crap-from-you-buster" attitudes tickle the stew out of me everytime I go. That particular morning I especially needed something like breakfast at the Loveless and dug into those delicious vittles with good appetite.

Harrison, by the way, put the quietus on my Roger Miller-type song entitled "She's Got

Waitress Legs," saying a good country music singer does not kid hard-core traditions like the Loveless Cafe.

He's a wise man and I listen to him most of the time—except of course when he wiggles his ears.

Chapter Eight

The letter that was waiting for me when I got back from breakfast made my heart stop. I recognized the spidery handwriting as Celeste's. I tore into the envelope with shaking hands.

There were only two lines: "Royce and I are going away. Don't tell anybody." She didn't even sign her name. I looked at the postmark. The note had been mailed from Hendersonville the day before.

I raced to the phone to call Donna and stopped midway through my dialing. Celeste had said not to tell anyone. I forced myself to sound calm and casual when Donna answered. "Hey, I'm thinking about taking a spin out to your place today. Will you be home?"

Donna assured me she would be pleased to see me. "We'll have lunch by the pool."

"No, I've just had one of those lumberjack-sized breakfasts at the Loveless. I'll just pop in and pop out."

I drove very slowly down Lake Valley Road until I reached the house where my sister lived. It was as tightly closed as ever, the gates double-locked. I wasn't sure what kind of car they'd bought after the Lincoln, but I was pretty sure it was gone. A call phone had been added to the front gate. I tried it, knowing there would be no answer. Sure enough, there wasn't.

Donna wasn't at all curious about my asking her to take me for a boat ride. She's familiar with my love of cruising the lake. Nor did she wonder greatly about my wanting to go slowly by the house. She did, however, wonder about what she noticed when we got up to the McColl dock. "Hey, their boat's gone! That's funny. Austin and I were all over the lake this morning and didn't see a sign of them." Then she observed something that I had missed. "Look, that ramp where the boat trailer usually sits is empty, too. Maybe they hauled The Wanderer down to the coast and put in for some ocean boating."

"Maybe so."

Azalea's grey mist turned out to be true prophecy. Less than a week after I'd gotten the letter from Celeste, Deputy Laney Ford paid a call on me and my parents. I could tell from the minute he walked into the living room that he had bad news. "Miz Devereux, sir, Miss

Fable, we just got a call from Hendersonville. The police down there at Key West called Tennessee." He worried his hat some more and then just blurted it out. "Your daughter, she's dead." My mother made a little sound like a wounded animal, and my father turned white around the mouth. I was in shock and couldn't say or do anything. I listened numbly as the deputy gave us the details and tried to comfort my mother, whose thin shoulders were shaking with her pitiful sobs.

"A boat? Somewhere off Key West?" My father became angry, which is how he deals with shock. "What would they be doing way down there?"

Laney Ford and I exchanged knowing glances. "Apparently, Sir, she and her husband were on their way to Bermuda or some island or other when the boat blew up. A boat way off saw the explosion and put out an S.O.S., but by the time anybody got there they wasn't nothing left but a few splinters."

I gasped, thinking of the Lincoln, and Laney Ford gave me a warning look. I knew then that he had no plans to tell my mother and father the whole story and didn't want me to, either. But I'd think about that later. Right now my heart was hurting from pain that mostly sprang from guilt. I had failed to make up with my sister and now she was dead. I started crying, and my father said sharply, "Be strong for your mother's sake, Fable." To the deputy, "Surely the Coastguard searched for survivors."

"Mister Devereux, there weren't no way in hell anybody could've survived that explosion. I'm sorry as I can be about being the one to tell you all this, but there ain't a chance of a snowball in hell of finding those folks alive." He added somberly, "Or finding 'em, period. Them sharks out there . . ." My mother shivered and gave a little cry. Deputy Ford looked even more mournful as he went on with his grim report. "I hate being the one to break this tragic news, but Key West said there were no remains to be sent back to the family."

"I presume this accident is being officially investigated. What do they think caused the explosion?" My father's anger was colder now. I think the mention of "no remains" brought the reality of the horror into true focus for all of us. Beautiful Celeste—or what was left of her—to be savaged by sharks! The image was terrible.

"Like I said, Sir, there just wasn't anything left to investigate. They got the registration number from the marina at Key West where The Wanderer left off from. That's how they got ahold of Hendersonville." Deputy Ford was a nice fellow. He showed real sympathy when he took his leave of all of us.

I offered to walk him out to his vehicle. Mainly I needed to talk to him where my parents couldn't hear. "Do the police think my sister and her husband were murdered? Laney, will all this come out? Will they go after the people who did this?"

"Whoa, I won't be involved. It'll be the Key West people, maybe Miami since that's kind of in their bailiwick, too. And I guarantee you, they'll find out more than we know before the week's up. As for pinning this to somebody specifically . . ." Laney shook his head. "No way. It's hard enough to get these guys even with live eyewitnesses."

I thanked the deputy for his kindness and went back in the house to find Azalea. Somebody had to break the news to her that her grey mist had indeed foretold a death.

The memorial service for Royce and Celeste was held in a little country church on our family property. My mother and I wept openly, as did Celeste's friends. My father stared stoically ahead, not shedding a tear. I wondered what he was thinking as he looked at the picture of Celeste smiling and radiant over one of her early contest wins.

I know what I was thinking—that my sister's life had been a long, empty waste. I should have been a better friend to her, I thought, should have guided her into more fulfilling goals than the meaningless ones that had led her to value herself only physically. My anger toward myself was exceeded only by anger at the man who had deluded first me and then my sister. Royce McColl was the real villain in this tragedy, I was certain. I shed no tears for him and vowed to remove his headstone one day when I was sole owner of Moncoeur.

Apparently no one else had any tears for my sister's late husband, either. No one showed up for Royce, which of course did not surprise me. Deputy Ford told me after the service that Key West had tried to locate next of kin but without success.

They had located his first wife, they said, and informed her of Royce's death. I thought about what Laney had said about the woman probably not being eager to have her missing ex-husband found. How strange it must have been for her to learn he was actually dead after all the years of not being sure!

Harrison Judd and some of my Music Row friends brought out a beautiful willow tree, which they planted close to the little church's graveyard where Celeste and Royce would have symbolic headstones. Azalea surprised us by singing after the service let out. Her quavery voice singing "In the Bosom of the Lamb" made me sadder than anything that had gone before.

My sister's life had been cut short before she had ever really learned what real life was all about. That was the saddest part of all.

My father closed us out completely after Celeste's death, and my mother and I did our best to give each other comfort. I did my best to talk her out of putting herself to bed each night with her little pills, but it was no use. Finally I gave up on trying to relate to my mother or my father. The former was on a self-destruct course with Valium and vodka, and the latter was totally consumed with the political horse race he was considering running. After all, I had my own life and career to think about.

My singing career had taken off, and I had been offered a chance at making an album that would include all my songs. That wasn't the most exciting part, though. I was being handed the real plum for any country music performer—I would make my first appearance on Grand Ole Opry almost a month to the day after Celeste's death. The timing was actually good for me, taking my mind off the haunting memories of my sister.

Anybody who has ever been on this famous old show will tell you it's like a zoo on stage and backstage during the strictly live performance. There are usually about thirty to fifty people milling around both places even while the stars are performing. The backup singers (the "doo-wahs") chat and socialize while the performer they're backing is doing her or his part. Then by some uncanny timing, they put their heads together and harmonize where they are supposed to. One employee does nothing but sit right there by the piano and keep a list of everybody who does anything at all during the show. Fans who've been given stage privileges wander all over, gawking and getting autographs, and the various bands change over with every performer. It's all totally confusing and wild and exciting, and somehow nothing ever goes wrong!

I was on the Roy Acuff part of the show and nervous as a cat in a room full of rocking chairs when my turn came to sing. Roy—who's a darling; everybody in Nashville loves him to death—pulled me out to face all those packed seats, and I felt as if I might faint dead away. But somehow I got into "Hand-me-down Love," and before I had sung even the first verse I knew I was a hit and I started enjoying it.

By the time I was ready to do my encore, I was an old Opry pro. I stepped up to that mike and told the fans that Clyde Edgerton's song "She's a Quiche Girl in a Barbecue Town" was being performed tonight in honor of my late sister, Celeste, "The most beautiful girl in America." And my voice shook the rafters with that raucous undertone that made one reviewer describe my singing as "a young whiskey voice that would bring the hogs up from anywhere."

Harrison took me out afterwards and that night was the closest we had gotten yet to exploring some of that electricity between us. But I would have been in love with any man I was with that night, and Harrison had the sense to know it.

He took me home and we had our usual little peck on the cheek. But I noticed that he stood outside on the veranda for a long time before leaving.

I'll never forget that night for more than one reason. I've described the first one.

The other reason I'll never forget that night is that it was the first time I saw the woman on the mountain—the ghost of my long-gone grandmother Deirdre. I thought about what Azalea had said about Deirdre's ghost appearing when there was something bad happening at Moncoeur, and I shivered.

Maybe her appearance was after the fact, I tried to reassure myself. But somehow I knew something was about to begin, something that I would be a very significant part of.

Oddly enough, my parents approved of my going to a psychiatrist. My father even offered to pay for it, adding that I ought take Mother with me.

But my mother refused to go, and I know now it was probably because the doctor would make her stop taking her Valium.

Dr. Velkoff was, as I've described him already, a funny little man. Over the months of visits, I became very fond of him. I stopped keeping things back, like the dreams and the little sparkles of light I sometimes saw before having a vision. My trust was complete by the time a year had gone by. I told the doctor everything there was to tell about my sister's and my relationship, about Royce, about my father, about Harrison and my music.

When I went for my session the week after the strangest and longest-lasting experience, I was ready to discuss every detail and try to make some sense of why everything seemed so real.

"Dr. Velkoff, you've told me about patients who've had regressions, visions—whatever they are—and imagined they were living in someone's specific past. But this was different! This was real! I was actually there."

"Have I told you about universal memory?"

Sometimes Dr. Velkoff forgets things. That endears him all the more to me. "A little. You said that we all have innate knowledge about certain things like Atlantis and familiar taunts or songs that show up even in remote villages. You also said that earthworms that are fed ground-up earthworms that have been taught certain reactions have those reactions without having to be taught."

"You have a thought on your face. I just saw a little light-bulb go on over your mind."

"It's silly, crazy, but I just happened to think about something. If I'm going back and living as Deirdre, is it possible that she's coming back and living through me?"

Dr. Velkoff pondered that. "I like the genetic memory theory much better. We've learned that certain chromosomes and genes pass on generation through generation, that they have memories, and that those inheriting them have been observed to act certain ways or have a particular characteristic because it's 'in their blood'."

"When do you think I can go back?" I was deeply worried about my ancestor and what might happen to her when Andre returned to Moncoeur and found her living there. What if he threw her out, along with Sean and the coming baby? Maybe all this stuff was inside my head, but these people were becoming very real to me and I was anxious to know what happened to them.

I held all of Deirdre's past in my head, but only up to a certain point. Now I was eager to know her future. "Dr. Velkoff, I want you to help me control these journeys into the past."

"I'm reading your mind, young lady, and I don't like it."

I gripped his arms excitedly. "Oh, come on, you know it would be safer if we were in control."

"You're asking me to use hypnosis to put you into regression. I can't do it, Fable. Right now, your mind is going through some kind of spontaneous process that your subconscious is directing. If I manipulate your mind through hypnosis, you may not even live the same life. I don't know everything that's stored in your mind. I may reach some part of your memory that's best left buried."

My enthusiasm waned at his logic. "I hadn't thought about that. You're right. One of my ancestors might have been riding with Genghis Khan or something."

"Better with him than his enemies." Dr. Velkoff patted my knee paternally. "Best just leave things alone for now. Somehow I think someone is watching over you to make sure you're not harmed by these strange experiences. If we start bringing in modern psychological techniques, the chain between your century and Deirdre's might get all kinked up."

Or broken. That possibility desolated me. Deirdre loved Andre so much that the knowledge of her love had filtered through the years to my awareness. I could not bear the thought of her never being in Andre's arms again. I may be living her life again, through some strange warp in time, but her love for Andre was separate from me somehow, as was his for her.

I had my own twentieth-century heart problems. I didn't need any additional ones from another era.

I left the building at Church and 4th to walk back to my car, wondering if the people I passed were aware that these streets were full of history that had nothing to do with the souvenir shops and record businesses that now characterized downtown Nashville.

On my way home, I pondered what Dr. Velkoff had said about someone watching over me. "Like a guardian angel," I said aloud in the car. It was a nice thought, one not new to me either. Ever since I was a little girl I had felt an occasional benign presence, sort of like the brush of an angel's wing.

This rather New-Agey line of thinking led me into an idea for my next song, which kept me occupied from that point on. I was humming tunes and filling in words for "On the Wings of an Angel" when I walked up to the kitchen house. As I walked through the door, I could smell one of Azalea's famous gumbos cooking on the old wood stove she still liked to use.

"Boy, that stew smells good enough to eat with yo' mouf!"

The black woman at the stove turned around and gave me a big warm smile. I realized then that the pot on the stove held chicken and dumplings and that the cook was not Azalea, but her ancestor, Prudy.

I had walked into the kitchen at Moncoeur of the past and Deirdre was as hungry as any woman could be who was "eating for two."

Chapter Nine

Fall 1859

"Aren't you lookin' fine this beautiful mornin', Miss DeeDee." Prudy, along with her husband, Rufus, had fast become Deirdre's good friend. In fact, Deirdre loved everything about her new life—the fresh green rolling hills of the countryside, the mountain rising behind the big house, the warm kitchen and even warmer friendliness of the slaves at Moncoeur, the instant sense of belonging, like family.

Deirdre was beginning to get past her morning sickness—she was a little over two months along, she figured—and did feel better than she had in a while. "That pot of chicken and dumplings smells wonderful, Prudy. I think I'll take a tray up to Miz Aurelia. She looked mighty pale when I took her coffee and sweet rolls this morning."

Deirdre had already become attached to the mistress of Moncoeur, too. Aurelia Devereux was a lady of the first tier, she had decided upon their first meeting.

"I hope she's not comin' down with her sickness again," Prudy said, dishing out a healthy portion of the scrumptious stew into a fine china bowl.

"What is her sickness, Prudy?" Deirdre worried about that, too. Miz Aurelia was as sweet and beautiful a lady as one could imagine, but she was terribly frail. In the three weeks Sean and Deirdre had been working at the plantation, she had seen its mistress often too weak to rise in the morning and totally exhausted by the smallest activity. Jean-Paul Devereux had made it plain to Deirdre from the start that she was to look after his wife ahead of all other duties, and Deirdre had taken that admonition to heart.

Prudy shook her head as she took out a tin of perfect biscuits from the oven and split them deftly, putting freshly churned butter on them and arranging several on Aurelia's tray. "Doctor Hollins says it's some kind of blood weakness, but I've often wondered my ownself if it wasn't something to do with the heart. When Miz Aurelia was being courted by Mister Jean-Paul, she was a Creole belle in New Awlins. I don't think she's never got over leavin' that place and comin' to Tennessee."

Deirdre could not imagine a more beautiful place than Moncoeur, or this part of Tennessee. But from what Aurelia had told the girl about her home, it was not just the place that she missed, it was the whole culture of the city.

"New Orleans is a fascinating town," Deirdre said, then hastily covered her tracks. "Or so I've heard. Let me have that tray, Prudy. You've got plenty to do without having to tote things upstairs. I'm young and strong."

Deirdre was deliberately using words like 'tote' these days, since she was determined to be assimilated by the South as quickly as possible—unlike Sean, who still stuck to everything Irish.

"And fillin' out some, ain't you, since I first saw you." The black woman gave Deirdre a broad wink and the girl blushed, knowing that Prudy had already guessed, through some kind of female bond, that she was pregnant.

"It's all your good vittles," Deirdre said, arranging a spray of flowers on the tray and refolding the napkin to give herself time to recover her composure. Prudy, like all the other Negroes at Moncoeur, had been taught to read, write and figure. It wouldn't take much counting to work out that Deirdre McAfee had been pregnant before she came to the plantation as a newlywed. "Gracious, is that Sean I hear coming up the back walk already? I better take this on up and get back down here to see to my husband."

Deirdre loved Aurelia's bedroom. It adjoined

the one that Jean-Paul used on the nights that his wife was not feeling well. "Let me open this window a little so you can feel the breeze that's coming off the mountain." Deirdre put the tray down on a pretty little Louis XVI table. Aurelia had filled the old plantation house with beautiful French furniture, but she spoke longingly of her former home in New Orleans.

"Merci, chérie. I told Jean-Paul last night that I don't know how we ever got along without you and Sean. It's as if you were dropped off at Moncoeur by the wings of an angel."

Deirdre's skin prickled with a strange chill. "You're the angel," she said quickly. Sometimes words used a certain way caused prickles on the back of her neck, and images flickered in her head but were gone before she could grasp them. Quickly she arranged the napkin on Aurelia's lap and sat in one of the pretty French chairs, thinking how much her new mistress did indeed resemble an angel. "Now eat up, every bite."

Long, taffy-blond curls framed a heart-shaped face whose brown eyes were huge and black-ringed with thick, curling lashes. The lace-trimmed gown and negligee disguised the too-thin limbs but accentuated smooth, unlined ivory skin that held not a flaw. Letitia, the black servant who had come to Tennessee with her mistress, had told Deirdre that Miss Aurelia's skin had never once been exposed to the sun.

Deirdre believed that story, as well as all the

ones about Aurelia being the most sought-after belle in Louisiana. She loved Aurelia's stories, too, about the Creole culture, of the balls and societies and carefully monitored courtships. She marveled at her new mistress's tales of how strictly the duennas guarded their Creole wards. New Orleans society with its separate customs, even balls, for young ladies of mixed color and great beauty fascinated Deirdre. She enjoyed very much listening to Aurelia tell about these things. The older woman had once even, when she was feeling particularly well, modeled one of the fabulous gowns that filled her closet.

"Oh, Deirdre, I cannot eat another mouthful. You eat it, so Prudy won't scold me."

"I'll be eating with Sean later. He was just coming in when I came up here." Deirdre told her, taking the still-full tray away. "But Prudy won't scold you. She just wants you be happy and healthy. We all do."

"I know." Aurelia gave a deep sigh. "Poor Jean-Paul more than anyone. The darling, he wants so much for me to be a normal wife to him. Why can't I be that way, Deirdre? You left your home country and came here and are not languishing. You make your husband happy." Another deep sigh. "I miss Andre. He always cheers me up, makes me laugh." She turned to Deirdre, her face lit up with a happiness that hadn't been there before. "Oh, but you've not met Andre, have you? He's Jean-Paul's brother, and they are so different, almost opposites. My husband . . ." Aurelia pleated the bedspread between thin fingers. "My husband is the dearest man in the world, but he can be so . . . so *gloomy.* Andre acts as if the world is one big ball. So gay, so cheerful always. He makes me remember my girlhood, the parties, the joy."

Deirdre sat quietly through Aurelia's animated chatter, thinking of the man who was in both their minds. She wondered about Aurelia's feelings for Andre. How deep did they go? "Well, perhaps he will come soon to cheer you up again. In the meantime, it may perk you up to hear that Gabrielle is coming home at the end of the week."

Aurelia laughed and covered her face. "Oh, *mon dieu!* That spoiled child at home again. Chérie, you will have to help me think of ways to entertain her. She exhausts me with her boundless energy and demands to be constantly amused. Andre has spoiled her so. He became her guardian when she was quite small, you know. His and Jean-Paul's sister died with her husband quite tragically, and Andre has been the only father poor Gabrielle has ever known."

Deirdre knew quite well how spoiled Gabrielle was. She just hoped that her own hair had grown out long enough and her newly matured figure was different enough that the girl would not recognize the waif from the boat to Nashville. "I'll help all I can. Perhaps she's interested in some young man around here. We could encourage that since she's at the age to be thinking about suitors."

Aurelia laughed again. "Gabrielle has every young man in the county after her, but to settle down with one . . . ! My dear, I'm sure poor Sean is wondering if you are ever coming down! He must be as eager for your company as we always are. I'm very naughty for monopolizing you so much."

Deirdre hugged her before taking the supper tray. "I love every moment with you. I came from such a poor family, as I told you, though my mother was from the upper class, and you make me feel I'm with her again—though you're far too young to be my mother!"

"I'm flattered! *Chérie,* do be a darling and stick your head in my husband's study. Order him to stop worrying with those books and come to me." Aurelia fluffed up her hair and rearranged the lacy trim of her negligee. "He spends far too much time with his accounts and far too little enjoying himself." Aurelia was actually feeling a bit guilty for going on so about Andre and sounding critical of her husband.

"I'll tell him you'd like to see him," Deirdre said with a smile. She knew that Jean-Paul adored his wife but had very serious concerns about the plantation. There was much talk these days about the precarious position of Southern slave-owners and rumblings of deep dissatisfaction with the presidential candidate,

Abraham Lincoln. Jean-Paul had confided to Sean and Deirdre that he had sent more money than he could really afford to boost the campaign of John Breckinridge, the Southern Democratic party's choice, and was afraid it was lost money.

Deirdre knew nothing about politics, but she sensed that the South was going into a troubled era that had to do with more than the slavery issue.

"Mister Devereux? Your wife sends the message that she's lonesome and would welcome a visit from a certain charming gentleman." Deirdre smiled at the disheveled hair of the man sitting deep in thought at his desk in the darkened study off the foyer. "Oh, I'm sorry, sir. I didn't mean to startle you."

"You didn't startle me, Deirdre, these figures did." Jean-Paul Devereux ran his big fingers through his graying brown hair and rose to greet her. One of the regional characteristics that pleased Deirdre more than any other was the total courtesy shown by Southern men to women—even Irish refugees working at menial jobs. "I swear, in these times it's getting harder and harder to realize a profit. But no more of that. Have a seat for a minute."

Deirdre settled herself in a large armchair near Jean-Paul's desk. "Thank you. Is there any way I can help you with your accounts? My mother taught me how to do figures and keep what meager records we had in my family."

"I may call on you. But I may need more than

your accounting skills if the country goes the way it seems to be headed. I may call on you in the future to help us learn how to survive on very little, like you Irish folks did. I'm afraid the South is headed for hard times."

Deirdre grinned. "If you can provide the land for a patch of potatoes, I promise you this plantation will eat well no matter how lean the larder gets. I can fix potatoes two hundred different ways and all different and delicious." She retracted a little. "Well, maybe not delicious, but satisfying and nutritious."

Jean-Paul laughed, and Deirdre was glad to see that the lines in his forehead had relaxed. "You're wonderful, Deirdre. My wife and I agree on that. I hope you're happy here."

"I've never been happier, Mr. Devereux. Now, can I get you a glass of port or something before dinner?"

"You can get Prudy to pour me a whiskey. Better yet, why don't you get that husband of yours to come in and join me for a drink so we can talk about the new horse he's been working with." He immediately looked apologetic. "Oh, but he'll be wanting to spend time with you, of course."

Deirdre laughed and said truthfully, "Nothing that I could talk about would interest Sean so much as that horse out there! But I think we should make a deal. You go visit with your beautiful wife for a bit and I'll go fix Sean his supper. Once you two get started on horses, there's no getting you stopped!"

Jean-Paul looked a little sheepish. He felt guilty about discussing plantation business with Sean and even Deirdre more than he did with Aurelia these days. But she always seemed bored with the horse talk, and his hints about financial difficulties only distressed her. "Tell Prudy I'll have a tray upstairs while I'm visiting with my wife. And tell Sean that we'll get together after Aurelia's retired for the night."

Deirdre's smile was broad. "Yes, sir. Shall I get that whiskey for you now?"

Jean-Paul nodded. "And maybe a small glass of sherry for my wife." He closed up the books he'd been working on. "We may have to start buying that rotgut liquor Lem Joe Bartow has been peddling around the county. Prices have been going up on everything."

Deirdre had ridden in the wagon with Rufus and Prudy to get supplies in Franklin, and they had pointed out the old rundown farm where the local moonshiner lived and made his questionable whiskey. "I wouldn't be drinking that stuff if I were you, Mr. Devereux. From what I've seen of that operation, a person could get poisoned or worse."

Jean-Paul laughed and patted Deirdre on the shoulder as he passed her on the way up to see his wife. "You're some little lady, Missy. Some little lady."

Deirdre took care of her duties and went to the small cottage attached by a long breezeway to the kitchen. This was now her home with

Sean. Her husband was stretched out on the spool bed, and she went over to kiss him tenderly. "Tough day, sweetheart?"

"Huh? Oh, yeah. And it's not over yet. One of the mares is due to foal maybe tonight. I may have to spend the night out at the barn."

She told him about Jean-Paul's request, and he dutifully got up and put his pants and boots back on, wolfing down the plate of food she'd brought him in the meantime. "I was thinking," she ventured a little shyly, "that you and I could walk up on that mountain tonight, watch the moon and the stars and maybe talk a little more than we've been able to do lately."

Sean's eyes took on a distinct male gleam. "Talk? Or do this?" He pulled her to him and pulled her dress up, pressing himself against her.

"Sean, that's not what I . . ." her words were cut off by his fervent kisses and then she was being pushed back onto the bed, with him driving into her. She turned her face away from the heavy breathing that was fanning her face and closed her eyes until it was over, till his gasps and moans had subsided and he had rolled off her.

"There," he announced proudly. "That's what you wanted, wasn't it?"

Deirdre waited until he had washed himself off, brushed his hair and left whistling to go talk about horses with Jean-Paul. Then she scrubbed her face and body with the cold water from the pump on the back porch, scrubbed till her skin was red and stinging. She talked to herself all the while. "He's not really like that. Just because your wedding night wasn't perfect and he doesn't make love like you think a man should to his wife, that doesn't mean he's a bad man. He works hard, he's kind to you, he gets along with everybody, and he's making you a good husband. You mustn't think about somebody else. You mustn't do that, Deirdre O'Shea McAfee."

She went up on the mountain and watched the moon and the stars all alone, and when the owls hooted their mournful cacophony, she felt like joining in.

Deirdre kept putting off her news about being pregnant, although she knew she would soon start showing and Sean would resent being the last to know.

Sean was spending more and more time with his beloved horses, and his wife spent as much time as she had free on her beloved mountain. Even Jean-Paul and Aurelia started teasing her about being part mountain goat. "I declare, girl, you must have some kind of Cumberland blood in you," Jean-Paul told her one day.

"I do," Deirdre admitted. "In my part of Ireland, the mountains reach clear down to the sea. It is so beautiful." Her heart constricted with just the tiniest pang of homesickness, until she remembered that she had nothing waiting for her in her homeland but more poverty. "In fact, my mountain here is just as pretty as the ones back home. I love the white oak tree that stands up there tall and proud like a lone sentinel. I wrote a little song while I was sitting under it this afternoon."

"Oh, sing it, Dee-Dee, please." They were all sitting in the parlor together, Aurelia having had one of her good days and able to join the others downstairs.

"I have no accompaniment."

"Aurelia can play the piano for you. She's quite good."

Aurelia clapped her hands together. "I have a better idea! My mother was quite musical and bought one of the Jurado guitars while she was abroad in Spain. I can play it a little."

While Jean-Paul fetched the instrument from Aurelia's special storage closet in the barn, Deirdre tried to figure out why she had that peculiar goosebumpy sensation again. "Will you teach me how to play it?"

"Of course I will." Jean-Paul had returned with the instrument, and Aurelia reached for it eagerly.

"Oh, how badly out of tune!" she wailed after a few experimental strums.

Deirdre watched, mesmerized, as the other woman started making rhythmical sounds come from the guitar. She could not restrain her fingers from tattooing the chair arms in imitation. "May I try it myself?" she said after Aurelia had gone through a run of basic chords.

Aurelia laughed. "You said you wanted lessons! But, *oui,* you may try it if you wish. I heard you at my piano one day. I think you have a natural gift of ear."

It was the strangest thing. The moment Deirdre nestled the guitar in her arms, her head filled with echoes of song after song, some with lyrics whose meaning she could not understand at all. Almost in a dream, she started crooning the song that had come to her on the mountain when she was digging up the fruit jars of peaches she had buried weeks earlier to make brandy. The brandy was to be a surprise for Jean-Paul at the party they would give for Gabrielle.

"Coffee grows on the white oak stump,
The river flows with brandy-oh.
Go choose you one that'll stand by you
As sweet as sugar candy-oh."

Jean-Paul and Aurelia's mouths gaped wide at the perfect performance. "That's incredible," Aurelia finally said. "How did you *do* that?"

"I . . . I'm not sure. It's just as you said, I guess. I inherited my mother's ear for music of any kind."

"I love the song. Do you have any more you've written yourself?"

Deirdre knew she could not tell them about the strange compositions that swirled through her mind when she first picked up the guitar. "No, but I know a couple of Irish ballads that my mother taught me. And one that my father taught me which my mother never allowed me to sing in public."

Aurelia laughed with delight. "We're not 'public.'. By all means, sing the naughty one first."

It was a very bawdy ballad, but Deirdre could tell that their little impromptu musicale was doing her mistress more good than Dr. Hollins's tonic, and she lit into the song about a rowdy Irishman who could not tell his mistresses apart.

After the lively little band had parted, Jean-Paul sought Deirdre out in the kitchen, where she was seeing to the proper storing of her peach brandy. "I have not seen my wife enjoy herself so much since my brother's last visit. Thank you, Deirdre. You are a ray of sunshine in this house which has been gloomy too long because of my worries about our country."

Deirdre had overheard Jean-Paul and some of his friends discussing passionately the events of October 16 which had all of the country stirred up. "Do you truly think Mr. John Brown will be hanged as a traitor for what he did at Harper's Ferry?" Deirdre had not grown up with slavery and sometimes had private thoughts about it that made her feel disloyal to the people who were so good to her. Sean had flat forbidden her ever to voice those thoughts aloud when she had timidly expressed her doubts to him. And she reflected that the majority of her Irish compatriots worked harder and lived meaner than the black people at Moncoeur.

"If he isn't, there's nothing left for the South except to secede as some states are already talking about doing," Jean-Paul said fervently. "It's ironic, Dee-Dee. It was federal troops that captured that damned abolitionist sympathiser. Not all the North's against us down here. Why, they sang that song "I wish I Was in Dixie's Land" in New York and everybody's been whistling it ever since. That reminds me. I got the words to it, and since you're so good at singing and playing, I think we ought to copy out some sheets of the words and have us a singalong when we have that party."

"I'll be glad to do that, Mr. Devereux." Deirdre was glad Jean-Paul was like most Southern men, who felt that discussing serious issues with women was simply not productive or proper. Her thoughts were so mixed on the matter, since she knew how well everyone at Moncoeur was treated and how they loved Jean-Paul, that she was sure that her confusion would not have made for an intelligent discussion.

Gabrielle came home in a flurry of bags and boxes and cries of girlish energy. The moment of encounter that Deirdre had dreaded finally came after the girl had made her rounds of the house and let it be known what changes she wanted immediately implemented.

"Don't worry," Jean-Paul chuckled when he came into the kitchen to find Deirdre helping Prudy bake the seven-tier chocolate cake that

Gabrielle had demanded along with all her other favorites for her first night at home. "She's like a hurricane, and the force dies down after the first rush of wind. She loves to ride and I've got Sean's promise that he'll keep a fresh horse saddled up for every time she stops to catch her breath."

Gabrielle burst in at that moment asking why her clothes had not yet been pressed and hung up.

Deirdre stepped forward and said quietly, "I'll be glad to do that for you, Miss Devereux. Is there a particular dress you'd like to wear tonight at your first dinner home?"

The girl's pretty face showed only the briefest moment of passing perplexity. Then, seeing that Deirdre's beauty was encased in homely adornment and that the Irish girl showed no visible case for competitiveness, she chose to be gracious. "That's very kind of you . . . Deirdre, is it? Your husband told me about you when he was showing me the new horses. And, yes, I would like to wear the maroon moire taffeta tonight. Your hair is very pretty—quite fashionable, in fact. Perhaps you could dress my hair along with your other duties?"

Jean-Paul stepped in. "You'll be looking after your own personal toilette after tonight, Gabby, my sweet. Deirdre has her hands full looking after your aunt."

Gabrielle looked a bit miffed but apparently accepted Jean-Paul as the authority around the plantation. Deirdre was very glad of that. She had no desire to become the personal servant of this haughty young woman.

After Deirdre finished with her duties in the kitchen, she went up to help Gabrielle with her dress and hair as she'd promised. As her masses of black hair were being arranged quite becomingly atop her head, Gabrielle watched her hairdresser critically in the vanity mirror.

"You're really quite pretty," the girl finally said with an edge of disapproval. "I don't mean to be critical, but you might want to leave off some of Prudy's cakes and pies, though."

Deirdre drew in her stretching stomach, realizing that Gabrielle had noticed her thickening middle and breasts. "That's sometimes hard to do, as I'm sure you know firsthand."

"Do I ever!" Gabrielle played with the ringlet her hairdresser had curled around her finger and let fall to the creamy neck. "That's very nice. I like your husband, though he treated the horses as though he liked them a lot better than me. He still has a sort of foreign sound in his voice that you don't have. Aren't you both from the same country?"

"Yes, but I seem to be losing my Irish brogue around your family. I like the way people talk here and don't mind at all that I'm losing my old way of talking. Sean doesn't talk as much as I do," Deirdre said with a little laugh. "He tells me I talk too much."

"Well, that's a man for you. When I get married, I shall marry someone like my Uncle Andre, who talks as much as I do and thinks women are more wonderful than horses. Ouch!"

Deirdre really hadn't intended to pull the girl's hair too hard, but she wasn't particularly repentent. The remark about Andre was forgivable since Gabrielle didn't know Deirdre's history with her uncle, but the comment about Sean's noticeable neglect of his wife was not. "I'm sorry. There, you look lovely."

Indeed, the girl did look beautiful. Deirdre felt a tiny pang at the thought of the plain dress she would wear that evening—but then, she was not a Devereux and never would be.

That thought brought a pang, too.

After dinner, at which Deirdre was enjoined to sit with the family, the peach brandy was brought out and presented to Jean-Paul for tasting. He took his time and great pleasure in sniffing the cork on the decanter and then rolling the liquor dramatically in the fine Waterford snifter Prudy had brought him. "Umm, wonderful bouquet. Ah!" The first sip brought a stream of compliments to Deirdre, who sat pleased and flushed to have Jean-Paul recognize her little gift to him.

"I helped my family make rye whiskey in the old country. I had never worked with peaches, but since they don't have the rye around here . . ."

"They use corn, Deirdre," Jean-Paul said, finishing off his glass of brandy and pouring another. "Perhaps you could try it. Lord knows, you have a better knack at this whiskey-making than Lem Joe Bartow. I'll have Rufus help you set up some barrels and a still if you'd like to try your hand at a bigger operation."

Gabrielle daintily wiped the chocolate off her mouth and made a derisive sound. "Whiskey! I cannot believe that this family is considering being associated with making corn liquor."

Jean-Paul said quietly, "The plantation is undergoing some financial difficulties, Gaby. I guess I need to remind you that the last few years of stability and growth in Southern industry have kept you in luxury in that fine young ladies' establishment where you've learned how to crook your little finger just right and not much else. And something else I guess needs saying. I'll thank you to start treating Deirdre as a member of the family—which she's become in your aunt's and my eyes and everybody else's around here."

Gabrielle's look in Deirdre's direction held no warmth, but her words were polite for her uncle's sake. "I'm sorry if I've acted cross, DeeDee." Deirdre knew the use of her nickname was deliberately intended to annoy—as it did. Deirdre did not care for her father's pet name for her to be bandied about without the true affection that came behind it.

"I accept your apology, Gaby," Deirdre said sweetly, enjoying the wince that the other girl made at the use of her own nickname. "I'm sure you and I can become friends. We aren't that far apart in age, after all."

But, oh, the other differences, Gabrielle's look said, as she pointedly swept her gaze over Deirdre's dark-blue merino dress and plain shawl. "I'm sure you're right. As a step toward that friendship, please call me Gabrielle."

Deirdre smiled just as sweetly. "I shall. It's such a lovely name that it's a shame to have it shortened to something as homely as Gaby. And you may indulge me with the same privilege of being addressed by the name my mother chose for me."

Jean-Paul's chuckle broke the deadlock between the two young women. "Sean, let's you and me get out of this henhouse before the pecking and scratching gets worse. We need to see what we can do about making our stables warmer this winter. Last year, one of our best mares got pneumonia and we came close to losing 'er."

He and Deirdre's husband were on their way out of the dining room when Rufus burst in. "Mister Devereux, I rode hell for leather all the way back from Nashville to tell y'all. They done had the wuss flood on the Cumberland anybody's ever heard tell of."

"Slow down, Rufus. What about the steamboats? Any of 'em caught in the flood?"

Rufus's breathing slowed down, and he drank the tall glass of ice tea Prudy brought, not stopping till it was all gone. "Nobody knows how many, but a slew of 'em was crippled. Some of the folks got killed. I couldn't find out nothing about Mister Andre. They didn't know which boat he was on anyways."

Aurelia turned even paler and looked as though she might faint. "Help her upstairs, Deirdre," Jean-Paul said, his eyes showing a sadness that Deirdre knew wasn't all associated with learning his brother might be a casualty of the Cumberland flood. "Don't worry, my darling. You, too, Gabrielle. You know Andre. He'll survive and he'll be in touch with us to let us know he's all right as soon as he can. I promise."

Deirdre put Aurelia to bed, promising her that she would wake her if there were any news through the night. She mixed some of the peach brandy with milk, and the older woman finally went to sleep.

For Deirdre, the night was a lot longer. When she got to her cottage and found Sean in bed, she thought he was asleep, but he wasn't. He was in a state of excitement over all that had happened that evening and reached for Deirdre almost before she was in her nightclothes. "Did you hear what he said about us being family and all? DeeDee, we've got ourselves a home here, and that's for sure. You sure looked pretty tonight, sweetheart, just as pretty as Gabrielle and her with all those fancy clothes."

Deirdre was thinking about Andre too hard to notice that her husband was paying her compliments such as he hadn't in a long time. "We're not really family though, Sean. We need something of our own, even if it's not close to being this fine. Sean, I guess now that we're talking about family, it's time to tell you the good news."

Sean was kissing her and unbuttoning the high-necked gown that Deirdre had just finished painstakingly buttoning up. "The good news is that Mister Devereux likes us both, and we can stay here as long as we want."

"I'm going to have a child, Sean." Deirdre felt him freeze and then grab her so tight she could hardly breathe. "Is it the truth you're telling me?" He gave a little yell and hugged and kissed her till she was breathless and laughing.

"I take it you're happy about becoming a father," she teased him.

"Happy? I can't think of anything in the world that could make me any happier. Except maybe that new walker we got bred to Barksdale's Night Wind giving us a winning foal next spring."

"We'll have our own winning foal coming next spring," Deirdre chided, not a little piqued at having her coming baby upstaged by a horse.

"That we will," Sean said, grinning from ear to ear. He looked at Deirdre's full breasts spilling from the nightgown he had opened and enthusiastically put his mouth to one, sucking with great vigor. "Just to remind you that these are mine till that baby gets here to take over," he whispered hoarsely.

Deirdre tried to pull away. "Sean, be careful!" Her husband was rigorously pursuing his course of amorousness, one that always led, as Deirdre knew too well, to the same end—

groaning satisfaction for him and quiet tears afterward for her.

"I want to show my wife how proud I am to have her pregnant with my child," Sean whispered. "You're not that far along. I can still have my husband's privileges with my pretty little wife."

"Dr. Hollins said I might be having some problems." Deirdre made up the lie before she even realized she'd said it. "He said it would be best to—uh, lie apart as husband and wife for a few weeks—at least till we know everything is all right."

Sean pulled away immediately. "Oh, sweetheart, I'm so sorry. I wouldn't hurt you or our baby for anything."

Deirdre felt the weight of guilt added to her growing middle. "Sean, you're such a good husband. You'll be a wonderful father, too, I know."

She kissed him and blew out the lamp beside their bed. Long after her husband was asleep, Deirdre thought about the man who had fathered the child she was carrying. What if he were dead? Well, she had never intended to tell him the truth, anyway.

What if he were *not* dead, came the companion thought to the grimmer one. Dread and excitement were so mixed at the thought of seeing Andre Devereux walk into Moncoeur that Deirdre lay half the night trying to calm herself into sleep.

* * *

The news of Deirdre's pregnancy was received with great joy by all the residents at Moncoeur except Gabrielle, who said she certainly wasn't planning to ruin *her* figure having babies until she'd had all the fun out of life she could have.

Aurelia's joy was mixed with sadness, partly arising from her anxiety about Andre's safety, but also coming from her long disappointment about not having children of her own. "Oh, Deirdre, I am so happy for you! You must stay here forever and let us have a part in rearing your little one. I have always dreamed of holding a sweet baby in my arms. Now I shall be able at least to share in your happy motherhood, though mine is not destined to be."

Deirdre wondered what Aurelia would say if she knew that the coming baby belonged to Andre and not to Sean. She prayed that the woman would never learn the truth and vowed again to keep her secret forever safe. "I would be honored if you and Jean-Paul would be its godparents."

Aurelia was overjoyed and wept a little. Then she and Deirdre spent the morning thinking up names for the coming child, finally deciding on Thomas Sean if it was a boy and Margaret Erin if it should be a girl.

Prudy pampered Deirdre to high heaven, making her drink glass after glass of the rich milk that came from the fat cows that were milked each morning at Moncoeur. She also made sure the girl did not do any more of the heavy kitchen work.

The pall over the house about Andre's uncertain circumstances was thus lightened, then lifted for good when Gabrielle's shout was heard from the veranda. "Uncle Andre's home! Everybody, here's Uncle Andre!"

Deirdre was in the kitchen helping Prudy arrange platters of ham and vegetables when she heard the commotion. Her heart beat so fast she was sure she would faint. "Prudy, I'm going to slip out so the family can have their reunion together. Please make my excuses."

"You all right?" The Negro woman felt Deirdre's flushed forehead. "Don't you be getting overheated now. That's not good for that baby of yores."

"I'll go back to the cottage and lie down," Deirdre said, hearing Jean-Paul greeting his brother and nearly fainting again to hear Andre's voice in answer. "Please don't make a fuss. I'll be all right."

"Well, we'll be having a big homecoming tonight, so you git to feelin' better." Prudy's wise old eyes were watching Deirdre closely and seeing more than the girl wanted her to see. "You sure you gone be all right? I could call yore husband in, get him to take you to Doc Hollins."

"I just got hot from the cooking stove." Deirdre thought momentarily about getting Sean and packing their things and leaving before Andre even knew she was there. "Don't worry about me. I'm just sorry about leaving you with the rest of the work."

"Ain't much else to do."

Gabrielle stuck her head in the kitchen door just then, her face even more flushed than Deirdre's. "Uncle Andre wants some of your cold biscuits to go with his whiskey, Prudy. And he says you better have some hugs ready when he comes in here to check on what's for supper." To Deirdre, "Aren't you coming out to welcome my Uncle Andre home?"

"I'm not feeling too well. I may have to throw up," Deirdre said truthfully.

"Well, yuk. I don't think Uncle Andre would enjoy that much. He's very fastidious." Gabrielle took the tray of tiny biscuits that Prudy kept in a big jar for nibbling at teatime and between meals. "Isn't it a miracle?" she asked happily. "Uncle Andre said the steamboat he was on missed the worst part of the flood by twenty minutes, and he was already safely on his way back here when the disaster struck. He brought me some lovely things from New Orleans, he said. And a huge bag of sweet potatoes from Georgia for you, Prudy."

Deirdre slipped out while the other two were talking excitedly about Andre and all he had brought them.

All he had brought Deirdre was a quandary about what she was going to do and say when Andre found out she was now a fixture at Moncoeur.

worry about me. I'm just sorry about leaving you with the rest of the work.

[illegible]

[illegible] any of them that I was to bring them back

Chapter Ten

Deirdre knew it was only a matter of time before she must reappear in the big house, but she stretched out her plea of illness until that time came.

Sean was the one who forced her to resume her place in the household. "Deirdre, you'll feel better if you get up and about. Miz Aurelia keeps asking about you, and she says if she doesn't see you at the celebration for Mister Andre tonight, she's personally coming over to root you out."

"Sean, I don't have anything to wear to something that fancy."

"She said you'd make that excuse, so she's sending Letitia over with some dresses for you to try on. She told me to tell you if you didn't like any of them, that I was to bring them back and swap them till you found something you did like." Sean opened the bag he was carrying and proudly showed his wife the shiny suit that Jean-Paul had given him. "See? You're not the only one who's going to be dressed to beat the band."

Deirdre made her husband leave when Letitia came with the dresses. "I'll get Letitia to help me pick one. Men have no sense when it comes to what looks good on women."

The black girl shook her head when Deirdre modeled the first gown. "Not yo' color, Miz DeeDee. And too high-cut. Miz 'Relia, she never had the big bosoms you got, even at her fattest."

Deirdre laughed as she pulled the second gown over her head. "Aurelia may be too thin right now, but she's still beautiful. Oh, look at this, Letitia! I love it."

Deirdre whirled about, feeling transformed into a fairy princess. This dress was the perfect fit and color. Of shimmery bronze, it almost matched her hair. Deirdre pirouetted in front of the chifferobe mirror, not believing how lovely she looked. The empire style of the dress disguised her thick waist and showed off to advantage her full breasts and smooth shoulders. Suddenly her face fell in disappointment. "Oh, dear, I can't wear this one, Letitia." She had turned to admire the back and caught sight of the dimple in her shoulder. She could not have Andre greeting her and seeing that first thing!

Letitia had dressed enough ladies in her time to know how to handle this one. "Miz DeeDee, if you don't wear that dress tonight, I gone sic Miz 'Relia on to you. And you know she ain't gone take no backtalk off you." The Negro gathered up the extra gowns and left. At the door, she turned and grinned wickedly. "I ain't seen no dimple in *that* place before! Bet it drives Mister Sean crazy."

Deirdre thought ruefully as she had her bath and spilled soapy water over her shoulders, *Sean has never even noticed her funny little dimple.* And he had certainly never licked champagne out of it. That dangerous line of thinking made her finish her bath quickly. It would probably take her an hour to fix her hair.

That exasperating mass had grown down to her shoulder blades. Experimenting, Deirdre pulled the red curls up on top of her head and turned from side to side. Finally she arrived at a style that she liked and that complemented the neckline of the dress. Now she needed some kind of ornament.

"I could get some of those copper-colored mums that Prudy planted by the kitchen stoop," she murmured, "and pin them in my hair, maybe add a few of those ribbons Aurelia gave me to tie my hair up off my neck . . ."

When Sean came home to dress, he was agog. "Oh, Deirdre, my beautiful sweetheart, I've never seen you look so lovely. You have a glow to you that I've never seen the likes of." He embraced her, careful not to muss the cascades of hair, flowers and ribbons. "It's proud I am of you. Mister Andre keeps asking when I'll be showing my wife off to him—says he knew a Deirdre in Nashville once, and he's never met her like. . . ."

Deirdre's heart froze. "People have been talking about me to Andre?"

"Oh, yes. Singing your praises, in fact. Well, mostly." Deirdre knew Gabrielle hadn't been singing her praises to her uncle. "Looking at you, I'll bet he'll forget about that other Deirdre!"

I hope so, Deirdre thought passionately. She helped Sean scrub up in the galvanized tub in the back room of their little cottage and complimented him on the way he looked when he dressed in the suit Jean-Paul had given him, then made herself ready for the night that she both dreaded and desired.

"My goodness, Deirdre, don't you look beautiful!" Aurelia, resplendent in one of her New Orleans gowns that she'd had taken in to fit her slender form, hugged the younger girl as she entered the festive dining hall. "Isn't it wonderful that Andre has come home to us after all our worries about him? He's eager to meet you, by the way. Keeps asking us where this incredible woman he's heard so much about is keeping herself. I didn't tell him about your expecting a baby, but I'm sure all he has to do is look at that glow about you to figure that out for himself."

The spread of food was sumptuous. Prudy had made her honey-baked hams and glazed turkeys, in addition to huge platters of vegetables and spiced fruits. The table groaned with every kind of dish dear to Southern palates.

Aurelia introduced Deirdre to some of the neighbors who'd come to socialize and share news about what was happening in the country. Deirdre was particularly interested to hear about the "Pike's Peak or Bust" phenonemon which had a hundred thousand prospectors following the gold strike in the Colorado Rockies. "That's something my papa would go after," she told Aurelia after she'd heard some exciting discourse about the gold strike in the Kansas territory. "I'll bet that's where he is right now."

All the time that Deirdre was mingling with the guests at Moncouer she kept thinking that at any moment she would come face to face with Andre. In agony, she finally asked Aurelia where Andre was.

"Oh, Andre's down with the horses, I'm sure. He hates being indoors unless he's at the tables. I don't see your husband or Jean-Paul, so I'm sure they're all down there talking horses—boring, boring, boring. You will sing tonight, *chérie?* Jean-Paul said you had practiced the new song we spoke of. Oh, what a treat that will be!"

Deirdre saw Gabrielle over by the piano and smiled and waved. Gabrielle stared in open-mouthed astonishment at the bronze-red vision and turned back to her escort, blocking that young man's view of the most spectacular beauty in the room. "Aurelia, I really think we should let this night be Andre's and put the attention on him. I'm not really part of the family, and I'm afraid Gabrielle is going to start resenting you and Jean-Paul treating me as though I were."

"Oh, pooh. I shall treat you any way I please, and Jean-Paul feels the same way. Ah! There's my darling brother-in-law coming in now! Don't you dare run off. I've been dying for him to meet you. *Chérie!* Andre! Over here, my sweet!"

Deirdre kept her head turned away until she heard the familiar voice almost in her left ear.

"Aurelia, Jean-Paul has outdone himself with the new stock. I swear, that new mare makes all the other horses in the next five counties look like goats with three legs. Sean put her through her gaits and I swear . . ." Andre's voice trailed off as he moved into the little circle and Deirdre's face, up until now kept in profile, was visible in full.

In a daze, she met his eyes, saw the astonishment on his face, and kept inside the full impact of seeing him again.

He recovered with remarkable aplomb, kept his composure as Aurelia introduced him to Deirdre, even made some light remark that his sister-in-law could laugh about. But his eyes told Deirdre what her heart was already saying—that this was a moment no one else in the room could share.

She tried to get away, knowing that if she did not escape, he would somehow capture her privately. She was not able to handle Andre alone, not yet. Perhaps not ever. "Aurelia, I know you and your brother-in-law have so much to catch up on that an outsider like me could not share in. I'll check to see if Prudy needs help with the dessert."

Andre's hand on her arm was like steel, as was his voice when he said very softly, "My sister-in-law will agree, I'm sure, that her kitchen is being well looked after. By my last count, there were eight people in there jumping when Prudy said 'jump.' " Andre took a slow, deliberate sip of his whiskey, his eyes never leaving Deirdre's face. "I met a woman by the name of Deirdre once, in Nashville. When I went back to see her again, she was gone without a trace."

"Oh, Andre, you know women in every port city!" Aurelia said, laughing and tapping him with her fan. "Our DeeDee's not the type of woman you're talking about. She's a married lady, expecting her first child in the spring. Oops! I let it out, Deirdre, darling. How indelicate of me."

Deirdre could not bring herself to look at Andre, whose sharp intake of breath told her that this was unexpected news. "Oh?" He watched her face carefully for any sign of what she was determined not to reveal. "Your husband told me you were married just before you came here. You certainly didn't waste any time starting your family, did you?"

Aurelia made a sound of feminine shock and slapped him with her fan. "Andre! Talk about indelicate! Where are your manners? Deirdre, *chérie,* you must forgive my dear brother. He stays out on that river and wanders much too far from his civilized upbringing. If you could see how he lives on those steamboats he loves so dearly. . . ." Aurelia rolled her eyes.

"Oh, yes, Deirdre would enjoy seeing my humble stateroom sometime, I'm sure."

Deirdre blushed, remembering the bath, and she knew that was what Andre was thinking of, too. "I don't foresee that ever happening," she said finally. "Aurelia, I really am sorry, but I'm still not feeling too well. If you and Mister Devereux will excuse me . . ."

"They're motioning for you to come lead the singing, darling," Aurelia said. "You can't leave now. Everyone is dying to sing that new song."

"No, you can't leave now," Andre joined in, his hand still strong on Deirdre's arm, guiding her toward the piano and the group of people gathered around it at the far end of the dining hall. When Aurelia moved ahead, he whispered, "I swear, if you keep on trying to avoid me, I'll tell them everything. We have to talk. Meet me up on the mountain tonight after everyone's in bed."

"I can't . . . !"

Andre said between his teeth, "Deirdre, I swear it. If you're not there, I'll call a breakfast meeting with your husband included, and tell them everything I know. Everything."

Deirdre felt the imprint of his hand long after he'd let her go and she was beside Aurelia at the piano. The mark burned like the devil's handprint.

"Brava! Brava!"

The resounding echoes of "Dixie's Land" at last died down, and Deirdre found herself the center of enthusiasm about the new song that roused everyone in the room to energetic patriotism. She was not released from her role of entertainer until she had sung several Irish ballads—not including the rowdy ones learned from Riley O'Shea. Finally, though, Aurelia took her place as singer, and Deirdre was released to make her way back into the sidelines.

Andre, though, had not released her. Deirdre, listening to Aurelia's lilting French songs, felt his eyes on her even when she did not turn her head toward him where he stood next to Gabrielle. Sean was no help at all. Having drunk more than was his custom, he had slipped away to the cottage after a sloppy kiss on his wife's cheek.

Andre did not miss that, either. Deirdre felt herself blushing at the look Andre gave her when Sean made his excuses to his wife and slipped away. That look clearly reminded her that now there was nothing keeping her from appearing for the rendezvous he demanded.

Deirdre's misery was half dread and half longing, but she knew that Andre would not hesitate to disgrace her if she did not keep keep their rendezvous.

Deirdre had no allies to save her from keeping her dreaded, yet longed-for tryst on the mountain that night. Sean was dead asleep, snoring and sprawled over their bed when she crept in to change from her finery. As she pulled on her plainest merino frock and took the frippery from her hair, she looked at her sleeping husband and said a little prayer.

The night itself was no ally, either, being unusually clear and fresh with a moon brightly overseeing the business of the new fall season moving in. Deirdre heard the owls, once her friends, asking the question "Whooo" as she made her way. How well she knew the answer to that question!

"Andre."

He was waiting for her under the white oak tree. "I wasn't sure if you would come."

"You gave me no choice." Deirdre pulled her dark shawl closer about her and faced him defiantly. "You had no right to force this meeting. I owe you nothing."

"I had every right." He stepped up to her and took hold of her upper arms, forcing her to look up at him and making the shawl fall from her shoulders. "You bamboozled me, in more ways than one, made me miserable after I left you and couldn't find you again, and now you show up in the bosom of my family, bound to another man, about to have his baby. Hell's bells, what do you expect me to do? Let my naive brother go on thinking he's got some kind of saint living in our family's house? And what about that husband of yours? He seems like a nice enough fellow. Does he know you were one of Madame Julia's prime pieces for whoever had the cash?"

"I met Sean . . . afterwards. Please leave him out of this. I don't want him hurt."

Andre shook her so that her head rolled. "And what about me? What about my hurt? Do you think I left you after that night in heaven with no intention of coming back to rescue you from hell? Even though you told me you liked your job and had every intention of keeping on with it, I wouldn't have let you stay there another minute if Julia hadn't had me thrown out."

"I didn't see you hanging around after that," Deirdre said in a strained voice. All of this was very hard to hear after her agonizing doubts about Andre following that one night. "Even Lillianne talked about how you never came around anymore."

"I was trapped up-river on a damned crippled steamboat and couldn't get back to Nashville, dammit! When I finally got back to Julia's, the girls wouldn't tell me anything about what had happened to you, where you'd gone, anything. Julia wasn't there, but she'd apparently threatened the lot of them about divulging your whereabouts. I finally choked it out of Pegean that Lilianne had gone to work for Justine's. I thought you might be there, too, so I went to see her."

Andre felt a jolt of remembered pain at what he'd heard from Lillianne. She pretended to be sympathetic with Deirdre's "plight," as she described it. Andre had felt she was hiding something from him about Deirdre but decided, agonizingly, that it had to do with what she told him about the other girl's fate.

"Madame Julia just couldn't control her," Lilianne had told him when Andre faced her in the scarlet and royal-blue parlor at the house on third. "Deirdre acted like a little tramp everytime one of our clients asked for someone else besides her. She started acting like the Queen of the May and didn't even want to give Madame Julia her cut of the money. The other girls told Madame, finally, that if Deirdre didn't go, they would." Lilianne had shrugged her bare shoulders, swinging into the lies without blushing. "So, of course, Madame had no choice. You know how it is in a place like that when one girl starts thinking she's the top draw. The cats' claws come out, and the clients start looking for a more peaceful place to seek their pleasure. Madame Julia helped her find a place up east. I have no idea where, but I'm sure it wasn't as nice."

Andre had not been suspicious of Lillianne at the time, but he was curious. "Why did you leave Julia's? She always said you were one of her best girls."

Lilianne had thought of the undelivered letter tucked deep under her corsets and drawers and shivered delicately. If Madame Julia ever discovered that she had not delivered that letter to Andre Devereux, she would be better off far away from that lady's formidable wrath. "Humph! I'm not planning to stay in this business forever, certainly not working for someone else. Justine gives me a better cut. I'll save my money and start my own place some day." She had fluttered her eyelashes at Andre then, saying seductively, "But in the meantime, you might as well sample the wares at my new venue. I can assure you, some things only change for the better. . . ."

Andre jerked himself back to the present, glad that he could face Deirdre right now with the memory of not having succumbed to Lilianne's charms. "I suppose you couldn't take the life up there. At any rate, this was the last place I expected to find you. All those miserable hours I spent worrying about you, and where do I find you? At Moncoeur, my own home—married, pregnant and totally involved with my family."

Deirdre clamped her lips on the defense that would have sprung to her lips had she not been convinced that Andre would never believe her now, not after all the lies between them—not to mention Lillianne's. "Then why did you force me to see you like this?"

Andre took a deep breath. "Because I haven't been able to get you out of my mind for a damn minute, and seeing you tonight I knew I never would again." Andre took another shuddering breath.

"I go back to find you, to try to talk you out of that damned crazy business—I was even going to pay Julia whatever she asked, like a dowry or something—and you're gone. Dammit, gone! And so was Julia, and everybody was closemouthed about you. Finally, Lilianne told me, among other things, that you'd gone to another house somewhere farther north." Deirdre stiffened at the lie and started to correct Andre on that, but clamped her lips together at the hopeless thought that she wouldn't be believed. Not after all the lies she'd told Andre.

Andre took another shuddering breath. "When I saw that damned dimple, I swear to you, I almost took you in my arms on the spot."

"I'm married," Deirdre said, knowing as she mouthed the words that they had nothing to do with what she was feeling. "I'm going to have a baby."

He shook her arms and cursed again. "That's the only thing that's saving you this moment from my taking you and making love to you like I've dreamed of ever since I was with you. I don't know how all this happened, Deirdre, but I'll damn sure tell you this—we aren't through with each other yet. Not by a long shot. Husband, baby, whatever—you and I have got something that has to be settled one way or the other."

"Andre, you're forcing me to take desperate measures. I'll . . . I'll talk to Sean, we'll go somewhere else, find another place." Even as she said it, Deirdre knew Sean would never leave, not unless he knew the whole truth about Andre.

"Jean-Paul needs Sean, and from what I hear, Aurelia cannot live without her sweet *chérie.* Don't run away again, Deirdre. That's your way of dealing with things, I know, but I won't allow you to hurt my family just because you can't accept what's between you and me."

"There can never be anything else between you and me. Never." Deirdre pulled her shawl tight about her and denied passionately what was in her heart. "That night happened, but it has nothing to do with us now. Nothing!"

His hands gentled on her arms, and Deirdre felt the betraying goosebumps from the touch she remembered so well. "Can you look me straight in the eye and tell me I mean nothing to you, Deirdre? Can you?"

She tried, but she could not. Her stumbling words of denial indicted her, and she turned to pleading. "Please, Andre, do not torment me any more. Please have mercy on me. . . ."

He saw her face turned up toward his in the moonlight and could no more have resisted taking her in his arms than he could have walked away from a winning poker hand. "Deirdre," he whispered, pulling her close and putting his lips on the fragrant hair. "Deirdre, my love. If you only knew what my torment has been, thinking about you in that place, thinking about other men knowing your beautiful body—and now seeing you married and carrying another man's child. . . ."

His lips founds hers, and Deirdre could not tell whether the passionate groan came from him or from herself. She felt his hands in her hair, tangling it and forcing her mouth to give in to his thirst for her. "Andre," she whispered, "we must not . . ."

He looked into her eyes and took a deep breath. "One more kiss, I swear that's all, though I want you so much I almost can't restrain myself." He put his mouth on hers softly, tantalizingly, moving his tongue lightly to evoke sweet shivers in her insides. "Say you want me, Deirdre, say you want me as much as I want you. Say you remember what it was like that night."

She resisted, and he made stronger demands till finally she gave a little cry of surrender and whispered the words. She felt the strength of him and knew that if he wanted to pursue their passionate embrace to its limits, she could not resist. "Yes. Yes."

"Then, as much as I ache to hold you in my arms for the rest of the night, that's enough for me right now." Andre let her lie back in his arms. "Now that you're being honest, tell me—was there another man while you were at Madame Julia's who made you feel like I made you feel that night we were together?"

She shook her head, wanting to cry about his misconception of her and knowing she could never convince him that she had not been one of Madame Julia's girls. "Not until Sean."

Andre's arms dropped like stones. "You have to remind me, don't you, that another man possesses you now." A new note entered his voice when he asked, "So Sean met you through Julia's business?"

"No! He never even knew what business she was in. Sean and I met in a very nice way. We . . . we fell in love right away." The lie was like straw on Deirdre's tongue.

"What would he do if knew the truth about you?" Andre's voice still held that hard note of a stranger.

Deirdre felt anger cutting through her daze. "My husband is a good man. I'm sure he would believe me when I told him the truth—that I never really worked for Madame Julia, that all of that was accidental."

Andre's smile was as cold as his new tone. "Perhaps I ought to engage Sean in a game of poker. He sounds like the kind of sucker who falls for every bluff in sight."

Deirdre wanted to slap him. "My husband has more important things to do than waste his time at cards."

They glared at each other, both conscious of the still unextinguished fire between them and feeling helpless to do anything about it but argue. "Well, I hold the aces where you're concerned, Deirdre, and I'll tell you this. I've seen how you've burrowed into the heart of my family and that's just fine—unless you hurt them. So help me, if Jean-Paul starts thinking a little bit too highly of you and Aurelia gets hurt, you'll have me to answer to."

Deirdre's anger flared up. "That's a horrible thing to say! They've been nothing but good to me, and I love them like I loved my own family!"

"Fine, then. I'll tell Gabrielle that her concerns are unwarranted. She was afraid you might be trying to take advantage of my brother and his wife, but I reminded her that Moncoeur is not all that solvent right now, and even if it were . . ."

Deirdre's hand would not be held back this time. The stinging slap startled the nightlife on the mountain, bringing a halt to the chorus of crickets. "How dare you suggest that I'm after Devereux money! How dare you!"

Andre put his hand to his cheek. "I see you still have that fire in you that made you such a hellion. Lilianne said that was what made you such an attraction to the customers."

"That's a lie!" Deirdre's fury was more directed at Andre for believing Lilianne than at the girl herself. "Please leave. I have nothing more to say to you."

"So now you're ordering me off my own property." Andre made a mocking bow. "The lady is getting to be quite mistress-like. I notice you've even developed Southern speech habits. And that was one of my sister-in-law's gowns you were wearing tonight, wasn't it?"

"Aurelia is very kind and gracious. If you're insinuating that I'm trying to take her place, you're totally wrong. I could never take her place, not with her husband, not with the servants, not as mistress of the plantation—even if I wanted to, which I don't."

Andre bowed again. "As you say. Just remember, this time I hold all the cards, and if you pull one out of your sleeve, I'll play the Ace to your Queen of Spades."

"I'll remember that," Deirdre said coldly. "Now please go. It wouldn't do for you and me to be seen coming down together."

"You can find your way down in the dark?"

Deirdre smiled grimly, "That's how I earned my living, remember? Besides, I come up here all the time. I know every inch of my . . . this mountain."

She waited till he was gone before going over to the clear, cold stream that came down from a spring high on the ridge. As she splashed the water on her flushed cheeks, the stinging cold liquid washed away the disturbing traces of Andre's kisses.

She cupped her hands and drank huge gulps of the delicious spring-fed water. This could be the place for the still, she thought suddenly. She stood up, Andre momentarily forgotten, at the exciting realization that the incomparable purity of the mountain spring water would lend itself to corn whiskey. "Jean-Paul will be so pleased!"

But her excitement disappeared at the reminder that Andre would only interpret her enthusiasm for finding a way to keep Moncoeur from going into debt as another way of worming her way into the Devereux affections.

"Blast him! Blast him to the devil," she cried. "And damn Lilianne, too, that little sneak. I'm going to write to Madame Julia and tell her what that snake in the grass did to me!"

Before she went to bed, Deirdre peeked out a window and saw Andre silhouetted on the veranda. The red tip of his cigar glowed and waned like a firefly. "Good. He can't go to sleep, either," she told herself with satisfaction.

She crept in beside Sean and adjusted the arm he flung across her so that she could breathe. It seemed like hours till the dawn finally broke and she could get up and put on a pot of coffee.

Deirdre could not believe it when she took a breakfast tray up to Aurelia and learned that Andre had left in the middle of the night. "I'm so angry at that man!" Aurelia fumed. "Leaving without telling a soul good-bye or having the courtesy to at least ask Jean-Paul if he needed help around here for a few weeks." Aurelia sipped her coffee. "Poor Jean-Paul looks so worried these days. With all these political tensions building all over the country, I declare it's hard to meet anybody without hearing the voice of doom." Aurelia, hunched in a girlish position, hugged her knees and beamed at

Deirdre. "Enough of that. How did you like our brother Andre? Isn't he just the most devastating man you ever saw in your life? I saw how he looked when he first laid eyes on you. I vow, if Sean had been there, he would have been jealous as all get-out. I was even a little jealous myself." Aurelia dropped her eyes, not wanting Deirdre to see the seriousness behind the teasing words.

Deirdre cleared her throat carefully. She certainly hoped Aurelia hadn't overheard her brother-in-law's demands to see Deirdre privately. "He is very . . . handsome. I didn't get to talk to him very much, but he seems quite . . . devoted to all of his family." Deirdre added softly, knowing it was what the older woman wanted to hear. "Especially to you. When we did talk, he let me know that he joins Jean-Paul in wanting me to take the best care of you I possibly can."

Aurelia was thrilled to hear her friend mention Andre's obvious affection for his sister-in-law.

"And you certainly do that, *chérie!*" Aurelia hugged Deirdre tightly. "Now what are your plans for this beautiful day? Prudy says she's not going to have you doing any more kitchen duties, that she thinks it's time we all started pampering you until that 'chitlin' comes." She gave her charming trill of laughter. "You know, of course, that I would never dare defy anything Prudy says. So, how are you going to busy yourself in these months of waiting?"

Deirdre said eagerly, "I plan to start my whiskey-making enterprise. Your husband has given me all the encouragement in the world, and I know he's excited about it too."

"Ah, Dee-Dee, you are so refreshing in this land of stuck-up notions about what women can and cannot do. Imagine either of the Misses Jarmon who were here last night coming up with an idea like yours."

They laughed together over that. Deirdre said a little wistfully, "I expect by the time it gets out in the county that I'm making whiskey—and selling it, as I plan to do—my reputation won't be worth a flip. But, then, I'm not a Southern aristocrat, born and bred, like you and Gabrielle."

"And the Misses Jarmon," Aurelia added wickedly, putting her little finger up to her nose in a pantomime of the half-glasses the sisters used to peer at everything and everybody.

"And the Misses Jarmon," Deirdre added with a puckered-up look of disapproval that made Aurelia trill with laughter again. "Now I must try to catch Jean-Paul before he gets off on his ride. I need to find out where we can get the barley we need—and the hard sugar-maple wood. It seems, too, that we might have access to rye, which will add a wonderful flavor to the corn and barley."

"Oh, you are so smart, you amaze me. I wish I were a whiskey drinker, but I'll stick to my coffee and sweet tea."

* * *

Jean-Paul was thrilled with Deirdre's plans to put the still house on the mountain. He congratulated her for realizing that the spring-fed stream would be perfect for the operation. "Rufus is yours, along with any of the other field hands to do what you need done. There's a vat and barrel-maker in Holly Gap who can construct the containers you'll need. He's also good with working up any kind of apparatus you might need for the distillation. Just charge anything you need to me. He still owes Moncoeur for a foal we sold him."

Deirdre thanked him, but he turned that aside. "It's I who thank you for your loyalty. That's the finest quality a person can have, I've decided. I hear all the talk these days about how we have to stay loyal to our country, and I'm all for that. But between you and me, the time's coming when I think some of us are going to have take a long look at loyalty to an America that's coming down hard on the South." He shook his head sadly. "I see things coming that I don't like the looks of. But Aurelia's always telling me that I'm too gloomy these days, always looking at the negative side of things. Did you enjoy the party last night?"

"I did indeed, thank you. I'm sorry your brother had to leave unexpectedly." Deirdre felt she had to bring up Andre's name; his brother would think it strange if she didn't.

Jean-Paul looked perplexed for an instant, then laughed. "Oh, that brother of mine has a restless foot, always has. He's not a bit like me, as my wife will be quick to tell you. Andre loves the cards and chasing after beautiful women. But I happen to know that if push came to shove, Andre would be right here. He's even more of a zealot about our South than I am. Speaking of which, everybody loved the singing. Do you know, a few people said we need ourselves a marching song for the South and that 'Dixie's Land' is just the trick."

"I enjoyed it, too," Deirdre said truthfully. Then she excused herself and went to find Rufus. If she were going to get this still operation underway, she needed to do it before her body got too cumbersome for her to trek up the mountain.

Sean was not totally pleased over his wife's new venture and let her know his feelings. "It's just not seemly, my wife making whiskey and everyone in the county knowing about it."

"Sean, you have your horses and hardly ever spend time with me. At least it gives me something to do now that I've been cut off from the kitchen work." Deirdre almost said something about the way Sean kowtowed to Gabrielle's every whim about riding and spent countless hours currying the young woman's favorite horse, but she held back the sharp words. She didn't want to argue with her husband. He had been sulky with her ever since she had gotten involved in the whiskey-making enterprise.

"I've heard men talking about Moncoeur turning to the liquor business and you being the Whiskey Mountain Woman, and I don't mind telling you, I don't like it. Over at Donald Bull's store in Shelbyville, when I drove over for the horse linaments and special feed, they were laughing at me, making me feel like a fool for having a wife that makes whiskey."

Deirdre had experienced a few of the same reactions, having women at the quilting bee she'd gone to with Aurelia actually cut her dead when she'd walked by. "I'm sorry, Sean. We will be able to help Jean-Paul this way, though, and he's the one I work for, not those hypocrites that you're talking about."

"Somebody said Lem Joe Bartow is really mad that you're cutting into his territory. He may be a weak little weasel physically, but he makes up for his lack of size with meanness. He's a dangerous man, Deirdre, and I'd hate to think of someone like him having an ugly notion against you. He's sneaky and doesn't do things out in the open. He's been known to run the other bootleggers out of the county, and he's even said to have killed a man or two in his time."

"He's killed plenty of them," Deirdre said hotly, "with his rotgut. Lord knows what he mixes in it! I'm not frightened of Mr. Bartow, and if you're any kind of man, you won't be either."

Deirdre was sorry she'd said that as soon as it was out of her mouth. Sean didn't need deprecating remarks from her. His insecurities about himself were becoming more and more apparent as she grew to know him better, and they needed no nurturing. She just wished he would stand up for her more, though, when men made remarks about her in his hearing. In a way, she was afraid that he shared their sentiments about her enterprises making her unfit as a wife and a mother.

Making whiskey wasn't something to be ashamed of, Deirdre reminded herself fiercely. Why, her family had been renowned in the county for their fine malt product. There had been no one in all of Wexford, maybe not in all of Ireland, who had known as much about the whiskey-making as her father's family. Her mother had been disdainful, being of a higher clan whose head had banished her when she married beneath her. But Deirdre had seen how the whiskey kept food on the table, even through the worst of the famine, even after potatoes had to be bought dearly with the products of the O'Shea still.

Their local priest had preached vehemently against the "still worm" that was used in boiling the beer in a large wooden vessel, calling it the "serpent from hell." But Riley and Deirdre had stubbornly kept on distilling the beer into whiskey, knowing it was all that kept their family from the starvation that was to take close to two million lives in their country. Her father pretended that he went into town only to trade for vital food and medicine for the ailing O'Sheas, but Deirdre had known he was on another gambling spree.

She would never forget the night her father came home after a week away in the town of Duncormick. He'd left her to mind the still and look after her mother and the small children while he tried to swell his pockets to whisk them all away to America for a new and better life.

Her mother was ill with a high fever and the two younger children not much healthier. Only Deirdre was robust and well, though she was near hysteria by the time her father showed her his empty pockets and wagon bare of provisions.

That night, the men whom Riley had recklessly accused of cheating when they'd taken his money at cards came by stealth and burned the O'Shea still to the ground. While Deirdre and her father were trying to put out the fires that were melting the serpent from hell to twisted metal, the fire crept into the thatch-dry cottage where the rest of the family were sleeping and there was no saving anyone or anything.

After the grieving period, Deirdre and her father left for New Orleans, paying for their tickets by selling the remnants of whiskey they'd buried in the barren fields and scraping together what they could to make a new life in the new world.

Deirdre threw herself into her whiskey-making with great enthusiasm once she'd worked out the basic needs with Jean-Paul and schooled Rufus as her assistant.

Boiling cornmeal, ground a little coarser than the meal Prudy used for cooking, in the huge cauldron was hot work even in the cooling fall weather, and Deirdre let Rufus take it over when it got close to boiling. After it cooled, she added the rye to give starch and flavor to the mash. After adding the barley malt, the mixture was transferred to the fermenter that Carl Tuten had designed for her. Yeast and strained stillage were then added, and the main fermenting process was underway.

Deirdre was very proud of her precious hard sugar-maple wood, which Jean-Paul had found for her at considerable trouble. The stack was carefully ricked not far from the still; Deirdre planned to dry it out and use it to flavor the whiskey in the final step of distilling. In Ireland, they had used another type of wood, but the maple, Deirdre sensed, would bring an even deeper flavor out in the distilled whiskey.

Just before she was ready to distill the fermented mash in the still Carl had also made for her, she had Rufus ready the big vat. Then she went back to the cottage, tired but happy over her accomplishments.

Life at Moncoeur went on, with Jean-Paul looking uncharacteristically happy over the success with the still. "Dee-Dee, I don't know how you managed to come up with something that workable," he told her one day when they were going over the costs of the operation. "You amaze me, and Aurelia too, being such a young woman and knowing so much about the whiskey business."

Deirdre was more than glad that she was contributing to the well-being of the plantation. She and Sean were enjoying benefits that she had never expected. They were treated like family and lived comfortably, though their personal relationship was far from perfect.

Deirdre often thought that Sean suspected more than he let on. He never talked about Andre, but she noticed that he looked up sharply whenever Andre's name was mentioned.

Deirdre and Rufus toiled at the still, smoothing out the process that would produce the corn whiskey that they hoped could be sold by spring. Night after night, they monitored the bubbling vat, kept the still going. They often talked about how Moncoeur could become the seat of a statewide, even nationwide industry, one that would put Tennessee on the map. If only they could come up with the exact recipe that would set Whiskey Mountain squeezings aside from all the rest!

Deirdre was so tired some nights that she fell into bed with her clothes on, even her boots which were usually dirty from trudging up the mountain.

Sean often spent the night in the stables. On one such night, Deirdre waked from a nightmare, thinking she saw Moncoeur burning as she had seen her family cottage burn.

It was not a nightmare, it was real. Only it was not the plantation house afire, it was the still on the mountain. Deirdre, running toward the blaze, stumbled on her way up. Rufus caught her and she grasped wildly at him, half-crying as she saw the results of long, hard labor going up in smoke. "Oh, Rufus, it's burning up! Our still is burning up! We must have left the coals too hot, must have—"

"Miz Dee-Dee, we didn't do nothin', but some'un else did. They done put a torch to it, that's what. Ain't nothin' else could happen. I checked them fires 'fore I went to bed." He started crying, holding tight to her arm and trembling just as she was. "Lookit that! The whole mountain's burnin' like the second flo' of hell!"

Deirdre remembered her family and tears flowed down her cheeks as she thought of the long-ago, nightmarish night in Ireland. Only this time her father was not to blame. She gathered her strength and let it pour from her into Rufus's tightly clutching grip. "Maybe we're in time, Rufus, maybe we're in time."

Together, they ran to the site of the arson. With the help of everyone roused by the ruckus, they managed to save the still and the other equipment, but the stack of precious hard sugar-maple wood was burned to the ground.

"Oh, Rufus, look! It's burned to coals!" Deirdre just sat down and cried. She and Rufus guarded the place till dawn, when the last flame went out. Sean could not convince her to leave to go back to the cottage and finally returned alone.

"It was that no-good, sorry Lem Joe," Rufus told her, wiping the soot from his face and handing the cloth to her to wipe hers off. "Prudy said she saw him ride by fast after this place started going up in smoke."

"Well, he didn't destroy the main of it," Deirdre said fiercely, going over to kick the coals of smoking wood. "Rufus, look!"

The Negro came over to see. "They's all crumbley, Miz McAfee."

"Yes, but what if we ground it even finer—I'm sure Carl's got a fertilizer bone-grinder—then packed it so the whiskey could seep through it. Think of the flavor." She picked up a handful of the charred residue and sniffed it. "Just smell it. Rufus, it'll work, I know it will."

"The barrels are all charred from the fire." Rufus's face lightened. "Wait a minute. That's what my grandpappy did when he made his whiskey—burned the insides of the kegs. Took the corn taste out, he 'lowed. Miz McAfee, I believes you's on to somethin'."

"I know I am," Deirdre said gleefully, dancing with the black man in a fit of delirium.

She knew if Sean saw her doing an Irish jig with an old black slave, he would be horrified, but Deirdre didn't care. All she could think about right then was that she had not been beaten. Moncoeur would one day be known as the biggest, best whiskey distillery in the South, and she would be the one who made it happen.

And what would the high and mighty Mr. Andre Devereux have to say about that?

Chapter Eleven

Margaret Erin McAfee was born on March 4, 1860.

The celebration of the birth of Deirdre's first child provided an excellent opportunity for the members of the Devereux family to think of something other than the grumblings of Southern secession. For at least this time, Moncoeur was a haven from worries about where the South was headed. Deirdre's first keg of leached Tennessee whiskey was brought out for the celebration when Prudy made her joyful announcement of the birth. "It's a beautiful little girl," she reported, her face still shining with perspiration from assisting at the difficult birth. Deirdre had perpetuated the myth of her baby's premature arrival, and everyone believed it since the infant weighed only five pounds.

"She ain't bigger'n a gnat's eye, but just about as perfect a little chile as you ever laid eyes on."

Sean's whoop of joy was matched by Jean-Paul's, and Aurelia wept for happiness. Even Gabrielle acted excited, especially when Aurelia reminded her that Deirdre planned to name the two of them as godmothers.

Jean-Paul held up his glass of whiskey, admiring the color, before he took his first sip. "I don't know what to drink to first—that fine new baby girl, this liquor that Rufus says is going to change the whole state's drinking habits, or the idea of the South seceding from the Union if Lincoln's elected."

Sean held up his own drink. "I say we drink to all three." His eyes widened after he'd downed the whiskey. "Great Irish ghosts! I believe we need to drink to each one separately, and then to anything else anybody can think of."

Jean-Paul, after his first sip, nodded. "I agree with you, Sean. Deirdre has given you a fine little daughter tonight, but she's also given something fine to the country. I'd be hard put to remember wrapping my tongue around any whiskey this good." He poured himself another. "You know, I had my doubts about that charring business, but I mean to tell you, it worked really well. Aurelia, you must taste this."

"You men can get drunk on Deirdre's whiskey if you want to, but I'm going over to see her and that newborn baby. Sean, I think your wife would probably appreciate a visit from the baby's father, too."

Had Deirdre been there, she would have smiled ruefully at the irony of Aurelia's words.

Sean looked abashed and put down his glass. "I just didn't want to get in the way. To tell the truth, babies scare the hell out of me."

Aurelia took his arm. "Well, you'll just have to get over that now that you've got one of your own."

Sean woke Prudy up in her cabin, where she'd gone to rest before taking over the care of the infant the next day. "It's DeeDee, Prudy—she's burning up and babbling like she's out of her head! Come quick, I think she's dying."

Deirdre's fever raged through the night in spite of the cold sponge baths and rubdowns that Prudy administered. Jean-Paul had one of the field hands go for the doctor, but everyone was worried that he wouldn't make it back in time to save the new mother. "Who's this Julia she keeps asking for?" Jean-Paul asked Sean.

"That was the woman in Nashville who took Deirdre in when she first got to town. She's the one that got us together."

Jean-Paul put a sympathetic hand on Sean's shoulder. "Man, you are no good to Deirdre right now, and I think maybe this Julia could be just the tonic to get her through this. Why don't you take the rig and go to Nashville? Perhaps you can bring this lady back with you."

Sean was off like a shot, obviously eager to be out of the sickroom. Aurelia scolded her husband. "Why did you do that, Jean-Paul?

Sean should be here with his wife."

"The boy was falling apart and needed something to do. Besides, this Julia woman is the only family Deirdre's got except us, and I truly do think a visit from her will help the girl get well faster." Jean-Paul patted his wife's hand comfortingly. "You're not up to looking after Deirdre, darling—look at you now, pale and shaking all over. And Prudy's got the little one to care for. If Sean succeeds in bringing this Julia to Moncoeur, it'll be good for everybody."

"I'm just so worried about her, Jean-Paul," Aurelia said, starting to cry again. "Look at her, lying there so still and feverish. I just wish Andre were here. He would know what to do." Aurelia was weeping so that she did not see the look of anguish that passed over her husband's face.

"Andre followed the other gamblers to the Cherry Creek gold rush. He won't be leaving Colorado for Tennessee as long as the money and cards are flowing." Jean-Paul's voice held more resignation than bitterness.

"Are you sure about that?" a voice spoke from the door.

Aurelia turned and saw Andre standing in the doorway and gave a little cry. "Oh, I'm so glad to see you!" She ran to him and embraced him and said with chagrin, "Oh, we mustn't make a fuss. Poor Deirdre . . ." Aurelia motioned toward the bed beside which Prudy sat rubbing the girl's forehead with wet cloths.

"I know. I passed Sean on his way to Nashville. He told me the news, good and bad. How is she?"

"Still delirious with fever. Did you see Doctor Hollins on your way in?"

"Yes, he's coming right behind me." Andre's eyes stayed on the still figure on the bed and did not see the penetrating look his brother was giving him. "The little girl's fine, Sean said. Would it be all right if I looked at her?"

Aurelia led her brother-in-law over to see the baby in the ruffled bassinet that Jean-Paul had had made months before the birth. "Isn't she beautiful?"

Andre touched a perfect little hand, and his throat caught when the tiny fingers curled around his finger. "Yes, beautiful."

"Andre, I cannot believe you're home," Aurelia exclaimed. "We were sure you would stay in Colorado."

"My country's in trouble. I decided I needed to be here." To his brother, "Jean-Paul, I know Tennessee is still undecided, but there's talk of secession from some of the deep South states that makes me wonder. You keep your ear to the ground. What do you think?"

"I think this time it won't be like when South Carolina seceded all by herself in '32. I think this time we'll get out together."

"That won't be good for the country, Jean-Paul—you know it won't."

"I know that, but I know, too, that we're being pushed against the wall. You know yourself that what's called industrialism up East, using child and immigrant labor, is called slavery down here. They're industrialists, we're monsters. But slavery isn't the only issue. The South's prosperity and demands for more states' rights haven't set well with some folks in the upper half of the country."

"I know that we're in for some troubled times. Here's Doc Hollins." Andre took another look at the sleeping baby and the woman on the bed. "There's nothing you and I can do here, Jean-Paul. I could use a drink. The letter I brought to Deirdre from her father can wait till tomorrow." At his brother's look of surprise, Andre made up a quick lie. "I ran across Riley O'Shea, and when we started talking, I found out that Deirdre was his daughter. He was out prospecting at Cherry Creek and came into the saloon one night." Andre hid a smile, remembering Riley O'Shea's embarrassment when he sat down at the table where Andre was dealing. But the fellow had offered to pay him his money and came back with a hundred questions about Deirdre, finally entrusting the letter to him.

"It seems our Deirdre has more family than we thought. Let's go have that whiskey. I think you're in for a treat. Aurelia, come with us and get some rest. I'm sure Prudy will let us all know when there's a change. Deirdre will be just fine now that Doc Hollins is here. Come, darling."

Toward dawn, Deirdre's fever hit its crisis point and she tossed and moaned, throwing off the covers. At the same time, Andre paced restlessly on the veranda, smoking one cigar after the other and looking anxiously toward the cottage where the girl lay.

"Why the devil did I come back here?" he muttered. "The country's in trouble, the South's in for hellacious times, I ought to just stick to the good times and gambling and stay the hell away from Moncoeur." He saw Prudy come out on the stoop of the cottage and strode over to her, asking anxiously, "How is she?"

"She's gone make it," the black woman said wearily, tossing out the pan of water and wiping her forehead. It was brisk March weather, but Prudy was still sweating from her efforts to cure her patient of the debilitating fever. "She been sayin' some strange things, Mistuh Andre, mighty strange. Yore name come up a few times. You do something to that girl, Mistuh Andre?" Prudy fixed him with one of the looks that had brought confessions from him when he was a little boy.

"Can I see her? Is she awake?" Andre wasn't anxious to have Prudy find out any of his secrets involving Deirdre. He was pretty sure she would skin him alive.

Prudy put the dishpan down and folded her arms. "I ain't sure it's proper, you not bein' her husband and all."

"Prudy, I swear I won't do anything improper." Andre wanted more than anything to see Deirdre and make sure for himself that she was all right. "I have a letter for her from her father.

I know that'll make her feel better."

"She's a wore-out little woman, so you behave yoreself."

Andre kissed the black woman's wrinkled cheek. "I will, I promise. Why don't you get yourself some coffee over at the house. I smelled some being brewed while I was outside. And you can bring me a cup after I've had a chance to tell Deirdre about her daddy."

"All right. But don't you be upsetting that little lady. She's had a rough time of it. And keep an eye on that little baby. It wakes up, you come git me right then."

Deirdre's eyes flew open when Andre whispered her name. "Andre?" She could hardly speak, she was so weak.

"Shh. It's all right. You're going to be fine. I just wanted to check on you, to be sure you really are better."

"What are you doing here? The baby? My baby . . ." Deirdre tried to rise, but fell back weakly against the pillow.

"Your baby's just fine. Beautiful, in fact, just like you."

Deirdre's eyes, fully aware now, darted around the room. "Sean . . . where's my husband?"

"He's gone after Julia. You kept asking for her. Jean-Paul thought you might need her in the next few days, to help you get your strength back."

Deirdre gasped. "Oh, no! Sean will find out . . ." Her eyes were wide and full of fear.

"He doesn't know about her, about the business she's in. Oh, God, Andre, you've got to stop him!"

"Shh." Andre stroked her hair off her forehead. "Julia has closed down her business. He won't find anything but a respectable middle-aged lady living alone in a respectable house on Second Avenue. Now, are you up to hearing about your father?"

"My father?"

"I have a letter for you. We crossed paths in Cherry Creek." Andre laughed. "He was surprised to see me in that saloon, I can tell you that. But after I assured him that I wasn't going to skin his hide, we had a nice talk—mostly about you. He was most contrite about running off and leaving you."

Deirdre gave a little snort. "So he was back to his old ways, in the saloon and no doubt gambling."

"No, in fact he wasn't. He'd staked a little claim, mined some gold—not much, but enough to keep himself up and have enough extra to pay what he owed me." Andre put up his hand before Deirdre could protest. "I know, Julia paid off that debt for you. I refused the money from Riley. But when I told him you were married and expected a child, he insisted on sending some money to you. I'll put it over here in the chifferobe." Andre tucked the envelope into a small drawer and came back to the bed.

"Why are you being so kind to me?" Deirdre asked, a catch in her voice. "When you left here, you acted like you hated me."

"I never hated you, Deirdre, hard as I tried to. When I left here I went to find Julia. She'd been away visiting her sister in Philadelphia, right after she closed down her house on Second Avenue. I forced her to tell me where you went after you left her place. She said Lillianne lied about you going up East, that you never did that. She said you never stayed in the business at all after that one night, that you stayed with her until you married Sean, but that you never had another client, and she wouldn't let you anyway." Andre lifted her weak hand to his lips. "Oh, Deirdre, I never believed deep in my heart that you lived that kind of life! If only I'd listened to my heart about you!"

"Hearts have a way of lying, too," Deirdre said, with a crack in her voice. "Mine lies to me all the time."

"Does it lie to you about me? About how you really feel about Sean? Deirdre, I hope to God your husband knows the truth about everything—about the house, about Julia, about . . ."

Deirdre withdrew her hand so Andre wouldn't know her reaction to his referring to the truth. "Sean never knew what business Julia was in. I feel badly about deceiving him about that, but what purpose would it serve to have him know that I once worked in a brothel?"

The gasp from the door made Deirdre and Andre turn simultaneously to the source of the sound of anguish. "Sean!" Deirdre cried. The look on his face devastated her. His eyes were wide with horror and repulsion, and his mouth worked to get out the words that Deirdre knew would haunt their marriage for the rest of their lives.

"I can't believe it—you pretending to be an innocent Irish girl, bent on finding a good man and a good life. Now I find out that you deceived me from the start. And you!" Sean spat out the words to the woman who had followed him into the room and immediately placed herself protectively between him and Deirdre. "You! 'Mrs. Poston, a respectable lady.' I can't believe you did this to me, the two of you. I only wanted a good wife, a person who would stand by me and work at my side to make a good life, a woman who would bear my children and help rear them while we worked to better ourselves."

"Sean . . ." Deirdre's plea was muffled by Julia's strong arms. "Sean, please understand. I tended the garden, I looked after the others' clothes, helped in the kitchen. I swear it—ask Julia—I was not one of her girls except for . . . except for . . ." Deirdre's eyes sought Andre's face for help. "It was that one time only," she whispered. "Just that one night."

"Why should I believe that? Why should I believe anything you say, you or Madame Julia? I don't even know now if that child lying over there is really mine. You let me think so, but how can I take the word of a—of a *slut* that I'm the father?"

Andre moved toward him and said in a dangerously soft voice, "Watch it, McAfee. Deirdre has told you she was not a prostitute, and I think you need to either take her word for it or get the hell out of her life and off Moncoeur property."

Sean glared at the other man. "What the devil do you have to do with any of this? I work for Jean-Paul. He's the man who hired me, not you."

"Just watch what you say to your wife. She's come through a difficult time tonight, and I don't think it's the right moment to confront her with something that seems to me to be more your problem than hers."

Sean looked at Julia and Deirdre, wrapped up in each other's arms on the bed. "Look at you. I'm sure you laughed behind my back at the smitten Irish rube who was willing to marry a girl he thought was sweet and innocent and pure." He went over to the bassinet and looked down at the sleeping infant. "I don't know whose daughter she is, but I'm damned if I'm going to play father to a bastard coming out of a brothel."

Deirdre hid her face in Julia's bosom.

Andre stepped up to Sean, his fists clenching and unclenching in a menacing way. "If that's the way you feel about it, I hope you won't waste any time getting the hell off our plantation. This morning wouldn't be too soon."

"I told you, I work for Jean-Paul, not you. I have a contract with your brother for the breeding and training of his stock over the next two years." Sean looked at Deirdre with a stony face. "You're still my wife, and legally that little girl is my daughter. I'll say this in front of witnesses so you can hold me to it. I'm an honorable man. I'll continue to be a husband to you and father to Erin, but in name only, till I've managed to save up enough to move away and start my own horse business. In the meantime, I'll thank you to keep Jean-Paul and Miz Aurelia out of this. They've been real good to me, and I want to see what I started here at Moncoeur finished."

"Where will you stay?" Julia asked.

"There's a room off the stables where I can be comfortable." To Deirdre he said, "Can I leave my things here so the Devereuxs won't be suspicious? And can I depend on you not to speak of this to your brother?" This to Andre.

"I don't know how this will affect Deirdre and her little girl, but I'll go along with what you ask for the time being. I agree that Jean-Paul and Aurelia don't need an upheaval around here right now. Especially my sister-in-law. Aurelia is not strong at all."

"And neither is this young woman who just delivered a baby and nearly died from birth fever!" Julia declared hotly, pulling the covers up to Deirdre's shoulders and feeling the girl's forehead. "And that child over there is innocent in all this and just needs her morning feeding, so I kindly ask—no, make that *demand* that you men get out of here and be about your business. I'll take care of my darling Deirdre and her baby, and if I hear one more mean word to her from you, Sean, I'll be changing ends with you before I leave this place."

Deirdre said with a wan smile, "Julia, I don't think I want you to leave Moncoeur, ever." Her smile grew brighter. "Julia, I want to see my little girl. Isn't she beautiful?"

"That she is, just like her mother." Julia latched the door after the two men left and went over to lift Erin from her bed. "I just wish this wee one could have a real father." She transferred the tiny bundle to Deirdre's welcoming arms and beamed down at mother and child when the baby started suckling noisily. "You know, Andre never got that letter. I think maybe Lilianne intercepted it."

"You didn't tell Andre that Erin's his!" She was sure Andre still thought the baby was Sean's in spite of her husband's damning words.

"No, it's not my place to—now," Julia added the "now" pointedly. "But I was certainly tempted after seeing how Sean behaved. That boy has certainly changed."

"Sean isn't a boy any more, Julia. And he changed when he began to realize that I didn't love him and never had."

"Well, you've been a good wife to him, and he had no business showing that Irish temper at a time like this." She cooed at the child, who was more interested in breakfast than all this grown-up talk. "You widdle darling, your mother's between a rock and a hard place about you. If she tells Andre the truth now, there'll be a big scandal, her being married to another man. And if she doesn't tell him and Sean abandons his family, there'll be the devil to pay. Andre would be such a good father."

Deirdre laughed. She was feeling ever so much stronger now, and she was sure it was due mostly to having Julia at Moncoeur. "I'm not so sure! He reminds me of my own father in some ways." She told Julia about Riley O'Shea and the chance meeting with Andre in Colorado. "Can you believe he sent the money he owed Andre after all this time? It's in the chifferobe, Julia. Please take it. You paid off my debt, remember, and the money should go to you."

Julia refused, saying she wanted the money to be put away for little Erin. Then she insisted on Deirdre going to sleep while she and Prudy cared for the baby. "You've had a very long, very hard ordeal, sweetheart. Get your rest and don't worry about anything but getting strong again. I'll be here just as long as you need me."

Julia had returned to Nashville long since, and little Erin was a healthy eight months old, totally spoiled by Prudy and Letitia. The latter had become so attached to Deirdre's baby that she would hardly let the other two do anything.

Deirdre and Sean maintained a civil relationship that appeared normal on the surface. No one but Andre, who was in and out of Moncoeur in his efforts to help Jean-Paul get the plantation back on a stable financial basis, knew that

Sean and Deirdre no longer lived together as man and wife.

The November election was fast approaching. Deirdre's kegs of mountain whiskey were in great demand all over the county. She and Rufus spent almost every day hauling the product to points of distribution like Donald Bull's store in Shelbyville.

When she and the black man rode by in their wagon, people stopped to stare and point at "the Whiskey Mountain Woman." Deirdre had adopted a rugged costume for the dusty, rough rides, a fringed deerskin skirt and jacket, boots and dark leather hat. She carried a bullwhip, which she cracked expertly over the horses' heads. She had practiced untold hours mastering that whip, knowing the day might come when she would have to use it. Now she could snap off a dandelion's head at thirty yards.

It was at Donald Bull's store, a general gathering place for gossip and information about the increasing unrest in the South, that Deirdre learned that Abraham Lincoln had been elected President of the United States. There was strong talk about the South electing its own president after the states voted to secede.

"We've got ourselves a black Republican heading the country now," the store proprieter told Deirdre as he unloaded her kegs of whiskey. "He only took forty percent of the popular vote, they say, but them sons of bitches put 'im in. The South ain't got a chance now. We got to get out and run our ownselves."

The old men who sat around the iron stove that was kept going from dawn to dusk agreed. "I heerd that South Carolina took down the flag in Charleston day after Lincoln was elected. They'll be the first to secede, you can count on it, and the other cotton states will be right behind." Everybody nodded.

Deirdre drove the wagon home that night, empty of her kegs of whiskey but with her heart heavy at the talk of coming troubles in the South. "Rufus, I can't help thinking about what this will do to Moncoeur. If we do go to war, as some people are saying we probably will, Jean-Paul will be the first to join up, then Sean, and Andre certainly won't stay behind. How will we look after things at home?"

The old Negro shook his head sadly. "I sho' don't know, Miz DeeDee. I sho' don't know. Miz DeeDee, they's somebody up ahead, blockin' us." Deirdre reached for her bullwhip as she spied a clutch of men lounging around a broken-down wagon.

"Just don't say anything, Rufus. I'll do the talking." Deirdre recognized two dangerous things immediately—Lem Joe Bartow was in the middle of the group, and the men were all drunk—no doubt on Bartow's rotgut. "All right, Bartow," she called out as her wagon rumbled up to where the other vehicle blocked her way. "Move it out of the way." *You despicable little runt,* she added silently.

"Oh, my, if it isn't the Queen of Tennessee Whiskey herself." Bartow gave a mocking, unsteady bow. "I do declare. Well, what if I was to tell you that we ain't happy about that bastard in Washington getting to be President, and we're out here talkin' about what we got to do to git him out."

"And what if I were to tell you that I'm due home, and if you don't move out of my way, I'm coming through over you."

"Well now, ain't you the big talker, bein' a woman out by herself with just one worn-out ole nigger to hep her. Hey, you got any o' that liquor on your wagon? We might could talk trade."

Deirdre's bullwhip snaked out with the speed of lightning, snapping with a sharp crack over the head of Bartow's horse-drawn wagon. The startled animals took off through the nearby field scattering everybody around the wagon and clearing the road. Bartow jumped a ditch as Deirdre moved her wagon past, ignoring the yells that followed her.

"Boy, Miz DeeDee, you 'bout the toughest white woman I ever laid eyes on," Rufus said admiringly, looking back at the debacle they had outrun. "But I think you done made yo'self a mean enemy."

"Lem's just a cowardly little sneak who talks big when he's drunk." But Deirdre was sure Rufus was right. She was sure, too, that there was no way to deal with someone like Bartow except as a foe.

* * *

In the midst of all the upheaval after the election and the dark talk about Southern secession, a new romance was born. Aurelia was ecstatic about Gabrielle's infatuation with Charles, the highly eligible heir to Barksdale Plantation, a fine old estate adjoining Moncoeur.

"I can't believe that girl has finally made a decision about marrying one of these young men who have been after her all the time. I can't believe, either, that the child has accepted the suit of one of the most marriageable young men in the state. I always thought the silly girl would run away with a gambler like Andre or elope with a farmhand. Deirdre, you must help me plan the engagement party. Everyone is so upset about the state of affairs, this must be the event of the year. No gloom, no doom. We shall have a party that will make everyone happy, happy, happy!"

They planned the party for the night of December twenty-third, as close to Christmas as they dared, inviting everyone from miles around. Julia sent word from Nashville that she would not miss the occasion and would bring Deirdre the new recipe for the latest local drink, the mint julep.

Andre appeared the eve of the party and captured Deirdre as she was watering the pots of mint she'd carefully nurtured from the summer garden. "They told me you were out here," he said, ducking as he came into the little garden shed which Deirdre had transformed into a hothouse for her special herbs and plants. "How long has it been since you and I have been alone? Every time I come home, you run from me." Andre closed the door firmly. "But not this time."

Deirdre felt her heart beat its usual tattoo. "I have a million things to take care of. . . ." She tried to press by him, but he stopped her with a hand on her arm.

"They can wait. This can't. Deirdre, I've watched you trying to put a good face on your marriage, but it doesn't work. You and Sean have nothing left but a shell. You and that little girl deserve better. I want you to divorce him."

Deirdre looked at him, horrified. "I could never do that!"

"Why not? It can be done. You can't go on, a full-blooded woman like you, living in a sham marriage. Sean deserves better, too."

"He and I are getting along all right. He's kind to Erin, spends time with her. Sean's a good man. He'll do the right thing by us."

Andre pulled her arm up so that she was forced to move closer to him. "And what do you do," he whispered, "a woman like you who's beautiful and passionate and needs to be loved? What about the nights, Deirdre? I know that loneliness, and I know how much you have to offer a man. What about your own needs?"

"Andre, please don't do this." Deirdre felt her body's betrayal and knew that Andre was aware of it as much as she. "You're making it so hard for me."

"That's what I want, to make you see that you're hurting yourself every day that you stay in a loveless marriage." His voice dropped to a low, impassioned whisper as he moved his hands slowly up her arms. "How long since you've made love to a man, Deirdre? Remember that night, remember how I made you surrender to your feelings, remember how it was when we . . ." His intimate reminders made Deirdre shiver; his warm breath on her face and throat were almost unbearably delicious.

"I can't, Andre," she said, pushing him away and putting the potting table between them. "You mustn't do this to me. It's . . . it's unfair. When I was with you that night, I was not a married woman. Now I am. Please respect that and let me be. I can't just turn my back on Sean. I can't."

"You plan to live the rest of your life like this, Deirdre? I can't believe that. You're too vital, too much woman, too alive. The Whiskey Mountain Woman isn't somebody who would lack the courage to do what I'm asking you to do."

Deirdre picked up the bowl of mint leaves she'd pruned to use at the party. "I have to get back to the house. Gabrielle was looking for you earlier. I think she wants to ask you to make the announcement of her betrothal tomorrow night."

Andre sighed deeply. "You won't let us talk about you and me, will you? I'll see Gabrielle later. Right now, I'm not through with you. I'm a patient man, but only up to a point. Deirdre, the day will come when it will just be you and me. That's a promise."

Everyone who was anyone from Nashville to Shelbyville was at the party for Gabrielle Devereux that night of December 23, 1860. It was as though the residents of the area were saving up lightheartedness for the grim times they knew lay ahead.

The house was festive and beautiful. Deirdre and Prudy had stripped holly and pine trees of their finery, arranging it on mantels and in corners everywhere in the big house, putting candles and sweet-smelling evergreens all over. The dining room table groaned with delicacies and the traditional holiday foods Southerners dearly loved. Aurelia's prize cut-glass Christmas punch bowl sparkled with the ice Deirdre had had Rufus bring down from the crest of the spring. Mint juleps in the special silver cups that Aurelia's mother had brought back from England were an instant hit. Aurelia was very pleased to be the first hostess in the area to serve the delicious iced sugar, whiskey and mint drink.

"It's Deirdre's whiskey and Julia's recipe that make it so good," she told everyone who begged for the secret.

When Gabrielle and her fiance, whom Deirdre liked very much, were brought into the center of the room by Andre, everyone smiled and clapped at the announcement of their coming marriage.

"Now, that's a fine young pair," a neighbor whispered to Deirdre. "I just hope this country doesn't come down to fighting a war like some folks are saying. That young man would be one of the first to go."

So would the Ragland boy, the Lunsford twins, the Boatwright fellow who'd just gotten married, thought Deirdre, losing her festive spirit as she looked around the room. Andre would sign up, too, she realized gloomily, even Jean-Paul and Sean. "There'll be a lot of our friends going."

"But if it comes to it, the South can lick those Yankees with a musket in one hand and the other tied behind our backs."

Deirdre was not given a chance to answer, for a wave of excitement rippled around the room when Jack Tarver, a latecomer from Shelbyville, came bursting in and got everyone's attention for a startling announcement. "It's starting, y'all, like we all knew it would when they put that damn' black Republican in the White House. I just got the news from my cousin, who came down from Beaufort late last night. South Carolina seceded from the union yesterday, and they say Mississippi and Florida ain't far behind!"

The clamor in the room was overwhelming. Most prevalent amongst the excited remarks were the questions about what Tennessee would do. Jean-Paul circulated around the room, promoting sentiment for Tennessee's secession if the cotton states all followed South Carolina's lead. "We can't let one of our sister states stand alone," he told everyone who would listen. "Tennessee men can't go against their own kind and join up with Lincoln's federal armies."

Deirdre's mint juleps were rediscovered in the enthusiasm of the mood brought on by the news from South Carolina. There were many toasts to the sister Southern state who, according to many, had set the course for the South. "We'll show those bastards we mean business," someone said to Deirdre. "South Carolina showed 'em we ain't bluffing."

Gabrielle came up to Deirdre and said a bit petulantly, "I declare, everybody's clean forgotten what this party was all about. Why in the blue-eyed world do men get so excited over politics and war? Even Charles, fresh upon his wedding announcement, is talking to somebody about how he can't wait to get his hands on a musket and go off to war."

"Maybe it won't happen, Gabrielle," Deirdre said comfortingly. "I pray it won't, but if it does, you'll have to be strong for your Aunt Aurelia. I don't think she could stand it if your Uncle Jean-Paul and Andre went off to battle."

"What about me? I'm getting married next month, and if things start going the way people are saying, I could be a widow in six months."

"Shhh. Don't even think things like that. Just concentrate on Charles and how happy you two are."

Deirdre thought about Andre and wondered how she could bear it if he went off to war and something happened to him. He was constantly in her thoughts these days as Erin grew to look more and more like her father.

Chapter Twelve

Late 1988

"Honey, if you don't take them mint juleps to the living room, they gone ferment 'fore anybody can drink 'em. This gumbo is jest about done to a turn, and I don't want supper ruint 'cause of yore daydreamin.' "

I took the tray of mint juleps that Azalea was handing me and stared down at the silver julep cups that my mother has collected since her wedding. There are now enough to have one for each guest at our annual Kentucky Derby party. "Azalea," I asked, a little timidly since I didn't know what I had been doing between the time I walked into the kitchen and into Deirdre's world and now. "How long have I been here—I mean, since I got home from town?"

"Honey, you been home maybe twenty minutes, but you might as well've been on Planet Mars for all the help you give me fixin' supper. I must've ast you five times to slice the bread, and all you did was sit there in that daydreamin' state you stay in a lotta the time these days." Azalea went back to stirring her gumbo. "Now git out there with that tray 'fore yore daddy starts yellin' at us."

Twenty minutes. How on earth had I lived all that time as Deirdre in just twenty minutes? I had a feeling even Dr. Velkoff wasn't going to be able to satisfy my questions about that.

My father and mother were waiting in the formal living room where we met for cocktails each night before dinner. They had invited another of the Belle Meade young eligibles for me, a habit they'd perpetuated since my sister's death.

"Fable, this is Keith Moncrief. I'm sure you remember meeting his family at their box in the Shelbyville Celebration last August."

I held out my hand to the nice-looking young man and smiled. After all, it wasn't his fault that my parents had decided they had to make a suitable match for their rebellious daughter. "Of course. Hello, Keith. I think I was in school with your younger sister." I handed him a mint julep, took one myself, and passed the tray to my father, who was looking pleased with me for a change.

"I've been hearing your songs lately," my suitor said eagerly. "You're really getting to be a celebrity around town."

"Oh, you like country music?" I looked at his preppie outfit and doubted that Keith Moncrief had ever heard more than one country music recording in his life.

"Well, I don't like the twangy stuff, but I really enjoy good music, no matter what the style."

We talked on like that until it was time for dinner and I found myself wishing when we went into the dining room that Deirdre, Aurelia, and all the Devereuxs were sitting here tonight instead of people I knew hardly at all and cared even less about.

I excused myself politely as soon as my father and Keith were safely engaged in discussion about politics and went upstairs to mull over my latest visit to another time.

Andre Devereux was a big part of my musing. How would he win Deirdre back with all the obstacles ahead of them? What would happen to Moncoeur when the South went to war (as I knew from my historical hindsight platform that it would)? I got out my guitar and played the Irish ballads that I could remember and heard new ones coming into my head. Before I went to bed, I half expected to hear Aurelia clapping her hands delightedly and crying, "More, DeeDee, more!"

I was living in two worlds and increasingly intrigued by the old one.

* * *

Strange things had been happening to me for such a long time now that I really wasn't surprised at some odd occurrences that took place in the next few weeks. I did my usual routine of going to classes at Belmont, having a few social engagements, riding Gambler, and going to the recording studio. My performance at the Grand Ol' Opry had gotten me all the personal spots I could use, so I fit all those in the best I could.

The first odd occurrence came during my trip out to Hendersonville to finally clean out my sister's effects from the house she and Royce had lived in. Because the title to the place had been left in limbo and Royce's claim had been quite uncertain, none of Celeste's family had been given clear access to the property for all this time. Finally, though, the title had been cleared up, and with none of Royce's relatives stepping forward to make a claim—or indeed, step forward, period—I was advised that Celeste's family could dispose of the estate. This unpleasant task fell to me since there was no one else to do it.

It was a peculiar feeling, I swear it, going into that house that I'd never entered before and seeing my sister everywhere. Every photograph she'd ever had made was displayed, making the whole house a kind of shrine to a vanished beauty queen. I saw her smiling visage every place I went, even in the kitchen and bathroom.

There were no pictures of Royce except the wedding picture. I looked at that and cursed it soundly. "You two-timing son of a bitch. I don't know what you did to my sister, but I sure as hell know what you did to me."

He grinned back at me, and I picked the picture up and dropped it in the wastebasket. "Wait a minute. You can't do that. From what Laney said, there may not be any other photos around." I retrieved the picture and put it in the box I'd brought up to put personal effects in.

The bed was one of those Las Vegas honeymoon types with silk drapings and heart-shaped pillows and mirrors everywhere. I looked at it with a grim smile, remembering the grass mattress that had been the site of my sexual crimes with Royce. "I don't even want to think about what took place here," I murmured.

It didn't take long to pack the personal effects in the bedroom. Actually, the McColls had had few intimate belongings except for clothes and the pictures of Celeste. I had no use for the clothes since Celeste wore a size five—I by now fit into an eight—so I put those in a bag for the Salvation Army. Royce's I packed up for Harrison to take to the Mission on Union Street. The winos and bums would love my late brother-in-law's rather cowboyish taste.

I walked into the bathroom and smelled the scent of Celeste's favorite perfume. "That's odd." I looked for a deodorizer, but there was none. There had been no bottle of "L'Air du Temps" in the stuff I'd packed from her dressing table. "That's really odd." Perfume doesn't last that long. I began to get the prickly goosebumps that I get when something's going on that I can't put my finger on. "Let's get the hell out here. This is creepy."

Azalea had once told me about smelling her brother in the room with her after he'd been dead several weeks. "It was that turpentine he dipped in Georgia and his chawing tobaccy. Folks laughed at me when I tol' 'im my brother was hangin' around, but there was no mistakin' his smell."

Shivering as if a rabbit had walked over my grave, I left the bedroom so quickly I knocked over one of Celeste's pageant pictures.

That's when I heard it, the almost imperceptible sound of a door closing downstairs. I froze in my tracks, not knowing whether to run or lock myself up in the spooky bedroom. I opted for the former. There was a fifty-fifty chance that the door was closing on someone leaving.

Of course there was that other fifty-fifty chance, too, but I didn't want to think about that. I eased down the hall to the stairs, picking up a heavy onyx cat that smirked on a marble table, and crept downstairs.

There was nothing, no one there. I looked out the back door and surveyed the quiet, unrippled lake. Nothing.

I left after making sure all the doors—especially the back one—were locked.

Halfway down Gallatin Road, I realized I'd driven off without the boxes I'd packed. "Damnation! I don't want to go back in there." I drove on a little farther and then cursed myself for being a superstitutious fool. There was nothing back there that could hurt me. If Celeste was haunting the place, she was just a ghost and powerless to do bodily harm—if the myths were right about spirits.

I turned around at the "House of Cash," Johnny's museum and gift shop, and drove back to the lake.

That's when the second strange incident occurred. I had my key in my hand, about to insert it into the lock when a voice spoke clearly inside my head. *Don't go back in there. Leave things be.*

Startled, I jumped and the house key fell from my hand into the thick, prickly shrubs that flanked the front stoop. Ten minutes later, I cursed at the scratchy bushes which made my search for the lost key futile. "Well, I guess that settles that. The boxes will just have to wait for someone else to pick them up."

This time when I got almost to the Interstate, I didn't turn around. I'm not much into sixth senses or ouija boards or spirit channeling, but I'm not stupid. I can take a hint when the stranger inside my head hollers *stop*.

The best news I'd had in a long time came after a taping of my new song was completed. I'd known that day in the studio that there was something magical happening. When the sound crew and the technicians go real quiet after a performer's finished before breaking into applause, she knows she's just done something outstanding. It happened when Patsy Cline recorded "Sweet Dreams," when Loretta sang "Coal Miner's Daughter," when Tammy Wynette sang out her heart in "Stand By Your Man."

It happened that day when I let the last note of "Whiskey Mountain Woman" echo to a stop, and the lead technician signaled a take. The quiet was deafening as I stepped out of the soundproof taping room; after that came the applause. My toughest critic, the lead guitar of my back-up band, Wally Privett, who has been backing up singers and Opry performers since before I was born, looked at me and nodded slowly. That's as close to being complimentary as he ever gets with anybody.

Harrison came up and hugged me, not saying anything either. That's his way. "I've got stuff to do in my office, but I'm taking you to dinner tonight. No excuses."

At dinner, he told me I was being nominated for a Grammy Award in two categories—best single and best album. Right there in Nashville's most elegant restaurant at the Peabody Hotel, I let out a rebel yell. Since the maitre d' and the manager knew me and my music, and I'd had at least six people come to our table for autographs, my crude behavior was overlooked and we were allowed to finish our dinner.

I could tell by the time coffee and dessert arrived that Harrison had more on his mind than the Grammy. He kept looking at me as if I were completely alien to the singer he'd known before.

"All right, Harrison." I put my cup down and shut out the noise of a rowdy Christmas party that was going on at the next big table. "Out with it. You've got something cooking under that ponytail, and this is as good as time as any to put it on the table."

Now that Royce McColl was permanently out of my life, I could look at Harrison Judd and realize that I hadn't been paying him enough personal attention. He was damned attractive, I thought, in his unaccustomed dark suit and formal tie. I felt a couple of little tingles that I knew had very little to do with our business relationship.

But Harrison was a proud man, too proud to let me pull his strings in a rebound situation. I knew that and respected his feelings.

"In fact, there is something. Fable Devereux, you know that I'm not a prying, nosy kind of man. I have never once interfered in your private life or asked you questions, even when you were going nuts over that red-headed cowboy that I could've told you was no good for you."

"You've saved all your nosiness up for this one time—right? And now you're going to ask me all those questions you've kept holed up all this time." I held up my hand. "Sorry! Go on. You were right about Royce, but that's history. What else have you got? Gossip about me on Music Row?"

"Only the good kind. People in the business like you, really like you. No, this isn't gossip, it's head stuff. I've just had some really weird feelings about this song that you came up with."

"'Whiskey Mountain Woman'? Did you really like it as much as I think you did?"

Harrison said solemnly, "It's the finest piece of work I've seen out of the studio since Kristopherson's first ballad and 'Billie Joe.' But that's not the weird feeling I'm talking about. I know the song will be a big hit and probably get you all kinds of awards next year, but there's more to it than that."

I leaned forward and whispered, "Then why don't you tell me?"

Harrison pushed his cup back and looked me dead in the eye. "All right, I will. Fable, you didn't write that song, although your name's on it. I know you, I know your style, your rhythm, the way you put words together and the musical sequences you use. Whoever did write it is damn good. You're damn good, but you didn't write 'Whiskey Mountain' and I know it sure as I'm sitting right across from you at this table."

I pleated my napkin carefully before saying slowly, "Are you trying to say I've stolen some poor sucker's song and am trying to pass it off as mine? Is that what you're hinting at?"

Harrison looked unhappy. "Look, I know that Music City is crammed to the gills with kids trying to make it in country music and a lot of 'em have real talent. They'll do anything to get their songs sung, and what I'm saying is that if you felt sorry for some mountain kid who came to you with a good song and agreed to do it under your label, that's a big mistake.

Not morally—the morality is between you and your conscience—but from a legal standpoint." Harrison gave me another steely look. "Do you realize that if we produce this song and it becomes the mega hit I know it will be, the real writer could pop up and cause us troubles like you would not believe. *Comprendez?*"

I was silent for a long moment, making up my mind about whether I could trust Harrison with the truth. He was a down-to-earth, hardnosed business guy; would he believe me when I told him that the song he questioned composed itself in my head one morning when I was walking on the mountain?

I decided to take a chance that he would. Harrison, after all, was a good listener. "Harrison, I have a story to tell you about the real 'Whiskey Mountain Woman,' one that you probably will have trouble believing. . . ."

When I'd finished, Harrison looked at me for a long, slow time, then: "You're putting me on, aren't you? You're telling me that that song came to you from a lady who lived back in the War Between the States? That you've got a hot line back to this Deirdre person and you know everything she had in her head?"

"Not everything. But her songs always stay with me. 'Whiskey Mountain' is about what she did. I don't know where it came from, I just know it came."

Harrison looked at me for a long, long time. "Does all of this have something to do with your sister?"

"I think so. Dr. Velkoff thinks so, too." I had leveled with Harrison a while back about seeing a shrink. He hadn't asked any questions, probably assuming I was getting therapy for dealing with rapid success or something.

"Have you worked through the Royce business with him?" Harrison asked this pretty carefully.

"Some of it." I took a drink of cold coffee and felt anxious to leave the restaurant. "Harrison, let's go. They're going to start charging us rent on this table."

"We'll go, but I'm not through with you yet." He counted out some bills and put them on the table. "I want to hear more about this going back in time."

Once we were on the highway out of Nashville, I tried to explain. "I've told you everything, Harrison. I don't understand it, my psychiatrist doesn't understand it, but I swear I am reliving a life that happened well over a hundred years ago. Go ahead, tell me I'm crazy. I've thought that a few times myself."

"I don't think you're crazy, but I do think you're letting your imagination work overtime. Look, you went through a lot back there with your sister and all. You spent your young life seeing her put ahead of you in every way imaginable, then had her take your boyfriend from under your nose. Add that to having her treat you like dirt after she married somebody we know had something funny about him and then she's dead—boom!—like that."

"You sound like Dr. Velkoff."

"Well, God help me, I sure as hell don't want to do that. I'm not one of your touchy-feely guys and I hope you know me well enough by now to realize that. Look, I don't understand what's been happening to you or how much I believe it, but I do know that that song you sang tonight is a winner. As long as you can promise me that nobody living today helped you write it, I'll go with it big-time."

I leaned over to give him a peck on the cheek. He smelled good. "I promise. And Deirdre won't come back to slap us with a lawsuit—that's a guarantee."

Harrison turned off on Franklin Road and drove past the turnoff to my house.

"What in the world are you doing? You missed our turn."

"I know. We're going on to my place." Harrison adjusted his rearview mirror as he drove on out to Wilson Pike, the twisty, turning road that goes by Dolly Parton's farm and others belonging to big-name stars. Harrison had built himself a stone and cedar house near Nolansville on a hill overlooking the beautiful countryside and a gorgeous lake. I had been to his house for parties but had never been there with him alone.

I was a little nervous about going there now. I hadn't had any serious romances since Royce and, though my attraction to Harrison had been sneaking up on me lately, I was still a little raw from rejection. "Harrison, it's awfully late. Maybe we'd better . . ."

"Fable, I'm not putting the make on you, although I've thought about doing that more than once. I just didn't want to turn into the road to your house back there."

"Now who's sounding mysterious! Why in the world not?"

"Because," Harrison said quietly, adjusting his rearview mirror again, "someone has been following us ever since we left the Peabody, and he's still behind us. Don't turn around! I don't want him to know we're on to him."

"Why would anybody be following us?" I whispered, my throat suddenly dry.

Harrison feigned lightness. "Maybe one of your more persistent fans. You had a few hanging around the restaurant. I was beginning to think I might have to break a couple of heads."

"Nobody would follow me home, for God's sake." It was almost all I could do to keep from turning around to see the car behind us.

"They camp outside Tammy Wynette's house all the time. And Dolly has full-time security at her place."

"You're putting me in elevated company there, Mr. Judd," I said, trying to sound lighthearted instead of scared, which I was. I knew none of those people back at the Peabody would follow us home.

"Hold on. I'm going to pretend that I'm going up my driveway, but I'm going to turn around and face the bastard—run him off the road if I have to."

He whipped around with a squealing of tires

and got back on Skinner Road. "Where did he go?" I whispered. There was no sign of a car.

"Must've turned around down at that old abandoned house." Harrison stopped the truck and took a deep breath. "He's gone. We scared him off, I'm pretty sure. I think we could both use a drink."

"Make mine a double," I said.

It had been quite a day, all around. You could say it was a mixture of the good, the bad and the ugly. One thing for sure, though. My ancestor was not mixed up with this incident. As far as I know, ghosts do not drive cars.

Maybe it was the fear we had both felt, or maybe it was a natural build-up of the repressed attraction between us, but I do know that by the time Harrison and I had finished our drinks in his raftered great room, the air was heavy with "what now?"s.

"I make a mean omelet," he told me during a loaded silence. "Your parents won't worry about you if you stay for a late breakfast, will they?"

"My parents never worry about me," I said truthfully, "except as my actions affect their lives. I'm a grown woman, Harrison, in case you haven't noticed."

"I've noticed," he said. "By the way, if I haven't told you lately, I'll tell you now. You look great." He reached over to touch my hair, which I was letting curl nearly to my waist these days. I felt the current from his hand and had prickles along my scalp.

"Thanks. I finally lost all that baby fat." I dared not look at him because I knew things were moving toward a natural conclusion that I wasn't sure I was ready for.

"Fable, please don't stiffen up on me. I think you know what I want tonight, and I think you want it, too." He took my drink from my hand and placed it on the coffee table in front of the decadently cushioned sofa we were sitting on. "I'm been patient from the beginning, even through all that garbage with Royce. But it's time we faced what's going on with us. You said you were grown-up now. Prove it."

"That sounds like a line left over from high school," I said. "You've been around people who write romantic lyrics too long. You can do better than that."

"All right, how about this. I don't tell lies and I don't play games." Harrison reached over and pulled me into his arms. "This is for real, Fable." He stroked my hair away from my face and looked into my eyes while he gently outlined my mouth with his thumb. "You've never really kissed me. I think it's time you did."

If I could write a song about what happened to us with that first "real" kiss, I could retire a wealthy woman. We were both totally rocked by it. After I managed to come up for air, breathing almost as hard as Harrison was, I did my best to postpone the inevitable. "I think we'd better stop right there. It's getting awfully late." I was very much aware that if what I wanted to happen happened, the sun would be up before I left this man's arms.

"You're damn right it is," Harrison growled as he reached for me again.

After the next kiss, I was too weak to resist, almost too weak to whisper as he gathered me up in his arms and headed toward the bedroom. "I don't believe this. You, the strong, the silent, the unemotional, turning into Rhett Butler."

"There are a lot of things you don't know about me yet, Fable Devereux, but you'll know a lot more before morning."

One thing I found out very quickly was that Harrison was all male, physically and otherwise. He had my clothes off so quickly and efficiently, I hardly had time to protest. "I bet you can change your pick-up's gears with your knees," I murmured, pretending to have my eyes shut while he stripped himself, although I was actually watching with great interest to see if the actual unveiling lived up to the earlier promise. It did.

"I've rehearsed this all night in my mind," he murmured back as he came onto the bed next to me. "I knew where every button, every zipper was."

Before the night was over, I realized that the lovemaking I'd experienced with Royce was just a preliminary to the awakening I was experiencing with Harrison. He played my body's responses like a fine-tuned guitar. I had never felt my body was beautiful, but Harrison made me feel it was. He treated my breasts like shrines, and when he had made them ache with desire, he moved on to the rest of me, paying delicious homage all along the way.

He braked our passion at one point to take care of protecting me, and I teased him, "So you planned this ahead of time."

"I have planned this from the first moment I saw you." The deep kisses resumed, this time with a strong movement of his hands over my hips and thighs. I felt myself parting for him at his urging and then melting at his entry.

"You feel wonderful to me," he whispered, "just the way I've dreamed you would be."

We made love till the sun came up, and then we made love again. Harrison mixed up mimosas and gave me a warm robe since the December mornings in Tennessee are pretty chilly. He wasn't crazy about leaving his cozy bed and the fire he'd built, but I insisted on shivering out onto the deck so we could see the pond coming awake.

When we went back to bed, I teased him, "Do you realize that you didn't wiggle your ears even once last night?"

"I was too busy with some much more important body movements."

"Well, do it for me just once," I whispered, putting my tongue inside his ear and tickling it.

Harrison Judd proved that he was a good sport. He also proved a few other things before I left his arms.

Chapter Thirteen

To be perfectly honest, I was glad that the following week's calendar was too full to allow much private time with Harrison. I had been rocked by the physical impact our night had on us both, but I still wasn't ready to throw myself into a new romantic commitment.

Harrison didn't push it, though I knew he was thinking about what had happened between us every time we ran into each other. He talked about other matters, though, for which I was grateful. "Anybody been tailing you lately?" he asked after a photography session for pub shots to be used in the hoopla planned for my new country hit.

"Only my shadow," I said flippantly. But my flippancy was surface-deep only. It would be a long time before I got over the jitters I'd felt that day at Celeste's house or that night when someone tried to follow me home.

The real estate agent who was handling my sister's house called just before I left the studio and told me some news I could have done without. "I'm real sorry, Fable, but the deal fell through. That couple with the pending contract just couldn't come up with the down payment the bank wanted. But we'll find another buyer, I'm sure. It's just that property on the lake is so expensive! There aren't that many people with the kind of cash required up front."

I thanked her for her efforts. "Okay, Betty Lou, I know you've done your best. Just keep me posted."

She had something else to tell me that had nothing to do with potential buyers or contracts. "Fable, have you been in that house lately?"

I told her I had, but I didn't tell her everything about my visit out there. "Why? Something wrong?"

"I'm not quite sure. I may have just seen a reflection of some boat lights from the water, but I could swear somebody was inside the house last night when I went by to take off our 'pending' sign. I saw this light moving around upstairs, like a flashlight or something."

I'd never been exactly sure what hackles were until that moment. Mine rose big-time. "Betty Lou, you told me the electricity was being kept on until the house sells."

"You better believe it. Plenty of buyers like

to see houses after dark. That's what worried me. I figured if that was someone who had any business prowling around, they'd turn on the lights."

"Well, I just hope you didn't go in to investigate all by yourself!"

"Oh, no. But I did call one of the guys at the office to come out with me to check this morning to be sure nothing had been vandalized. Maybe we scared whoever it was off, if they were still there. I saw some boxes with the McColls' personal stuff. 'Course I have no way of knowing if any of that was taken. It didn't look as if a burglar had been in there or anything, but there was something kind of funny about the place."

I was getting those goosebumps again. "Funny?"

"I just had this feeling that somebody had been there, you know what I mean?"

I did, but I wanted her to tell me where she got *her* feeling. "I'm not sure I do."

"Well, I've been in the real estate business for quite a while. I know my properties inside out—that's my job. Maybe this was nothing, but I noticed anyway."

I was getting impatient. "Betty Lou, I'm not one of your clients that you have to circle a hundred times before moving in with the hard sell! Get to the point."

"Somebody had been up there looking for something. There was a drawer not quite closed here, a closet door cracked there, stuff slightly out of place. I've been through that house with clients a hundred times. I know this property backwards and forwards, from the water stains in the basement to the crack in the kitchen sink."

"You never told me about the stain and the crack." I couldn't care less about those, but I did care about Betty Lou's instincts. I had no doubt that someone had been prowling around my sister's house—someone who didn't want to be seen. What I couldn't figure out was *why?*

"Think you ought to report this to the police? 'Course the lock wasn't forced, and nothing we know of was taken. Could it be that the McColls gave a key to one of their friends?"

I didn't point out that, to the best of my knowledge, my sister and her husband had no friends, but I did point out that anybody close enough to be given a key would know about the accident. "Tell you what, I'll hold off on the report until I check those boxes to see if anything was taken. Which reminds me, I'll need to pick up a key from your office. I lost mine on the way out to my car the other day. Tomorrow morning okay?"

"Fine. Sure you don't want to take one of the men with you?"

I pondered that, then decided against it. I didn't know what was going on in that house, but I was pretty sure it had something to do with my late sister. I didn't want any outsiders along if I did find something. "No. I'll make sure nobody's lurking around when I get there."

Betty Lou ended the conversation with a reminder that if ever my family decided to sell Moncoeur, she would like to have the first crack at it. This was a long-standing joke between us. Betty Lou is well aware that the Devereux plantation house will never be for sale.

I performed my part of the ritual. "Betty Lou, I assure you that when Moncoeur goes on the market, you will be the first to hear about it. You will also get the first snow-cone in August at the open house."

She laughed and I did, too. But that was the only comical note in the entire conversation. Whatever was going on in the McColls' vacant dream house was not funny at all, not one bit.

We had one of those rare light snowfalls during the night, and I bundled up more than usual the next morning to make my trip to Hendersonville. The roads weren't icy, a blessing since I'm not great at driving on bad roads. Few Southerners are, as transplanted Yankees are quick to tell us when Dixie ices up.

The gorgeous houses on the lake road looked like something from a Christmas card. Everybody in the area would take pictures, I knew, and send photo holiday cards the next year with their very own "White Christmas" places pictured.

I passed Donna's house and smiled to see that she already had the old sleigh trimmed with lights. Judging from the number of cars in the driveway, her voluminous family had already begun descending upon her and Austin.

This time I didn't falter as I let myself into the empty house on Lake Valley Road. "Okay, all you ghosts and goblins—scoot outta here. Lulu's back in town, and this time she ain't leaving till she finds out what's going on here."

I stomped up the stairs and entered the bedroom, where I'd left the two biggest boxes. When I finished sorting through them, I sat back on my heels and thought about this newest puzzle.

Why would someone sneak into the house after dark and take only three items—none of which had any real value?

I stood up. "The picture of Celeste winning her first crown and the dress she wore that night. Why would anybody steal those?" The third item missing was the picture of her and Royce at their wedding.

As I drove back to Hendersonville I wondered who had broken into the house and why. Had my sister and her husband left something of great value behind when had left for their fatal voyage? Or was there a cache from Royce's past that meant a great deal to those people who had driven him into hiding all those years ago?

I came to hopeless dead ends in my speculations. Hardcore criminals might have been responsible for driving my sister's husband into the secret life that he had been living before he was killed. They might have been the ones who blew up the car and later the yacht. But why would they take the innocuous pictures?

My head started aching, especially when I thought about the car following me the night I'd spent with Harrison. What did all of this have to do with me?

The Hendersonville police didn't have any updates on the yacht explosion investigation, when I stopped by to check with them. Or at least they had none they were willing to share with me. They were apologetic and eager to assure me, however, that they would make sure the lake house was patrolled frequently. When they asked me what had been taken from the house, I answered truthfully, "Nothing that was of any value."

They promised to call me if there were any future signs of break-ins and to keep me posted about news from the Miami police. As I was getting ready to leave, one of the detectives called me aside and, looking a little embarrassed, asked me about Celeste. "You think maybe your sister left, uh, a stash of crack and somebody knew about it?"

"Cocaine," I corrected him. For some reason that made a difference to me. Crack had such ugly street connotations. "I thought about that, to be honest with you. But if she was an addict, that would've been the last thing she'd leave behind, wouldn't it?" I still had a lot of trouble dealing with the idea of my sister being on drugs.

He shrugged. "Hop-heads do crazy things. No offense to your sister," he added hastily.

"None taken." There was no use getting mad. "Thanks very much, officer. I'll wait to hear from you if anything comes up."

I slid my car into the noon-day traffic on Gallatin, glancing into my rear-view mirror to be sure the lane was clear.

The bland dark car parked two autos behind me slid out, too. I switched lanes a couple of times, and so did the dark car behind me. I slowed down. Ditto.

When I got on the expressway, my tail was close behind. I sped up. So did he.

I decided I'd had about enough. Without using my turn signal, I whipped around two cars, squeezing in between them and an eighteen-wheeler, then took a hair-raising exit. The two drivers I'd scared were telling me about my dubious heritage, I was pretty sure, but all I really cared about was that the car following me had to keep going on the expressway. I broke a couple of speed laws getting back to the entrance ramp on the other side of my exit and came up one car behind my quarry.

We had now reversed roles, and I was the stalker. I was determined to get a glimpse of him or, even better, a license number. A white Cadillac in the left lane blocked me from getting any closer. "Move it, lady," I muttered between clinched teeth, but that damned Cadillac sat right there, and I watched helplessly as my hunter-turned-quarry darted into an opening in the fast lane and vanished while I stayed behind my slow-moving tortoise.

"Well, at least he knows I'm on to him," I said with a remnant of satisfaction. Next time I would run him off the road, so help me God, and get some answers to things I didn't even know the questions to.

The manager out at our family's whiskey distillery was thrilled to death when I agreed to sing my hit song about the Whiskey Mountain lady at the traditional Christmas Eve party for employees and their families. "Fable, we've sold about twice as much whiskey since that song came out and folks found out it was about our product."

Daddy had more or less disassociated himself from the distillery since he'd sold his stock majority to a liquor conglomerate. But the management still liked having a Devereux around to help celebrate the distillery's continued success. I usually wound up being the one to go.

I invited Harrison to go along with me, since the roads were tricky in December. Harrison did a very thoughtful thing without saying much about it beforehand. He brought along a crate of my records with a special commemorative cover that he'd had made up at company expense.

After I'd performed, we sneaked away from the noisy party and all the kids and found the path up to the spring. Of course, it wasn't the same spring Deirdre had used. A new one—miles from Moncoeur—had been found around the turn of the century. From the spring we could look back down on the lights of the huge distillery complex. As I looked at the array of vats, tanks and buildings, I wondered what Deirdre would think about her tiny operation turning into one of the largest, most famous distilleries in the world. I said as much to Harrison. "Look at all that! Deirdre wouldn't believe this if she were here right now."

"I think she is here right now—at least where you're concerned. She's gotten to be real to you, Fable."

"That's because she is real." I knew Harrison was looking at me and not at the complex below. "She's as real as I am."

He put his hands on my face and turned it up to the moonlight. "Not to me." He looked down at me for a long time and said softly, "I like you in moonlight, but I'd like you even better in firelight. Can we get out of this place and go to mine? I want to give you your Christmas present in private." He laughed at the look I gave him. "Not that kind of present, although it's an idea. No, I mean a real one."

I said with true regret, "I can't. Daddy would have a hissy if I didn't show up for our traditional Christmas Eve toast at midnight. We always hoist the mint juleps to all the dead ancestors and the future heirs to come."

"You're the only people I know who drink mint juleps year round. What about eggnog?"

"Do you think I'm crazy, Harrison?"

"For drinking mint juleps when the snow's on the ground? Nah." But he knew what I was talking about and said more solemnly, "No. I think you've been put through the mill and are trying desperately to make sense of it all in the best way your mind can devise."

"Thank you for that," I said sincerely.

"And thank you for this." Harrisson put his mouth on mine and kissed me long and lingeringly. "I want you to accept your destiny, Miss Fable Devereux," he said after we came up for air. "Before we leave this magical place, I insist on it."

"Now who's sounding like the lead-in to 'Twilight Zone'? What do you see as my destiny, o great swami?"

"To become the greatest little country music singer since Patsy Cline. And to be my girl."

I was flattered by the allusion to my all-time favorite performer, but I loved even more the old-fashioned ring to the second part of his statement. "Aw, shucks. You asking me to go steady with you, boy? Is that what you mean?"

"This is what I mean." Harrison put his mouth on mine and proceeded to kiss me in a way that showed exactly what he meant. It was a cold night, but by the time we broke apart, we were both steamed up to the boiling point.

"That was what I call a bedroom kiss," I said tremulously.

"You're damn right it was. Forget the mint julep, forget your father. Come back home with me tonight, Fable."

I was sorely tempted. In Harrison's arms I

felt safe and desirable, as I had never felt in my life. "I can't. I'm sorry. It's just that Christmas is really lonesome with just the three of us there. It's tough for my mother. On Daddy, too, to be fair."

"And what about you?"

I nodded. "Me, too."

We went down and said our Merry Christmases to everybody, I autographed record covers, and then Harrison took me home. He left me at the front door, refusing my invitation to come in. "I don't think your father would accept me as part of your family tradition."

I stood on the veranda and admired the magic Christmas-card look of the landscape, especially the mountain with its gleaming cover of snow. I felt the tingle of remembered kisses on my lips and smiled, letting the warmth of memories insulate me against the coldness of the night.

"Will You Be My Girl" started coming into my head, the lyrics first and then the music fast behind. The song would not be recorded until a year later, but it was born that night, right there on the veranda not far from Deirdre's mountain. When I went into the house, "Little Drummer Boy" was filling the air, but my heart was holding fast to its new song.

Daddy and Mother were awaiting me in the living room, where our huge tree sparkled with its ancient decorations and the fire glowed merrily. It was a Norman Rockwell scene, and I fit myself right into it. My father and I were getting along these days, mainly because I spent a lot of time smiling sweetly and holding my tongue. In fact, he made a remark about my new "attitude" tonight, saying that I was turning into a "right genteel young Southern lady."

I wasn't sure that was what I was turning into, but I wasn't about to start an argument on one of our rare pleasant occasions. Exchanging gifts fell into this category. Daddy really liked the soapstone carving I'd found at an antique show to add to his collection. Mother was thrilled with the old opal drop earrings I'd bought her. As for me, I made lots of oohs and aahs over the four settings of Francis First sterling to add to the collection that had been started at my birth. In short, we all behaved very well, in spite of the fact that not one of us was unaware of the absence of Celeste, who had sung "Silent Night" to the accompaniment of her harp on every Christmas Eve since she'd been six.

I brought Azalea in for the big cash bonus we always give her, laughing when she looked at the same old red stocking and shook it and held it up to her ear. "Merry Christmas, Prudy," I said. "Now that you own your own home, that'll come in handy."

Everybody stared at me, and I realized that I'd made one of my crazy slips backward into the past. Except that this time I was still in the living room of the present. "Joke, everybody," I said weakly. "Azalea, if you've still got some of that Japanese fruitcake left over, I sure would like a piece with a cup of coffee."

Mother wanted some, too, and Daddy decided he needed a brandy, so the awkward little moment passed by.

I don't know what awakened me later that night, but awaken I did, feeling the familiar rippling of goose pimples. "Okay," I told myself, getting up and going to close the window, "Some snow has plopped down somewhere and you're not going to make a big deal about it."

I looked out on the snow-covered landscape. The moon lorded it over the whole outdoors, bright as a spotlight. "Forget it, you big hunk of cheese. I'm not going to be lured out there no matter how much you shine."

I saw it, then. A shape moving on the mountain. No flowing gown, no flowing hair, just a shape. My heart caught in my throat, and I felt those damn goosebumps again. I closed my eyes and counted to ten, then opened them.

Gone.

"So. I'm seeing shadows. Well, this time I really am going to bed and staying there."

I heard the big old grandfather clock downstairs peal two times and pulled my pillow over my head. Someone once said that this was the hour of the wolf, the time of night when all your anxieties crowd in on you and make the night a scary dark place where there's nothing but you and all your fears.

I closed my eyes, trying to conjure up sugar plums and fairies. It was no use.

My ski suit and warm boots were in the corner of the closet. I might be practicing folly, but at least I wouldn't freeze to death doing it. Tiptoeing downstairs, I carefully avoided the squeaky places. My mother can hear a mousetrap snap in the kitchen.

The flashlight was in its usual place by the back door. The moon was still lighting up the mountain, but I took the light anyway. I might need a weapon. If that was Deirdre up there, she wouldn't have malice toward me, but I couldn't be sure that was who I would find—if I found anybody.

The sound of my boots scrunching in the snow were all I heard as I made my way up to the top of Deirdre's mountain.

Who would be waiting for me? For some reason, my fear dissipated and I moved faster, suddenly eager.

Chapter Fourteen

Christmas 1862

"Andre! Oh, my God, look at you." Deirdre saw the gaunt, ragged man step from the shadows and gasped. She wanted to rush to him and embrace him, but dared not. The hunger in his eyes was not from lack of food, just as the hunger in her heart had never been satisfied since the night she spent in his arms. "How long has it been since you've had anything to eat?"

"Too long, but I don't see any signs of the rest of you eating high on the hog these days."

"Andre, it's dangerous for you to be here, with all your anti-blockade activities. They're saying that Murfreesboro is about to be attacked. That's not far from here. You mustn't be seen here."

"I won't be. I'm used to skulking in low, dark places. When Forts Henry and Donelson went under, those of us still left had to go undercover. They've got control of the Cumberland, Deirdre, total control. The bastards are going to starve us out." Andre's voice was full of weariness and despair. "But there's hope at Murfreesboro. Bragg held 'em off at Shiloh, and look at what we did in Fredericksburg. Trouble is, Grant's smart. He's been replacing generals right and left. Too bad Davis won't listen and get rid of some of the egomaniacs we've got leading our troops."

Deirdre was war-weary, too, but she was too glad to see Andre alive and well to be as downcast as he was. She had been the one running Moncoeur virtually single-handed since Jean-Paul's confinement. The year and eight months since Fort Sumter had matured her far beyond her twenty years. "Poor Jean-Paul is so frustrated that he can't join the rebel forces. He's so brave, Andre. The pain is constant from that bullet close to his spine, but Dr. Hollins says he can't operate with the limited medical supplies he has on hand."

"My brother should have had better sense than to get into an argument with an anti-secesh Kentuckian. People blow real hot over these things. Look at what they did in northern Virginia."

Deirdre was glad Tennessee had remained united, unlike Virginia. She would hate to see brother fighting brother within her adopted state. "You still haven't told me what you're doing here. Andre, you mustn't risk your safety like this. We can take care of Moncoeur."

"I've heard about that, about how you endanger yourself every time you have some whiskey to sell, about how you've kept this place in food and not let it fall apart."

"Well, when Sean left and Jean-Paul was disabled, there wasn't much choice. When the Emancipation Proclamation came out, most of the Negroes ran away, taking the livestock, even the chickens, and I had to figure out some way to help Moncoeur survive." Deirdre thought about the flour and beans that she'd made hard trades for and wished she'd been able to get some salt pork too. Andre was lean as a long drink of water. "Your brother was very generous to me in return. I don't know if you got a chance to talk, but maybe I should tell you what he did."

Andre nodded. "I know. He deeded this mountain to you. Aurelia told me, not knowing how I'd take it. But I take it just fine. After all your loyalty to the family, you deserve to have something all your own when this is over."

Deirdre felt relief. She had heard Gabrielle's reaction to "giving away the whole place to people who aren't even blood" and hadn't been sure that Andre's reaction would be any different. "I guess you know, too, that he deeded the cabin and an acre to Rufus and Prudy so they wouldn't be homeless after the war."

"And I approve wholeheartedly. They've stuck by us through thick and thin. They deserve to be rewarded." Andre stepped forward and nearly fell. Deirdre rushed to catch him.

"You're wounded!" she cried.

"No, no. It's an old wound I caught the first week we skirmished with the gunboats. But don't go away." Andre draped his arm around Deirdre's shoulder and managed to cup her chin, pulling her even closer. "Now tell me about your daughter. Is she getting to be as pretty as her mother?"

She's looking more and more like her real father, Deirdre thought, glad that Andre had not noticed the resemblance. "She's my little darling. If I didn't have Erin, I think I might have given up. She makes me remember that the world still holds innocence and hope, that we will somehow get through this war and go on with our lives."

"Sometimes I have my doubts that the South will even survive, much less go back to what it was. Deirdre, there are some terrible times ahead for all of us. Can't you and I, at this one moment in time, give each other comfort?"

Deirdre felt the warmth of him pressing against her. "There's still Sean," she whispered.

"He joined Forrest's Escort, Aurelia told me. She said he was really upset about Jean-Paul donating the horses to the cavalry and left without a word to anybody."

"He had nothing here," Deirdre said in a low voice. "You know how he felt about me and about Erin. As for going to war, he didn't have any notion of patriotism. He just liked the idea of being more independent."

"And where is Sean in your thoughts right now? Have you given more thought to what I said to you about divorce?"

Deirdre's thoughts held nothing of Sean at this moment. Andre was caressing her shoulder and sending delightful shivers all along her body. "Andre, even if my religion did not prohibit such a thing, I could not do that to my child."

"And what about what you're doing to me? To us?" Andre's voice was low and intense as he continued to make dangerous forays beneath the cloak Deirdre was wearing. "Sean has virtually abandoned you and Erin. How can you remain loyal to him? Any man worth his salt would never have left under these circumstances."

"All the men around here have had to abandon their homes and families. We're better off here than most." She didn't want to think about her husband. Andre did not realize what she had done to Sean. Her deceit had been far worse than anything he had ever done to her. "My father would laugh his head off if he knew I was making and selling whiskey after all the lectures I used to give him about his drinking."

Andre relaxed somewhat. "And what have you heard lately from that old reprobate? Is he still after the pot of gold at the end of the rainbow?"

Deirdre was happy to be on a more neutral subject. "Riley O'Shea is now on his way to being a big landowner. He wrote me that the Homestead Act makes it possible for anybody to stake a claim for just the ten-dollar registration charge—up to a hundred and sixty acres. The catch is that the homesteader has to live on the land and make some improvements."

Andre looked thoughtful. "Imagine. We in the South are being stripped of everything we own and made to suffer for being property owners. Yet, the Federal government is throwing out land right and left to every scalawag who can come up with ten dollars." He added hastily, "I'm not calling your father a scalawag, mind you. It's just the principle of the thing."

"I agree. And my father is something of a scalawag. Now, let me help you back down to the house before you faint. I left Prudy making a big pot of bean soup. There may even be a ham hock with it. Rufus caught an old razorback up on the mountain a couple of days ago."

Andre leaned heavily on Deirdre, his hand curling in the hair at her neck. "You really do have plenty of food?"

Flour and beans, Deirdre thought. She would go out early the next morning and trade a keg for some sweet potatoes she'd heard the Barbers at Holly Gap had banked. Maybe they would have some butter, too. They'd managed to hold on to their milk cow. "Did anybody look underfed to you?"

Andre laughed. "Especially not Gabrielle. She certainly didn't waste any time getting pregnant, did she? I just hope Charles makes it back. He's mighty young for this business." Andre came to a sudden stop.

"What's wrong?" Deirdre was afraid he was about to collapse.

"This." Andre pulled her into his arms. "I can do without food a little longer, but I can't do without you another minute."

The kiss knocked Deirdre off balance. This time it was she who staggered when Andre finally gave her release. "Andre, please don't do this."

"You want me as much as I want you," he said huskily, pulling her back to him. The wiry strength she thought he'd lost was still there. She was very much aware of his virility. "Tell me you don't want this . . . or this . . . or this. . . ." His lips and hands were making her weak with desire. Another moment and she would be lost.

"Andre, I swear I will leave tonight if you don't stop." Deirdre stepped back, breathing hard, her ultimatum issued between breaths. "I will, so help me. You can't just come in here like this and expect me to betray my marriage vows."

"They're as empty as that larder down there that you've been lying to me about."

"But Sean made them in good faith, and I . . ." Deirdre paused, realizing she'd been on the verge of saying too much.

"You what?" Andre said, his eyes narrowed in suspicion. "You didn't make your vows in good faith? Out with it, Deirdre. What are you hiding from me? What were you hiding from Sean when you married him?"

Deirdre's heart pounded. He was getting too close, too close. "You know that he would never have married a girl who worked in Madame Julia's house of ill repute. Sean's hard in some ways, maybe inflexible, but he was right to be offended at my marrying him under a cloak of dishonesty."

Andre looked at Deirdre with her streaming hair and full, proud body and said in a voice that held a catch of regret, "He's a fool to be offended at having you for a wife, no matter what he thought you had done." He winced when he slipped on the snow a little with his injured leg as they started toward the kitchen. "I need some food and I need some rest, but I promise you, Deirdre O'Shea McAfee, you are not finished with me yet. I am not going back into that bloody war out there again without a proper send-off from the woman I crave more than life itself."

It was a threat that made Deirdre shiver from a very different fear than that she'd experienced in some of her adventures peddling whiskey.

Andre slept non-stop for two days, and Deirdre took advantage of the respite from her emotional dilemma to try to shore up the lean larder at Moncoeur.

Though she knew Union soldiers could be roaming the countryside with the Murfreesboro battle still underway, she loaded the wagon up with several kegs of whiskey. Her ever-present bullwhip was at her side when she trundled down the road toward Holly Gap.

Her trade for sweet potatoes and butter was in her mind, so she didn't see the trio of men who stepped from behind a tree until they challenged her horses to stop.

"Miz Deirdre, look out! Them's Union soldiers!" Rufus reached for the big stick he carried in the back of the wagon, but Deirdre stopped him.

"No, Rufus, you let me handle this." She knew her chances of making it through by lashing the horses weren't good. Negotiation was the only way. "Hello. I'm carrying some supplies over to Holly Gap. Mind letting me pass here?"

The leader of the trio stepped up and grinned at Deirdre. "Now aren't you a pretty little rebel. Bet you've got something better than supplies on that wagon."

Deirdre pulled up her thick Irish brogue from somewhere. "Ah, it's right you could be about that, my friend. Tell me where 'tis you're headed and perhaps I can point you out a shortcut."

"We're headed anywhere Rosecrans ain't headed," one of the men said, fiddling with the burlap cover over the kegs in the back of the wagon. "Now what have we got here? Contraband, it looks like, Captain. Maybe we best take charge of this illegal booty."

Deirdre felt a sinking in her heart at the thought of losing her trading goods, but that was better than losing everything else—maybe her life. Deserters were dangerous men. "It's good whiskey. You fellows look like you could use a bit of the spirits. Try a cupful."

Deirdre reached back for the tin cups she always carried for customer sampling, but the three men were ahead of her with their own battered cups.

"And why don't you alight from that wagon, leave your nigger in charge, and come have a swig with us?"

Deirdre shuddered within. She could imagine how three drunken soldiers would act after they had control of a helpless woman. "What if I just leave the keg with you and go on about my business? By the time I come back through here, you'll be feeling real good and I can send Rufus home with the wagon." She fingered the bullwhip at her side, just in case. It would be very little protection against the men with their muskets, but she had no intention of being raped by three drunken soldiers without at least a fight.

The whiskey was already taking effect. The captain looked at her, up and down, then said in a slurred voice. "You have to come back by here all right. We know the roads. And if you don't . . ."

"I think you ought to get a kiss, Captain," one of the other men said, from his lounging position under a tree. "Every deal needs to be sealed with a kiss."

Deirdre's hand tightened on the bull whip as the man leaned upward and she felt the whiff of whiskey-laced breath. "How about that, rebel-girl? You want to give me a kiss?"

"I had the typhus a few weeks back," she said sweetly. "My baby died, along with half the Negroes, but I'll kiss you if you want."

He backed away like a snake had just offered to share his bed with him. "Come to think of it, you and your nigger do look kind of puny." He waved her off. "You come back now. Bring some pretty gals."

"Oh, I will," Deirdre said as she lashed the wagon forward. "I will."

She knew a shortcut through the fields and took the turn back to Moncoeur well out of sight of the Union revelers. She was coming home without sweet potatoes and butter, but at least she and Rufus were unharmed.

Aurelia waited on Andre hand and foot during his recovery from exhaustion, though Deirdre tried her best to get the woman to look after her own frail condition.

"I consider it an honor to be looking after one of our country's heroes," she told Deirdre. "You and Prudy do the bulk of the work around here, and it's time I started pulling my load, too. Besides, Jean-Paul says you're the only one who knows how to massage his legs so they don't hurt as much."

This was said in front of Andre, who was sitting up in bed eating potato-and-ham soup.

Deirdre saw the look on his face and wished Aurelia had not commented on the growing dependency of her husband on Deirdre. "But it's you, 'Relia, who cheers him up with your optimism." Deirdre turned to Andre. "It's true. You sister-in-law never loses her spirit, no matter how bad the news from the battlefields, no matter how hard our struggles to survive here at Moncoeur."

"Aurelia is a remarkable woman, all right. All the women of the South have shown incredible strength and courage. Julia, for instance, was almost as legendary as Captain Morgan during the Nashville evacuation. Why, she put together a cadre of women who provided every kind of assistance to the Confederates who were doing their best to torment Floyd. She and her little band even bashed a few looters on her street." Andre shook his head in disbelief. "Do you know that those Federal troups came into Nashville expecting to have a cheering welcome? Well, they got a reception all right—but not the kind they expected. And the women—those women whose men weren't there to protect them—held their own. I don't think any more Union troups will be invading Southern cities expecting welcoming committees."

"Oh, I'm so glad to hear Julia's safe. I hoped she would come to us, but after hearing what you just said, I know she would never have left her town even if Grant and wild horses had tried dragging her away." Deirdre and Andre exchanged smiles over the woman they both respected so much.

Andre put his bowl down and looked at the two women whose ministrations were like the touch of angels after the harsh horrors he had witnessed. His nightmares of the carnage at Fort Donelson had kept him thrashing and crying out during his sleep, to the point that Aurelia had stayed in the room with him to soothe him in the worst times. "You are both remarkable, too. But I can't stay here lying abed knowing what my comrades are going through. My clothes are all in rags, Aurelia. Do you think you could commandeer a set of Jean-Paul's more durable pants and shirts? A stout pair of boots, too, if he can spare 'em. We wear the same size."

Aurelia left to do as he asked, and Deirdre was left alone with Andre. She knew he was aware she'd been avoiding him and had invented the errand for Aurelia to have her to himself. "You mustn't overstir yourself until you're completely recovered. The war can do without you for a few more days."

"The South needs every man it has and then some," Andre said harshly. "Deirdre, I don't want to talk about the war, I want to store up memories of you that will carry me through. When I leave here, I may not come back—"

"Don't say that!" she cried. "Andre, you must come back to us!" She realized the passion of her words and added weakly, "Your family needs you, Moncoeur needs you. The South will need men like you more than ever after the war is over."

"How about you, Deirdre?" he asked softly, a smile of triumph showing at her uncautious revelation of her emotions. "Do you need me, too?" She could not speak, so he spoke for her. "I think you do. I think you need me more than anyone."

She had to leave before he said more. "It isn't proper for me to be with you like this, Andre, or for you to be talking to me like this. I must go."

"Deirdre." His voice, steely with demand, stopped her at the door. "You can leave this room now, but I will not leave Moncoeur until you've faced up to what lies between you and me. You may as well accept that."

She took the cowardly way out and simply fled.

Gabrielle, though still prone to hold herself above Deirdre as she'd always done, had taken a great liking to little Erin. She appeared at Moncoeur before suppertime, pleading with Deirdre to let her daughter spend the night at Barksdale. "It's still two months till I have my own baby, and it gets so lonely with so many of the servants gone and nothing at all to do but hear ol' gloomy war talk."

Deirdre thought of some of the things that Gabrielle could occupy herself with if she weren't so self-centered, but she forbore to comment. In fact, she was rather pleased that

Gabrielle gave Erin special attention, since Deirdre was always too busy to spend much time on the frivolous activities that little girls liked. "Just don't give her any more of those sweets that you're always eating." Deirdre wasn't sure how Gabrielle still managed to hold on to certain luxuries in these deprived times, but she didn't ask questions. "And make sure she's in bed early and doesn't go out by herself." There were still rumors of marauding Union soldiers who'd detached from their units, and Deirdre wasn't taking chances. Her own trips were getting more and more dangerous. Only by using rough back roads had she been able to visit Donald Bull's store, where she could trade for priceless provisions.

Gabrielle flung her dark curls. "Erin and I get along just fine. We're like blood kin. In fact, she doesn't look one bit like you and Sean." She eyed Deirdre's flaming tresses, then tossed her head again, ruffling little Erin's black locks at the same time. "To tell you the truth, she looks enough like me to be my daughter."

Deirdre was caught between alarm and an urge to laugh. Erin looked enough like Andre to be *his* daughter, but he had not put two and two together. "I consider that a real compliment, Gabrielle. All right, you two. Have fun, but don't stay up late."

Gabrielle went off with Erin's tiny hand in hers. Just as she left the cottage, she turned to Deirdre and said, "By the way, you may call me Gaby now if you wish."

Deirdre laughed out loud. "Why, Gabrielle, I never thought I'd hear you say that. All right, Gaby it is. And while we're at it, why don't you call me DeeDee?"

Erin looked up, from one woman to the other. "Mummy DeeDee and Aunt Gaby."

Deirdre rushed over to give the adorable child a kiss. "And, you, precious, don't need a nickname at all. You'll always be Erin, forever and ever." "Forever and ever" echoed through Deirdre's head, and she had an odd vision of a sad little girl Erin's age but with straight blond hair reaching her shoulders. Deirdre gave her daughter an extra hug and a kiss for the forlorn child in her mind's vision.

Long after Gabrielle and Erin were gone, she sat pondering the peculiar image of the stranger and the poignancy of the child's pull on her heartstrings. She got her worn leather journal out for the first time since the Confederacy had been officially formed and wrote down the date, then entered, "January four, 1863. Today has been a most unsettling day. We are uncertain of a victory at Murfreesboro, and the war grows more terrible with each hour. But Andre is safe and well, and I have hopes of Jean-Paul getting strong again. I have had a strange sense of our future, having been visited by a sad little angel who I know somehow to be part of me. Perhaps the vision was sent from God to reassure us all that there will an end to the war and a new beginning for the South."

She put the journal back in its hiding place. Sean had once caught her at her writing and playfully taken it away from her, pretending to be shocked at what he was reading. That was, of course, before they'd had their rift at Erin's birth. She felt a catch in her throat at how much her husband had changed after learning that his wife had deceived him about her life in Nashville.

"Poor Sean." She had not revealed to him then or later that she knew the secrets in her journal were safe since her husband could not read or write.

Deirdre spent her usual hour before supper sitting with Jean-Paul, who always depended on her not only for the leg massage, but also for news. She had told him about the exploits of the beautiful spy, Pauline Cushman, elaborating a little here and there to make him smile, and ended her visit with a verse or two from the new song, "Old Black Joe," accompanying herself on the banjo she'd learned to play.

When Jean-Paul got very sleepy, he asked if Andre had left yet and Deirdre squeezed his hand, knowing how much he hated lying helpless. "I haven't seen him since lunch, Jean-Paul, but I'm sure he won't leave without saying good-bye."

"He's a good man, a good brother," Jean-Paul said sleepily. "Your husband Sean is a good man, too. I'm just sorry that he didn't understand why I had to give the horses to the Confederate cavalry. If he'd been fighting in Ireland, he might have understood better."

"Don't worry about Sean, Jean-Paul," Deirdre told him. "He may not feel strongly about the cause, but he'll fight his best."

She tucked him in and went to the kitchen to fetch the glass of warm goat's milk that she and Prudy had decided Aurelia ought to have nightly. Aurelia was sleepy, too, sipping at the glass of milk with murmurs of thanks before burrowing down into her bed.

"Make sure that Andre doesn't leave without saying good-bye to me," the older woman said before drifting off. "And make sure he carries food with him when he leaves."

Deirdre tucked Aurelia in, wishing that it were not up to her to deal with Andre's leave-taking from Moncoeur. She had not seen him since noon and was dreading the moment when he sought her out again.

"I will, 'Relia. Don't worry. Have a good night's rest and don't worry about anything."

Deirdre wished someone would say that to her. She worried about everything these days. But when she put on her old nightgown and banked the little fire in her cottage, she tried very hard to put all those worries behind her.

Her hair was standing up in the cold air. She plaited it carefully and put one of Erin's tiny pink ribbons on the end of the braid. There had been no sound of cannon fire tonight. She prayed that the battle at Murfreesboro was over, and that none she knew were among the dead.

Gabrielle had not heard from Charles in the months he'd been gone. Deirdre knelt by her bed and said a prayer for him and for Sean and for all the young men she'd seen march off to war.

Prudy had made her take a mug of goat's milk for herself, saying she needed it as much as Aurelia. Deirdre got up and put the thick mug on the edge of the hearth to warm it. With thoughts of Andre fresh in her mind, it would be hard to go to sleep.

The knock at her door brought her out of her reverie. When she opened the door, there stood the man who'd been at the center of those dreams since he'd come home.

"Deirdre, if you tell me I can't come in, I swear I'll howl at the moon all night until you'll wish you'd never kept me out." He looked at the braid lying delectably over her shoulder, his eyes stopping at the pink ribbon. "My God," he moaned. "You look like an angel standing there looking at me as if I were the devil. Well, the devil take all." He made a surge forward to take her in his arms that all the Union forces could not have stopped.

Andre slipped out of bed so he wouldn't awaken the woman lying next to him with her hands tucked under her cheeks like an adorable sleeping child. The braid had come undone during the night, and Andre smiled to see that the pink ribbon was lying on the pillow.

He could not feel guilty for making Deirdre admit to the passion they shared, though he wished he could have convinced her more thoroughly that she had not been wrong in allowing them this night together. "My darling," he whispered, touching her cheek oh-so-lightly as he stood over the woman he loved, memorizing every detail of her to take with him back into the nightmare of war. "Your courage has been wonderful, not just in what you've done for my family and my home, but in what you gave to me last night. I shall never forget it, even if I'm destined to die for the cause."

Every detail of that glorious night was imprinted on his brain, from the moment he had moved to take Deirdre into his arms to this moment when he stood looking down at her sleeping in peaceful beauty.

She had protested only until his kisses had melted the last barrier to their passion. Andre relived the scene as he brewed a cup of coffee on the dying embers of the fire which had lighted their stairway to ecstasy.

"I feel so wrong about this," Deirdre had whispered as he had carried her in his arms to the fire, his lips at the delicious hollow in her neck. He had ferocious plans for the dimple in her shoulder and had hardly settled her down on the lambskin rug before unbuttoning her nightgown to get to that place from which he had licked champagne all those eons ago.

"How can anything this right be wrong?" he whispered as he removed the last of the flannel barrier. He cupped her breasts and sucked the sweetness from their tips, savoring the tremors that he was causing in the body he held captive with his demands.

She had grown fuller and sweeter with motherhood. Andre drained from her the moans of desire and kept her on the edge of surrender for as long as he could bear it. "Say you want me, Deirdre," he whispered against lips that were swollen from his kisses, as were her nipples against his bare chest. "Say you want me as much as I want you."

She whispered the words he longed for, and with the hoarse cry of a triumphant warrior, Andre parted the secret softness of her and made her his own again.

There was no end to their lovemaking after that. Andre would not have it when Deirdre, embarrassed by the excesses of her response, reached for the flannel nightgown. That unfortunate item was burned to ashes, with Deirdre protesting half-jestingly, half-not. "Bolts of cloth are totally unavailable," she chided Andre. "I have only one other nightgown, and it is not half so sturdy as the one you just burned."

Andre pulled her to him and watched the last licking flames of the flannel sacrifice. "I will buy you a dozen silk ones after the war. That's a promise."

Deirdre looked at the ashes. "Jean-Paul thinks the South will be left at the end with worthless money. He says we won't be able to buy anything."

"And if Jean-Paul says it, it's so," Andre said with a tinge of sarcasm that went over Deirdre's head. She wasn't aware that he had started noticing his brother's special treatment of her. He loved Jean-Paul but still had problems accepting him as master of Moncoeur.

Deirdre said in innocent sincerity, "Your brother is so very smart about everything, and so kind. He hates it so that he's helpless and can't do the things he wants to do."

"And I hate leaving you. Deirdre, when I come back for good, I won't have it, your belonging to another man. You're mine, I don't care if you're married to Sean or to the Pope. You belong to me."

She didn't protest that or anything else as he carried her to the bed and deposited her on it with the greatest gentleness he had shown all night. In her weariness she drifted off, reminding him sleepily at the end that he must not leave without saying good-bye to Aurelia.

Andre thought of that now as he watched the sun coming up and sipped his warmed-over coffee. "I'll say goodbye to Aurelia, darling Deirdre, but it's you who keeps my heart safe at Moncoeur after I leave." He leaned over to kiss the sweet mouth parted in sleep. "I will be back to reclaim that heart and everything that goes with it."

When he left the cottage, he did not see the man watching from behind the cherry laurel hedges that lined the entrance to Deirdre's little house. He did hear the skinny cock that was all that was left of the poultry stock at Moncoeur, and he laughed out loud. "That's it, Barnaby. Crow in the dawn. The South's not done yet, and you need to tell the world."

He went in to tell Aurelia good-bye, hoping she wasn't aware that his bed had been unslept-in the night before.

Deirdre sat up in bed with a cry at the dark shape that had appeared out of nowhere. She was so deep in sleep when she was awakened by the man at the foot of the spool bed that she didn't remember to cover her nakedness.

"Look at you," Sean said disgustedly. "Lying here after a man's left, like the slut you were in Nashville when I met you." He jerked the covers off her, glaring down at her body. "The child's not even around. Did you give her away to somebody so you could turn this place into another brothel?"

Deirdre pulled on the old robe that she'd left on a chair and faced her husband. There was no use trying to justify herself. She didn't try. Then she forgot herself and her untenable situation when she saw the shape Sean was in. He was gaunt, drawn, hungry-looking, and his blue eyes blazed out with bitterness. But that was not the worst of it.

He was missing a leg. The cloth-wrapped stick that served as his cane was stained with dirt and had obviously carried him limping for many a mile.

"Oh, Sean! Your leg—how long, when did it happen? Let me help you." She moved to touch him in sympathy, but he pushed her away.

"I've lived without this leg since one of Johnston's soldiers shot it off. I've lived without a wife for longer than that, and I'll tell you right off that one's a lot more painful than the other."

"Let me get you something to eat. Oh, Sean, please don't look at me like that! I've been a good wife to you, I swear I have, but I thought you were never coming back. I was afraid you were . . ."

"Dead?" Sean hunched himself awkwardly over to the fire and sat in the wooden rocker, taking the torn rags off his one good foot. "I've come close several times, all right. Forrest is reckless with his raids, doesn't care about his men. I saw people like him in the rebellion back in Ireland. They want to make a name for themselves, no matter who gets hurt in the meantime." He leaned his head back, the stubble of his beard catching the last light of the fire. "You mentioned food."

She got him what there was, the last of the bean and ham-fat soup that they were stretching out until she could make it through for more supplies.

He fell asleep with the empty bowl in his hand. When she tried to get him up, his eyes flared in the blankness of dreaming about horrors that she could not imagine. "My horse! It's crippled, like me. I've got to shoot it, got to put it out of its agony. Oh, God! Somebody shoot me! Damn you, shoot me! Can't you see? I'm not a man anymore, I'm not even half a man!"

Deirdre felt the tears streaming down her cheeks as she managed, with a supreme effort, to help her husband into bed. She covered him up and felt the guilt and pity overflowing into tears. "I'm so sorry, Sean," she whispered, touching the red stubble on his chin and wishing that she loved him as he deserved to be loved. "I'm so sorry."

She tucked the quilt in over his missing leg and his one good one and wept inconsolably. Of all the casualties she had seen and heard of, this one was somehow the saddest. Sean McAfee had not even believed in the cause, had not ever called himself a Southerner, had not had his heart in any of this.

Yet here he was left with a stump for a leg, a fine young Irishman whose life had turned from youthful ambition and hope into one of tragedy.

Deirdre did not creep in beside him, knowing that was not what Sean would want. She stoked the fire so he would be warm and made herself as comfortable as she could in the hard rocking chair.

She thought about the six kegs of whiskey that she'd saved to trade for hard-to-get essentials during the winter. She would use that booty for something else, for something special for the husband whom she had so betrayed.

Sean slept soundly, with only a few fitful murmurs about his war memories. Deirdre, hearing these and having her own memories, slept not at all.

Chapter Fifteen

New Year's 1989

I awoke in my bed, not knowing how I had gotten there. The dream I was having of Sean riding the new black mare that Deirdre had bought him dissipated with the tap on my door. I was again in my own world at Moncoeur.

It was Azalea, bringing me coffee and juice and her special homemade coffeecake. Azalea looks on breakfast in bed as the lowest form of human laziness, so I knew she must be pretty worried about me.

"Merry Christmas!" I caroled.

Azalea looked at me as though I'd lost my mind. "What's the matter with you, girl? This here's the last day of December. And if you ask me what you been doing since Christmas

Eve, I'll tell you right fast that you been mopin' around on that mountain."

I gave her an astonished look.

"Chile, you got to watch yo'self. Mistuh Devereux, he been noticing how different you is these days since your pore sistuh passed. He axed your mother how them treatments with that doctor are doin', had she noticed any good comin' of 'em."

I was not alarmed. Daddy has always expected full value for his dollar, and my psychiatry sessions with Dr. Velkoff were not excluded from this practical concern. "I'll have to get ol' Siggy to send him a report card with all 'A's. Azalea, has anyone called?"

"You mean from this planet or from the one you stay off on half the time?" She sniffed. "A whole bunch of folks, but I ain't puttin' 'em on to you when you goin' off in a daze ever' time I look at you lately."

She had put my messages under my coffee pot. I didn't see anything exciting except a note to call Harrison. I thought about our last time together and smiled. "When did Harrison call? He never did give me my Christmas present."

"He said to be sho' and tell you he was off to Georgia for Christmas Day through New Year's Eve but to be sho' and save him the first kiss. He havin' a party at his place and says you be there or else. I tol' him I don't much like you bein' out on the road with all the drunks, but he said he would see to it that you wasn't."

My smile got wider at that. I could pretty

well figure out how he planned to keep me off the road. "Did he say why he was going to Georgia?" I'd never heard Harrison mention having relatives that far down South.

"Nope, and I didn't ax since it ain't none of my business."

I drank the rest of my coffee and dreamed a little about the life I had left behind. Would Andre come back and force Deirdre to leave Sean? Would Andre realize that Erin was his child and use that to make Deirdre face up to their love for each other? I felt sorry for Sean, but I hoped that Deirdre would not remain in the marriage that had become unbearable with Sean's new bitterness.

My morning ride on Gambler was a somber one. All I could think about in the cold crisp morning was how Deirdre had sacrificed half a wagonload of her precious whiskey to get her husband a fine horse.

Gambler stumbled on a rock at the little cemetery we had reached and I pulled him up. "Whoa, fellow. This is far enough. I don't want you breaking a leg like Sean's horse when he rode with Forrest."

I got down and left Gambler happily munching on grass while I wandered over to the newest tombstones—my sister's and Royce's. I should have brought some pretty flowers, I thought tardily, as I walked around the graves.

Someone had beat me to it. On Celeste's stone rested a huge bouquet of yellow roses, Celeste's favorite flower.

"Daddy brought them, of course," I told myself without conviction. Our father has always lambasted the florist industry for commercializing every event and occasion for their own gain. He never sends flowers to anyone.

I stood there for a few quiet moments, pondering. The answer simply would not come. I could not think of anyone who was still grieving over my sister enough to make a secret visit to her grave to bring her favorite flowers.

That was a sad thought for such a beautiful day. I wandered over to the old graves in the cemetery and found Deirdre's tombstone with its simple inscription lifted from Coleridge: *Sleep, thou art a gentle thing.* "Do you really lie here?" I whispered. "You don't feel dead somehow, and I still can't make any sense of any of this. Why am I reliving parts of your life?"

The wind whistling through the willow tree was my only answer, and I went back to Gambler to finish my ride. Cemeteries, especially the old family ones, keep the dead's secrets from the living—which is probably best for all of us.

Azalea had a message from Harrison when I got back home. "He say to call him right away, and he ain't takin' no excuses for you not being at his whing-ding tonight."

I got a cup of Luzianne from the pot that Azalea keeps on the stove all day long and sprawled out at the kitchen table. "Azalea, what do you think about Harrison?" I trust that woman's instincts more than anybody else's in the world, and I remember how she tried to warn me about Royce being one of those men "who can hurt a body." "You've always shot your mouth off about every guy I've ever gone out with and I have yet to hear you say one word about Harrison, good or bad."

"That's 'cause I still ain't made up my mind about that dude. It's that funny hair he's got. I don't set much store by the menfolks wearin' pigtails."

I laughed. "Oh, come on. You're not one to go by physical appearance. Besides, I like Harrison's ponytail. Tell me what you really think about him."

Azalea sat down opposite me and pulled out her Luckies, offering me one without thinking. "I think," she said puffing away, "that he suits you better'n anybody I seen you with. Way he looks at you when you ain't lookin' . . ." Azalea shook her head. "That boy would eat you up with a warm spoon even when you wasn't givin' him the time o' day."

I blushed. "Azalea!"

"Don't you give me none of that cow dooky. I know you ain't no virgin, Fable Devereux! I been knowin' what you was up to just about every minute of your life, and I ain't fooled by that innocent act you pull on your daddy."

I finished up my Luzianne real fast because once Azalea gets on my case about something, she turns me every which way but loose. "You think my mama would mind if I borrowed that snappy new jumpsuit she bought last week and wouldn't wear 'cause Daddy said it was too lowcut?"

"I think you axing for trouble wearin' somethin' that has your boobies hangin' out anytime, but don't pay no 'tention to this ole nigger." Azalea grinned at me, and I realized she'd been putting me on all night. "Wear your mama's pretty outfit and don't call me to come get you outta jail."

I gave her a big hug. Azalea is probably the only reason I'm not in the loony bin.

"Don't be too impressed by the fact that everybody who is anybody is here tonight," Harrison told me when I climbed the stairs to the deck where stout-hearted guests were braving the cold to admire his view. "Wow, look at you." Harrison took my wrap and eyed my mother's jumpsuit in a way that made me feel that maybe I hadn't zipped everything up. Actually, it wasn't the jumpsuit he was looking at but the parts it didn't quite cover.

"Down, boy," I said, feeling festive already. "How was Georgia—still on your mind?"

Harrison sort of lobbed that one. I decided that maybe I'd better find out a little more about this man's past before he became too important a part of my present. Later, though. Everybody started coming up and wanting to hear about what I was planning now that I had another sure hit coming up on the charts.

"What's next, Fabe?" I got a kiss from Andy Dickens, who can take a banjo and play Handel's *Messiah.* "Let's duet together, make Dolly and Kenny cry in their beer."

"I'd like that. But I think we're more Loretta and Conway. Hey, want to get me some of that champagne?"

I didn't have another free moment after that, and by the time we counted down the minutes to the New Year and toasted and ate the black-eyed peas and hog jowl that Harrison had ready for us, I was back in the real world. Deirdre would not have fitted in here, I thought at one point. That was kind of a sad thought. Did that mean that my world didn't hold fast to the Southern, American values that she had adopted so painfully?

"Hey, you're too serious. A beautiful woman cannot possibly be that serious on New Year's Eve." I smiled at the inebriated man who breathed heavily into my ear and hoped he was not the new executive at my recording company. If he wasn't, I planned to get rid of him *tout de suite.* I can't stand men who glue themselves to women they don't know on New Year's Eve just so they can get a big wet smacky-mouth at midnight.

"Are you a singer?" I asked sweetly.

"No. Guess again." He was being cute.

"You work at B.M.A.?"

"Uh-uh, but I know Frances Preston."

Ha, I'll just bet you do. "That doesn't count. Frances knows everybody in Music City and isn't one bit stuck up. Okay. I give up. What are you doing in Nashville?"

Mr. Bad Breath gave me another whiff. "I came down from Ohio to Grand Ole Opry. I'm not even supposed to be at this party, but I saw the lights and cars. I'm staying at the Rodeway not far off and I thought, what the hell."

"Gatecrasher, huh? I wouldn't be broadcasting the fact that you came here uninvited. See that man over there standing by the bar, the guy that looks like Hulk Hogan, only twenty years younger?" I pointed to Sonny Robison, who is a piano player and weight-lifter and one of the gentlest men I've ever known. "He's the bouncer for the Purple Poodle in Printer's Alley and is very likely to throw you out." My nose grew an inch.

The jerk went for it and turned as pale as his turtleneck sweater. Real country music lovers do not wear turtlenecks. I love all my fans and the folks who sincerely appreciate and enjoy my kind of singing. People who come to Nashville for their beloved country music are the salt of the earth, for the most part, but, boy, are there some jerks! This was one of the latter, and I was very glad to see him leave after I'd pointed out the "bouncer" to him.

"Why don't these people go home so I can give you your Christmas present?" Harrison looked very sexy in a tailored white silk shirt and stonewashed jeans. "Why don't they go home, period? Guy Lombardo is dead, for God's sake. These people should go home to their loved ones. I want very much to be alone with you. You are in serious trouble for wearing that jumpsuit. I've had all night to figure out how it works."

"Well, aren't you the negligent host, ogling your female guests while you're supposed to be dispensing your famous Southern hospitality." I was secretly pleased that Harrison had been keeping tabs on me all evening. There are plenty of women who've tried to snag this man. He's eluded more stars and demi-stars than I could count—or so the gossip goes.

"Ogling only one female guest. Look, find yourself a cozy place in front of the fire while I do some serious herding out of these bums. Designated drivers are all in place. I sure as hell don't want anybody getting a bad start to the New Year."

He was pretty good at clearing the room. My fresh glass of champagne was only half-gone when Harrison came over to report that the last guest had been wished Happy New Year. "Now for that kiss. I couldn't get through to you when the clock struck twelve."

I was very glad to oblige. Harrison really knows his stuff when it comes to making love to a woman. For one thing, he knows how much we like to be kissed. Most men don't bother with serious kissing after they've been to bed with a woman. Harrison does. His kisses are long and slow, and they drive me totally wild. For another thing, he doesn't do things that most men do, like go immediately for the erotic parts. He makes every part of me feel desired and special—even the dimple on my shoulder.

We had just gotten down to some serious smooching on the sofa when the doorbell rang.

Harrison sat up and cursed soundly. "Hell's bells, if some drunk bastard has run off the road, I'll send him to a motel for the night." He went to the door and let in Laney Ford.

"Sorry, Harrison, for coming by so late. Just wanted you to know I watched out for all your party guests like you asked, made sure they got to the main road. Them one-way railroad tunnels have caused some mighty bad accidents."

Harrison was still a bit irritated, though he was polite. "Well, I appreciate your coming by to tell me that, Laney, but it's mighty late and I'm sure your wife and kids would like to have their daddy home tonight, so . . ."

Laney looked over at me. "Evenin', Miss Fable. Fact is, I wouldn't've come up here, 'cept I saw your car was still out front. I need to talk to you kind of serious."

Harrison looked alarmed. "Laney, nothing's happened to her folks or anything like that?" When the deputy shook his head, Harrison conceded, "Well, whatever it is, I gather you want it to be private. I'll make us some coffee while you two visit."

"Thanks, Harrison. Some coffee would sure hit the spot." The deputy waited till Harrison had left for the kitchen before coming over and sitting on the ottoman by the fire, twisting his hat in his hand as he looked at me worriedly. "I don't know what this is all about, Miss Fable, I just know there's something going on and it involves you."

I leaned forward. "Does this have something to do with the man following me, with the break-in at my sister's house?"

Laney nodded. "The F.B.I.'s in on it now. I got a good buddy in Miami I go fishin' with down in the Keys. He wasn't supposed to tell me anything since the whole thing's under strict wraps, but he's done me favors before, like I have him."

"The F.B.I. But why, Laney? Is that who's been following me? And if it is, why? What have I got to do with anything that could possibly involve the F.B.I.?"

"I don't know all the details, but my buddy says they think you can lead 'em to something they want real bad. And it's not just the Bureau involved. There's somebody else after the same things the Fed boys are after."

"You didn't answer my question, though. Am I being followed by the F.B.I.?"

Laney looked at me real sharp and then looked quickly away. "I shouldn't be telling you any of this, Miss Fable. I could lose my job."

"You won't lose your job because of me, Laney. Dammit, I need to know. Is it the F.B.I. following me? Are they the ones who were in the house that night?"

"They been following you all right, Miss Fable," Laney told me with a nervous look at the door to the kitchen. "But what's funny about the whole thing is that there's somebody else watching you, too. It was in the F.B.I. secret file my buddy got to see. You been having somebody else tail you since the night your sister and brother-in-law got blowed up in that boat."

I was aghast. What on earth did I have to do with the unsavory business Royce had apparently fled years before he came to Tennessee? "Who? Who besides the F.B.I. is tailing me? And why, for God's sake?"

"Miss Fable, I swear if you let it out that I told you this, I'd be nailed to the closest barn door."

I crossed my arms over my chest. "Cross my heart and hope to die. Go on."

"It seems like there was some kind of book your brother-in-law got hold of when he was working for the Louisiana Bureau. That book was gonna be used to convict these high-ups that they was after. But when your brother-in-law disappeared 'fore he come down here, so did the book. Folks want it back—both sides—real bad."

"Is that why they killed my sister and her husband? Because they couldn't get the book from them?" That didn't make any sense. Why would they blow them up, whoever "they" were, before the book was back safe in their possession?

"My buddy thinks McColl was playing both sides against the other, that he let both parties think he was ready to deal. He had a bank account in the Cayman Islands that you wouldn't believe. I think he got a bunch of money from both sides, promising delivery when he went down to Florida. I think he pulled off a shell game."

"But why was he killed? They didn't have the book, you say. How would it profit either side to blow up the boat with my sister and Royce and possibly the very thing they wanted most?"

"Miss Fable, I don't know how you gonna take this, her being your sister and all and you with all the grief, but they got a theory down there that's crazy as all get-out."

I wondered if all this was part of another dream. Celeste had never been involved in anything more nefarious than giving a pageant judge an extra peek at her cleavage. "Crazy or not, I want to hear it."

He told me what his friend had related to him, and I sat listening in total shock, trying to make sense of it all. When he'd finished, I couldn't say anything in response because my mind was juggling everything and putting some pieces in place.

"Laney scooted out of here mighty fast after drinking his coffee. Did you have a good talk?"

"Let's call it interesting. Harrison, if this next year shapes up to be anything like the past one, I may give up New Year's Eve."

He grimaced. "I don't like the thought of you not being with me when the next one rolls around. Hey, we got interrupted in something very important." He kissed the tip of my ear and got up to stoke the fire. "But there's all night for that. Right now, I want to give you your present."

I couldn't believe it when I unwrapped the large package. "Harrison," I breathed, rubbing my hand over the old stone jug that had an 1862 date and Deirdre's name on it. "Where in the world did you find it? I thought all the jugs had been lost or broken. I can't believe you're giving me one of Deirdre's original Whiskey Mountain jugs full of the real stuff."

"I heard about this antique dealer down in Georgia. That's where I was, you know. I stayed with some friends who raise ostriches now, which brings me to my second present for you." He gave me a large box and I squealed in delight to find a pair of handmade ostrich-skin boots.

"They're gorgeous!" I hugged him and then made him sit tight while I went to get my gift for him.

Harrison loved the set of silver mint julep cups that had the name and date of every hit song, with the performer's signature, that he'd had anything to do with. Some of mine were included in the set, and he was especially thrilled about those.

"Fable, you make me look like a piker. These are wonderful."

"So is this," I said, touching the jug that had been one of Deirdre's first whiskey products. "I can't believe you went to all that trouble.

As for the boots . . ." I rubbed the soft skin of the boots. "These are the best boots I've ever owned. Thank you."

The kiss we shared was full of holiday festivity, but then it changed to something more serious.

Harrison put on a CD of slow dance music, including some recorded by his favorite, the late "Gentleman" Jim Reeves, and we moved together with that close fit that we seem to have together in everything we do.

I liked the hunched-up muscles under his shirt and the way he played with the hair on my neck. I thought about Deirdre and wished she and Andre could be here tonight, dancing together cheek to cheek like Harrison and I were.

"You're a thousand miles off again," Harrison whispered in my ear. "I want you here with me tonight, Deirdre."

I jerked away, not believing what he had just said. "Harrison, what did you just call me?"

He didn't believe it, even when I swore to him that he had called me by the name of my long-gone grandmother. "That's crazy. I'm not living your fantasies. I don't know that woman, it's you I'm after."

That night, in Harrison's arms, I had the strongest feeling that it would not be long now before Deirdre revealed her purpose to me.

I was not wrong. While I lay in Harrison's arms, the moonlight streaming over us in a bed rumpled by the excesses of our passion,

I made the transition back again to Deirdre's world.

Deirdre woke in Andre's arms, her mind filled with anxiety about the war. The Battle of Franklin in November had been a disaster under General Hood, and the Battle of Nashville was about to begin. Would it bring devastation or new hope to her adopted home?

She and Andre went up on the mountain that day to watch the seige, taking comfort in each other's arms as the horrible bursts of fire from the satanic Gatling gun and other gunfire lit up the sky. "Oh, Andre, we can never be a country again, after all this! Atlanta was burned, and Sherman's march to the sea has ruined everything in his path. And now, look at this! Oh, I pray that Julia got out in time."

"Julia's a survivor," Andre said grimly, his arm tightening around her.

They were in a close embrace when Sean burst up on his mare, Shenandoah. Andre and Deirdre split apart guiltily as Sean slid off his mount, his eyes blazing as he lashed out at them. "You! Look at you! The moment my back is turned, you're all over him. He comes home with a wound that's nothing, and you can't stop fawning over him, you and Aurelia and all the rest of the lot. Look at me! Look at this!" Sean shook his stump of a leg at them, holding on to his horse and trembling with rage. "I came up here to show you that I'm still a man. I honestly thought you would be happy to see that I can still do what a man does. . . ."

"Sean, please don't take it wrong, what you saw here. Don't you realize, don't you know, can't you hear it? They're destroying Nashville! Look at it!" Deirdre swept her arm out over the glowing horizon where sunset did not hold the gentle rays of the sun but was afire with battle. "Sean, don't be against us. You're a Southerner, too, now; you've fought and paid dearly. Stand with us! Help us weep for the South that is almost gone!"

Sean got back on his horse and glared down at them, his eyes filled with bitterness and contempt. "You'll pay for this, Devereux," he said hoarsely. "By everything that's Irish in me, and that's what my blood still is, by God, you will pay."

Deirdre called after him, but he would not stay, wheeling his horse around and going down the mountain at a breakneck speed.

"I'm afraid, Andre," Deirdre whispered after Sean had gone. "He hates you, so. I'm afraid for you."

Andre pulled her closer into his arms and buried his chin in her hair, watching the glow of battle over her head. He silently cursed Hood and Pillow, who had let their egos command rather than their good sense. He cursed the circumstances that had brought his beloved South to this terrible point, and he cursed the horrors of war that had reduced good men like Sean McAfee into bitter shells of humanity. "Don't be afraid, my darling. Somehow, we will survive."

"Oh, Andre, I'm so afraid for you! I saw Sean's face when he left here. He knows you're an anti-blockade hero. You've got to get away, hide!"

"If I do, they'll take it out on my family, probably burn down Moncoeur. No, my darling, I can take care of myself." He kissed her long and deeply. "It's you who must be careful. They mustn't catch you up here with me when they come for me." Andre buried his face in Deirdre's hair, closing his eyes against the thought of being separated from her for the duration of this war. "Promise me," he whispered, "Promise you'll be here waiting when I get back. The nightmare won't last forever; the South will be a place where we can make a life together someday. Promise."

"I promise," Deirdre whispered back, her tears staining his face as well as hers. "Oh, Andre, there's still time. You can run, you can escape. I can't bear it, thinking of you in prison!"

"I can bear it if I know you'll be here waiting for me when I get out. Now, you must leave. Hide, Deirdre, until I'm gone. No matter what happens, don't show yourself. Sean isn't himself, but he won't have betrayed you—I know him that well. Now hide, quickly! They mustn't find you here with me." Andre brushed her hair from her face and kissed her passionately, then pushed her from him as the crack of underbrush marked the approach of the enemy. "Now!" he hissed.

She whispered brokenly, "I love you!" before she secreted herself behind the large shield of brush and scrunched down in fear as the Union soldiers loudly accosted the lone Confederate awaiting them.

She put her hands over her ears and wept silently as she heard Andre calmly state his military rank and unit. She cringed when she heard the sharpness of the Union captain's voice as he made the arrest of "a known war criminal and enemy of the Union."

She longed to catch one last sight of her beloved as she heard them order him to march ahead of them back down to a waiting envoy, but knew that she could not risk it. Moncoeur depended on her. She must keep it safe until Andre's return.

She waited until it was almost dark before making her way down the mountain, her heart heavy with the news she must bear to Aurelia and Jean-Paul.

Her bitterness toward Sean was partially toward herself. If she had loved him as he deserved, none of this would have happened.

But there was no use berating herself about something that could never be—then or now. Her heart belonged to Andre Devereux forevermore, and she would pray from now to the war's end for his safe return.

Chapter Sixteen

Deirdre had always known that Aurelia was deeply in love with Andre, but she never allowed that knowledge to diminish her affection or respect for the older woman.

Her heart was heavy with her own grief about the horrors of prison in store for the man she loved. She dreaded telling Aurelia about Andre's fate and prayed for the courage to be strong for her friend even as her own heart ached. Maybe, now, Aurelia could freely vent her pent-up feelings for the man they both loved. They could hold each other up.

Deirdre felt the weight of being the sad messenger as she entered Aurelia's bedroom and was greeted with an eager smile. "*Chérie?* Is there news?" The smile faded as Deirdre approached the bed, her face still streaked with tears. "Oh, mon Dieu, how you look . . . it can only mean . . . he's dead! You've had news of Andre and he's dead!" Aurelia's wail of anguish came straight from the heart.

Deirdre's description of Andre's capture was heard in mournful silence. At the end of it, both women burst into tears and held each other tightly, not having to give words to their feelings of bereavement, nor their mutual sympathy. The tears said all that needed to be said.

Deirdre held the frail body of her friend as Aurelia rocked back and forth in tearing grief, her own grief contained with the secret that Aurelia must never know—that Deirdre and Andre had made a pact of the heart that could never be broken, not even by years apart while Andre suffered in prison.

She held Aurelia until the racking sobs finally subsided and the woman fell into exhausted slumber. When Gabrielle came into the room, Deirdre held her fingers to her lips. "Shh, don't wake her. I'll meet you downstairs."

Gabrielle was in hysterics by the time Deirdre joined her. "Oh, Dee-Dee, how could Sean do such a thing? Now he's run off and there's no one left to protect us." Gabrielle's wail was on par with that of a child Erin's age and Deirdre realized with despair that it was up to her to keep Moncoeur from disintegrating into helpless mourning. Her own sorrow must await its turn, she realized with sadness.

"There, there. We'll have to protect ourselves, and that means you must be strong. It's up to us, Gaby, to try to keep Moncoeur from more harm. You say Sean's fled." Deirdre was glad of that. She would not have been able to see her husband without showing her hatred for his treachery. "Where's Rufus?"

Gabrielle sniffled into Deirdre's shoulder. "He said he was trying to hide what whiskey and food we've got left."

"Good." Deirdre patted the girl's shoulder. "I told Prudy and Letitia to keep Erin with them every minute and to hide in the storm cellar if they heard anything at all. We've come this far, Gaby. We'll make it somehow."

Gabrielle started crying all over again. She knew as Deirdre did that there had been horrible incidents all over the county involving deserters and marauding looters. "Oh, DeeDee, what will we do? One of Colonel Barksdale's nigras came back from Nashville last night and said it's just awful over there. He said that Hood's lost over six thousand men, a slew of generals amongst 'em. He said there are trenches full of dead soldiers, mostly ours, some of 'em still standing up, propped up by the other dead ones." Gabrielle's sobs got louder. "What if Charles is with them? What will his little son say when I tell him his daddy will never even lay eyes on him?"

"You'll tell him like all the other brave women in the South are telling their children every day that his daddy died with honor, that he died fighting for what he believed in. But don't give up on Charles coming home, Gaby. I have a feeling he will. He'll come home to you when the war's over, I just know it." Deirdre hugged the girl tightly, her words more confident than her heart. She knew that after the terrible battles of Franklin and Atlanta, after this battle in nearby Nashville where the Gatling gun had spewed death like a machine made in hell, the South was lost. "Now, we must think. It's up to you and me right now. Did you bring your father-in-law's gun, the one that you said he had hidden away at Barksdale?" Sean had taken the guns from Jean-Paul's study when he came back down off the mountain in a fury, determined to turn Andre in. Except for the pistol Gabrielle had brought, Moncoeur had no firearms.

Gabrielle lifted her head from Deirdre's shoulder. "It's up in Aurelia's bedroom. I took it out of my pocket when we were helping her into bed."

The sound of something or someone on the veranda made the two women freeze in terror. "What was that?" Gabrielle clutched Deirdre fearfully. "I heard something."

"Shh. Don't make a sound." Deirdre's heart was pounding so hard she could barely hear her own whisper above it. "Here, help me move this. Quickly." They tugged at the heavy oak halltree in the foyer, trying to move it against the door, which was rattling by now.

It wouldn't budge. Deirdre closed her eyes and said a quick prayer, then tried again, but it was no use.

"Go upstairs, Gaby. Run! Get the pistol and hide until you get a good shot. I'll try to hold them." Deirdre leaned her back against the bulging door. "Hurry! Hurry!"

She felt the door give way and was thrust across the room as three men forced their way in. Gabrielle sank in paralyzed fear onto the bottom stair, and seeing the men, started screaming hysterically. One of the men ran over to her and picked her up like a sack of meal, putting his rough hand over her mouth. "It's like we heard on the way out of Nashville. They ain't anybody on these places but women and a few old niggers." Gabrielle squirmed and gave out muffled cries, and the Union deserter grinned at her, dodging her flailing hands and laughing when she tried to bite him. "Look at you, sweetheart, trying to get away from old Fred. You don't want to do that—or you won't after we've gotten a little better acquainted. Bet you ain't had a man since Johnny went marching off. Well, you got one now."

Deirdre kept her eyes on one of the other men, who appeared to be the leader of this pack of deserters. He was in the dining room, checking the drawers in the buffet for silver, sweeping off dishes to the floor, looking for anything valuable. She shifted her eye to the heavy brass candlestick on the table in the foyer.

When Gabrielle squealed and struggled with her captor, who was trying to kiss her and open her bodice, Deirdre picked up the candlestick and moved swiftly. "Let her go," she hissed. When he continued pawing at the girl, Deirdre brought the weighty candlestick down on the man's head. Gabrielle fell free of him as the man collapsed in a pool of blood.

Deirdre whirled around to see the leader standing there, looking from the injured, moaning Fred to her, murder in his eyes as he saw her with the bloodied candlestick.

"Well, now you've done it, you little rebel bitch." He pulled out his pistol and started toward her, fury all over his grimy, bearded face. Deirdre backed away, girding herself for the bullet she expected to tear through her flesh at any moment.

But then he stopped, and worse than the fear of being shot was the sight of the slow, terrible grin that came to his lips. "Naw, that'd be too quick, too easy. I'll probably shoot you later for what you done to my friend, but for right now I'm gonna teach you a lesson or two about how to treat a man." He started toward her again, moving in slow, snake-like moves. "Now just put that candlestick down real easy and I'll put my gun away. See?" He stuck his pistol in his belt and hitched up his filthy pants. "We better have our fun 'fore ole Fred over there wakes up and gets real mad about what you done to 'im. That's it, put it down, real slow and easy-like."

Deirdre's hand trembled as she dropped the candlestick with a clatter. Her eyes darted around for another weapon, one he wouldn't see, but there was none. "Don't . . . don't come another step closer."

"Is this too close?" the man asked, towering over her and putting his hand on her throat. As Deirdre stood frozen stiff, he slid his big hand down, down, over her shoulder, down her arm, over to her breast. Then with a swift, fierce move, he ripped the front of her bodice down to her waist. "How about this? Too close?"

Deirdre gave a sharp cry, and the third man, who'd stayed out front to guard the door, stepped in and ogled her, giggling hysterically. "Shut up, Heck," Deirdre's captor said menacingly. "Get back out and watch for rebs. They don't take kindly to us messing with their womenfolks, and I'd just as soon not get a bullet in my back."

Deirdre stayed rigid as her captor buried his stubbly face in her chemise and she held her breath when the stench of sour hair and skin rose to her nostrils. The pawing at her body grew more fevered, and Deirdre prayed that she would not faint. If she were unconscious, she would not be able to fight him off.

Just as he had her pinned, helpless, to the wall, about to take her down to the floor, a voice spoke from the top of the staircase. "Let go of her, you filthy bastard." Gabrielle rose to her knees, Deirdre's and her tormentor's eyes turned upward to where Aurelia stood, her face as pale as her filmy white peignoir, Colonel Barksdale's mean-looking pistol in her hand.

"I said, let her go." Aurelia moved slowly down the stairs, her usually fragile-looking body as straight and unafraid as an avenging angel's. "Get his gun, Deirdre."

Deirdre wasted no time taking the man's pistol. "There's another man outside the door," she whispered. "But I don't think he's armed."

"We'll see about him later." As Aurelia moved toward her, around Gabrielle, Deirdre saw a movement and screamed, " 'Relia, watch out for the man on the floor!"

Then she was too occupied with her own danger to see what happened next. Her tormentor was grappling with her, and she managed to point his gun right at his big belly. Then, closing her eyes, she pulled the trigger.

There was a deafening echo. Deirdre felt heavy hands grabbing at her throat, then sliding down her arms, then slipping away. Deirdre opened her eyes and saw the man at her feet and started sobbing. "I killed him. Oh, God, Aurelia, I killed a man."

Gabrielle pointed out the front door. "Look! The other man's running away."

"Let him go," Deirdre said contemptuously. "He's a coward like the rest of them." Under ordinary circumstances, she would have laughed to see the fleeing deserter jumping fences and leaping over streams and falling down and getting up and running as fast as he could. But these were not ordinary circumstances. "Check those other two, Gaby. Make sure they're both dead. If either one so much as twitches an eyelid, shoot him between the eyes." Deirdre went over to where Aurelia had slumped onto the staircase. The poor dear had probably fainted from all this horror, she thought tenderly.

"They're both dead as doornails," Gabrielle said with uncompassionate satisfaction. "Is Aunt Aurelia okay?" She knelt beside Deirdre. "She's a good shot. She shot that animal that attacked me right in the neck."

Deirdre moved Aurelia's hand from her chest and saw the spreading crimson and said with a catch in her voice. "He was a good shot, too. Gaby, she's been shot. Oh, God. Oh, 'Relia, you were so brave! Please don't leave us! Gaby, quickly, go get help. Quickly!"

Aurelia held Gabrielle's wrist, her eyelids fluttering as she tried to speak. "No. It's too late. Don't go. Stay with me. We got them, didn't we?"

"We sure did. Those are some dead Yankees, thanks to you."

"Wonder what Andre will say about all this?" Aurelia's face gained a bright, almost happy look. "He won't believe it, will he, when you tell him I actually shot a gun."

Deirdre squeezed one hand, Gabrielle the other. Both women's tears dripped down their faces, but Aurelia's eyes were closed again and she was smiling even more happily. "He'll believe, just as we do, that you're the bravest, most courageous, wonderful woman that ever lived."

"I hear his voice out there. I thought he was in prison, DeeDee. Is that really Andre, come home to Moncoeur?" Aurelia tried, but could not rise. Deirdre gave a warning look to Gabrielle, who had started to sniffle loudly.

"I believe it is Andre come home again. Oh, 'Relia, won't we have a wonderful life together, all of us."

"Andre is really home again? He's safe and well?"

Deirdre and Gabrielle looked at each other, and Gabrielle said strongly, "He looks fine, Aunt 'Relia, and he cannot wait to see you at our celebration tonight."

Aurelia smiled. "I . . . may not . . . be up . . . to . . . that. You take care of him, DeeDee."

"I will," Deirdre whispered, but Aurelia did not hear.

"May the angels that brought you take you back to heaven on their wings," Deirdre murmured brokenly, folding her friend's lifeless hands over the ghastly stains on her gown.

With the help of Rufus and the two remaining loyal Barksdale servants, Gabrielle and Deirdre managed to drag the bodies of the dead Union deserters to the abandoned well on the back of Moncoeur property. "Unless they follow their nose a week from now, no Federal soldiers will find this carrion," Deirdre said grimly after they had finished the unsavory task. "I'm just sorry to cheat the buzzards."

Gabrielle looked at Deirdre with awe. "I declare, DeeDee, I've never known any woman quite like you. You've got a streak of iron that just won't quit."

But that streak of iron melted into butter when they buried Aurelia in the little family cemetery. One of the hardest chores Deirdre had ever performed was telling Jean-Paul about his wife's death. She'd waited till the morning after the attack, when he seemed to have a little more strength than usual. Deirdre tried hard to comfort the man, telling him about his wife's great courage in saving both Gabrielle and Deirdre, but Jean-Paul was almost inconsolable.

Deirdre heard him weeping long into the night, but did not go to him. She knew he had to face his grief alone.

Jean-Paul, pale and on his crutches, had appeared at the little graveside service for his wife. "I want you to sing for her, DeeDee," he said after the prayers were done. "Sing 'Dixie's Land'—that was her favorite—and then the 'Brandy-Oh' song."

Tears coursed down Deirdre's cheeks as she fulfilled Jean-Paul's request. As the last note of the second song trailed off, she heard a harmonizing echo inside her head.

Grief lifted from her heart, and Deirdre walked back to the house with less heaviness to her footsteps. The next morning, she hugged her daughter Erin and sang some Irish ditties while they looked out the window at Erin's new kitty. "See that mean ole blue jay chasing poor Marmalade? They say that blue jays report to the devil every Thursday. But you and I have another saying, don't we? Seeing a blue jay outside our window means that winter won't last forever."

The long, hard winter of the South would end before long. Deirdre got out her worn volume of Coleridge and Shelley and read aloud to her daughter from the "Ode to the West Wind."

If winter comes, can spring be far behind?

Chapter Seventeen

There was a story about Savannah being presented to President Lincoln as a Christmas present; horror tales about the deprivation following the South's defeat abounded. A story circulated about General Lee offering an honored Southern general two sweet potatoes for a festive meal, and it was totally believable. The South had been cut off from almost every kind of supply.

Hope for victory had eroded with each successive defeat and ended completely when General Lee surrendered to General Grant at Appomattox on April 9, 1865.

Deirdre, now a true daughter of the Confederacy in every important sense, wept for the death of the cause, but more for the devastation, death, and misery the war had left behind. Then she set herself to doing what she could to help her family survive. All spring, she toiled at her still. One bright June morning, she and Rufus loaded up the wagon and struck out. Deirdre was determined to trade her whiskey for provisions to help Moncoeur regain its strength.

When she reached Donald Bull's store, she found a happy surprise awaiting her—a letter from her father.

I planned to show up without you knowing about my coming but thought better of it since you've not seen your ole papa in so long you might wonder who the bearded old geezer was. I'll be loading on the steamboat Sultana out of St. Louis to New Orleans, on or about July 25th. Hope that Jesse James character doesn't decide to switch from robbing trains to robbing sidewheelers. . . .

This happy news was somewhat diminished by another news item that made Deirdre feel uneasy. Lem Joe Bartow had split off from the new citizen protection group called the Ku Klux Klan and formed his own unsavory bunch of riff-raff. The proprieter at Donald Bull's shook his head as he related this to Deirdre. "It's all right that we've got men riding the countryside to protect our women and homes from some of the trash that's crawled out from under rocks. But Lem Joe and his crowd ain't no better'n what we're trying to keep under control."

He was reluctant to add his last bit of news concerning the unprincipled vigilantes. "Hate to tell you, Miz McAfee, but your husband

Sean's said to be riding with the Bartow gang."

Deirdre nearly dropped the crate of brown eggs she'd swapped dearly for. "Sean! What could he be thinking of?"

The storekeeper shook his head. "War's changed a lot of folks." He carried out the huge sack of flour and another of dried beans. When Deirdre was seated on her wagon next to Rufus, he handed her up a bag of hard candy. "The missus wanted little Erin to have something special. I don't know how long she's been hoarding these goodies."

Deirdre, touched, thanked him graciously. "Tell Mrs. Bull that Erin sends a whole wagon full of hugs."

"One more thing. Rufus, you better keep an eye on your place. I've heard some things that don't sound too purty about how Lem wants to put the fear of God in all the black folks herebouts." To Deirdre, "Miz McAfee, if your husband does come home to you, don't be shocked. When I seen him, he had that look about 'im makes you think of these crazy fanatics. Got a peg leg now that he's carved all kinds of symbols on. Those pale blazing eyes looking down at you makes a body shiver. Rides like the devil, too, they say, with that long dark overcoat he took off a dead Union soldier flapping in the wind like a big crow's wings."

Deirdre closed her eyes at the picture of her husband, trying hard to conjure up the old, bright-eyed, smiling Sean. "Surely my husband would not join in terrorizing helpless old people."

"Maybe not, when it comes to your own place." The storekeeper looked at Rufus and beckoned Deirdre to lean down so he could whisper something to her.

Deirdre was horrified to think that Sean would take part in the sort of atrocity Mr. Bull related. She headed for home as fast as her horse and wagon would take her.

That must not happen!

Jean-Paul's medical condition was improved. With treatment, the illness from lead poisoning was now under control and the pain from the bullet near his spine had lessened. Dr. Hollins had told Deirdre privately that nothing more could be done and that the best thing to do was to let Jean-Paul do whatever he was capable of physically.

Aurelia's death had brought new, different lines of pain to Jean-Paul's face, but he made a courageous effort to take his place in keeping the plantation going.

He made that clear to Deirdre on her return from the general store in Shelbyville. He was leaning on his crutches outside his study to which he'd had a cot moved so he didn't have to struggle with the stairs. "It's time I took my part in this business of putting Moncoeur and the South back on their feet again," he'd told her the week after they'd buried Aurelia. "Time

I took my place as the man in the house. If I hadn't been lying abed, she'd still be alive and you wouldn't have had to do what I should have been up doing. I would have been down here protecting her and you like a man's supposed to do."

Deirdre had done her best to reassure him that he could not be held to blame for the murderous actions of soldiers gone bad. But she was glad to have the moral support and bookkeeping help that Jean-Paul could provide even though he was still too debilitated physically to do much else.

She missed Aurelia terribly. The late mistress of Moncoeur had always been cheery and bright, spurring Deirdre to keep on going when everything seemed bleak and hopeless.

Jean-Paul was telling her the bad news. "They've burned out Barksdale's nigra shanties, the ones that the Colonel gave to the blacks that stayed on even after he granted them their freedom. Shiloh and his wife were threatened with hanging or worse, but your husband stopped 'em, saying the burning was enough."

Deirdre closed her eyes, breathing a prayer of thanks that the incident had not ended even more dreadfully. If Sean had taken a role in physically harming those old Negroes, she would never again have been able to look at him without loathing. She was not far from that now. "This wasn't what was intended when the Klan was formed. Our men banded together to protect our property and the helpless, not to terrorize and maim and kill."

"Tell that to Lem Joe Bartow and the scum that's falling in behind him," Jean-Paul said grimly. Then, "I'm sorry, DeeDee, I didn't mean to imply your husband is made of the same cloth as these bullies."

"But he is if he's going through with these atrocities! He's just as bad as they are, maybe worse, since he ought to know better." Upset as she was about the sorry business carried out at the neighboring plantation and Sean's hand in it, there was no time to be wasted. The same thing could happen at Moncoeur if she didn't do something to prevent it. "I'm going down to Prudy's and Rufus's cabin. I heard when I was at Bull's Store that Lem Joe and his crowd are planning to go after more Negroes tonight."

"I'll go with you." Jean-Paul hunched up his shoulders over his crutches.

Deirdre did not miss the spasm of pain that passed over his drawn features. "Jean-Paul, I think it's better if I approach Sean by myself. He won't let any harm come to me, I just know it. There's still good down deep inside him, I really believe that. Besides, you're needed here to protect Moncoeur. I'll have Letitia come over with Erin so she'll be safe. With you in charge, I know my daughter will come to no harm."

Jean-Paul's shoulders straightened as he said with passion, "You're damned right that nobody will hurt that little girl, not while this body's got a breath of life to it! You're right.

They may decide to attack here, too. I've got that pistol Charles brought back with him from Appomattox. He sent it over to me before you got here, saying he would've brought it and himself if he'd been able. I know how frustrated he must have felt, lying half-conscious from the dysentery he's had ever since he came back."

"Poor Charles. But with Gabrielle nursing him night and day, I have a feeling he'll soon recover. Charles says Gabrielle's really grown up since he went off to war," Deirdre said with a smile, momentarily forgetting the ordeal ahead in her recollection of the younger woman's new maturity. "I guess we all have. Well, I'm off." Deirdre gave Jean-Paul a sisterly kiss.

"Maybe you need this gun more than I do," Jean-Paul said worriedly.

"No, you need to sit right here where you can see anybody coming up in time to shoot. Besides, Sean is more likely to listen to reason if I'm unarmed." Except for my bullwhip, Deirdre thought grimly. She hadn't forgotten the way Lem Bartow enjoyed preying on a lone woman when he thought she was helpless.

She found Prudy and Rufus inside their cabin eating their lean meal of mashed turnips and cornbread. Shaking her head at their offer of some supper, she quickly explained what had occurred at Barksdale Plantation. "Rufus, you and Prudy must go up to the house for your own safety. I'll try to talk some sense into my husband."

Rufus went over and got the big knotted cane that he used when his rheumatism was bothering him. "I ain't leavin' this cabin, Miz DeeDee. It's the fust home my wife and me's ever had, and I'm stayin' right heah to protect my propity. That no-good Lem Bartow, he make a move on my house or my woman, I'll knock him cross-eyed."

Deirdre tried to calm the old man down, knowing that the last thing she needed was Rufus brandishing his walking stick at a bunch of edgy scoundrels. "You stay in here, Rufus, until I need you. It's best that I face that bunch by myself. Sean won't let them hurt me, but he may not be able to stop them if they see you ready to fight."

"All right, Miz DeeDee." Rufus shook his head and sank down at the kitchen table. "I jest don't understand it, how a man like your husband could throw in with a crowd of no-good rascals like that."

"War does terrible things to everybody, Rufus. This wasn't Sean's war, and he didn't want to fight it. He lost his leg and . . . and some other things a man can't bear to lose. And now it's all for nothing. All he's got left is the bitterness."

Deirdre went out on the porch. "Shove the latch on the inside, Rufus, and don't come out unless I say to." She looked at the sunset lighting the beautiful hills and the pastures that didn't look quite so scraggly with the sun on them. The devastation in the South, in hard-hit places like nearby Nashville and poor, destroyed Georgia, was not so evident in the countryside, at sundown.

The Union had been incredibly brutal about many decisions, like Grant's concurrence with Sherman's cold-blooded destruction of a sixty-mile strip through Georgia, all the way to the sea. Yet that same commander-in-chief had humanely allowed surrendering Confederate officers to retain their sidearms and horses when they left Appomattox to return to their homes. Nothing about war made any sense, Deirdre was rapidly concluding.

The sound of horses' hooves pounding over the wooden bridge on the old road to Holly Gap brought Deirdre back to present harsh realities. She braced herself as the band of hooded men came to a stop in front of the little porch. She recognized Lem Joe's horse at the head of the pack and said contemptuously, her hand on the bullwhip secreted in the folds of her skirt, "It's just like you, Lem Bartow, to hide behind a sheet. I would not have expected any less, given the cowardly things you've done in the past." She turned to the rider on the black mare. She had sacrificed a great deal to get that horse for her husband—and now look at how he was using Shenandoah! "You, Sean, though, I would never have expected to hide behind a mask and burn down the cabins of your old neighbors! I know you had cause to turn bitter, but those poor old Negroes were never anything but kind to you."

Sean slowly pulled off his hood, and Deirdre was shocked at the changes in the once handsome face. Deep lines of unhappiness and perhaps pain were etched there, making her husband look twenty years older than he actually was. "I had no real part in that, Deirdre, though I was there. But we have to stand up to these people before they start doing what they're doing everywhere all over the South." Sean's blue eyes burned with the fire of the fanatic. "If you could see what they're doing in the towns, you'd saddle up and ride with us! The little that's left is being grabbed up by the scalawags and carpetbaggers, land's being confiscated, taxes raised sky-high. Nobody in the south's got the money to buy anything now that our currency's worthless. The freed slaves are acting like they own everything now—and if we don't do something, they *will* own everything!"

Deirdre cried out, "But that's not Shiloh's fault, not Rufus's. Sean, you mustn't let anything happen here. I know you feel wronged, I know the war did something to change you, but I know there's a good, decent man beneath that—that costume you're wearing. Sean, as your wife, I beg you to make these men leave and not commit a crime that you will never be able to forgive yourself for."

Sean looked away, for the first time appearing uncertain, and Deirdre would have moved in to take the advantage, but Lem Bartow jumped off his horse with a snarling curse and was on the porch before Deirdre had a chance. "Bitch! You haven't been a wife to the poor devil, so what makes you think he'll listen to you? Now, git out of our way and you won't get hurt. We ain't after white people. We just aim to shake up them niggers enough so's others around with ideas of stealing what's ours will get the word."

With a lightning move that caught everybody off guard, Deirdre's hand snaked out with the bullwhip. It lashed around the startled ringleader, pinning his arms, and in a flash Deirdre had the thick part of the whip around Bartow's throat. "One more twist and I'll crush your jugular." She saw one of the men ease a gun out and told Lem Bartow harshly, "I mean it! If I catch a bullet from one of your scoundrels, I'll still use my last breath of life to tighten the noose that you should've had around your neck long before now."

"Put the gun away, Randy," Lem rasped to the man who'd sneaked his firearm halfway out.

Deirdre had been shocked to find that Bartow was not struggling against her. *Why, he's just a little coward who's always hidden behind his bullying!* "Tell them to leave this place. If they don't, their ringleader is the one who'll pay for it."

Lem rasped out the order. He added in a whisper meant for Deirdre's ears only, "You got the upperhand this time, but we'll be back just when you've stopped expecting us. Arghh." The tightened noose made him choke. "You're killin' me! Sean, make this devil of a woman turn loose of me."

Deirdre reached for the pistol stuck in the outlaw's belt and stuck it in Lem's back. "What I told the others holds for Sean, too. If he tries to shoot me—and I don't think he's gone down that far—you'll go with me." Deirdre looked at Lem's horse waiting patiently. Without either remaining man realizing what she was about to do, she shot the pistol up in the air. The horse took off like a bolt.

"My horse! Damn you, how'm I gonna git back?"

Deirdre looked down at his feet. "Those look like pretty sturdy boots to me."

The outlaw, rubbing his bruised throat after she unwrapped the whip, gave her a look of sheer hatred but said nothing as he turned around toward the main road. "You comin', Sean?" he asked the other man.

Sean did not look at Lem. He had not taken his eyes off Deirdre since she'd bested his cohort. "I'll meet you back at your place tonight sometime. Right now, I've got to talk to my wife."

Lem grunted something unflattering and then cursed. "Gotta damn stone in my boot." He stopped not far from where Sean was dismounting and bent to slip his hand inside his boot.

Deirdre was looking at Sean and didn't see the knife appear in Lem's hand, but her husband did.

"Look out! Deirdre, look out!"

Sean made a dive for the porch and went down on top of his wife. Deirdre felt his dead weight and screamed, "Sean! Oh, no, Sean. Oh God, oh God." She struggled to move him and saw the handle of the knife sticking out of his back.

And then she saw Lem Bartow, his face set with fury, pointing the rifle he'd taken from Sean's saddlebag straight at her head.

She closed her eyes and prayed. When the shot rang out, she saw the exploding colors of a hundred battles raging inside her head.

Miraculously, she was still alive. But Deirdre dared not open her eyes for fear that she would see Lem Bartow's hateful face looking down to see if she were dead. When she felt Sean's body being lifted away, she squeezed her eyes even more tightly shut. "Go ahead and shoot me, you cowardly bastard. Our soldiers will be coming home, and they won't let the likes of you get away with murder."

"You can say that again."

Deirdre thought she was dreaming to hear Andre's voice. She opened her eyes and quickly shut them again. "I'm dead and the angels are playing tricks, making me think I'm seeing Andre Devereux's face."

"My darling Deirdre, you are not dead and you're not dreaming." Andre lifted her gently in his arms and put his lips against her hair. "I'm so sorry I didn't get here earlier. Maybe I could've saved Sean."

"Sean!" Deirdre pushed Andre from her and struggled to her feet. She knelt beside the still body of her husband and sobbed. "Oh, Sean, I'm so sorry, so very sorry." She took his rough hand in hers and put it to her tear-streaked cheek. She pushed the once butter-yellow hair that was now dark with grime away from his forehead. "You saved me. You were still the man I knew you were all along." Deirdre squeezed her eyes shut on the burning tears.

Andre gently pulled her to her feet and held her trembling body close in his arms. "I'll have Prudy and Rufus see to him, Deirdre. You come with me now."

Deirdre opened her eyes and saw the gaunt face of the man she'd never expected to set eyes on again. She'd heard about the way prisoners were treated at Elmira. "Oh, Andre, it was so horrible!" She started crying uncontrollably, even as she did so thinking how ironic that she should have stood up to a band of cutthroats without so much as a tear—and now that she was safe, she was squalling like a baby. "Poor Sean, nobody could've saved Sean. He was lost a long time ago." She tightened her arms on Andre's neck. "He saved me. At the end, he was Sean again and not that horrible stranger."

"I never really held it against him that he turned me in. He wasn't himself. He'd lost a leg and you, more than any man could bear. Oh, it was no picnic being in that hell-hole, I can tell you! I've heard the stories from the other side about how brutal Andersonville was, and I'm sure they're true. But at least our side had the excuse of not having the food and medical supplies. They had 'em at Elmira, but just didn't always choose to use them."

Deirdre's heart contracted at the underlying pain in Andre's voice. "How could you forgive Sean for putting you through that hell?"

Andre brushed Deirdre's hair back from her tear-stained face. "Because he'd lost you, and I knew that you and I would be together forever. Sean didn't have that knowledge to keep from going under. I did."

They stayed there entwined for a long moment, then Deirdre had a terrible thought. "Oh, my God! Lem Bartow's still probably out there lurking around, waiting his chance."

"Bartow's lurking days are over, my darling—or didn't you hear the shot that you mistakenly thought was Gabriel's horn calling you to heaven? As for his cohorts, they ran into the men I was with—and you talk about mad! Some of my friends have homes around here, and they didn't waste any time telling that bunch of riff-raff what they thought of them prowling on private property and terrorizing helpless blacks and women."

"Thank goodness," Deirdre sighed. "Is that how you found out about me?"

Andre nodded. "After a little—uh, friendly persuasion of one of the more talkative chaps to tell us what such a raggle-taggle crew was running from and why." His eyes, sunken though they were in deep sockets, took on a distinct twinkle. "Do you know what he told us?"

Deirdre tried her best to look innocent. She wasn't sure how Andre would feel to find out he was in love with a she-devil. "I . . . uh, guess they told you I had Lem . . . uh . . ."

"By the short hairs, I believe the expression goes. I don't think any of these rag-tags will be back—not because we scared 'em out of it, but because not one of 'em was willing to face the fury of a whip-toting, bad-talking, red-headed wild woman."

Deirdre's laugh turned back to tears as Rufus and two other Negroes carried Sean's body up to the big house. She stood with Andre and watched the somber little procession. "I wish he'd never left Ireland, never met me. I feel so sorry for Sean. I have for a long time."

"I have, too. For a man to deny himself the joy of knowing his own child . . ." Andre shook his head sadly. "If little Erin were mine, and her mother my wife, I'd be the happiest man alive."

Deirdre turned her tear-stained face up to Andre's and almost said it. *Sean was right about one thing, Andre. Erin was not his child.* But somehow she could not bring herself to tell Andre the truth. It would be a deep betrayal to the man who had just given up his life for hers. "At least you are alive. Poor Sean . . ." Deirdre broke into sobs again.

It was as Azalea had always said to her, Deirdre thought as Andre's arms enveloped her. "The ol' worl' goes thisaway sometimes, then it goes thataway."

Azalea? But Deirdre had no time to ponder the strange name. The South might not be a safe place to be for a long time to come, but right now she felt very, very safe in Andre's arms.

Chapter Eighteen

With Jean-Paul's and Andre's wholehearted approval, Deirdre held a true Irish wake as she knew her husband would have wanted. Jean-Paul brushed aside Deirdre's hesitation to honor Sean, since he had brought harm to Andre and participated in the arson at Barksdale. "Andre and Charles feel the same way I do. Sean wasn't himself after he lost his leg. And mind you, we don't take it lightly that he lost it defending the South. That and his final heroism exonerates your husband in our eyes."

He also insisted that Sean be buried in the family cemetery. "After all, he was married to you, DeeDee, and you're part of our family now."

The Irish settlement near Holly Gap had been

Sean's source of friendship during the peaceful times. Many of its inhabitants came at Deirdre's request to give their fellow countryman a proper send-off. Though Gabrielle and some other women were initially shocked at the levity and high spirits of those attending the wake, they soon joined in the mood of celebration that was the tradition in Ireland.

Everyone was tired of sorrow and hardship. Deirdre's whiskey made up for the meagerness of the funeral foods, and everyone complimented her on the "finest batch ever."

Although she had never really loved Sean McAfee, Deirdre wept with sincere grief at the brief graveside service. She had chosen a spot where a wild rose vine grew. Sean had told her their first summer that the flower made him think of Ireland.

Deirdre was grateful to Andre for giving her time to mourn her husband's death. Though both knew the marriage had not been a real one since Erin's birth, they were also aware of propriety. In fact, to keep tongues from wagging, Andre made a decision to leave Moncoeur for a few weeks.

"Maybe," he said to Deirdre, "I could somehow get to New Orleans in time to meet your father's sidewheeler." He grinned at her. "If you'll recall, your father got into a lot of trouble the last time he traveled from New Orleans to Nashville. With luck, I can keep him away from the tables this time."

Deirdre knew Andre's joking offer hid a more serious purpose. Travel on the once beseiged Cumberland River was not what it had been in the old days. Rogues and thieves made up most of the passenger lists on the river in these times. "I'm sure my father would be very grateful to have you as escort and bodyguard. Would you please, please see if you can get word of Julia when you go to Nashville? I'm so worried. I haven't heard anything since before the battle."

"I had already planned to do just that." Andre and Deirdre were sitting on the veranda waiting for Gabrielle and Charles to join them. The younger pair had sent word that they had happy news, a rare commodity this postwar-scarred summer. "I know Julia's just fine. She's a survivor." Andre added in a low tone since the voices of their visitors could be heard on the walkway up to the veranda. "Deirdre, I know it's too soon, and I know I promised not to press you, but when I come back, we have to talk about our future." His eyes searched hers hungrily. "If you only knew how hard it's been, not being able to hold you, to make love to you."

Deirdre took a deep breath, not daring to say how much she wanted the same thing. How many times lately it had been on the tip of her tongue to tell him about Erin! But she knew that Andre would throw propriety to the winds if he knew the truth. He would learn it after they were married, and not until then. "You must be patient, my darling. Sean gave his life to save me. The least I can do is show proper respect for his memory."

"I know. But I want you to know, too, that it's killing me, holding you at arm's length," Andre whispered. He rose to greet their visitors, kissing his niece on the cheek. "You are blooming, my darling. Could it be from having your husband back in charge of Barksdale? Charles." Andre shook Gabrielle's husband's hand. "I haven't had a chance to tell you this, but your wife turned out to be quite a little trouper. She and the Colonel kept your place up with only a few workers even during the worst times."

Charles bent his sandy head over his wife's dark one. "I'm really proud of her. I guess you know, though, that we probably won't be able to keep Barksdale with the taxes owed. Some carpetbagger has already been out with the assessor looking the place over." Charles tightened his arm around his wife. "But, here, that's not the news we came to tell you. Gaby is expecting another child!"

Deirdre clapped her hands with joy, and Andre congratulated the beaming couple. "Might I ask when the blessed event will occur?"

Gabrielle blushed and Andre teased, "I warrant exactly nine months from the day Charles came walking in that door." Andre slapped the father-to-be on the back. "Good work, Charles! Deirdre, won't you see if you can get Jean-Paul to join us out here for a spot of whiskey to celebrate?" After Deirdre had gone inside, he said to the others, "My brother has these very black moods and only Deirdre seems to be able to get him out of them."

Gabrielle chirped, not intending malice, "Uncle Jean-Paul misses Aunt 'Relia, I know, but if anything ever happened to his DeeDee, I declare he would probably go crazy." She missed the look on Andre's face as Deirdre came out on the veranda just then with Jean-Paul. "Uncle! I'm so glad to see you! Just wait till you hear my news. . . ."

Andre got Deirdre away from the others and whispered, "I wish I were the one giving *you* a child, my darling. After we're married, naturally. Of course, I already love your daughter as much as if she were mine. But I intend to give you another as soon as possible."

Deirdre lowered her eyes to hide what she was thinking secretly. *You already have, my darling!* She smiled down into the cup of unadorned whiskey she was holding to await the toast to the coming baby. When she and Andre celebrated their next child, real mint juleps would be on hand! Right now, the sugar could not be spared.

Ironically, Gabrielle chose that moment to complain, "Where are Aunt 'Relia's silver mint julep cups?" Gabrielle looked down distastefully at the plain glass in her hand. "DeeDee, don't tell me some Yankee broke in and stole 'em."

"DeeDee traded them for the sugar and corn she needs to make the whiskey," Jean-Paul said quietly. When all eyes went to Deirdre, he added, "With my permission, of course. We can do without silver dishes. We can't do with food."

Gabrielle looked shocked. "Those cups were worth a *fortune,* Uncle Jean! Aunt 'Relia would just die!" She realized what she had just said. "I mean . . . I didn't . . . Uncle Andre, isn't there any money left over here, either?"

Andre smiled grimly. "The only commodity we have right now is Deirdre's famous whiskey. And I agree with Jean-Paul that the sugar and grain to keep her still going are worth a helluva lot more than silver cups."

Charles patted his wife's hand. "Don't you worry, my pet. After we get our place back on its feet, I'll buy you all the silver you want."

He was whistling in the wind, and he and the others knew it. But they all raised their glasses when Andre lifted his in a toast. "Hear, hear! To the South, may she rise again in our time—and to your coming child, who will see it happen, to be sure."

They all drank, though Gabrielle took only a sip of her whiskey and handed the rest to her husband, whispering, "Not good for the baby."

Before the Barksdales left, they entreated Deirdre to be the godmother and Andre to be godfather to their expected child. Deirdre could not bear to look at Andre when she gladly accepted. But Andre looked at her long and meaningfully when he told Gabrielle that he would be honored to be godfather to her baby. She knew he was thinking of what he had confided to her about his eagerness to give her a child. She was thinking about Erin and what a wonderful father he would make when he found out he was one.

Deirdre could not believe it when she straightened up from her backbreaking task of helping Rufus hoe the pitiful remains of their summer garden and saw a horse and wagon turning into the lane up to Moncoeur. She shaded her eyes to see if the hallucination she was having could be real. "It is!" she shouted to Rufus, throwing down her hoe and lifting her skirts to run down to meet the wagon. "It's Julia! Julia, is it really you?"

Madame Julia hardly had time to say "whoa" and pull the horse to a stop before Deirdre was up on the seat beside her, hugging the woman till Julia laughingly begged for breath and a chance to tie the reins. "Well, that's the best greeting I've had from anybody since Andre came by to see me."

Deirdre helped the older woman lift out her big canvas bag. "How are the girls? Did Pegean finally marry that old shopkeeper who was after her?"

Julia chuckled. "Yes, and she has him wrapped around her little finger from what she says in her letters. They left Tennessee before the worst, thank God. Lilianne and Andre had a long visit together, by the way. Can you believe that girl, after all her self-centered shenanigans when she was working for me, opened up her own sewing and alteration business? Not only that, during the seige, she let her place be used for nursing the wounded soldiers." The woman shook her head. "War brings out the worst and the best in people, doesn't it?"

Deirdre was too happy to see her old friend to talk about the war. "I can't wait for you to see Erin! Oh, won't she be thrilled to see her Julie-Ma!"

"I can't wait to see her, either, but before we do that, I need to tell you a couple of things that may change your mind about being so happy to see me."

Deirdre set down the canvas bag and stared at Julia, dread starting to erode the joy of seeing her dear friend safe and well after the horrible battle that had devastated Nashville and its citizenry. "Nothing could do that, Julia. But tell me, please, and quickly. You said, truly, that war brings out the best and the worst. Well, it brought out a strength in me that I wasn't aware of. Sean's death was one of the hardest things to bear, not because I loved him but because I didn't. Yet, I've been able to get past that and see that I have to get on with a life for me and Erin."

"With Andre in it, I hope." At the answer on Deirdre's face, Julia added gently, "Don't wait too long, darling. It's always later than we think."

"Andre and I have an understanding about that."

"Good. As for your inner strength"—Julia put her hand on Deirdre's face, tracing the firm jaw—"I knew how strong you were the moment I found you sleeping on my porch in that ridiculous urchin's disguise. Deirdre, I'm sorry about Sean, but we both know that he was never the man for you."

"Julia, you must tell me what it is that has you upset."

"Andre left for New Orleans to meet your father as he told you he would."

Deirdre's heart came close to stopping. "Something has happened to Andre!"

Julia shook her head. "No, not in the sense that you're worried about. Andre learned from Lilianne before he left that you bore his child. She was contrite about destroying the letter I wrote to him. Andre, I don't mind telling you, was overcome to learn he's Erin's father."

"Oh, Julia, was he angry with me for not telling him?"

"I really can't say. When he came by to see me after seeing Lilianne, he was still in a state of shock. He wanted to confirm what she'd told him, and, of course, I did. He was angry with me, I can tell you that! He said I had no business keeping the secret from him after Sean abandoned you and Erin the night she was born."

"That's not fair, his blaming you! You thought he'd gotten the letter and just didn't want to be recognized as the father," Deirdre cried.

"Andre realized that after he thought about it. Before he left, we were friends again. Deirdre, I know this is enough for you to take in at one sitting, but there's more I have to tell you."

Deirdre girded herself. "It's my father, isn't it? You've heard something about Riley O'Shea."

"Yes, but it's still uncertain. The *Sultana* exploded on the Mississippi before it reached New Orleans. There were twenty-three hundred people on board. Over sixteen hundred were killed." Deirdre was crying by now, and Julia pulled her into her arms. "Oh, sweetheart, I'm so sorry to be the one to tell you this after you've been through so much! But there's still hope. Your father could be one of the survivors. From what you've told me, he's come out of worse scrapes than a plain old explosion."

Deirdre dried her cheeks and eyes. "You're right. Papa always lands on his feet, no matter what."

"Andre will find him, you can count on it. If your daddy came through this disaster, as I'm sure he did, Andre will bring him home to you." Julia gave her friend another squeeze and then forgot all about Riley O'Shea when a squealing, ecstatic little girl with flying black curls threw herself into the maternal warmth of Julia's bosom.

When a grinning Riley O'Shea came striding into the kitchen where Julia and Deirdre were boiling jars for the canning, a triumphant

Andre right behind, the whole place went crazy. After her father had finally put her down after whirling her around till she was dizzy, Deirdre tried to be stern.

"You might've sent word before just showing up here and scaring a body to death."

"Now, DeeDee, me darlin', don't start off fussing at me before I've been here more than five minutes." He looked at Julia, "And this fine figure of a woman has to be Madame Julia, who's been so good to my little bairn since I had to jump ship."

"Call me Julia, please. Leave off the Madame and you and I will get along just fine."

"That we will," Riley said with a look at the other woman that made her turn pleasurably pink. "That we will."

Andre had been waiting his turn and would not be denied a welcoming hug from the woman he loved. When Deirdre's shyness would not permit him to get the real kiss he wanted, he complained. "Your father knows all about you and me and that little granddaughter of his that he's aching to see, just like her father is. Julia, of course, has known all along how much I love you. Why shouldn't I have a real kiss from the woman who will be my wife as soon as we can line up the preacher?"

Riley said to Julia in a wistful voice, "Look at those two. So much in love and together for the rest of their lives. This poor old reprobate Irishman will probably never again know a good woman's soft lips and warm heart." At Julia's laugh directed at the obvious, bogus attempt at eliciting pity, Riley joined in. "It's a smart lady you are, as well as fair, to see through me blarney. Ah, you and me, we'll be friends for sure. But right now, I'm rarin' to see the child that carries the name of me blessed mother. Come show me to my grandbaby and let's let the lovebirds be. God knows my daughter could use a good man in her life for a change."

Julia laughed heartily as she tucked her arm into the Irishman's. "Me, I've had my share of both kinds, and I have to confess I find myself getting restless when a man is *too* good. Come on and let's have you meet the most beautiful little girl a body could see. And I don't doubt this house will be echoing with more little footsteps not too long from now."

Deirdre and Andre were unaware of the other two departing. They were too busy reveling in the joy of their reunion.

Andre finally lifted his head, though his arms still held their captive tight. "I have never been so happy as I am at this moment, knowing you and I will never be separated again, knowing that Erin is my child, too, and that her mother will soon be my bride. Oh, darling, how much time we've wasted being apart! If only I'd known."

"We mustn't dwell on that. It's behind us now, like the war. We have each other and Erin, and thank God for that. Others have so much less to be thankful for."

Andre's eyes clouded momentarily as he

thought of the men at Elmira who'd died miserably, knowing they would never lay eyes on their loved ones again. "Yes," he agreed in a low voice. "I'm one of the lucky ones. Thank God, thank God, I was able to get back to you and Erin."

Deirdre cradled his head against her chest. "I'm lucky too, my darling. I have my father back, I have Julia, Erin . . ."

"And me," Andre interjected jealously. "You have me forevermore, my darling, like it or not."

"I like it very much," Deirdre whispered, turning up her face for another kiss. She only came up for air when she heard the pot of jars on the stove hissing and gurgling dangerously. "Oh, my lord, the jars!"

With Andre's help, she rescued them just in time.

"There are things I'd much rather be doing than this," Andre complained when he was impressed into the canning preparation.

He found that the reward when they were done was well worth the bit of domestic duty.

There had been enough sad occasions during the past four years. When the community learned that there would now be a wedding joining two stalwarts who'd endured the pain and suffering of the South, the rejoicing was great.

Even the women who'd snubbed Deirdre for her unladylike hawking of whiskey to help Moncoeur survive came through. Though most families were suffering the pangs of Reconstruction scarcities, cakes were somehow baked, hams and chickens turned up roasted for the big celebration that was to follow the wedding.

Deirdre was insistent that her wedding would take place on her mountain, on the very spot where so much of her important history had taken place.

Andre laughed at her about the romantic notion but had no objections to anything that his beloved bride-to-be wanted. "Hell, we can be married in the outhouse, and I'll be happy as a pig in the sunshine," he told her. "But just don't think for one minute that we'll spend half our honeymoon surrounded by people using our wedding to feed their starved need for socializing."

Deirdre promised him that the honeymoon would be a chance for them to be with each other, unmolested by the world outside.

The path up the mountain was strewn with buttercups by the adorable little flower girl, Erin. Deirdre and Andre had both wanted to tell the world that she was their joint child, but Julia persuaded them to wait. "You wouldn't want the little darling to be hearing things when she goes to school. Let Andre wait a decent interval, then adopt Sean's child in a legal way. No need putting a little smudge over the child's birthright when there's no need for it. She knows who her father is now, and he does, and the people who matter do. Leave it be."

They had agreed to accept Julia's wise advice. Now, as Deirdre waited halfway down the mountain, her arm linked with a proud Riley O'Shea's, her bridesmaid Gaby and friends widowed by the war marching up to the be-flowered altar, she thought only about the happiness that lay ahead.

Times were hard and might get harder, she knew, but with Andre at her side, she knew they would make it. Together they would help rebuild a South that would provide a safe, happy place for their children, and their children's children, to grow up and prosper.

"Do I look all right?" Deirdre whispered to her father, who was resplendent in fancy dress and the latest hairstyle. Julia had gotten the clothes from a friend in Nashville and created his neat beard and haircut, saying that no father worth his salt would give his daughter away looking like a runaway gambler turned logger.

"You look beautiful, me love. Andre's a lucky man, and he knows it. Look at 'im. Can't take his eyes off you."

Deirdre was indeed a picture coming up on the crest of the hill, her peach-colored gown trailing, her wispy veil catching the breeze. The cloth for her wedding ensemble had been sent by, of all people, Pegean, whose shopkeeper husband was, it was said, opening a whole chain of fabric stores up East.

"I love him so much, Papa," Deirdre whispered, a catch in her voice at how handsome

Andre looked, though still too thin in his cutaway and trousers. "Oh, please put your blessing on our marriage."

"You've had that, me darlin', since I came back and saw how 'twas. Now, put your thoughts on that man up there and say the words that people say at times like this, only say 'em with the fervor of the Irish in ye."

Deirdre did that. And when Brother Perkins said the magic words, "I now pronounce you man and wife," she added enthusiastically "And amen to that!"

Andre laughed along with everybody else and then stopped laughing when he put his lips on hers for the first kiss as her husband.

They ate and danced and drank celebratory mint juleps and then, amid a flurry of rice, kisses, and well wishes, managed to slip away in the carriage that Andre had waiting almost from the time the ceremony had ended.

He had kept the honeymoon plans a secret, but as Deirdre told him, it could be anywhere and she wouldn't know the difference or care.

"The Cherokee Indians called these Smoky Mountains 'the great blue hills of God.'" The farmhouse tucked into the side of the mountain just outside Walland, Tennessee, belonged to the McCarters, old friends of Andre's.

The family were away in Knoxville, helping with the birthing of their first grandchild, and had gladly offered the retreat to Andre for his honeymoon.

Deirdre loved the view from the wide porch. The valley seemed untouched by the war and offered natural peace and quiet such as she had long wished for.

Andre had barely given her time to unpack before bringing her out to enjoy the scenic view of the Smokies. "I just wanted you to see some *real* mountains before we go back home to settle down at Moncoeur," he told her.

They took a picnic basket and walked down to the stone-cobbled brook in the valley. As they lay on their blanket, whispering words of love and listening to the music of the bubbling water, Deirdre was almost certain she could hear other voices as well.

"Shh." She sat up, putting her finger to Andre's eager mouth. "There's someone else here!"

Andre kissed the tips of her fingers, one by one. "Mr. Squirrel and maybe one of McCarter's stray cows."

"No." Deirdre strained to hear, but the lilting sound of a far-off couple was no longer audible. Was it her imagination, thinking she'd heard a throaty voice singing, accompanied by an unusual-sounding instrument?

"Well, my darling, I've done my best to wait until the sun goes down, but I can wait no longer. Since we've been driving almost day and night to get here, I've had to put off the occasion that I've been longing for—getting you into that huge bed I saw first thing when we got here."

Deirdre teased him. "I was planning for us to go to sleep early so we could get up and pick blackberries for breakfast. The old man at the corners told us that this area is just bursting with huge, juicy blackberries."

"The blackberries will be there when I let you go."

Andre's kiss went to Deirdre's head like the champagne they'd been drinking.

But there was something she had a deep impulse to do before they left the beautiful glade by the brook. "I want someone to know we were here. I want us to leave our names behind, some kind of mark."

So Andre, under Deirdre's supervision, carved their names together in a huge tree trunk, low enough so it would not grow out of view in the years to come.

That night, as Deirdre went into her husband's eager arms, she wondered aloud, "Will someone as happy as we are see the names and maybe hear our voices in the brook?"

Andre was more interested in enjoying the present than speculating about the future. "My darling, the voice I hear is the one in my heart telling me that if I don't make love to a certain delicious woman before long, it won't be held responsible for what happens."

As Deirdre's lips met Andre's, she offered a prayer of thanks for sending her beloved home to her to share passion and joy in the "great blue hills of God."

Chapter Nineteen

New Year's 1989

I lifted my head from Harrison's comforting chest and listened to the sound of the train that rumbles through not a mile from his house. "The railroads can't ever replace the steamboats," I said in a voice that I'm sure didn't sound like my own. "And Riley will love that Stetson hat Deirdre bought him for Christmas."

Harrison rolled over and propped himself up on his elbow to look down at me. "Let me guess. You've been back in that other world of yours. Give me an update. What's Deirdre up to now?"

Somehow I didn't feel right about telling him. Deirdre had let me into the most intimate part of her soul; to violate that trust was to violate myself. "I think she's finally going to make it.

Her father did live through the explosion, I know that somehow, and when Andre comes back, those two will finally get together."

"Andre and Riley?" Harrison quirked his eyebrow comically.

I slapped him playfully. "Andre and Deirdre, you big nut." I looked down at myself, realizing that except for the sheet, I was totally nude. "Harrison, what have you done with my underwear?"

"I'm wearing it, of course," Harrison said with a fake lisp, which got him another slap, harder this time. "If I were writing the script for your saga, I'd have Riley fall in love with Madame Julia."

I lay back on the pillow smiling at the thought. "That would be nice. You're a romantic, Harrison Judd."

He kissed me and pulled the sheet down very, very slowly over my breasts, making the goosebumps rise as well as certain other parts of anatomy between us. "I think it's almost over between us," I said when Harrison pulled me close to him and began doing the things that had earlier turned me into melted jello.

He was jolted. "What do you mean 'over between us'? It's just begun, you crazy woman."

"I mean it's almost over between me and Deirdre," I said drowsily. Harrison did have a way with his hands and mouth that made me feel I was in some kind of sensuous hot tub with everything but the water. "I felt it this time, like reading a book and knowing

I'm getting to the last chapter."

"Reading in bed is for people who are all by themselves." Harrison rolled me over toward him and proceeded to bring me out of my drowsy state. "You and I are not alone right now. Let's make the most of it."

We did.

Harrison thought it was peculiar that I wanted to leave before dawn but was good-natured about it. "I had visions of our having a big breakfast and making New Year's resolutions together over bloody marys and football games."

I just had this need to visit Deirdre's mountain and told him so. "Something's coming to a close, and I don't want to be too far away from the center of where it started."

My visit to the little cemetery included a stop at Sean McAfee's grave. I vowed to make sure that the rose vine was pruned and fed the next spring. The yellow roses on Celeste's grave were dead. I replaced them with a cheerful pot of red poinsettias that I'd brought from Harrison's.

I stood the longest at Deirdre's tombstone, feeling closer to her on this bright, cold morning than I ever had. "Don't leave me forever," I whispered. "I know you are not going to let me stay a part of your life after you work through what you're working through, but please don't leave me without saying good-bye."

The ripple of goosebumps I felt weren't from the cold morning wind.

I don't know to this day what possessed me, but I went up on the mountain that morning and took out the tiny tape recorder that I keep with me always and recorded what happened after that.

It was a very quiet day, made for echoes. When I sang the song that I had always known, I paused at the end of each line and waited for the echo.

"Coffee grows on the white oak stump.
The river flows with brandy-oh,
Go choose you one that'll stand by you
As sweet as sugar candy-oh."

The echo of each line after I paused came back strong and clear and I listened to it with a sweet aching. "Oh, Deirdre, I'll miss you so. I'll miss you so."

I heard the whisper of the wind in the oak tree and felt the chills that signaled my last trip back into Deirdre's world. How did I know it was my last journey? I've thought about that since. I think the oak tree told me. When I looked at it that night, it seemed to be growing and aging and shedding leaves and putting on new ones all at once. And then I was at Deirdre's eightieth birthday party, being treated like a matriarch by all the grandchildren and great grandchildren. Andre, I thought, with great sadness—where's Andre?

Deirdre leaned on the cane that she had spurned when it was given to her by one of her grandchildren years before. She looked out at the spread of tables on the green lawn, each with its cut-glass punch bowl filled with mint juleps, and marveled at the spilling array of rich food. "Could have fed a Confederate regiment for six months," she grumbled to no one in particular.

Her son Paul came up to her. "Mama, is all this tiring you out? Shall I take you up to your room?"

He was the most like her beloved husband Andre in looks, the least like him in temperament. Deirdre felt the veiling film of inarticulate pain that she'd been quietly experiencing for the past six months and looked at her son. "Of course I'm tired, but I have no desire to go to my room. Did you take care of that little task I asked you to attend to?"

"The metal box? Of course, Mama. I have it wrapped up over there with all your other presents."

"It'll withstand the weather if it's left outdoors for a very long time."

"Yes, Mama. I had it made specially. It will last forever, the toolsmith said. What in the world have you got planned for that box—are you putting all your love letters in it and burying it, or something?" Paul lifted his mint julep to drink and, realizing that his mother's silver cup was empty, raced off to refill it.

She was glad he was gone without waiting for her answer. The journal she'd made her last entry in the night Andre had died was ready for burial—as was she, Deirdre thought laconically. Why on earth didn't people die before everything inside them withered up? She wondered.

"Grandmama?" Erin's granddaughter Germaine stood in front of Deirdre, holding a bundle of scrawny buttercups. "Are you asleep or just thinking?"

Deirdre hugged the child who was the most like her of all her progeny. "I think they're both the same with this old, worn-out brain of mine. Oooh. Aren't these pretty? I like them so much better than those your father grows in his greenhouse." The dull disturbance in her chest gave a sturdy kick, and Deirdre dropped the bouquet. She caught her breath again and managed to smile at her daughter's grandchild. "Tell you what. Are you good at keeping secrets? Do you think you could keep one between you and me?"

"Grandmama, you looked funny just then."

"All old people look funny. Would you do a little favor for Grandmama?"

Germaine looked a little uncertain, and Deirdre was considering choosing another favorite amongst her grandchildren. But the little girl said after a moment, "I was just worried about you, Grandmama. What do you want me to do?"

"There is a square package on the birthday gift table in the dining room, about this big, with my name and your Great-Uncle Paul's name on it. Bring it to me, please, but don't make a fuss."

"You're opening one of your presents before you even blow out your candles?" Little Germaine looked horrified.

"My dear," Deirdre managed calmness, though the tumult that sometimes occurred in her breast was starting up, and she knew she had very little time for what she wanted to do. "Please just do as Grandmama says."

Deirdre sat down quickly as soon as her great-granddaughter was out of view. She was dizzy and experiencing lapses into the past as she'd been doing for the past few weeks. "Julia?" she knew her old friend was long dead, but the woman coming up to her was as real as her three-tiered birthday cake. "What are you doing here? I thought you and Papa would be busy with that saloon I know you've got opened up right outside the pearly gates."

Julia gave her hearty laugh. "Oh, didn't we have a fine time, that daddy of yours and me, once he finally realized I wasn't letting him out of my clutches! He outlasted me on this earth, but not long. I've got him back now, Deirdre darlin', and we won't be parted ever again."

"I'm so tired, Julia, so tired. There's no one here now who remembers—even Gaby and Charles are gone, 'way down in Florida somewhere. I just hated it, their losing the plantation, and us with no way to help them." A tear seeped from Deirdre's eye, coursing down the still-smooth cheek. "Why am I the only one left? Why can't I go too? I just know Andre's waiting out there for me, but there's something, there's something I have to do before I go. Julia? Julia?"

"Grandmama, you were talking to yourself again." Germaine held out the square package she'd been sent for. "Is this what you wanted?"

Deirdre mustered her senses once more and sat up straight. "Ah, that's it, my precious. Now, if you will go to my bedroom and open the middle drawer of my dresser, you'll find a leather-bound book. It's under my Coleridge volume. Bring both to me, but don't show them to anyone. To anyone, you understand?"

Germaine grinned widely. "Grandmama, you are being so mysterious! Can I take one peek? Is this your diary with all the dirt on the Devereux family?"

Deirdre laughed and ruffled her great-granddaughter's dark curls. "You little dickens, I'm not telling. And not one peek, mind you! Just do as I say, and be quick about it. They'll be bothering me about cutting the cake or some such foolishness before long, and I want to take care of my business ahead of that."

Germaine ran off, and Deirdre received her next ghostly well-wisher. "Happy birthday, darling DeeDee. I always admired you for your stamina and look at how you outlived us all!"

"Oh, 'Relia, I missed you so! You were so brave that night. And I know it was always Andre that you loved. Did it hurt you terribly that he and I married and had our family here? 'Relia, our life together was so wonderful. Through it all, we felt your loving presence."

"DeeDee, I loved Andre but he never returned that love in the way I dreamed of. I wanted his happiness, and that could only come through loving you."

"Stay, Aurelia, don't go!" Deirdre reached out and embraced the air, then whispered to the dark shape moving toward her through the mist. "Andre? Oh, my darling! I have missed you so. I have missed you so!"

"They're wonderful children," Andre said, sweeping his arm out at the throng of laughing, playing children and chattering adults. "We brought the best into the new South, DeeDee darling. They'll make us all proud, just as you did."

"And you," Deirdre whispered, afraid to reach out to this, her dearest vision, for fear it would fade away with the others. "Andre, I loved you so. And when you came back and took Erin into your heart with never another question, I loved you even more."

"My regret was missing those years in between when you and I could have lived in the old South before it was destroyed. We survived the holocaust, but we missed out on the pretty years."

"But look how happy we were! And look at our family and their families. Have you ever seen a handsomer lot? Oh, Andre, I've missed you so! I'm ready to go, too. I'm ready, Andre. Please take me with you, darling!" The sigh was lost on thin air, and Deirdre sat up with a jerk when Germaine touched her knee.

"Grandmama, you were talking to yourself again."

Deirdre sat bolt upright. "Hmmph. That's the prerogative of old people. Ah, you got it." She put the book of poetry aside and took the leather book in which she had recorded her life and rubbed her fingers lovingly over the cover. "Now comes the tricky part—you and I sneaking out of here without anybody noticing. Ah, I have it. I'll have Prudy come out and gather everybody up behind the kitchen for a championship game of horseshoes." At the child's puzzled look, Deirdre hastily amended, "Just a slip over names. I know Prudy and old Rufus have been gone a long time. I meant their daughter, Dixie."

When Germaine had gone off to perform yet another mission for her great-grandmother, Deirdre leaned back in her chair, not sure she had the energy for yet another visitor from the mists surrounding her, but one came and she whispered hoarsely, "Not you, Sean, not now. I'm too tired."

His baleful look faded with the rest of him, and Deirdre clutched the gold locket at her throat that held Andre's picture on one side, Erin's on the other. "Too tired," she murmured, unclasping the locket and placing it inside the metal box with the journal and the volume of Coleridge. She dozed off for a bit and then Germaine was shaking her arm gently.

"Grandmama, they are all back of the house like you wanted. It's all clear now." Germaine's face was alight with the delight of the conspiracy, and Deirdre summoned up her energy.

"Then let us be off," she said, rising with some spryness and taking her cane. "You carry the box for Grandmama and let her rest from time to time, you hear."

The mountain loomed as high as Olympus, but Deirdre girded her remaining strength and struck forth with her little supporter. Her breath was ragged, and her limbs felt like stone by the time they reached the top. Breathing hard, Deirdre leaned against the white oak, pointing out the remnants of the original still and the view of the valley to her companion. "This is where it all began, my darling." *And this is where it shall all end,* her mind added. "The old tree will outlive us all. Oh, the stories it could tell!"

"What will you do with the box, Grandmama?"

"Let me catch my breath, sweetheart, then I'll show you." Deirdre gasped as the thunder inside her breast gathered momentum, then died down. "Ah. Now. See the hole in the old tree, where squirrels have hidden their nuts for more years than you and I can count together?"

Germaine nodded. "You want to hide your treasure there?"

Deirdre nodded, smiling at the word 'treasure'. Well, maybe the journal would be a treasure someday to the right person. "Can you think of a safer place? Houses are sold or torn down, but this old mountain, this old tree . . .

thank you, my darling. Now come here and let me sing you a song."

Germaine came and cuddled into Deirdre's embrace, hearing the erratic thump of the old woman's heart and knowing in her own young heart that this was a precious moment that would not last.

"Sing after me as I sing each verse. The mountain will carry it out into the valley, and our voices will be part of Moncoeur forever."

Coffee grows on the white oak stump,
The river flows with brandy-oh,
Go choose you one that'll stand by you
As sweet as sugar candy-oh.

As the last sweet note ended, Deirdre's eyes closed, and her arms loosened on the little girl she was holding. When Paul, Deirdre's oldest son, appeared on the rise, Germaine put her finger to her lips. "Shh. She's sleeping. Grandmama's sleeping."

Paul saw that what the child said was true and sent her down to join the other children at horseshoes and croquet. Then he went over to kiss Deirdre's cooling forehead, not hearing or noticing the fussy squirrel who was scampering out the white oak hollow to complain about the invasion of his domain.

He picked up her limp form, which weighed no more than a large sack of corn, and carried her down the mountain, which was now cast in the rosy glow of Deirdre Devereux's last sunset.

Chapter Twenty

The white oak tree! I sat bolt upright in the middle of the night after my long dream. How could I have forgotten about the hollow that had intrigued Celeste and me when we were very little? We had used that old hollow as our private post-office, sending letters to our movie idols and secret boyfriends. Celeste had once planned a birthday party and put the invitations in the hollow. She had cried all night when no one showed up. I think it was then that we lost faith in our "mailbox."

I got up and put on my jogging suit. The night was cold and clear, with a half-moon. I felt jittery as all get out about going up there to find what I knew I would find. There was something else making me nervous, too. I sensed that Deirdre's life had something to do with the present. It was as though Deirdre had hung on, sick and tired and old as she was at the end, to make me some kind of present of her past.

"My God!" I encountered my image in the mirror at the end of the hall and jumped. Everything about me looked wild-eyed and bushy-tailed. Why was I so afraid? I knew what I would find in the hollow of the old oak tree.

I didn't count on the cacophony of night sounds. Surely it wasn't normal for owls to be hooting and bobcats to be screaming on nights this cold. The animal life of a place, they say, reflects the history it contains. The local War Between the States buffs had accounts of rabbits jumping into the arms of soldiers during the murderous battle at Murfreesboro. Whiskey Mountain had always held a life of its own—I can attest to that personally.

"Deirdre," I whispered as I neared the crest of her mountain. "I'm scared, and I don't know why. Please don't leave me." I felt the familiar ripple of goosebumps and knew she wasn't far away. That knowledge gave me the courage to go directly to the hollow in the old oak and reach down for the box I knew I would find.

That was not all that I found. After I'd retrieved the aged metal box that I knew held Deirdre's precious journal, I fished around to see what else had survived the years of squirrel residency. It tickled me to find the bundle of birthday party invitations that Celeste had "mailed" when she was five. I found my old fan letter to Ronnie Milsap and giggled to see I'd sealed it with a big sticky lollypop kiss.

I found something else, too, something that did not make me laugh with nostalgia or giggle at silly adolescence.

It was a plastic-bound book that definitely did not belong to either Deirdre's era or my childhood. My heart thumped as I opened the packet and then the notebook. Deirdre had led me to this, a part of my mind told me as I thumbed through the pages of data and realized that what I held was an incriminating bible of evidence against a group of men who were holding office in the State of Louisiana and the people who were corrupting them.

"Celeste," I whispered after taking a deep breath. "She put it here." My sister was the only other one I knew who was aware of the "mailbox."

I heard the night sounds stop suddenly and realized that I was alone in an isolated place with an extremely valuable piece of evidence against an extremely powerful syndicate. "Deirdre," I whispered, "Thank you for leading me to this, but now I need your protection."

I never told anybody about this, but I swear it really happened. There was a huge crack like a bullwhip cutting through the night, and then the moon appeared from behind a cloud and some birds started up a friendly chirping and I was back home safe in my bed before you could say "night-night."

* * *

I decided my loyal little deputy friend from the Franklin sheriff's office ought to be the one to get the credit for cracking open one of the biggest criminal rings in the deep South. In exchange for me and my family being left out of the subsequent investigation, I let Deputy Laney Ford "find" the little black book with all its incriminating information on the passenger's seat of his vehicle.

By the time the crap hit the media fan, half of the political slate in Louisiana was under indictment or out of the country, and a few arrests were made in New York that made the D.A. there ecstatic.

It pleased me that some criminals were being put out of commission thanks to Celeste, Deirdre, and me, but I had a more intimate concern now. I placed a little personal ad in the *Nashville Banner* and sat back and waited. When I got my answer, I went to Dusty Roads Saloon and ordered a pitcher of beer and waited some more.

When the slim girl with short-cropped dark hair came up to my table and sat down, I knew it was finally at an end.

"Hello, Celeste," I said with just the tiniest tremor in my voice. "I expect you could use a drink."

She had been the one on the mountain that night when I thought I was seeing the ghost of Deirdre. "I thought of the hollow and how it would be the perfect hiding place. I couldn't take it to the police. I didn't know who to trust anymore. I was so scared, Fable! Royce had been playing both sides against each other, and they all wanted that book. I couldn't believe it when he forced me to go with him to meet those crooks off-shore Key West. They won't let us leave here alive, I told him, and even if they do, the side you doublecrossed will get us! Well, when I learned he was planning to doublecross both sides, I realized I had to do something to get out of there!"

I couldn't believe half of what she was telling me, but I could believe her terror when she discovered Royce was bent on blackmailing people who could have him killed at the crook of a little finger. "How did you get hooked on cocaine?" That was as bizarre to me as any of the rest. Celeste had never even smoked a cigarette.

Celeste blew her nose. "You didn't know that man at all, none of us did, least of all me. He was totally without morals or feelings, Fable. He had a way of using me, manipulating my emotions without ever getting involved himself."

"Sounds like someone else we both know," I pointed out drily.

Celeste shuddered. "At least Daddy isn't a criminal. Royce was far worse. Do you know that he was married to a woman years ago, someone whose family's political connections he could use, and he abandoned her on their wedding night, letting her go on thinking that he was dead?"

I nodded. "The mob caught up with him that night, and he had to disappear or get cement shoes. Go on."

"About the cocaine—that wasn't the worst of what he did to me. Did you realize that he set out to marry me even before he met you?"

"Yes, but it doesn't hurt quite so much now."

"He'd seen me at some contest and decided I was just the right bait to use for some of his deals." Celeste turned her head away. "He used me like—like some kind of bonus that went along with the deal."

I was horrified. "You let him do that to you?"

"I was hooked on cocaine by then, really hooked, and the worse things got, the more control he had over me. I agreed to anything he wanted me to do when he withheld my dope and, Fable, some of those things were pretty awful."

I put my hand over hers.

"Finally, I got up my courage and decided to go to the police. He found out and showed me a video he'd made of me in some pretty . . . pretty awful circumstances. Oh, Fable, he was so awful, so evil! And yet—and yet, there was this excitement at first. You know what my life was like after I lost the big contest. I had nothing. I can't believe that I'm saying this, but I loved being on the edge—at first. Royce recognized that about me when he asked me to marry him, said that I was more like him than you were. He said you couldn't handle the excitement that he wanted in his life, but I could."

I thought about that. "He was right, you know. I don't mean about you necessarily, but about me."

"He was right about me, too. At first I did love it. The hiding out, the secrecy, the meetings with dangerous men, the scariness of not knowing whether we'd be killed. I was on cocaine and felt very glamorous, doing all these exciting, bad things." Celeste's voice cracked. "That was before, of course, my husband started 'lending' me to special friends, and I found out what he really was."

"Royce is really dead, right?" She nodded. "Well, how did you escape being blown to smithereens, too? What happened on that boat?"

My sister shook her head. "I guess I just wasn't meant to die that night. I mean, when I think back to how I escaped being blown to bits, I shudder. You see, that was part of Royce's plan. He said that once we met up with the other boat and made the exchange for all that money, we'd go off a little ways and take our skiff and leave the *Wanderer* to blow up. People would think we'd died on it, and we could go off and start a new life. He knew how to do that, he said, and of course he did. He didn't trust those people, either side. They would come after us, he said."

"He was probably right," I said. "But you still haven't explained how you got out and Royce didn't."

Celeste closed her eyes, remembering. "He set the timer on the device for an hour after we'd be making the deal. I had two books in my windbreaker, the real one and a fake one that I was supposed to let them have." She buried her head in her hands. "Fable, I knew he was probably going to doublecross me, too—that is, if I survived the scam. I waited till he went below to set the device and then I got in the dory and rowed myself off. I was scared to death, more of my husband than anybody."

"What happened then? What went wrong with Royce's plan?

"I saw the explosion from two miles off. It lit up the sky. Then I looked down at my watch and realized what had happened. We'd spent a couple of nights in Alabama making some contacts, and I had set both our watches on Central time so my husband wouldn't be late to one of his precious deals. I guess he didn't realize that I'd done that. Don't you see? The explosion happened an hour before it was supposed to."

My sister didn't fool me. She may have been floundering morally, but she was not a conscienceless killer. I knew it had probably devastated her when she realized that she had been the instrument of her husband's death. I let her cry a little bit. There were still some things to be ironed out, and I wanted her thinking clearly when we talked about them. "I'm sorry, Celeste."

Celeste dabbed at her eyes and sipped her beer. "You don't know how many times I thought about letting you know I wasn't really dead, but I couldn't take the chance. Those people were still after that book, and I knew they would be watching you."

"Yes, I found out about that. Deputy Ford told me Miami suspected that Royce had pulled another of his arranged deaths to get the heat off. I expect the people after the book had the same suspicions."

"They couldn't find him, and they couldn't find me, so they figured you were the only possible connection."

I was glad I didn't have anyone on my tail these days. "Why in the blue-eyed world did you take those things out of your house?"

"I don't know. Just stupid, I guess. I was living in this dumpy halfway house for druggies and I felt like I was turning into a nobody. I don't know! The pictures, that dress, they made me remember that I was once somebody." Her voice hardened. "I cut the picture of Royce and me into a zillion pieces."

She told about her life in the halfway house after she'd kicked cocaine. "I was lucky. Nobody cared who anybody had been or was. I took a long hard look at my life."

I was proud of her and told her so. "What now?" I asked, drawing stick figures in the moisture on the beer pitcher. "Do you go home and present yourself to the folks, say 'Hi, honeys, I'm home!' "

"Do you know, I've thought about that a lot, especially now that I'm not in danger of being hunted down and killed. Fable, I've never had a chance to be anything but what some man wanted me be, first Daddy and then Royce. I think I want to stay dead for a while, at least until I find out what I want to be in real life. I never had a real life, you know that. I don't want to go back to the one back there."

I didn't try to urge anything on her because I had to agree that my sister was better off dead than leading the so-called life she'd had before. Besides, Daddy's heart condition probably wouldn't withstand the shock of having his elder daughter show up alive, and Mother was too far gone in her Valium and vodka to comprehend. "You're really okay now on the drug business?" She nodded, and I believed her. "Will you at least keep in touch with me?"

"Of course I will. One of these days you might need me."

I felt a little bit like crying myself. I knew that Celeste had been let down by her parents and by the man she'd married, but maybe I had let her down, too. Sisters ought to be good to each other. I vowed on the spot that when Harrison and I had daughters—whose names I'd already chosen, by the way—I would make sure they looked after each other in the way sisters ought to. "I hope you'll let that hair grow back," I managed finally.

"I will," Celeste said with the old million-dollar smile. "And I hope you'll hang on to that Playboy figure you've got now, as well as the curls. They both look great."

"Thanks." I reached into my purse for an object wrapped in tissue that I'd brought on a hunch. Maybe I'd known at the outset that Celeste wouldn't be coming home with me this time. "I've got something here for you to remember your roots by, until you get back to the real thing."

I dangled the locket that Deirdre had packed in the metal box, and Celeste's eyes filled with tears when she opened it. "Oh, Fable, this should be yours."

"No," I said firmly and truthfully, "It should be yours. You are most like her, it's just that you haven't learned that yet. But you will."

She held the open locket and gazed for a very long time at the picture of Andre. "Why is it I feel that I know him?" she asked softly as she closed the heart and put the locket around her neck.

"Because you probably will—or someone very much like him," I said with a smile. "I'm jealous, you know."

Celeste kissed me and left, and I finished up the beer and listened to a very bad singer try to sound like Garth Brooks. Then I saw our sound engineer from the studio come in. I waved him over. I needed company.

"Damn, Fable, what a coincidence. I was going to call you tonight. You know that tape you gave me to send over to the voice analysis guy at the lab? You're not going to believe what he said."

I knew I would. "He said that the echo had a different pattern from the original, therefore making it impossible for the two to be from the same person."

He looked at me in astonishment. "Now how the hell did you know that?"

I patted his shoulder. "Because I rigged up the whole thing as a joke to play on Harrison." What a bald-faced lie. I knew sure as hell that nobody would ever hear that tape again but me. Harrison would just think I'd had someone dub it, anyway.

But I knew better.

"Hey, I feel like singing. Do you think maybe these people would mind if I got up and sang?"

The people at the next table who'd recognized me started applauding, and soon the whole room had joined in.

I got up there on that podium and I sang "Whiskey Mountain Woman" as I had never sung it before. I'm sure nobody else but me in the room heard the ghostly soprano echo. Maybe Deirdre Devereux had passed down her looks and other characteristics to my sister Celeste, but I know who she deeded her musical talents to.

Our duet in Dusty Roads ended, but I knew Deirdre's harmony would stay with me forever.

Epilogue

The Present

My four-year-old twin daughters, Deirdre and Aurelia, and I had returned from a glorious, exhausting vacation at our family's favorite retreat. I was still basking in the memories the visit had brought back about my honeymoon there in the great Smokies.

Lord knows mine and Harrison's wedding had been something to remember. People on Music Row still talk about it.

"Fable, this thing is turning into a country music three-ring circus. Can't we just elope and forget all the hoopla?"

Harrison had not been as enthusiastic about making our wedding day a celebration for all our country music friends as I was. I had read

Deirdre's account in her journal of the joyfulness that had rung over her mountain with the wedding bells, blotting out much of the gloom and doom of the past. I wanted to duplicate that special day in my own way, and country music had a big part in it.

"Harrison, this is the only time I ever plan to get married, and I want it be an event we will never forget."

Our wedding was exactly that. *Billboard* took pictures and did a spread that looked like a Willie Nelson charity concert gathering. I was sorry my sister wouldn't be there to be my maid of honor, but Donna was pleased to fill in.

The ceremony was to take place beneath the old oak on Deirdre's Mountain. I had the florist hang huge baskets of garden flowers and wild roses from the limbs and arrange an arch of yellow roses where Harrison and I would say our vows.

The best guitar player since Chet Atkins provided the background music, and Jackie Lucas, who everybody says is headed for fame like Reba McIntyre's, was to sing the traditional solos I wanted: "O Promise Me" and "The Lord's Prayer." You see, deep down I am and have always been a traditionalist who believes deeply in sticking with the tried and true.

I spent a fortune on my wedding gown, because I wanted it to be worn by the daughters I would have, and maybe their daughters after then. *The Nashville Banner,* in its account of the wedding, described my dress as one that "might have worn by Scarlett O'Hara in her first wedding if there hadn't been a war."

Everyone teased my new husband about his "monkey suit," but I found him devastating in the pearl-grey and pinstriped ensemble. In fact, I was finding myself getting a bit impatient, too, about getting on with the honeymoon. Harrison (reluctantly) and I had decided upon our engagement announcement that we wanted our wedding night to be a new beginning to a passionate life together.

Neither of us had found the period of celibacy easy, but on our wedding day, we were both happy that we'd made that choice.

I know I sound like a bossy bride, but I was the one who planned the honeymoon, too. After all, not many brides have a great-great-great grandmother's personal journal to use as a bridal manual.

I found out that the heavenly spot where Deirdre and Andre had spent their honeymoon was now a five-star country inn resort. I had met the couple who manage The Inn at Blackberry Farm at a Foothills Cuisine charity affair in Knoxville near which the thousand-plus acre farm was located. I had been intrigued to find that the fifty-year-old inn was now part of the place where the Devereuxs had honeymooned.

Harrison told me that all he asked for our honeymoon was a very large, very comfortable bed—and no telephone.

He was a good sport at the reception following our wedding on the lawn at Moncoeur, not showing impatience to make our getaway until well after the dancing and merrymaking had gotten under way. I'd had Loveless Cafe cater the later breakfast that featured all the famous foods of the Southern hunt table—country ham and biscuits, grits and hash-brown potatoes, all those low-calorie dishes, and everybody ate till the overflowing tables were empty.

"*Now* can we leave?" Harrison and I were dancing cheek to cheek over one of Jim Reeves's old songs, and the neck nuzzling and close contact were having their effect on both of us.

"Soon," I assured him. "After I go up and change into some real clothes."

I had decided against the traditional going-away outfit, since we would be spending our honeymoon in the "great blue hills of God," and it was a good little drive to Walland, Tennessee, where the Inn was located. I had had my seamstress make some tight-fitting jeans out of a shimmery soft, lightweight leather and a pearl-grey silk shirt that matched my beloved boots that Harrison had given me. The grey Stetson had been a wedding gift from my band. I loved it.

When we were poised on the veranda, dodging rice and calling out farewells, I was treated to a final, lovely surprise. My band serenaded the newlyweds with a medley of the hit tunes that Harrison and I had made together.

Nobody, not even Deirdre, has ever had a nicer wedding and send-off. If we'd been married in the old Ryman Opry House—as we discussed at one point—and had our reception at Opryland with the dancing waters and the harpist playing the wedding march, we might have topped what we actually did, but I've always remembered that day with great joy.

And, oh, that honeymoon in the beautiful Smokies!

When Harrison and I arrived, we were shown directly, without the check-in hassle, to the renovated old farmhouse that the current owners use when they're staying at the Farm.

It would be ours for five glorious days. Harrison and I found the fresh flowers and iced champagne in the master bedroom and proceeded to celebrate the first night of the rest of our life together with a toast.

"Here's to Deirdre and her mountain. She climbed it with great courage. May I do the same in my life."

Harrison tipped his glass to mine. "You will, my darling. And I'll be right there at your side."

His kiss sealed the magical moment.

"Mrs. Harrison Judd," I whispered against his lips. "I like the sound of that."

"And I like being alone with you at last." Harrison took off my prize Stetson. "No wonder cowboys used to kiss their horses instead of the girl. Do you think maybe you could put on one of those sexy outfits I saw in your suitcase?"

"You peeked!" But I was as eager as my husband to seal our union.

He was waiting for me, his chest shamelessly bare above the covers, the candlelight from the bedside table illuminating the muscled arms that were reaching out for me.

"Do you think it's possible that I'm a virgin again? I declare I feel like one." I did, too. My insides were doing their own rocket show, and I was suddenly as shy as the time . . . well, the first time.

"There's only one way to find out," Harrison whispered wickedly. Then I was in his arms and everything was right as mountain rain.

My journal is a haven for my private thoughts and all the strange things that happened to me before I married Harrison. But I think I'll leave the details of my wedding night to the imagination of anyone reading this.

I'll say this much, though. If I could write music and lyrics with the kind of feelings that my husband and I enjoyed together on that night of nights, I'd have the number-one hit song in the world. As all of us in the trade know, country music dwells on despair, but I may swap that in for passion and sheer pleasure in life and love on my next song.

Ten light years of lovemaking later, Harrison and I finally decided we had better have something of actual substance to eat. Maybe honeymooners can live on love but both of us are healthy carnivores who enjoy our vittles.

I'd had it in my mind all along—well, when I wasn't being distracted to madness by my sexy husband—to seek out the place Deirdre had described in her journal. I found out upon talking with the innkeeper, Bernadette, that this was Hesse Creek, a true mountain stream often using for the guests' fly-fishing activities.

She arranged to send a gourmet picnic basket to us. I'd heard of the incredible cooking in the Inn, but when Harrison and I unpacked our basket and found goodies like prosciutto-wrapped prawns and gorgonzola-coated croutons, along with homemade soup that would send normal taste-buds into shock, I just gave in to the newfound realization that I'm not a true country girl, but a hedonistic sensualist.

Making love with Harrison was the peak so far, but the rich chocolate almond rum torte, known as "Queen of Sheba", that Bernadette had devilishly packed along with two kinds of wine, was running a close second.

We basked in our contented stupor of repleteness in food and drink—and our love—afterwards by the bubbling stream. "I think I can hear its voice," I said drowsily. "It's singing to us."

"Do you know, one of the things I love about being with you is that I feel like a permanent resident of the Twilight Zone."

I cuffed him soundly for that. "I suppose you think that I made it up about Deirdre being right here when she and Andre came for their honeymoon. She wrote that she heard someone singing, and a guitar playing."

Harrison quickly turned off the portable tape player he'd brought to listen to the demo tape of my new song, "Two Outta Three Ain't Bad."

"Well, what I hear in that stream is nice, fat bass and luscious trout talking about finding their way onto somebody's line."

I laughed. "Does this mean the honeymoon's over, when the groom starts talking about going fishing?"

He hugged me tight. "Our honeymoon is for life, baby. For life."

A squirrel jumped to a new limb on the big tree near the stream, and I sat straight up. "What would you say if I told you that Deirdre and Andre left a sign for us to find, right here on this very spot?"

"I'd say 'da-da-da-da-da-da-da.'"

I ignored that, getting up and going over to inspect the tree. "It should be . . . she said she wrote it very low so it wouldn't grow too much . . . Harrison, here it is! Here's Deirdre's initials—and Andre's! Oh, my lord, I never expected . . . oh, look darling, they carved them out so we'd see them all these years later, on our honeymoon like they were."

Harrison said nothing, but I knew that he was rethinking his skepticism about my stories of my strange links to Deirdre and the past. He looked at the initials and then down at his wife. "Know what we should do?" He took his pocket knife out and opened up. "I'm not big on mutilating the natural landscape, but I think we owe it to the future to leave our mark here, too."

We left the heart-shaped design with our initials inside it for future lovers to find and went back to our rooms, hand-in-hand. I didn't tell Harrison, but I felt that this was truly good-bye to my ancestor. She was on her honeymoon, after all, and didn't need any more intrusion on my part.

My mental excursion into the happy experiences of several years past ended, I settled back in the present—equally happy, I might add.

I called out to Azalea, who was bringing us a pitcher of lemonade. "Has Harrison called in yet?" My husband had gone straight from Knoxville to Atlanta, where he was working with the new public relations firm. I usually went with my husband on his trips, but now that I was five months pregnant with number three, I had started taking it easy. The visit to the Inn at Blackberry Farms had been wonderful but would no doubt be the last one for a while.

"No, but guess who just blew into town." Azalea's broad face was beaming.

"Surprise!" Celeste, once again in her red-haired glory, stepped out from behind the old housekeeper.

We hugged and cried and cried and hugged and finally caught our breath and got down to being sensible. I found out that Celeste had visited Mother in her suite and been received quite calmly. Our mother has retreated into her own world since Daddy died, and it made perfect sense to her that Celeste should come to visit her as all good daughters ought to.

"Well, tell me everything. How's that big job of yours? And what about that man, the executive you said was trying to talk you into getting married right away?" My sister and I had agreed that old wounds and scars required very cautious healing. Our relationship over the past few years had been slowly repaired through letters and phone calls. Celeste's psychiatrist and my dear old darling Dr. Velkoff—who had dismissed me years ago—agreed that a visit in person needed to be delayed until we were both ready for it.

Well, I'd been ready for a long time. Apparently Celeste was too, now.

"Hold on, hold on. I want to see these darling children first. They don't know their Aunt Celeste . . ."

"I've told them all about you and how you were the prettiest fairytale princess in the whole world and."

"Oh, no," Celeste said with sincere alarm. She looked at me, her arms protectively around my twins. "Don't make young silly me their role model, Sis! Fable, you aren't putting these children through that dreadful pageant business, are you?"

"Believe me," I said, crossing my heart, "I am not. They'll be Little Leaguers all the way, not a diadem in sight."

When Azalea took the children for their baths and supper, Caleste and I fixed mint juleps and wandered down to the little cemetery. I knew she wanted to talk about the journal I had mailed her to read.

"She was a remarkable person, wasn't she?" Celeste paused at the gravesite of our illustrious ancestor. "I felt after reading her diary that I knew her."

I said nothing. Celeste didn't know how well Deirdre and I had become acquainted, and I had no intention of trying to tell her. "I think that's what she wanted," I said truthfully. Looking at my sister was like looking at a copy of the woman I had come to know so well. "Everyone says you're just like her."

"But I wasn't for a long time. I wasn't anybody, not even myself. That sad little blond girl she often wrote about. That was a prophecy of you, wasn't it?"

"I think so."

"Look at you now!" Celeste said with a smile. "You're happy as can be, you have that gorgeous husband who adores you, two precious children and another one coming—and a great career to boot! If Deirdre saw you today, she would picture her future great-grandchild very differently."

"And what about you?" My sister had never been so beautiful or so successful. She had taken her Whiskey Mountain stock and parlayed it into enough to get her a seat on the major stockholders board. She was now Chairman of the company and making its profits soar. Celeste's picture had appeared on several business magazine covers. She usually turned down bids from the women's magazines because, she said, they always wanted to play up her past as a beauty queen and she had had enough of that for a lifetime.

We wandered on to the newer part of the graveyard. Celeste studied the tombstone that bore her own name. "It was so strange that night I came down here, seeing my own grave. I knew putting the flowers on the tombstone was risky, but I felt so damn forgotten and alone!"

"I had them file the date off," I told her. I'm superstititous about things like that."

Celeste fiddled with the locket at her throat. "You haven't asked me why I came home, besides just to see you."

"Why did you come home, besides just to see me?"

"Well, I heard the old Barksdale house is up for sale and I was thinking . . ."

My disappointment was enormous. "Oh, Celeste, how terrible! It sold right away. I had no idea you wanted that place, or I would have had Betty Lou call you the moment it was put on the market. What a shame. How we would have loved having you right next door! But what about your fabulous job, what about the executive in Atlanta, what about . . ."

"What about 'em? My roots are on this mountain. I started finding those roots in Deirdre's journal, and I'd like to find some more."

"You must live with us, of course. There's oodles of room."

"I'll do no such thing. You've got all the family you need. Besides, I want my own place." Her eyes twinkled. "The new man I met when I was negotiating to buy back the whiskey distillery may be just the one to help me."

"You bought the distillery? Celeste, that's wonderful." I looked at the sly expression on her face. "That's not all you bought, you little sneak. You're the one who bought Barksdale, aren't you?

At her grin, I whooped out a rebel yell and hugged her. "I'm going to run the distillery myself," she told me as soon as I let her catch her breath. "I'm keeping on current management, but I'll be the one who sets the pace and tone for production. Plus, I'm changing some logos and such."

That rather disturbed me. "Not too much, I hope." Deirdre wouldn't want the basics of her whiskey business tampered with.

"Just to the extent of making sure that everybody who buys our whiskey knows that there was a damn strong woman behind it." At the look on my face, Celeste laughed. "No, silly, I'm not putting my picture on the labels, I'm putting Deirdre's. I want the whole world to know that we're proud of our ancestor and what she did."

My pride in my sister made it difficult to speak. "Deirdre will love that," I whispered.

"I know she will." Celeste made it seem the most natural thing in the world to be talking about our ancestor as if she were still alive and right there with us.

The sunset was exploding around us, and I noticed that Celeste's eyes kept going to the mountain. "Do you see anything up there?" I finally asked.

"I just keep hoping . . ." Celeste bit her full lip. "Nothing. You go on in. I think I'll take a little walk before dinner. Maybe I will spend the night with you tonight instead of going back to the motel."

I assured her that would be fine and left her still gazing up at Deirdre's Mountain.

When I looked out from the veranda, she was already half-way up, her face full of eagerness that could mean only one thing.

She was going up to meet Andre Devereux.

COMING IN FEBRUARY!
HISTORICAL ROMANCE
BITTERSWEET PROMISES
By Trana Mae Simmons

Cody Garret likes everything in its place: his horse in its stable, his six-gun in its holster, his money in the bank. But the rugged cowpoke's life is turned head over heels when a robbery throws Shanna Van Alystyne into his arms. With a spirit as fiery as the blazing sun, and a temper to match, Shanna is the most downright thrilling woman ever to set foot in Liberty, Missouri. No matter what it takes, Cody will besiege Shanna's hesitant heart and claim her heavenly love.

_51934-8 $4.99 US/$5.99 CAN

CONTEMPORARY ROMANCE
SNOWBOUND WEEKEND/GAMBLER'S LOVE
By Amii Lorin

In ***Snowbound Weekend,*** romance is the last thing on Jennifer Lengle's mind when she sets off for a ski trip. But trapped by a blizzard in a roadside inn, Jen finds herself drawn to sophisticated Adam Banner, with his seductive words and his outrageous promises...promises that can be broken as easily as her innocent heart.

And in ***Gambler's Love,*** Vichy Sweigart's heart soars when she meets handsome Ben Larkin in Atlantic City. But Ben is a gambler, and Vichy knows from experience that such a man can hurt her badly. She is willing to risk everything she has for love, but the odds are high—and her heart is at stake.

_51935-6 (two unforgettable romances in one volume) Only $4.99

LOVE SPELL
ATTN: Order Department
Dorchester Publishing Co., Inc.
276 5th Avenue, New York, NY 10001

Please add $1.50 for shipping and handling for the first book and $.35 for each book thereafter. PA., N.Y.S. and N.Y.C. residents, please add appropriate sales tax. No cash, stamps, or C.O.D.s. All orders shipped within 6 weeks via postal service book rate. Canadian orders require $2.00 extra postage and must be paid in U.S. dollars through a U.S. banking facility.

Name ______________________________________
Address ____________________________________
City _____________________ State ______ Zip ______
I have enclosed $______ in payment for the checked book(s).
Payment must accompany all orders. ☐ Please send a free catalog.

TIMESWEPT ROMANCE

TIME OF THE ROSE

By Bonita Clifton

When the silver-haired cowboy brings Madison Calloway to his run-down ranch, she thinks for sure he is senile. Certain he'll bring harm to himself, Madison follows the man into a thunderstorm and back to the wild days of his youth in the Old West.

The dread of all his enemies and the desire of all the ladies, Colton Chase does not stand a chance against the spunky beauty who has tracked him through time. And after one passion-drenched night, Colt is ready to surrender his heart to the most tempting spitfire anywhere in time.

_51922-4 $4.99 US/$5.99 CAN

A FUTURISTIC ROMANCE

AWAKENINGS

By Saranne Dawson

Fearless and bold, Justan rules his domain with an iron hand, but nothing short of the Dammai's magic will bring his warring people peace. He claims he needs Rozlynd—a bewitching beauty and the last of the Dammai—for her sorcery alone, yet inside him stirs an unexpected yearning to savor the temptress's charms, to sample her sweet innocence. And as her silken spell ensnares him, Justan battles to vanquish a power whose like he has never encountered—the power of Rozlynd's love.

_51921-6 $4.99 US/$5.99 CAN

LOVE SPELL
ATTN: Order Department
Dorchester Publishing Co., Inc.
276 5th Avenue, New York, NY 10001

Please add $1.50 for shipping and handling for the first book and $.35 for each book thereafter. PA., N.Y.S. and N.Y.C. residents, please add appropriate sales tax. No cash, stamps, or C.O.D.s. All orders shipped within 6 weeks via postal service book rate. Canadian orders require $2.00 extra postage and must be paid in U.S. dollars through a U.S. banking facility.

Name______________________________________

Address____________________________________

City ____________________ State______ Zip______

I have enclosed $______in payment for the checked book(s).

Payment must accompany all orders.☐ Please send a free catalog.